PARADOX VALLEY

GERRI HILL

BELLA
B O O K S
2016

Bella Books, Inc.
P.O. Box 10543
Tallahassee, FL 32302

Printed in the United States of America on acid-free paper.

First Bella Books Edition 2016

Editor: Medora MacDougall
Cover Designer: Linda Callaghan

ISBN: 978-1-59493-496-4

About the Author

Gerri Hill has twenty-nine published works, including the 2014 GCLS winner *The Midnight Moon*, 2011, 2012 and 2013 GCLS winners *Devil's Rock*, *Hell's Highway* and *Snow Falls*, and the 2009 GCLS winner *Partners*, the last book in the popular *Hunter Series*, as well as the 2013 Lambda finalist *At Seventeen*. Hill's love of nature and of being outdoors usually makes its way into her stories as her characters often find themselves in beautiful natural settings. When she isn't writing, Gerri and her longtime partner, Diane, keep busy at their log cabin in East Texas tending to their two vegetable gardens, orchard and five acres of piney woods. They share their lives with two Australian shepherds and an assortment of furry felines.

Other Bella Books By Gerri Hill

Angel Fire	*The Killing Room*
Artist's Dream	*Love Waits*
At Seventeen	*The Midnight Moon*
Behind the Pine Curtain	*No Strings*
The Cottage	*One Summer Night*
Chasing a Brighter Blue	*Partners*
Coyote Sky	*Pelican's Landing*
Dawn of Change	*The Rainbow Cedar*
Devil's Rock	*The Scorpion*
Gulf Breeze	*Sierra City*
Hell's Highway	*Snow Falls*
Hunter's Way	*Storms*
In the Name of the Father	*The Target*
Keepers of the Cave	*Weeping Walls*

CHAPTER ONE

"I thought you liked her."

"I do. But I don't want to marry her," Dana said. "We've been dating for six months and she asks me to marry her? It's like everyone has gone crazy because they can get married now."

Her mother laughed as she handed Dana the plate she'd just dried. "And you said this day would never come."

"I know. Maybe that's why the thought of getting married terrifies me," she said as she put the plate away, waiting patiently as her mother dried the last one. "I do know, however, that Kendra is not the one."

"Then why are you dating her?"

Dana shrugged. "I like her. We have fun together. We have mutual friends, so it's easy."

"Only you're not in love with her?"

"No. I'm not even in lust with her," she said, then laughed as a blush covered her mother's face. "Sorry."

"Well, in fairness to her, you should probably let her know."

"You mean, instead of running away like I did?"

"We love having you here, you know that," her mother said. "And it gives your dad an excuse to have a barbeque and invite the family over."

"It's been a few years since I've seen them," she said. "I'm actually looking forward to the party tomorrow."

And she was. She'd left Seattle in such a rush—a panic, really—that she hadn't even considered whether her parents would mind an impromptu visit. A hastily written email to her boss had gotten her a two-week vacation on a moment's notice. She didn't know if that was a testament to the kindness of her boss or to the fact that she wasn't really as indispensable as she thought. She chose to think it the former rather than the latter. She'd flown into Salt Lake City and rented a car, heading east through the mountains then hitting the high desert of the Colorado Plateau, down through Arches and Moab. She drove through the Spanish Valley as she skirted the mountains to her north, driving the scenic La Sal Mountain Loop and crossing over into Colorado. The highway followed the same path as La Sal Creek through Lion Canyon and she'd felt the anxiety she'd carried with her from Seattle evaporate with each mile. Kendra—and her unexpected proposal—faded from her mind as she became mesmerized by the beautiful scenery that surrounded her.

She'd last been home at Christmas, two years ago. And while she loved the snowy scenes and white peaks that guarded the canyon and valley, there was something about the mountains in summertime that drew her like nothing else did. Well, late May, not quite summer but close enough. She would get reacquainted with some of her old stomping grounds, take a few hikes and hopefully talk her dad into some serious trout fishing over on the Delores River. Two weeks should be plenty of time to sort through the marriage proposal and come up with something better than the startled "Are you out of your mind?" response she'd blurted out to Kendra.

Yes, two weeks in the sparsely populated valley, where the closest town was nearly thirty miles away—tiny Paradox—should do wonders for her.

CHAPTER TWO

Squaw Valley hadn't seen much change in the last sixty-some-odd years. That suited Jean Bulgur just fine. She and Hal had married when they were both barely seventeen and had settled in the valley, moving in with his mother. They'd made a good enough living with the small farm, raising pinto beans and corn most years. They kept chickens, hogs and a few cows too, but it was hard work, she had to admit. Hard enough work that all three of their boys moved off as soon as they were of age. Hal Jr., moved only as far as Grand Junction, yet they saw him but a handful of times each year. The other two apparently forgot where they had been raised, she thought. She couldn't remember the last time they'd come by for a visit. Peter married a gal from Los Angeles and they had three kids. Jean had only seen them twice when Peter had bothered to bring them around. His last Christmas card said that he was now a grandpa himself. Jean figured she and Hal wouldn't ever see their great-grandchildren unless they made a trip to Los Angeles. She was fairly sure that wouldn't happen. Johnny, the youngest, followed the rodeo circuit and they'd gone up to Cheyenne to see him one year. That must have been eight or ten years ago now. Surely Johnny had given it up. He was getting too old to be riding bulls. Shame he didn't keep in touch more, she thought sadly.

"What's got you lookin' all dreamy?"

She turned from the window, not realizing she'd been staring out at nothing. She smiled at Hal and motioned to the table, which she'd already set for supper.

"Smothered some pork chops up like you like them," she said.

"I thought I smelled them. Fresh biscuits too?"

She nodded. "Need something to soak up the gravy." She moved to the oven and peeked inside, already knowing that the chops were ready. "You want a glass of milk?" She didn't wait for an answer as she filled a glass. After more than fifty-five years of marriage, she knew him well.

"I was thinkin' we could take a trip into town the next day or so," he said.

"Paradox? You need something from the feed store?"

"No. Up to Grand Junction. Maybe we could meet up with Hal Jr., for a meal."

She pulled the cast-iron skillet out of the oven and set it on the stove. The gravy had thickened nicely, she noted. "You talk to him?"

"No. Thought maybe we could call him up, though."

She nodded. "It would be nice to go to a real grocery store instead of that pitiful excuse for one they have in Paradox."

She took the empty plate in front of him and went about the routine of fixing his supper, putting a heaping spoonful of mashed potatoes down first, then a pork chop and gravy. The green beans were from the freezer and the last of the ones from last year's garden. She topped it all with two biscuits that she'd baked just that afternoon.

"Looks real good, Jean," he said as he took the plate from her.

She stood behind him and watched him eat for a moment. Hal wasn't much for endearments, but she couldn't recall a time when he hadn't said those same four words at suppertime. After this many years, she wondered if he even saw the plate before he spoke the compliment. She smiled contentedly and reached for her own plate to fill it. No, not much had changed in Squaw Valley over the years.

CHAPTER THREE

Corey sat up in bed with a jolt, her eyes wide, her heart pounding. She took a steadying breath. The dream. The damn dream again. She rubbed her face, trying to scrub away the memory, but it remained— the shooting, the screams, the fire. It wasn't really a dream, she knew. Her team. All dead. All but her.

That was a joke, wasn't it? She *was* dead. Dead inside, at least.

She got out of bed and shuffled into the kitchen. In the dim light of morning, she could make out the remnants of last night's dinner. The steak had looked good and for a moment, it was like old times— grilling a steak to medium rare while she watched the sun set over the mountain. Problem was, it was tasteless. Everything was tasteless lately. Well, except for the bottle of scotch. That went down like the fine whiskey that it was. It went down almost too well. But she reasoned it was better than the sleeping pills her doctor had prescribed. She hadn't even filled the damn prescription. She'd drink to oblivion before she'd start popping pills to help her sleep.

She took a bottle of water from her fridge, then opened a cabinet and took out the container of aspirin. That had become a morning ritual, it seemed.

The doctor had told her it would take time. It had been four months. How much longer would she be in this state of...of nothingness? She felt empty...numb.

Dead. Like her team.

She blew out a weary breath. She knew she had to get past this... only she wasn't sure how. She stood at the sink, looking out the window at the approaching day. Without thinking, she reached over and turned on the coffeepot. As it sprang to life, brewing up a strong pot that she'd set up the night before, her eyes were again drawn to the subtle pink that colored the mountain. She hadn't taken the time to enjoy a sunrise in more years than she could recall.

Maybe this morning would be a good one to start with.

CHAPTER FOUR

Anna Gail Filmore went about the chore of methodically restocking the shelf where the canned vegetables were kept. Their small grocery store wasn't large, but it carried the essentials, enough for most people to get by with. Of course, in the summer, when most everyone in the valley had gardens, the canned vegetables would sit undisturbed until winter.

"Hey, Mom? I couldn't find any more tuna cans in the back," Holly said.

Anna Gail looked over at her daughter and nodded. "Add it to the order list for Monday."

Holly's shoulders dropped. "I'm ready to go home. Can't you do it?"

"Are you going out with Butch tonight?"

Holly shook her head. "No. His cousin is in from Seattle and they're having a family party or something," she said.

Anna Gail stopped what she was doing and turned to her daughter. "You've been dating for a while now. Were you not invited?"

"Oh, Mom...yeah, he asked," she said with a shrug. "But you know, I don't go out to their farm much."

"He's such a nice boy. And his family too. I don't know what you've got against them."

"He's not a boy. He's over thirty. And yes, his parents are very nice," she said as she fidgeted with her watch. "I just don't like the whole farm thing." She waved her hands in the air. "I want to get out of here, Mom. Not marry some farmer."

Anna Gail had known for a while now that her youngest child was restless living here in Paradox. But after high school, she'd shown no desire to move away and go to college like her brothers had. She'd seemed content to work at the store and when she began dating Butch Ingram, Anna Gail assumed they would one day marry. Lately, though, she could feel Holly's impatience.

"So you want to leave Paradox finally?"

Holly nodded. "It's time."

"I guess we should have encouraged you after high school, but you seemed so young," she said. "The thought of you heading out on your own was frightening."

"I know. That's why I didn't want to leave. But I'm twenty-four now." She again waved her hands around her. "I can't stay here and work in the store forever, Mom. I want to get out and do something."

"Where are you thinking of going?"

"Over to Grand Junction," she said. "I can get a job there, I'm sure."

She seemed confident, at least. Anna Gail didn't point out that her only skills were stocking grocery store shelves. She'd never shown an interest in learning about the ordering, the inventory, the paperwork involved in running the store. She wondered what job she could possibly get.

"Maybe you should think about going to college," she said. "It's not too late, you know."

"I don't know. College is expensive."

"We'll help you, of course. We helped your brothers."

"Maybe. Right now I only want—"

A low rumble cut off her words and Anna Gail's eyes widened as the shelves began to shake—the cans she'd neatly stacked vibrating around her. She steadied herself as the floor seemed to move under her.

"What's going on?" Holly asked, her voice thick with fright. "Mom?"

Cans rolled to the floor, and Anna Gail managed to get into the next aisle, holding her arms up to prevent the glass jars of pickles from falling. Other items crashed to the floor around her and she heard Holly scream in the background as the lights went out.

It was over in a matter of seconds and Anna Gail peered through the darkness, imagining the mess of her normally neat store. She turned, nearly tripping on a box that had fallen from the shelf.

"Holly? Are you okay?"

"Yes. What was that? An earthquake?"

"I'm not sure."

She made her way slowly to the sound of Holly's voice. Darkness had settled over the town of Paradox and she looked toward the large windows in the front, thankful they had not broken. Most, if not all of the shops had closed up hours ago. She took Holly's hand and they walked toward the door even as the darkness enveloped them.

CHAPTER FIVE

Dana laughed as her cousin was recounting a tale from their childhood. She and Butch had been quite a pair, born only two days apart and growing up no more than a mile from each other. She knew everyone had heard this story plenty of times over the years, but it never got old.

"Covered in pig muck, head to toe," he said.

"I didn't even recognize her," her father supplied. "If not for her ponytail, I'd have thought Butch done drug home a stray."

"It was his fault," she said, pointing at Butch. "It's not like I *wanted* to try and catch a pig."

"You never could turn down a dare," he said with another laugh.

"I had Louis spray her down with a garden hose before I'd let her in the house," her mother added. "Threw her clothes away too."

Darkness had settled in the valley, but no one seemed to be in a hurry to leave. Besides Butch and his parents, another aunt and uncle had come over as well as their closest neighbors, Irene and Paul. Her father had cooked ribs and chicken on the barbeque, and her mother had made her special potato salad that Dana loved. Aunt Fredda brought two apple pies, and Dana had topped her piece with ice cream. It brought back all sorts of childhood memories, and she recalled many an evening with these very same people sitting around sharing a meal. Of course, there were more kids back then. Like her, most had moved away. Butch, however, still lived at home, content to work side by side with his father on their farm.

"This has been fun," Butch said. "You should come home more often."

"I know. Only it's hard to get away sometimes," she said. That wasn't really the case. At thirty-one years old, she had her own life, her own friends. But her parents were getting older, and she knew she should see them more often than she did.

"I wish—"

Her mother's words were cut off as a violent rumble shook the ground around them. Lights flickered on and off, losing the battle as they went out completely, plunging them into darkness on the back porch. Dana jumped up, afraid she would fall from the chair she was sitting in. She fell anyway as the earth seemed to shift beneath them. It stopped as suddenly as it had started, and she grabbed the porch railing, unable to see anything around her. She looked up into the sky, finding no moon this evening, nothing to cut the darkness.

"What the hell was that?"

"Is everyone okay?"

"I can't see a damn thing."

"Earthquake?"

"Didn't last long if it was one."

* * *

Jean noticed the light flickering before she felt the first tremor. Hal was in his recliner and she hurried over to him, cringing as their wedding china rattled in the hutch. She reached him seconds before the power went out, but as the house shook around her, she fell to the floor, unable to keep her balance.

"Jean?"

"I'm here," she said, grabbing his hand tightly.

In the darkness, they heard a crash and she knew the coffee cup she'd been using earlier had fallen off the counter. It was her favorite one, she thought crazily as she clung tightly to Hal's hand.

They sat there in silence for several moments after the shaking stopped, as if fearing it would start again. Hal finally stood up and helped her to her feet.

"Let me get a flashlight," he said. "You stay here."

She heard him shuffling toward the closet, and she turned, holding her hands out as she made her way back to the kitchen. Her shoes hit the broken coffee cup and it crunched as she walked over it.

"Jean? Batteries must be dead. I thought we changed them out a few weeks ago," Hal called.

"We did."

She pulled out the end drawer by the back door, the drawer that had become a catch-all. She felt inside it blindly, searching for the book of matches that she knew was in there.

"Where's another flashlight?"

"In the washroom. I've got matches," she said as she wrapped her fingers around them. She moved slowly back to the living room, feeling on the bookcase for the candle she kept there. The first match went out before she could light it, and she noticed that her hands were trembling. The candle lit on the second try, chasing some of the darkness away.

"You think it was an earthquake?" he asked as he came closer to the light. "They keep saying we're due a big one. Ever since they put that damn injection well in, ain't no telling what's happening around here."

"It didn't seem like it lasted long enough to be an earthquake," she said. "Remember the one back in 2000?"

She took the candle into her laundry room and opened the cabinet, seeing the small flashlight she kept there. She turned it on, but there was no light. That was odd. She'd used it just yesterday when she'd lost one of Hal's socks behind the dryer.

"The batteries must be dead in this one too," she said.

"Nothing ever works when you need it to," Hal said from the doorway. "I've got one out in my shop. Be right back."

"Best make sure the dog is okay. Lucky doesn't like thunderstorms," she reminded him. "This noise likely frazzled him."

* * *

"I told you we need to keep extra batteries around for this very thing," her mother said. "I can't believe that every single flashlight we own has dead batteries."

"I'll get the generator going in a minute. Butch? Can you give me a hand? We'll bring it over on the four-wheeler."

Dana pulled out her phone, remembering the flashlight app on it. She frowned as the phone remained off. Had she forgotten to charge it? No. She'd charged it that morning. In fact, it had been plugged in all night.

"Mom? Where's your cell phone?"

"It's in my purse. Why?"

"Mine's not working."

Uncle Joe pulled his out. "I'll call on up to the Bradford's and see if they've got power," he said.

Dana walked off the porch, thankful for clear skies, although the stars cast very little light down on them.

"Well, that's odd. The damn thing won't turn on."

Okay, she thought, it didn't take a rocket scientist to figure out something was going on. First the flashlights, now their cell phones?

"Uncle Joe, let's go around front and see if your car will start," she said.

"Why wouldn't it start?"

"Because I think we're having some kind of an issue with our batteries," she said. She looked through the darkness to her dad's workshop. They should have already had the generator loaded, but there was no sound of the four-wheeler's engine.

"Maybe we should head on home," Irene said quickly to Paul. "Make sure everything is okay. My phone is dead too."

The four of them made their way around to the front of the house, and Uncle Joe got in his car. The interior light did not come on, and Dana wasn't surprised when he turned the key and there was only a dull clicking sound.

"Let me try ours," Paul said, but he had no better luck.

"What the hell's going on?" Uncle Joe murmured.

* * *

The generator thundered outside and they finally had lights. They'd also determined that anything that used batteries was now useless. She couldn't even get her laptop to boot up. They plugged the TV into the power strip, but they couldn't get a signal on the satellite.

"I can't stand not knowing what's going on," Dana said, hearing the panic in her voice. She held her phone up. "I'm used to being connected."

"Calm down," Butch said. "We've got power to the fridge. We've got lights. We're fine. I'm sure they'll have the electricity restored tomorrow."

Irene and Paul had walked the half-mile to their house, but the others stayed. Butch and his parents lived only a little more than a mile away, but they would wait until morning to go home. Her other aunt and uncle lived over in Bedrock, so they were stuck here until they had a vehicle that worked.

"I need a drink," she murmured. "What do we have?"

Her mother laughed. "The only thing other than beer is your dad's whiskey that he hides up on the top shelf."

"Great. I'll find it," she said, going into the kitchen. "Anyone else want one?"

Butch was the only one who did, and he followed her. "You okay?"

"No," she said. "I hate not knowing what's going on. Was it an earthquake? Something else? I can understand the power but all the batteries?"

"Yeah, that is a little weird," he said.

She held up a Coke and he nodded. "What if the power doesn't come back on tomorrow? How long do we wait?"

"Well, it's not like we can drive anywhere to find out," he said.

She added her dad's whiskey to the glasses with ice, then topped them off with the Coke. "My old bicycle is here," she said. "Do you have one? We could use them to get around."

He laughed. "There's one in the barn, sure. It doesn't have tires, though. Not sure why we keep it. I think it was Tony's bike," he said, referring to his younger brother.

"What about that purple one you had when we were kids?"

He looked at her skeptically. "Dana, you do know that we're over thirty, right? I had that bike when we were seven or eight."

She sighed. "Yes, I know we're over thirty. God, where did the years go? It seems like yesterday I was heading off to college." She sipped from her drink. "Do you ever regret not leaving?"

He shrugged. "Sometimes, yeah. I'm content, though. It's a relatively stress-free life here."

"You still dating Holly Filmore from over in Paradox?"

"We still go out, yeah."

"Is marriage on the horizon?"

"No. She doesn't want to be a farm girl," he said.

"So why don't you move on to someone else?"

He shrugged again. "I like her…I'm content. Besides, out here in Paradox Valley, single women don't grow on trees. Like you, most move away."

"Well, maybe she'll come around."

"Yeah, maybe she will." His face turned pensive. "And maybe she won't."

She looked past him, seeing the others in the living room huddled together. They had two lamps hooked up to the generator, and they cast an almost eerie glow in the room. Her gaze drifted to the window where outside was nothing but the black expanse of darkness. She sighed and pulled her cell phone out of her pocket, hoping it worked now. It, too, remained dark.

CHAPTER SIX

He yawned as he held his thumb on the security scanner. It was 2 a.m. and he'd gotten to bed before eleven, for once, only to be woken up a few hours later by an urgent call. As he'd told Lieutenant Duncan…this better be good.

"Good morning, Colonel Sutter."

He glared at the soldier who saluted him. "Is it?" he mumbled as he walked past.

He went directly to the control room where Lieutenant Duncan had asked him to meet. He was surprised by the activity and the number of people in the room. They were all looking at various monitors and talking at once.

He cleared his throat loudly, waiting until they acknowledged his presence.

"At ease," he said as he tossed out a salute.

"Good. You're here, sir," Duncan said.

"It's goddamn 0200 hours on Sunday morning. What the hell is so important that it couldn't wait?"

Duncan turned to one of the soldiers at the monitors. "Peters, bring it up."

Sutter walked behind him, watching the screen. A quick flash of light, then nothing. "I hope you got more than that because I was in the middle of a very nice dream when you called. A redhead with big tits was about to give me a lap dance. So tell me this isn't what you hauled me in here for."

"This was picked up on radar, 2046 hours, local time, sir," Duncan said.

"So what's the thought? Drone? Missile? A damn meteor? What?" he asked.

"Unidentified. We've spent the last several hours going over satellite images, even telescope images. It doesn't show up anywhere. It was on our radar for all of four seconds."

"What's the conclusion? Hostile?"

"A craft definitely using stealth technology," Duncan said. "Where it originated, we have no idea. As you know, several countries have comparable aircraft to our B-2."

"Yes. But most are friendly."

"Russia has one."

Sutter pointed at the screen where the image played over and over. "It's not a bomber. It disappeared as if it landed. An aircraft the size of the B-2 can't land just anywhere. You got coordinates yet?"

"Without knowing the size of the object, we can lock it down to about two hundred square miles. Best guess is right across the Utah border into Colorado." Duncan turned and snapped his fingers. "Pull up the map."

When it appeared on the large monitor, he walked over to it. "Here's the area we're looking at," he said, making a circle with his finger.

"Any civilian reports?"

"Nothing yet, sir." He moved to another monitor. "Here is the current satellite image. It's remote country, most of it. But there are pockets—Squaw Valley, Paradox Valley—where people live. Farms, mostly, and a handful of unincorporated towns." He circled an area again. "Sparsely populated, but there should still be visible light. Bring up the satellite image from two nights ago," he instructed.

Sutter nodded at the difference. "So we've got a power outage in the area. Have you checked with the utility company?"

"Yes, sir. They have no reports of damage, no reports of outages from their customers. They only get feedback once a day from their meters so they'll be able to get us something Monday."

"They'll be able to tell what area is affected?"

"Yes, sir. That'll help us narrow it down." Duncan cleared his throat nervously. "But there's something else we need to consider," he said. "This thing...it could be something that...well, that didn't originate on this earth."

Sutter would have laughed if not for the seriousness of Duncan's voice. "UFO? Are you suggesting we have a goddamn UFO that landed out there in the middle of nowhere?" he asked, pointing to the map that was still up.

"I'm...I'm saying it's something we should consider, sir."

"You're out of your fucking mind if you think I'm going to General Brinkley with a goddamn UFO theory."

"With the power out to that area, it could be something with an electromagnetic pulse of some sort. That might explain why there have been no civilian reports. No power. Cell towers in the area are probably useless. I'd guess—"

"I don't want a goddamn guess, Lieutenant Duncan," Sutter said harshly. "Let's send out a Black Hawk at first light."

"A Black Hawk, sir? Are you sure? I mean, maybe we should—"

"I need something more than a guess, Duncan. Send a helicopter out." He stared again at the image of the flash of light on the screen as it repeated over and over. "I'll wait until morning to inform Brinkley."

"Yes, sir. Of course."

Sutter shook his head as he left the room. UFO? What the hell was Duncan thinking? That wasn't a goddamn spaceship. If word got out that he was even *thinking* that...they'd have another Roswell on their hands and the place would be crawling with conspiracy theorists thinking they were hiding little green men on the base.

"UFO," he muttered with another shake of his head.

CHAPTER SEVEN

Lucky started barking a few moments before they heard pounding on their door. Hal and Jean turned at the same time to stare at it. Breakfast had been a simple meal of fried eggs and bacon with the homemade bread Jean had baked the other day. Trying to save fuel for the generator, Jean had dug out their old percolator and they'd had their coffee the old-fashioned way, cooked on the gas stove. They'd managed just fine since the power had gone off and they hadn't lacked for anything. Well, except for information. They could only speculate as to what was going on. They'd heard the helicopter early that morning and had gone outside. It never got close enough for them to see it, but they'd heard the crash. Breakfast had turned somber after that.

"I'll see who it is," he said to Jean. As he walked to the door, he glanced against the wall where he'd put his rifle. Only as a precaution, he'd told Jean. He pulled the curtains back from the window, relaxing as he recognized one of his neighbors. "It's Carl Milstead."

He went out on the porch, extending his hand to Carl in greeting. Lucky was already there, sniffing Carl's boots.

"You and Jean okay?" Carl asked.

"We're making it." He glanced behind Carl where two others sat atop horses. One held the reins of the horse Carl had been riding. "Jim, Graham," he said in greeting.

"Hal," they said with a nod of their heads.

"Did you hear the helicopter this morning?" Carl asked.

"Yep, sure did. Heard it crash too," Hal said.

Carl nodded. "Sounded like it was over past the creek, up near the high ridge, maybe. Good ways west of the valley, I imagine. We're going to get a group to go check it out. Thought you might want to join us."

"Up past the creek? That could be anywhere," he said. "Only the three of you going?"

"Got Curtis and Dusty too. Just came from Dusty's place. His wife is putting together some supplies. They made a whole mess of elk jerky over the winter. We figure to only be gone a couple of days. Three at the most."

Hal glanced back at the door. He reckoned Jean could manage on her own. But hell, every last one of them was over seventy. Most nearing seventy-five, like him. What business did they have taking horses through the canyon along Paradox Creek?

"Be an easy ride, Hal," Carl said, as if reading his thoughts. "I suppose you're like the rest of us. Got no batteries? No phone?"

Hal nodded. "Nothing's working. Don't even know what time it is."

"Had to be an army helicopter," Carl continued. "Probably from over at the base in Utah."

"I suppose sittin' around here waiting ain't getting us nowhere," Hal said. "Daisy's not been on a trail ride in a while. I guess she wouldn't mind a trek through the canyon."

"Good. We're going to meet at Dusty's place. Come as soon as you can." Carl paused before getting on his horse. "You might want to bring a rifle," he said. "Ain't no telling what's going on."

Hal watched them ride away before going back inside. Jean was tidying up the lunch dishes.

"What's that fool got planned now?"

Hal smiled at that. The Milsteads had been their neighbors for over forty years, but they weren't exactly friends.

"He's rounded up a posse. Wants to go check out the helicopter crash," he said. "Wants me to go along."

Jean stared at him. "And are you?"

"Might as well. They figure it was an army helicopter. Shouldn't take too long to get there on horses."

"Hal, you haven't been on Daisy in more years than I can remember," she said. "She's likely to throw you right off."

"I'll be okay, Jean. Let me go fetch her." He motioned to the kitchen. "If you could put together something that I could eat for dinner tonight, that'd be real nice," he said. "I've got that old canteen out in the barn. I suppose that'll have to do for water 'till we get to the creek."

He knew Jean didn't like the idea of him going off, but he felt obligated. All of the other men were going. Even though he felt like it was probably a waste of time, he didn't want to be the only one to stay behind. Jean could take care of herself for a few days. He reached down and ruffled the dog's head. And she'd have Lucky. The dog wasn't good for much, but at least he'd be some company for Jean.

"Ain't that right, boy?"

Lucky seemed to be smiling up at him as he followed Hal to the barn. Hal smiled back, feeling a bit foolish. They didn't need or want a dog...not at their age. But a momma dog had strayed up over at the Bensons' place a couple of years ago. Momma dogs didn't usually last long out here, but the Bensons took a liking to her. Next thing you know, all the neighbors were being offered puppies. How he and Jean ended up with one, he'll never know. The momma dog was a half-breed black Lab. They didn't have a clue as to who the daddy was, but all them puppies were jet black and as fat and round as little piglets. The Bensons brought over two of them, and the next thing he knew, Jean had picked one up and was cuddling it and cooing at it like it was a baby. He knew right then that the Bensons would only be leaving with one puppy that day.

But Lucky was a good dog. Never caused them a bit of trouble. Except when he crawled into the water trough and made a mess of things. Hal guessed he might be more Lab than not...he sure did like the water.

* * *

Sutter ran his hands over his hair, back and forth. He kept it short, neat—military style. Always had. His wife hated it, but it was familiar to him. When he looked in the mirror, there was never any doubt who he was...what he was.

"Sir? Did you want me to notify the families?" Duncan asked again.

"Not until we know for sure," he said. Though by all accounts, the aircraft was lost. Disappeared off radar like someone had flipped a switch. Disappeared in the sector where the unidentified...*object* had disappeared too. "He could have made a landing."

"Yes, sir."

Sutter sighed, then leaned back in his chair. General Brinkley had chewed his ass out for sending up a Black Hawk in the first place. His only saving grace was that the target sector was mostly federal land and not state, or worse, private. Brinkley told him to sit tight until he heard back from him. Brinkley was following protocol and going through all the proper channels. Maybe that's why he was promoted to rank of general, and Sutter had been passed over for promotion yet again.

"Still no civilian reports? No one saw it go down?"

"No, sir. It's like there's nobody out there."

"What about the power company? They get back with us yet on which grid we're looking at?"

"They said they'd get something to us before noon," Duncan said.

"And the cell towers?"

"We're pinging them, sir. Nothing."

"Media?"

"As far as we know, there's been nothing reported."

He gave a humorless laugh. "Well, there's that going for us."

Duncan fidgeted with his hands and Sutter raised his eyebrows.

"Sir...if I may?"

"What, Duncan? You got another theory?"

"Communication with the crew was normal. There was no distress signal. Nothing out of the ordinary. Communication was lost in mid-sentence. The exact same instant they disappeared from radar."

"I know. I was there." He sighed. "Are you going to bring up this electromagnetic pulse crap again?"

"It's a credible theory, sir."

"Back on the UFO again, Duncan?"

"There could be any number of ways to jam communication signals, shut down power grids. It could—"

"I'm more likely to believe domestic terrorists before little green men from outer space," he said loudly. "Our airspace was breeched. *That's* what we should be concerned about. If it wasn't a meteor and it was indeed an aircraft of some sort, how the hell did it get all the way to the Utah-Colorado border without being detected?" He slammed his hand on the desk. "And if it's not domestic terrorists, then what goddamn country did it come from? Find *that* out, Duncan. Drop the UFO bullshit."

"Of course, sir. I'll get back to it."

Sutter stared at the closed door long after Duncan had left. He had a bad feeling about this. Was it terrorists they were dealing with? Was there going to be an attack of some sort? Bio-terror?

Brinkley had chewed his ass, yeah. But sending out a Black Hawk to do some reconnaissance seemed like the right move. What did Brinkley expect him to do? Notify the state and have a local sheriff go out and take a look?

He shook his head. No. Brinkley wouldn't go that route. Not with power and cell phones out. *Something* was going on and apparently no one on his staff had a clue…Duncan's UFO theory aside. No. Brinkley wouldn't notify the locals. Not yet.

CHAPTER EIGHT

Dana stared down the lane from their house to the road. It was a beautiful morning, cool and crisp. The sky was clear and blue, birds called from the trees and only a slight breeze rustled the leaves. It could have been ten, fifteen or even twenty years ago that she sat here. Things remained unchanged—timeless—in this little corner of the world. Life crawled at a slow pace here, following the ebb and flow of the sun as it rose and set. Early mornings, like today, it was a lazy breeze that blew, carrying with it the sounds of the chickens and rooster as they started their day. It seemed to be a perfectly normal morning in late May. It was nearly too quiet, too perfect. Even the generator was off for the time being, the absence of its constant rumbling creating a void in the stillness.

She assumed Butch and his parents had made it back to their farm yesterday. Aunt Tina and Uncle George had walked back with them. Butch and his family's house was bigger so they would stay there until someone could drive them over to Bedrock. Butch had been in a hurry to leave. They had chores to attend to, power or not. So did her parents, and Dana had found herself feeding the chickens, something she used to love to do as a child. She didn't, however, particularly enjoy eating dinner when chicken was served. Even at that young age, she knew where the food had come from.

"What are you staring at?"

Dana turned, finding her mother watching her from the door. She patted the seat beside her, inviting her mother to join her on the porch swing.

"Waiting on Butch to come back. We're going to make a run for it, remember?"

"We're managing fine," her mother said. "Your father has enough fuel to run the generator for a month, if need be."

Dana raised her eyebrows. A *month*? Did her mother really plan to stay here a month without knowing what was going on? Dana would go stark raving mad. In fact, a few more days of this might very well send her there.

"While I appreciate your sense of adventure," she said, "I can't just sit here and hope the power comes back on."

"Well, you were going to be here for two weeks anyway," her mother reminded her. "You should try to relax. The weather's been beautiful. I know you like to hike. You should get out."

Maybe Dana had been in the city too long. Maybe that's why she felt this underlying sense of panic. But to go hiking? As if nothing out of the ordinary was going on?

"How can you act like nothing's wrong?" she asked.

"Oh, honey, it's not like it's the first time the power's gone out. Why do you think everyone has generators? Besides, remember that freak ice storm we had a few winters ago? We were without power for four days."

"Not only the power, Mom. The batteries too. Our cell phones. There's no satellite reception, no TV. Something's going on."

"Well, the earthquake may have caused some damage. I'm sure we'll find out soon enough."

"If it even was an earthquake," she said. "It was obviously *something*. And I can't simply go on about my business as if it was nothing."

"You worry too much," her mother said. "Even when you were younger, you were always a worrier. What good is it going to do for you and Butch to go out?"

"Someone has to know something, don't you think?"

"Dana, the power *always* comes back on."

But Dana shook her head. It was the second full day without power. Something wasn't right. She didn't want to sit here and wait. Because she didn't know what they were waiting on. Waiting on the power to come back on? Waiting on someone to show up? Waiting on something *bad* to happen? At what point would her mother start to worry? At five days? A week?

"What if it doesn't come back on this time, Mom?"

"It'll come back." Her mother stood up, signaling an end to the conversation. "I best start on lunch."

Dana frowned. They'd barely gotten finished cleaning up the kitchen from their early breakfast. A rather large breakfast, in fact. Apparently her mother was more worried than she let on. Cooking had always been her outlet when she needed a distraction from something.

Dana let a heavy sigh escape, then turned her attention back to the road. It remained empty…and quiet. She hoped Butch hadn't changed his mind. They'd agreed that if the power was still out today, they'd take off and try to make it to Paradox. Or at least to someone's house where there was power. Since Butch had no bike and her old one had a flat, their mode of transportation would be by horseback.

She'd grown up with horses, but once she'd left home, her father had sold the two that remained. She couldn't remember the last time she'd ridden. Five years or more, she guessed, and that had been only a short ride with Butch on one of her rare summer visits.

So she told herself it would be fun. She tried to forget the fact that it would take them more than one day to reach Paradox. That meant a night out. And again, horseback riding and camping were two things she did frequently when growing up. Now? She hated to admit it, but she'd turned into a city girl after living so long in Seattle.

She pulled her phone out of the pocket of her jeans and ran her hand over it affectionately. God, who would have thought she'd miss the damn thing so much. She closed her eyes for a second, then pushed the button. The screen remained black and lifeless. With a sigh, she slipped it back into her pocket and resumed her wait for Butch.

CHAPTER NINE

The ringing of her phone startled her so much, she stared at it for several seconds before walking over to pick it up. Corey couldn't remember the last time someone had called her.

"Yeah, Conaway here," she answered.

"Captain Conaway? Please hold for General Brinkley."

Her brow drew together in a frown. Sounded like an official call. The last time Harry had called to check on her—a month or more now—he'd used his personal phone. She only had to hold a few seconds before his familiar voice sounded in her ear.

"Conaway? I know it's early but...you got a minute?"

"Yes, sir. Of course."

"We've got a situation," he said. "I need your help." He paused. "I need someone I can trust."

She ran a hand through her hair, noting the length of it. It hadn't been this long since she was a teenager. She found a little humor in that thought, knowing that it really wasn't long now. She'd lived in a military family all her life, had followed her father into the service, had moved up the ranks quickly. All the while, she kept her hair cut military short. She wasn't a woman concerned with her looks. She was a soldier. But now? Was she still a soldier?

"Corey? You there?"

She turned her attention back to the phone. "I'm not in any kind of shape, Harry," she said. "Mentally or physically," she added.

"I need you to get back in the saddle, kiddo. It's time. I can't leave you on special assignment forever, you know."

Yes, of course she knew that. She'd actually been surprised he'd let it go this long. But Harry Brinkley and her father had been best friends. She'd known him her whole life. When her father had been killed, it was Harry her family turned to for support. And when her team had gotten ambushed at a remote airport in Pakistan, Harry had been the steadying force when all she'd wanted to do was take her rage out on Colonel Sutter and his so-called intel. As her team had been lying dead on the tarmac around her, she knew Sutter was to blame. She, too, had been left for dead, yet somehow she'd survived. Her physical injuries had healed but not her mental ones. For all Harry had done, he couldn't heal that. But he needed her now. She owed him that.

She swallowed down her apprehension and nodded. "Yes, sir. You're right, of course. It's time to get back. What do you need me to do?"

"That's my girl," he said quietly. Then he cleared his throat, pausing only a few seconds before continuing. "I'll tell you what I know, which isn't much. Sutter's team spotted an object on radar. About four seconds of it anyway, for what it's worth. They've got a potential grid of where it went down. Sutter sent out a Black Hawk for recon. It disappeared off radar approximately in the same area as our unidentified object."

The mention of Sutter's name made her bristle, but she pushed her anger at him aside. "Assumed lost?" she asked.

"No radio contact, no distress signal. Disappeared."

"What area are we talking about?"

"Local," he said. "Colorado, across the Utah border. Paradox Valley, if that means anything to you."

"I've driven through the area," she said. "Desolate in places. A handful of farms and ranches."

"Power is out in the area. Cell towers are out too," he said. "Because it is sparsely populated, there's been nothing in the news. A unit for the salinity control of the Colorado River is out that way. A pumping station and an injection well, but there's been no indication that they've had any problems with power. The outage appears to be to the north and west of Bedrock."

She scratched the back of her neck, not really understanding. "So you think the power outage is a result of this...this object on radar? Or something to do with the Black Hawk?"

"Unknown at this point. Hell, it could be a coincidence, for all we know."

"Okay, so what's Sutter's theory?"

Harry sighed. "Several theories, all with no substance," he said. "Sutter's got a guy, Lieutenant Duncan, who is even going so far as suggesting it could be a UFO with little green men."

Her eyebrows shot up. "Seriously?"

"Seriously."

"Okay. So what's the *official* theory?"

"Unidentified object, possible meteor," he said. "Got a seismic reading from the area...2.3. Of course, since they put in that injection well, they've had thousands of small earthquakes, most not even detectable above ground."

"Harry, you're losing me here," she said truthfully. "A possible meteor went down, took out power. What's that got to do with us?"

"We need to be sure, for one thing, that it wasn't a hostile aircraft."

"If it was a hostile aircraft on a mission, wouldn't we already know something?"

"We have the greatest military in the world," he said. "Yes, we would know if it was a hostile. Our intel says it wasn't."

"Could it have been a drone or something?" she asked.

"Too large. I'm going to believe our experts that it was only a meteor...but like I said, we need to be sure. Especially with the Black Hawk going down," he said. "Obviously *something* took out the power grid, the cell towers. *Something* is causing batteries to turn useless."

"What do you mean...batteries?"

"Maybe Duncan's theory of an electromagnetic pulse is true. Maybe this meteor is radioactive or something."

"I don't understand."

"It's not only electrical power that's out, Corey. When we lost contact with the Black Hawk, we sent in a squad of ten. The transport vehicle lost power...battery, whatnot. Communication was lost. Wristwatches stopped working. Everything stopped functioning. They hiked back out, but we at least know where the western edge of the zone is," he said. "There's only one highway that goes into the canyon from Utah to Colorado. It doesn't appear to be affected. Our zone is to the north of that, including the town of Paradox. As a precaution, we're closing the highway. Using a rock slide as the excuse. There's not a lot of thru traffic anyway, but what there is, it's being rerouted to the south. The Department of Transportation is cooperating, but since there really is no slide, it's only a matter of time before word gets out."

"And the locals?"

"Haven't heard from them," he said. "There's no power, no cell phones, like I said. Our checkpoint is on a small unpaved county road. That's where our team lost power. From what we understand, the nearest residence is more than twenty miles down that road, heading toward Paradox, which is probably another twenty miles or so beyond that. We don't yet know the southern point of our zone, although the highway is not affected," he said. "And that's, like I said, to the south of Paradox. Inside this zone, phones go dead, batteries go dead. Obviously, it appears our helicopter lost power. We've designated this area as a no-fly zone for the time being."

She again ran her hand through her hair. "What do you want me to do?"

"I need you to get in there. Once you're in the zone, there'll be no communication."

"You want me to find the Black Hawk?"

"That's a start. Some of the locals could have seen it. We're sending in another squad, on foot. It's rough terrain from what I understand, and we don't have a firm location. It could take several days before they find it. If you think you can get to it, great. We need to locate the craft and more importantly, the crew. But I want you to go in and… and see if you can find whatever the hell it was that landed, whether it was a meteor or not. Someone had to have seen something out there."

"No offense, General, but wouldn't it be quicker to send in troops for this instead of merely one person?"

"We have no valid reason to deploy troops on private land… certainly not without causing a media stir, which is something we're trying to avoid."

"Why not call it a training exercise?" she suggested.

"That's been considered. But training exercises are planned months in advance, and the local and state authorities are always notified well ahead of time. We don't want to bring up any red flags. I've got a downed helicopter and three crew members missing and unaccounted for. I'll have enough explaining to do over that. We don't need to deploy troops and have the locals think they're under attack or something. Remember how crazy those Texans got when we started the Jade Helm exercise?"

"Okay. And this might be a stupid question, but why isn't the power company trying to get in there to restore power?" She heard him sigh before he answered.

"Let me be completely honest with you, Corey. This whole thing is going to turn into a clusterfuck if we don't find out what the hell's going on and quick," he said, causing her to laugh quietly. "I'm serious. We're telling the Department of Transportation that there's a rock slide. Someone under Sutter told the power company that a satellite fell from orbit and might be radioactive. That's how we're keeping them away. The radioactive part might be true, for all I know, but we're fairly certain it's not a damn satellite."

"How the hell did that not hit the media yet?"

"It's only a matter of time. Fortunately, we're dealing with a desolate area with very few people. The power outage affects less than a hundred residences. That's not gonna make the news."

"And why again are we involved and not the local or state authorities?"

"Because goddamn Sutter overreacted and sent out a Black Hawk that didn't make it back," he said loudly. "Sorry. But if it ends up being just a damn meteor, I'll have his ass for losing a helicopter and her crew."

"You won't get any complaints from me on that," she said.

"I know, Corey. I know you can't stand the sight of the man. But—"

"But you want me to go to the base," she said. "And report to Colonel Sutter."

"Yes. And please don't shoot him. I don't think I could explain that to the Secretary."

At that, Corey laughed. Then she sobered up. Was that really the first time she'd laughed out loud in the last four months?

"They'll have gear for you, maps, everything you'll need," he continued.

"Will you be there?"

"No. I'm in Washington. I have a briefing with the Vice Chairman of the Joint Chiefs in the morning."

"You probably shouldn't mention the UFO and little green men theory," she said with a smile.

"Let's just hope you don't find a spaceship."

"Yeah...let's hope."

"This mission is classified, Corey. Sutter knows you're going into the zone, obviously. And his Lieutenant Duncan does too. They know your mission. We're also sending in a squad from Sutter's command on foot, like I said. They'll know you're in the area as well."

"The last time I trusted someone under Sutter's command—"

"I know, Captain. And after review, Major Godfrey was transferred out. But Duncan—he's a good man from what I hear. Spotless record. You can trust him."

"Perhaps. But I don't trust Sutter in the least."

"Right now, we don't know what the hell is going on out there, Corey. You've got to trust him. You've got to trust *me*."

Corey still held her phone long after Harry had ended the call. This whole thing seemed a little far-fetched, and she wondered if he was fabricating some of it for her. If this was simply a benign mission that he wanted her on so that she could get "back in the saddle," as he'd said, why hint that it could possibly be something other than a meteor?

Well, first things first, she thought. She tossed her phone down and went into the bathroom, pulling out her hair clippers from one of the cabinets. She stood looking at herself in the mirror, hardly recognizing the image that looked back at her. Her face seemed pale, gaunt. Her dark eyes shallow. She always prided herself on her level of fitness. In the last four months, she'd done absolutely nothing that resembled exercise other than long walks. And she couldn't remember the last decent meal she'd had. She didn't seem to have an appetite for anything. She assumed she was about to pay for her lack of activity.

But at least she'd look the part of a soldier. She slipped on a Number Four clipper guard and turned it on. The familiar buzz was almost a comfort to her and she brought her hand up, pausing only a second to meet her gaze in the mirror before running the clippers through her dark hair. It had been a weekly chore for her in the past and even after four long months of not bothering, it was with a practiced ease that she trimmed her hair. Perhaps it was only symbolic, but as her hair fell around her, she could almost feel the pain of the last four months slip away.

She would never forget her team. Seven men and three women. Ten individuals working seamlessly as one. They had been as close as any family unit. They fought together, they cried together...and they laughed together.

And they were all gone, leaving her behind to carry on without them. She put the clippers down and ran her hand over her hair several times. It wasn't a military buzz cut, but it was short enough to remind her of what she was. She met her eyes in the mirror, then squared her shoulders.

"Captain Conaway reporting for duty," she said out loud.

As she stared at herself, a small smile finally appeared. Yes. It was time she got back in the game.

CHAPTER TEN

Dana stared up at the horse, then looked back over at Butch, who was holding the reins of his own ride. "Couldn't have found one any bigger than this, huh?" she asked dryly.

He laughed. "I know she's big, but she's gentle. Tough as nails too."

She reached up and tentatively stroked the horse's head. Well, she supposed her only other option would be to walk. Paradox was nearly thirty miles away. She shrugged and picked up her backpack.

"My mom made us some sandwiches," she said. "From last night's meatloaf. And she wrapped up some of those ribs from the other night's barbeque."

"Good. I've got some cheese and crackers," he said. "A link of that dried sausage we made in the fall."

She wrinkled up her nose. "Venison?"

"Oh, come on. You grew up eating venison."

"I grew up eating a *lot* of things I wouldn't eat now."

He smiled at her. "Remember how you used to love my mom's stew?"

She held her hand up. "Do not remind me. I didn't know it had bunnies in it until we were in high school."

"Wild rabbits, not bunnies," he corrected. He looked past her toward the house. "Where's your mom and dad?"

"Chores. They're not exactly thrilled that we're going off," she said. "Especially Mom. She thinks we should stick it out until the power comes back."

Butch nodded. "Yeah. My folks think we're crazy too," he said. "I think they're afraid we're going to get into some trouble."

Dana rolled her eyes. "We're not kids anymore," she said as she swung up onto the saddle. Thankfully, the horse never moved. She leaned down and patted its neck. "Good girl."

Butch nudged his horse and headed down the lane toward the road. Dana looked back over her shoulder, seeing her mother watching from the window. She raised a hand and waved, getting a small one in return.

"I figure we'll follow Cat Creek until it crosses under the road," Butch said. "At least we won't have to worry about water for the horses."

"We used to do that when we were kids," she said. "There's that section where it drops into the canyon. The horses can't make it, can they?"

"We're getting a late start," he said. "That'll probably be a good place to camp. Then in the morning we can skirt the canyon. The road is not that far after that. We'll just take the road on in to Paradox. Shouldn't take us but four or five hours tomorrow."

"Okay." She nodded. "Sounds like a plan."

He glanced over at her. "You nervous?"

She shrugged. "I don't know. I got a bad feeling," she said. She looked behind her one more time, but her mother was no longer standing by the window.

"Just going on a little trail ride," he said. "We'll be fine."

She brushed the blond hair out of her eyes, wishing she'd thought to bring a ball cap along. The sun was already getting hot. Of course, when she'd left Seattle, ball caps and horseback riding had not been on her mind. She pulled down the sunglasses which had been perched on top of her head, then she nudged her horse a little to catch up with Butch.

He glanced at her. "Your hair is longer than the last time you were here." He grinned. "It's also blond."

"I've always had blond hair."

He laughed. "Light brown, maybe with a touch of red."

"Red? Get real. It's blond."

"How else do you explain the freckles on your nose?"

"The freckles on my nose have absolutely *nothing* to do with me *maybe* having a trace of red in my hair," she said, pretending to be annoyed. "Besides, my hairdresser assures me that this color looks perfectly natural on me."

"Yeah, it does. I'm just messing with you."

"You hear about my marriage proposal?" she asked.

His eyes widened. "I didn't even know you were dating anyone. Who's the lucky gal and did she say yes?"

She shook her head. "No, no. It wasn't me who proposed. Kendra—a woman I've been seeing for barely six months—popped the question."

He laughed. "So let me guess…that's why you showed up here so unexpectedly. You ran."

She laughed too. "Yeah. And fast."

"So what's the deal?"

"I like her okay. And we have fun. But it's not like it's some big love affair. At least not on my end."

"I see. You like her, but you're not in love with her." He nodded. "I can relate."

"You mean with Holly?"

"Yeah. Only Holly is the one who isn't in love," he said with a quick shrug. "She made it clear to me that she had no intention of marrying a farmer and staying in Paradox Valley the rest of her life. It wasn't like we ever really discussed marriage, though. If she stayed around, I imagine it would probably lead to that, regardless if we're crazy in love or not."

"Yeah, well I don't want to be content. I *want* to be crazy in love."

"So what kind of woman are you going to fall for?"

She smiled wistfully. "I like strong women. Women who are sure of themselves. Women who aren't afraid to be who they are." She glanced over at him. "I'm not really into girlie girls."

"Ah. You mean butch women. I guess I can see that."

"I mean strong, independent women," she clarified. "No long nails, no nail polish…I don't like women who wear a lot of makeup."

He rolled his eyes. "Yeah. So butch women."

She laughed. "I prefer the word 'sporty.' Besides, I have this vision of her. I call her my Dream Girl."

"So why keep dating this other chick?"

She sighed. "I don't know. I'm kinda in a rut, I guess." She looked at him. "My job, my life. Everything."

"I thought you loved your job."

"I like it. I guess." She paused. "I got a degree in marketing because you can work pretty much anywhere with that. I took the first job that was offered to me and I'm still there." She shrugged. "So it's a job, that's all. I don't know that I'd say I love it though."

"Weren't you promoted recently?"

"Last year. To sales manager," she said. "It's been challenging coordinating the sales team so that was a good change. And I like the people I work with. I have an assistant under me who I can boss around, so that's a plus," she said with a laugh. "And I love my boss. There are no complaints where he's concerned."

"So what's the problem?"

"It's just a job and I feel like I settled," she said. "I mean, I've never even *looked* for another job. Some people my age have had three or four jobs already."

"I thought it wasn't good to job hop," he said.

"That's old school. Now? People change jobs every other year, it seems. It broadens their experience, for one thing. They get into their thirties or forties and maybe then they find that perfect job that fits their skillset."

"So it's really your job that's got you feeling stagnant. Not Kendra?"

"It's both, really. I don't want to settle in my personal life like I did in my professional one. That's all I'm saying."

"Then quit your job and get a new one."

"I'm kinda stuck now," she said. "I'm over thirty and this is the only job I've ever had. If I got another job, it would have to be in the same capacity. It's all I know. So I might as well stay where I am. I can't complain about my salary and I certainly don't want to start over." She sighed again. "Anyway, you're missing the point. It's not about my job. It's about my *life*. Yes, I feel stagnant. I haven't met my Dream Girl and I probably never will. I'm going to end up settling, like I did with my job. At what point do I settle? At what point do I accept a marriage proposal from someone like Kendra? Which, of course, would be so not fair to them. All because I've had this stupid dream since I was a kid."

"You're still young, Dana. Don't worry about having to settle. You'll meet your Dream Girl one day. You just need to have faith."

Faith? When she was in her twenties, she still had faith that she'd meet the woman of her dreams. Now that she was over thirty, however, that faith was dwindling, much like the years that were slipping away from her.

CHAPTER ELEVEN

Sutter leaned back in his chair, his glance going to the door then back to Duncan. Captain Conaway would be here any minute, and he was shocked that he felt apprehensive about their meeting. He was a colonel, for God's sake. But she was General Brinkley's pet. Anything they discussed would be reported back to Brinkley, no doubt.

"Is there something wrong, sir?"

"She's a goddamn nutcase, Duncan. That's what's wrong."

"Captain Conaway, sir?"

He leaned forward again. "She accused me of intentionally sabotaging a mission she was on."

"Major Godfrey took the fall, sir."

"Damn right he did. He was a good man. He screwed up, sure, but he was still a damn good man," he said. "Now he's in some godforsaken desert hellhole."

"I've heard of Captain Conaway, sir, but I've never met her," Duncan said.

"Consider yourself lucky. She's up Brinkley's ass. She's been on… *special assignment*," he said, making quotations in the air. "Been seeing a shrink too. I'm certain she's not the one for this job, but who am I to argue with Brinkley. He thinks she hung the moon or something."

"I hear she lost her whole team, sir."

Sutter narrowed his eyes at Duncan. "Yeah, she did. Maybe she should have shouldered some of the blame too instead of piling it all on Godfrey. She was the one on the tarmac, not him."

"Of course, sir."

"She's hotheaded, Duncan," he continued. "She'll never make it past the rank of captain. Hell, I don't know how she even got that far. I'm sure that was Brinkley's doing."

"Yes, sir."

"You be wary of what you say to her. Like I said, she's up Brinkley's ass."

"If you don't mind me asking, sir, are they…involved?"

Sutter stared at him for a few seconds, then laughed. "Involved? No. She's a goddamn dyke. Hell, she—" He stopped in mid-sentence as a quick, loud knock on his door signaled Captain Conaway's arrival. "Come in, Peterson."

Corporal Peterson nodded briefly at both him and Duncan. "Captain Conaway is here, sir."

Peterson stepped aside as Conaway walked into the room, then he left and closed the door behind him. Conaway glanced at Duncan before turning her gaze on him. Sutter saw the defiance in her eyes, and he wondered if she had the balls to refuse to salute him. She looked much the same as the last time he'd seen her although she appeared to have lost weight. Her uniform hung loosely from her shoulders. Her hair was cut military short, as she normally kept it. He held her eyes for a long moment, almost daring her not to salute. She finally squared her shoulders and raised her hand, holding it to her forehead.

"Colonel Sutter," she said in greeting. "Captain Conaway reporting, as ordered by General Brinkley, sir."

He returned her salute quickly. "Have a seat, Captain. This is Lieutenant Duncan. He'll be handling the briefing."

"General Brinkley said you would have gear for me. And maps," she said, addressing Duncan. "I'm not really familiar with the area. I understand I'm to get dropped off this afternoon."

Sutter stared at her. "You look out of shape, Conaway. Can you still haul a fifty-pound pack? That'll be quite a hike for you."

"I can manage, sir."

Sutter leaned forward, bringing a smile to his face. "You seem a little…hostile, Conaway. I'd hoped your sessions with the shrink would have helped. Yet I sense you still have anger issues."

She surprised him by matching his fake smile with one of her own. "I promised Harry I wouldn't shoot you, so I'm trying to play nice… *sir*."

Her casual use of General Brinkley's first name spoke volumes to him. He leaned back, acknowledging she'd made her point with a slight nod. "Duncan, why don't you take Captain Conaway to your office for the briefing. Shouldn't take long. Then get her the hell out to the zone."

"Of course, sir."

Duncan stood and Conaway did the same. This time, her smile was a bit condescending as she saluted him. He let out a frustrated sigh as the door closed behind them.

"Arrogant bitch," he muttered.

Something about Conaway had always irritated him. He hated to admit it, but she was too perfect a soldier, too competent. She did her job with little regard for the politics of the military, as if she couldn't care less about rank. But he didn't work his ass off to get where he was only to have some underling think she was above saluting him. Respect was respect whether you liked it or not.

He shook his head slowly. "She actually called him 'Harry.'" Again he wondered at the extent of their relationship. Brinkley kept his private life private. Sutter knew very little about the man outside of the military. And Conaway? He knew absolutely nothing about her private life. He, like everyone else, assumed she was a lesbian. But she seemed devoted to the military and he knew of no one in her personal life, other than her team. They were a close-knit group, very cohesive. He had to admit, they were the damn best he'd ever had under his command. Elite, in fact.

Of course, "were" being the operative word in this case. And that was the only reason he was letting her slide on her lack of respect for him. The *only* reason. He didn't care if she and *Harry* Brinkley were close or not. He was still her commanding officer.

"Arrogant," he murmured again.

* * *

"This way, Captain," Duncan said as he pushed open a door and waved her inside.

"You don't have to formally address me, Duncan," she said.

"Of course, ma'am. As you wish."

She turned to him. "And don't call me ma'am. You make me feel old."

"Yes, ma'am. Of course."

She flashed him a smile. "Lighten up, Duncan. I'm here for a quick briefing, some gear and maps, then I'll get out of your hair," she said.

"The day is wasting. Besides, Brinkley was pretty thorough in his briefing to me. I would like to see the blip on the radar, though."

He nodded. "Of course. There's not much to it, really," he said as he sat down at his desk and pulled his keyboard closer.

"Were you the one who spotted it?"

"Actually, yes, ma'am, I was." He smiled sheepishly. "Sorry. Habit." His turned his monitor around for her to see. "Don't blink or you'll miss it."

"Wow. Four seconds?"

"Four-point-three, to be exact," he said, spinning the monitor back around. "We spent hours going over possibilities, thinking perhaps a meteor had missed detection. Nothing showed up on any radar or telescope or any satellite image," he said.

She stared at him. "The official stance is that it *was* a meteor," she said.

He nodded. "Yes, ma'am. That's what people who make more money than me are saying."

She raised an eyebrow. "I understand you have a theory that goes against the grain."

He actually blushed before he answered. "Colonel Sutter thinks I'm out of my mind," he said. "I simply raised the possibility of...well, of something from another world."

"Do you actually believe in that sort of thing? UFOs?" When he hesitated, she added, "I'm not one to judge, Duncan."

He shrugged. "Well, I think it's more probable than not that there are other life-forms in this vast universe of ours. Surely we're not the only planet or star that has life on it. I mean, it's mindboggling to think that we're on this little piece of rock—one of so very many—spinning around in space...and space is infinite. Think of the possibilities."

"Star Trek fan?"

He blushed again. "Not as rabid as some, but yes," he said.

"Well, I get where you're coming from, Duncan. And I agree with you. There's probably something out there somewhere. But in this case, I can't see how something from *out there*," she said, pointing to the window, "could make it all the way here without being detected. There are satellites all over the damn place. And I'm fairly certain there are a lot of telescopes searching our sky for this very possibility. I don't think something comes in undetected."

"To quote a line from a movie, ma'am, 'it's a big-ass sky,'" he said.

She laughed quietly. "So you're convinced the object we're looking for is indeed a UFO?"

"Not convinced, no. But I don't think we should dismiss the possibility just because it seems implausible."

She nodded. "Okay. Since I'm charged with trying to find this alleged meteor, I'll keep that possibility in mind." She smiled. "And if I do happen to find a spaceship, what do you propose I do?"

He grinned. "Run like hell, Captain."

She laughed out loud, noting how good it felt to truly laugh again. "You're okay, Duncan."

"Thank you, ma'am. And despite what Colonel Sutter says, I don't think you're a hotheaded nutcase."

She laughed again. "Damn...he said that? He never did like me." Her smile faded. "The feeling is mutual."

CHAPTER TWELVE

Hal pulled Daisy to a stop next to Jim Holman. The six members of their little posse lined the edge of the canyon, looking down to the flowing waters of Paradox Creek. They'd been riding on the old Jeep road that followed the south rim of the canyon since that morning. He shifted in the saddle, trying to give his back end some relief. As Jean had said, it'd been a number of years since he'd been on Daisy. They'd gotten a late start Sunday afternoon. So late, in fact, that they'd only ridden an hour before stopping. He'd suggested that they wait until Monday to get started, but they were all packed. It seemed the others were looking forward to a few nights away from their wives. He had to admit, it brought back memories of when he was a boy. They'd had an amicable time talking around the campfire, just the guys. But sleeping on the hard ground the last two nights hadn't helped his back any. While they'd gotten an early start yesterday after breaking camp, this morning they'd lingered, as if all of them were feeling the effects of sleeping on the ground. And this morning when they'd headed out, he couldn't help but miss sitting with Jean and having their coffee together. He sure hoped she'd made it through the last couple days okay on her own.

"Should be around here somewhere," Carl was saying.

Hal shook his head. "You know how this terrain plays tricks on you. That thing could have gone down miles from here."

"I got a look at the smoke with my binoculars," Dusty said. "It went down way past the canyon, I tell you. Lived here my whole life, Hal. I know how to read the damn terrain."

Hal glanced over at Jim. "And suppose we find the helicopter. What the hell are we going to do then?"

"You've done nothing but complain, Hal," Carl said. "Maybe you should have stayed behind with the womenfolk."

The others laughed and Hal smiled, not taking offense. "At least I'd have had a decent breakfast these last two mornings. Not to mention coffee."

Dusty stood up in his saddle, scanning the area past the creek with his binoculars like he'd been doing on and off for the last couple hours. Hal could tell by the sudden straightening of his shoulders that he'd spotted something.

"I think I found it," Dusty said excitedly. "Hard to be sure, but it's definitely not a rock outcropping." He handed the glasses to Carl. "Out past the fork. To the right, about two o'clock."

"I don't see a damn thing," Carl muttered as he moved the binoculars around back and forth.

"No. More to your right. Two o'clock! Not three," Dusty said, pointing. "See it?"

"I can't find it." Carl handed the binoculars to Graham. "Can you?"

Graham, who was the oldest of the bunch at seventy-eight, took the binoculars with shaking hands. Hal watched as he took his glasses off first before bringing the binoculars to his eyes.

"Out past the fork," Graham repeated quietly to himself. "To the right. Three o'clock."

"Two o'clock!" Dusty corrected.

Hal waited as Graham scanned the area, going from noon on an imaginary clock all the way to six. Hal finally took the binoculars from him.

"Let me give it a try."

He found the fork in the creek and then refocused the binoculars for his eyesight, moving them slightly up and to the right. Part of him hoped it was nothing. He was ready to give up on this helicopter chase and head back home to Jean. But he found the pile of rubble and like Dusty said, it was no rock outcropping. He lowered the glasses.

"Dusty's right. I see it. A good ways past the creek. About five or six hundred yards beyond the fork, I'd reckon. Maybe more." He handed the binoculars to Jim to let him take a turn. Jim couldn't find it and handed them over to Curtis.

"Yeah, I can spot it too," Curtis said. "Let's go see what we got."

Hal brought up the rear as they headed down into the canyon one by one, following a wildlife trail to the creek. Conversation was scant on the way down and he assumed they, like him, were just hoping the horses didn't lose their footing. Daisy slid a couple of times and Hal pulled her up as he held on tight to the saddle. By the time they made it to the creek, his back felt like a tangled mess. It would be a miracle if he could even manage to get off Daisy. He was thankful that Jean had thought to put some of those ibuprofen tablets into his pack.

They stopped at the creek to let the horses drink, and Dusty was again scanning the horizon.

"You can see it pretty good now," he said. "Definitely a helicopter. Looks in bad shape, though."

"I imagine a crash and burn would do that," Carl said.

"How many crew you think that bird had?" Jim asked Carl.

He shrugged. "Two or three, I'd guess. Been a long time since I was in the military, though. Back in the day, it didn't take a whole crew to fly."

"Back in the day, we didn't have computers on everything," Dusty said with a chuckle.

Hal kept quiet. He figured he was the only one of the six who'd never served. Wasn't for lack of trying, he reminded himself. Of course, by then he'd already met Jean and the Vietnam War had started. When he was turned down after trying to enlist, he was secretly thankful for his chronic back pain. He'd learned to live with it over the years, and it hadn't slowed him down much. Well, these last few years, sure. But he was barely hanging on to seventy-five. More things hurt him than not at his age.

"Let's go see what we can find," Carl said as he and his horse picked their way across the wide, but shallow creek.

Hal figured his calculations must have been a bit off—it took them much longer to reach the wreckage than he'd imagined. They stopped a good thirty yards from it, all staring at the charred and crushed piece of machinery.

"Don't see no bodies," Curtis said quietly.

Carl finally swung his leg off the saddle and dropped to the ground. He put one hand to his lower back as he tried to straighten up. One by one, the others dismounted too. Hal struggled to stand, and he held on to Daisy until his back finally loosened up enough for him to walk.

"Back still bothering you, Hal?" Graham asked.

"Always," he said. "Ridin' down that canyon didn't help matters none."

He followed the others over to the wreckage. Despite the crash and obvious fire, the aircraft was still pretty much intact. Broken and bent, but still intact.

"You think they could have walked away from this?"

Carl walked closer and pointed. "Got blood over here. It's not fresh, though."

"I don't think anyone could have survived this," Dusty said. "Blood in the back too."

"Fire didn't burn everything," Carl said. "You never know."

Dusty picked up a twisted hunk of metal. "The crash did this to this pipe. What the hell do you think it did to a human body?"

"Let's look around and see if we can find some tracks or something," Jim suggested.

Hal nodded, but he didn't have hope of finding anything in this rocky desert landscape. They all walked the perimeter, shuffling along the outer edges of the wreckage. A few pieces of metal were strewn about, but Hal saw nothing else to indicate the crew had walked away.

"If they didn't walk away, where the hell are their bodies?" Carl asked.

"Even if they burned, they'd still be here. The inside is charred pretty good but not like it was incinerated or anything," Curtis said.

"Well, if they ain't here, they had to have walked out," Graham said.

"Maybe somebody else got here before we did," Hal said. "Maybe somebody from around Paradox made it over this way."

"No, I talked to Lou Wright before we left. He lives over near Paradox. He didn't even hear the helicopter or crash out that way," Carl said. "I'd bet nobody in town even knows there was one out here."

"Where'd you see Lou?" Hal asked.

"He was out on a bicycle, if you can believe that. He was trying to see how far the power outage went. I told him we were heading out this way. I believe he was on his way back to town."

"I guess with his wife gone, he's got nothing else to do," Graham said. "God knows he let his place go to hell and back after she died."

Hal laughed as did the others, but he could relate to Lou. If something were to happen to Jean, he didn't know if he'd have the will to keep up their place by himself. Hell, he didn't even know if he could put a meal on the table.

Curtis dropped the twisted piece of metal he still held and it clanked on the rocks. "Well? What now?"

Carl shielded his eyes to the late afternoon sun. "Got a lot of daylight left," he said, almost to himself. "I don't know about you all, but I'm not looking to be sittin' in the saddle again today, though."

"How about we ride back to the fork, make an early camp by the creek?" Curtis said.

Hal nodded, even though he wanted to head on back to Jean. "Sounds good to me. I imagine I can make it that far," he said. His back hurt just enough to make him accept a third night out.

They made the return trip to the creek in silence, only the sounds of crunching rocks breaking it as their horses ambled along. It was a pleasant enough day, Hal mused. A few clouds building in the west, nothing more. Should be another nice, cool evening for sleeping, but he'd be lying if he said he didn't miss his own bed. And Jean, of course. There'd only been a handful of times over the last fifty some-odd years that they hadn't shared a bed. When their kids were born, for sure. And then when Jean's aunt had taken ill and she'd gone over to their place in Utah to care for her for a week or so. Of course, there were a few hunting trips for him where he'd left Jean behind for a day or two. He figured it'd been fifteen or twenty years since he'd done that, though. Oh, hell, the years got away. He was seventy-five. It'd probably been closer to thirty years since he'd been on a hunting trip with the guys.

"Those nice two cottonwoods will make for some shade," Carl said. "We'll be hard-pressed to find a spot without rocks to lay our bedrolls, though."

"Sleeping out like this reminds me of how damn old I am," Graham said as he got off his horse.

Hal nodded. "I second that."

CHAPTER THIRTEEN

"Damn, my ass hurts," Dana said for the third time.

"You're a wimp," Butch said. "We're on the road. Riding doesn't get any easier than this. Not like yesterday when we were following the creek."

"I know. But it still hurts. I haven't been in a saddle for this many hours since we were kids."

"Well, your ass is a little bigger than it was back then."

She whipped her head around, glaring at him. "What are you saying?"

"That didn't come out right."

"Are you saying I'm fat? That my ass is big?" She arched an eyebrow. "Or both?"

He laughed. "You know what I meant. You're as thin as you always are."

Her shoulders sagged. "I am not. I've gained seven pounds in the last year. *Seven!* I swear, once I turned thirty, all I have to do is *look* at food and I gain."

"I'm going to guess that huge scoop of ice cream you put on your apple pie the other night might have something to do with it."

"I hate you," she muttered.

"And last night, you practically fought me for that last rib," he continued.

"I was *starving*," she said. She waved her hand around. "I'm not used to all this activity."

"But you slept okay?"

"When I slept. I kept hearing noises and imagining we were about to be attacked by a pack of wolves or something."

"Camping by the creek was great. I slept like a baby."

"Yeah…you sure didn't snore like one, though."

He laughed. "So I shouldn't tell you that you were doing your share of snoring too?"

"I do not snore," she said, mustering up as much indignation as she could. She was fat, she had a big ass and now she snored? Damn, it was hell getting old.

They rode in silence for a while and she again wished she'd thought to bring a cap. Butch had offered his, but it was dirty and stained with who knew what so she'd declined his offer. She brushed at her hair as the wind blew it into her face.

"It's weird not to have cars or trucks on the road," she said as she turned around, looking behind them. "It's so quiet. It's like we're the only people out here."

"We're coming up on the turnoff to Paradox," he said. "Then it's about four or five more miles to town. Makes me think that power is out there too. Batteries too since there's no traffic this close to town."

"You think anyone will know what's going on?"

He shrugged. "Hard to say. Like us, surely people have gone out, trying to find someone with power."

"Or a phone."

He pulled his horse to a stop and she did too. He was shielding his eyes against the sun as he stared up ahead of them.

"What is it?"

"Something's on the road," he said.

She squinted, trying to see, but the afternoon heat was shimmering on the road's surface. "I don't see anything."

He reached behind him and pulled out a small pair of binoculars from the leather bag tied to the saddle. "I'll be damned," he murmured. "There's some guy walking. Got a backpack."

Dana shoved her sunglasses on top of her head. "Let me see," she said, taking the binoculars from him. Sure enough, a guy with a backpack was heading their way. He appeared to be tall, though slight, his head covered with a ball cap. He was wearing sunglasses, but he was too far away to make out his features. But there was something about his walk that attracted her. She studied the gait closer, then smiled. "Not a guy. It's a woman."

"Carrying a big pack like that?"

She handed the binoculars back to him with a smirk. "It's a woman," she said again.

He looked once more, then shook his head. "A guy. It's a dude, Dana."

"Ten bucks your dude is a woman," she said.

"Let's bet twenty and make it interesting."

"You're on," she said.

As they got closer, she was certain she was correct, despite the very short hair that was mostly hidden by the ball cap. When they got to the turnoff to Paradox, Butch pulled up his horse. The woman was still at least fifty yards away.

"It's a guy," Butch said again.

"I think I know a woman when I see one," she said.

"And I don't?"

"Apparently not," she said with a teasing smile.

The woman continued to walk toward them, then stopped a good twenty yards away. She pulled fashionable Oakley sunglasses off her face, then looked them over, her glance lingering on the rifle strapped to Butch's saddle.

"I'm assuming you're friendly," the woman called, her tone indicating it was a question and not a statement.

"I'll be damned," Butch muttered. "It's not a dude."

"Told you so," Dana said with a smile. "Twenty bucks." She then stood up in the saddle, stretching her back. "We're friendly," she called back to the woman. "Are you?"

The woman came closer, but Dana noticed an alertness in her walk, as if she wasn't quite sure she trusted them. She gave her what she hoped was a reassuring smile.

"I'm Dana. This is my cousin Butch," she said, pointing at him.

The woman again stopped, still twenty or twenty-five feet away. "I'm Corey," she said. "My car lost power." She motioned down the road from where she'd come.

Butch pointed at her pack. "Camping trip?"

"Yeah. Backpacking trip."

"Don't get a lot of people backpacking around here," he said.

Dana glanced at him, surprised that he sounded so suspicious. The woman looked friendly enough. Harmless too. Even from this distance she could tell that.

"No. I was actually going to head south to the San Juans," Corey said. "There's a trail outside of Silverton that I like to take. Still a little cold up there now, at night especially, but I like to beat the summer crowds."

Butch nodded and Dana noticed that he relaxed some. Apparently the woman's answer appeased him.

"We're heading to Paradox," Dana said, pointing down the road to their left. "We lost power three days ago. Or is it four now?"

"It went out Saturday night," Butch offered. "At least we're assuming they're still without power."

"Anyway, we're trying to find out what's going on," she continued. "Cell phones don't work."

"Batteries either," Butch added.

Corey nodded. "Yeah, my phone is dead too."

"You want a ride?" Dana asked. She patted the rump of her horse. "I think she can handle both of us."

"I can take your pack," Butch offered. "That thing looks like it weighs fifty pounds or more."

"Yeah, at least," Corey said.

She finally walked closer and Dana got her first close-up look. Corey met her eyes with a smile, then slid her gaze to the horse.

"Thanks. Beats walking. It's been a while since I've ridden, though," Corey said.

She had an easy smile and a friendly face, but Dana noticed that there was still a little wariness in her dark eyes. Pretty dark eyes, she added to that thought.

"Me too," she said. "I'm from Seattle. Came down to visit my parents," she explained, which was sort of the truth.

"Oh. Okay. Not a local then." Corey's gaze drifted up to Butch. "You?"

"Yeah. I live out here," he said. "Why?"

Corey shrugged. "Just thought one of us should know where we're going," she said, the corners of her mouth lifting up in a smile. "Don't want somebody shooting at us."

The smile was genuine, Dana noted, and it completely transformed her. The wariness seemed to disappear from her eyes and her expression was open, inviting, friendly—and attractive. Their eyes held for a few seconds, and Dana returned her smile. Damn…she'd never really had a concrete image in her mind of what her Dream Girl looked like. It was always a blurry vision of a woman. But now, right at this very moment, the blurry vison turned crystal clear.

Corey finally turned her attention to Butch, who had gotten off his horse. Dana watched as Corey slipped the heavy pack from her shoulders and handed it to Butch.

"Wow…it really does weigh fifty pounds," he said. "You don't look big enough to even carry it."

Corey laughed good-naturedly. "I'll admit, I'm a little out of shape," she said.

Dana took the opportunity to look her over, thinking there was nothing whatsoever wrong with her shape. Then she pulled her eyes away, embarrassed. Now was no time to ogle a stranger's body. They'd been living in the dark for three days. They were on a mission. And that mission did not involve finding her Dream Girl. It involved finding some semblance of civilization. And a cell phone, of course.

Butch strapped her pack to the back of his saddle, on top of his own meager pack. Dana then realized that she needed to move hers if Corey was going to ride behind her.

"Hook it to your saddle horn," Butch suggested.

Dana did, then took her boot out of the stirrup so Corey could use it. She swung up behind her easily and rested her hands at Dana's waist. *Oh, my.* Corey scooted up a little closer to the saddle—and closer to her—before removing her hands from her side.

"Is this okay?" Corey asked.

"Uh-huh," Dana said, chancing a look at Butch, who gave her a wink before nudging his horse along.

CHAPTER FOURTEEN

Anna Gail swatted at a fly as it buzzed around her head, missing it badly. The doors were both propped open, letting in the late afternoon breeze. The store had been cleaned and the shelves straightened since the earthquake, but as there was still no power, there was little activity in town. She'd heard from Brenda over at the post office that surely by now help was on the way. If the mail truck from Grand Junction couldn't get to them, then someone had to know of their predicament.

"I'm bored out of my mind."

Anna Gail offered a small smile to Holly. "I know. I miss TV," she said, looking at the television that hung on the wall in the corner. When she opened up the store each morning, turning on the TV was the first thing she did. The silence without it was nearly unbearable.

"I miss my phone. How much longer do you think this'll go on?"

"I have no idea. You'd think the power would have come back on by now. The generators won't last much longer. Then we'll lose everything in the coolers," she said.

"Are you sure there isn't *somebody* who knows what's going on?" Holly asked.

Anna Gail sighed. "No phone. No cars. No TV," she said. "Nobody knows anything."

Holly walked down the chip aisle and picked up a bag and opened them. "It's weird, isn't it?" she asked as she shoved a potato chip in her mouth. "No cars or trucks on the street. It's so quiet."

"I know. That means that the outage goes out much farther than just Paradox."

Holly came closer and offered the bag of chips to her. Anna Gail took one out and bit into it. Without thought, she reached into the bag for another one.

"You think Daddy will be back tonight?"

"He said he would."

Richard had gone off with Leland Hilmer yesterday, up to the old garage outside of town. Leland had it in his mind that when they'd closed up the shop, they'd left barrels of fuel up there. The lone gas station in town couldn't pump gas without power. According to Richard, since they'd put in the new pumps and that fancy electronic system, Gilbert hadn't been able to get the pumps going with a generator. It wouldn't be long before folks started running out of fuel, them included. Richard had his mind set on finding some for them. But even if Leland was right and there was still fuel up at the old shop, how would they ever get it down here to town?

"Do you think we should be afraid?"

Anna Gail shook off her musings and turned to Holly. "Afraid of what, honey?"

Holly shrugged. "Daddy said if this goes on for much longer that people would start getting crazy."

Anna Gail shook her head, hating that Richard was putting thoughts like that in Holly's head. "We're all neighbors here," she said. "No one's going to get crazy."

She saw movement out of the corner of her eye and turned to the window, seeing two horses with riders coming down the street. She wasn't really surprised to see them since some of the town's residents had been out and about on horses and even bicycles. But she was surprised to recognize Butch Ingram up on one of the horses.

"Why, Holly...I believe that's Butch out there. Wonder if he knows what's going on?"

Holly had dropped the bag of chips where she stood and hurried out the door and into the street. Anna Gail followed, although not quite with the same enthusiasm as Holly.

* * *

Corey steadied her hands at Dana's waist as their horse danced away from the young woman who'd run toward them. She wanted nothing more than to get off the horse and stretch her legs and back. When Harry had suggested she get back in the saddle, she doubted he'd meant that literally.

"Power is out all the way at the farm too?" the girl asked.

"Afraid so," Butch said. He tipped his cap politely at the older woman who had followed the girl out. "Mrs. Filmore," he said in greeting. "This is my cousin Dana. And this here is Corey. Picked her up walking on the road." Butch looked over at her and Dana. "This is Anna Gail Filmore and her daughter, Holly."

Holly stared up at her. "Where you from?"

Corey offered a quick smile. "Utah. I picked the wrong time to go camping, I guess," she said, using the lie that she and Duncan had devised.

"Well, get down off that monster of a horse," Mrs. Filmore said. "Come inside and I'll get you a cold drink."

"I hope that cold drink involves a beer," Dana murmured as she kicked her boot out of the stirrup for Corey to use.

"I'll go for that," Corey said as she swung down off the horse. She took the bridle in one hand and held the horse still as Dana dismounted as well. She laughed quietly as Dana rubbed her butt.

"What can I say? My ass hurts," Dana said as she stretched both arms out to the side and bent backward to loosen up. She took two steps, then stopped. "No wonder cowboys are bowlegged. I may never straighten up again."

Corey's gaze traveled to her backside where Dana was still rubbing, then she pulled her eyes away, finding Butch watching with an amused expression. She lifted up one corner of her mouth in an apologetic smile. Well, at least that part of her hadn't died. But she was on an assignment to find a missing military helicopter and an alleged meteor—checking out pretty women's asses wasn't on her list. Of course, neither was horseback riding. She held the reins up questioningly.

"What should I do with the horse?"

"Take them around back, Butch," Mrs. Filmore said. "The old hand pump still works at the well."

"Need help?" Corey offered.

"I got it. I'll see if I can find a patch of grass for them to graze in," he said.

"I'll help," Holly said and walked with him.

Dana leaned closer to her. "They kinda date," she said quietly. "I've not met her before. She looks really young, but I think she's twenty-four or -five." She lowered her voice even more. "I don't think I like her for him."

"How can you know so soon? She's only said a handful of words," Corey reasoned.

Dana shrugged and followed Mrs. Filmore into the store. Corey turned around in the street, noting the quiet, the absence of people. No one seemed to be around. None of the shops looked open, and she wondered if the grocery store was open for business or if Mrs. Filmore was merely here to keep an eye on things.

She followed them into the store as well, immediately noticing the dark shadows inside. Even though the store faced west, the afternoon sun cast only limited light into the front of the store. She took her sunglasses off and clipped them in the collar of her shirt, then removed her cap as well and shoved the bill in her back pocket. She rubbed her hair with both hands, trying to give it some semblance of order.

"I've got some Coke," Mrs. Filmore said. "And bottled water, of course. Orange juice."

"I guess no beer," she whispered to Dana.

"Orange juice sounds good," Dana said to Mrs. Filmore.

"Me too," Corey said.

"Dana, I understand you're visiting from Seattle," Mrs. Filmore said. "I suppose this isn't how you thought your vacation would go."

"To say the least," Dana said. "Thanks," she added as Mrs. Filmore handed her a small plastic bottle of orange juice.

Corey took the offered juice as well. "Thank you, Mrs. Filmore."

"Call me Anna Gail, please," she said. "Did you both feel the earthquake?"

Corey deferred the question to Dana, not knowing the extent of what the tremor felt like. Harry had mentioned the seismic reading, nothing more.

"Are we sure it was an earthquake?" Dana asked as she ran a hand through her blond hair, brushing the bangs from her forehead and tucking a strand behind her ear. "I mean, we felt it at the house, but it didn't seem very strong or last that long."

"Strong enough to knock canned goods off my shelves," Anna Gail contradicted. "But you're right, it was very brief." She turned her gaze to Corey. "How about you? You were camping, you said?"

Corey nodded. "Up off the road there coming in from Utah. It was a little scary with rocks rolling around," she said vaguely.

"I imagine so. It was frightening in here," Anna Gail said. "Once the power went out, we couldn't see a thing. I did manage to keep the glass jars from falling," she said, pointing down one aisle.

Butch and Holly came in from a back room, and Holly immediately went to the cooler and pulled out a Coke for Butch.

"Got the horses staked up the hill behind the store," he said. "I hope somebody around town has some hay we can use." He looked over at Anna Gail. "Or does Tommy have the feed store open?"

"Richard said he'd seen him up there yesterday. Not much else is open," she said. "And I don't know why. If somebody needs something, just write up a receipt and take care of the business part of it later when the registers are working again, I say. But even here, only a few have come by. It's like people are afraid to leave their homes," she said.

"It's almost like the town is deserted," Corey said, voicing her earlier thoughts.

"The first day, people were out on foot, some even riding bikes, all wondering when the power would come back on. But with batteries out too and no phones, well, I guess it's got people worried that something's going on. Yesterday I only saw a few people out walking."

"I can't believe that no one's come here to help us yet," Dana said. "Surely someone knows that we don't have power, right?"

"I heard from Lou Wright that some of the men from up in Squaw Valley were going out to look for a helicopter," Anna Gail said.

"What do you mean?" Butch asked with a frown.

"Said they saw a helicopter fly over, then go down. Heard the crash too. They headed out on horseback."

"Close to town?" Corey asked as nonchalantly as she could.

Anna Gail shook her head. "No. We didn't hear anything around here. Squaw Valley is up to the north, other side of the creek."

Corey looked over at Dana and Butch. "Is that where you came from?"

"No. We live southeast of town where the creek flows through the valley," Butch said.

"You didn't hear it from where you were camping?" Dana asked.

Corey shook her head, wishing she'd had more time to study the maps Duncan had given her. She didn't even know what creek they were talking about.

"Did they say what kind of helicopter?" Butch asked.

"Military was all they said."

"Then someone must know we're without power then," Dana said.

"But they said it crashed," Holly said. "What good does that do us?"

"Then that means somebody will be looking for it," Butch said.

"Maybe it lost power too," Corey said, wanting to add something to the conversation. These people were strangers to her, and she felt no need to offer them hope that someone—like her—was out looking for the aircraft. And she was a stranger to them as well. But Dana and Butch hadn't left her out on the road to fend for herself, they'd offered help. Still, she had to bite her lip to keep from assuring them that yes, someone *did* know they were without power. They just didn't know what had caused the outage in the first place.

"That would be such a tragedy," Anna Gail said. "Sending someone out to help us and then they crash. You wouldn't think someone could survive that."

A freefall from the sky without any power at all? No, Corey doubted the crew survived. She did wonder if the men from Squaw Valley had any luck with their search, though. The locals would know the terrain, know which route to take. Sutter's squad would be hard-pressed to find the aircraft without knowing where it went down. Duncan only said they had a "best guess" based on satellite images, but that still left a lot of miles to cover on foot.

"I guess we need to think about what we're going to do," Butch said. "Somebody's got power somewhere. We just need to find them so that they can let the authorities know what's going on around here."

"Maybe head south toward the highway, but that's a good ride," Anna Gail said. "No water for the horses on that route, not until you reach the La Sal Creek."

"I was thinking we could follow Paradox Creek, east, all the way to where it hits the Delores River," Butch said. "That'd be up near the saline plant. We'd be sure to find help there."

"Oh, Lordy, Butch," Anna Gail said. "That's a long way. The creek goes through the canyon. Not sure your horses could make it."

"We've got to try something," Dana said. "I feel like we're totally cut off from the world."

Corey smiled. "That's because we are."

Dana glared at her. "You're not helping."

Anna Gail looked past them, out toward the street. "Oh, good. Here comes my husband. He and Leland left yesterday, looking for fuel," she said.

"What about Gilbert?" Butch asked. "His pumps aren't working?"

The man who entered the store was big and tall with bushy brown hair sticking out from an old dirty John Deere cap. Several days' worth of stubble darkened his face. It was the rifle he held, though, that drew her attention.

"Butch," he said with a curt nod. "Who are these people with you?"

"Oh, Richard, where are your manners?" Anna Gail said.

"My manners disappeared when we lost power on Saturday, and now three more days have passed and still not one word from the outside," he said gruffly as his eyes narrowed. "So who are you two?"

Butch stepped forward. "This is my cousin, Dana," he said. "She's Louis and Barbara's daughter. From Seattle."

Richard nodded. "Okay. I know Louis, of course." He turned his gaze solely on her. "And you?"

Corey wondered if he was always this rude or if it was as he said, the power situation had put him on edge. She gave a friendly smile and held her hand out in greeting.

"Corey Conaway," she said. "I'm displaced, I'm afraid. I was camping, on my way to the San Juans when my car wouldn't start." She shrugged when he ignored her handshake. "No phone either, so I started hiking. Butch and Dana found me, oh, I don't know…four or five miles from town, I guess."

"That's about right," Butch agreed. "We were hoping you had power here in Paradox, but I guess the outage goes farther than anyone thought."

"If I were you, I'd get back to your place and secure it. If this goes on much longer, people will get crazy," Richard warned, holding his rifle up. "Once the fuel runs out and no one has generators, that's when you'll need to worry. I can already imagine a pack of them coming to loot out the store."

"Oh, Richard, these are our neighbors, our friends. Our *customers*," Anna Gail said. "No one is going to come looting. If they need food, they'll buy it."

"With what?" he asked loudly. "Half the town lives on credit as it is. We got no power to run cards."

"I think you're overreacting," Anna Gail said, and Corey was inclined to agree with her.

"You think so? I already heard that Mac Woodson was out of fuel for his generator. Won't be long, the others will be too."

"And so will we," Anna Gail said. "Unless you found some up at the old shop."

"Nothing but empty barrels," he said.

"What about Gilbert?" Butch asked.

Richard shook his head. "He put in those new pumps not two months ago. They're all *computerized*," he said with disgust. "As if the old ones weren't good enough for Paradox, he has to go and get upgraded. Now they're useless."

"Have you tried to siphon from the holding tanks?" Corey asked.

"Siphon with what? The pumps are buried with the tanks, and Gilbert says there's some sort of safety valve around the cap," he said.

"What about—"

"Look, lady...we're not stupid. Don't you think we've already talked about how to get the fuel out?"

She held her hands up and flashed a quick smile. "Hey, you're right. What do I know about it?"

"She's just trying to help, Richard," Anna Gail said.

"I don't need help from her kind," he said as he walked away to the back of the store.

Corey glanced at Dana. "*Her kind?*" she whispered. "Is he saying what I think he's saying?"

Dana sighed. "I believe so."

"Don't pay him any mind," Anna Gail apologized. "He's been on edge. Everyone is."

"Maybe we should take our leave then," Dana said.

"Oh, no. It's late. You can stay up at the house with us tonight," she offered.

"I don't know," Dana said hesitantly, looking over at Corey with raised eyebrows.

"I've got to find some hay for the horses anyway," Butch said. "I think I'll ride on up to Tommy's and see if he's got the feed store open."

Anna Gail turned to Holly. "Why don't you take these ladies up to the house," she said. "I'm sure after being out all day they'd love to clean up."

Corey saw Holly's shoulders sag, but she nodded.

"I've got a chicken out thawing," Anna Gail said. "I'll make us up a nice stew for dinner."

Corey saw Dana's indecision so she stepped forward. "We'd appreciate that, Anna Gail. Thanks for your hospitality." She glanced in the direction of where her husband had gone. "Are you sure he's going to be okay with that, though?"

"Knowing Richard, he'll stay here at the store tonight." She smiled quickly. "To ward off all those looters, you know. Holly can sleep with me and you two can take her room," she said. She looked over at

Butch. "I'm afraid the spare room has turned into nothing more than storage. I hope you don't mind the sofa."

"I'm sure it'll beat the hard ground we slept on last night," he said. "Thank you."

"I should get my pack," Corey said.

"Yeah. I'll let you take mine too," Butch said. "Give me more room to haul some hay back."

CHAPTER FIFTEEN

Dana splashed water on her face and let out an audible sigh as the cool liquid touched her skin. She assumed everyone's first objective had been to run a line from the generator to the well house, like her father had done. Even without power, it was still comforting to turn on the faucet and have running water.

She looked at herself in the mirror, not even caring that her hair looked a frightful, windblown mess. She had no clue as to what time it was. She wasn't even sure what day it was. Tuesday? As she took her clothes off, she thought of her mother and wondered how they were faring. Her mother had said that they had enough fuel for a month. Was that really true? What if others didn't, though? Was Mr. Filmore right? Would people come with guns, wanting to take what they needed?

No. The farms and ranches may be separated by distance, but it was still a close community. Everyone knew their neighbors, and most everyone had lived here their whole lives. She couldn't imagine them turning on one another over fuel. Maybe food. But then, everyone was pretty self-sufficient out here. Of course, surely the power would come back on before it came to that.

Surely.

She let out a weary sigh and stepped into the shower, hugging the wall as cold water sprayed around her. She'd been prepared. While some people used propane to heat their water, the Filmores were not one of them. But a shower was a shower, and she finally stepped in, dousing her head with water before letting it run down her back. She was hot and dirty enough not to mind the cold, and she grabbed the soap, lathering herself. The water pressure wasn't much, but it was enough to clean her and rinse off. After washing her hair, she turned the faucet off and stepped out, grabbing one of the towels that Holly had left out for them.

She tried not to think of the Filmores as strangers. When she was younger and still lived here, she'd come into town with her parents. She'd been to the store before. Holly was younger and they'd never been in school together. She may have met her before, here at the store, but she couldn't recall. Regardless, Anna Gail had been kind enough to open her home up to them and she was grateful. Even if her husband scared the shit out of her with his rifle and dire predictions of rampant looting by the townspeople. She figured if there was anyone around here to fear, it was him.

"And he obviously doesn't like lesbians," she said to her reflection in the mirror. Of course, she doubted the Filmores knew of her sexual orientation. While she wouldn't consider herself overly feminine, she was no longer the uninhibited tomboy she'd been growing up. Although, with her jeans and hiking boots, all she needed was a baseball cap to bring her back around to those days.

That brought a smile to her face as memories of her childhood flashed through her mind. Maybe because she and Butch had been so close, but she'd always been more comfortable in boys clothes, stealing his on occasion. Her mother tried her best to get her into dresses, but on the few instances that she'd give in and wear one, she inevitably would end up tearing it or soiling it so badly that her mother wouldn't mention a dress again for months. By high school, though, she understood why she wasn't drawn to girls clothes and makeup and boys. The enormous crush she had on Susie Perkins confirmed her suspicions—and fears. Telling Butch that she was gay had been easy… he was her best friend. Telling her mother, not so much. She'd worked herself into a nervous wreck over it, only to find out her mother had suspected long before Dana herself had.

Well, she'd grown up since then. She no longer shunned makeup and girls clothes, although she still felt more comfortable in a pair of jeans than she did dress pants or the suits she wore to the office.

She shook her head. How did her train of thought get her there? Oh, yeah. Mr. Filmore didn't like lesbians. While she felt she could hide it if need be, Corey could not. It wasn't just her very short hair—which Dana thought looked sensational on her—or how she was dressed. It was the way she carried herself, the way she walked. She appeared to be capable and confident, and she had yet to make any statement that would indicate she was afraid or even worried about the situation they found themselves in.

Which made her wonder why. If *she* felt like a stranger here among the folks in Paradox, how must Corey feel? Corey had known her and Butch all of five hours, yet she'd blended in and gone with the flow as if she had not a care in the world. Why wasn't she more concerned?

Dana jerked her head around as a light tapping sounded on the door. She clutched the towel tighter around her.

"You okay in there?"

"Yeah. I'll be out in a minute." She paused. "Sorry. I was... daydreaming," she said truthfully. "I know you want to shower too."

"No problem," Corey said from behind the door. "I've got Gretchen tied up in back. Didn't know what to do with her."

Dana frowned. "Who is Gretchen?"

"Your horse."

"Oh." Dana smiled as she finished drying herself off. She hadn't even thought to ask her name. "Who names a horse Gretchen?"

"Apparently your cousin."

* * *

Corey found Dana sitting outside on a bench and she snuck up behind her.

"Psst."

Dana turned, eyebrows raised. Corey had both hands behind her back, and she wiggled her eyebrows teasingly.

"Look what I found," she said as she showed Dana her prize.

"Oh, my God! You stole beer from Mr. Filmore? The man with the rifle?" Dana reached for one of the cans with a grin. "Are you *crazy*?"

"Yeah. Living dangerously, I know." She sat down beside her. "What's up?"

Dana took a swallow of the beer before answering. "Just trying to put some semblance of normalcy in my day."

"I see. Catching the sunset?"

Dana nodded, then fixed a stare on her. "Where are you from?"

Ah. Corey had been wondering when the questions would come. She anticipated them coming from Butch, though, not Dana. Well, some things she could be truthful about. She stretched her legs out and leaned back comfortably.

"Over in Utah," she said.

"Really? If you were camping along the road, why didn't you hike back toward Utah instead of coming this way to Paradox?"

Corey shrugged. "I was hoping to come upon a house or something," she said. "I already knew there was nothing back toward the border."

Dana studied her intently. "Why were you camping here anyway? Utah's got a lot of wilderness to camp in."

"Yeah, you know, but I was heading down toward Silverton and the San Juans," she said.

"Paradox isn't really a direct route to Silverton," Dana said. "A little out of the way, isn't it?"

Corey arched an eyebrow. "Why all the questions?" She met her gaze and smiled, trying to keep things light between them. "What? Are you getting paranoid like Richard Filmore?"

Dana blew out her breath. "Oh, God…I am, aren't I? Sorry."

"It's okay. But I'm harmless. Really. No need to worry about me."

This time it was Dana who met her gaze. "I'm scared."

Corey frowned. "Why? I think we're safe enough."

Dana looked away and stared out toward the west. "I got a bad feeling," she said. "I don't know what it is, but I can't shake it. Even when it first happened and everyone thought the power would come back on in a few hours…I had this feeling." Dana turned to look at her again. "And when the power didn't come back, well, I just feel like something's going on that's really, really bad."

"Like?"

Dana leaned closer, her voice low. "You don't think we're like… under attack or something, do you?"

"Like who? The Russians?" Corey shook her head and offered another small smile. "I think if another country was going to attack, they wouldn't pick Paradox, do you?"

"No. But maybe it's not only Paradox. Maybe it's all over. Maybe no one has power. Maybe that's why we haven't had any help. Maybe—"

"Dana…you're overreacting a bit, I think."

"Am I? Then why haven't we had help?"

Corey shrugged, wondering if she should divulge anything to her. She decided against it. Even though her instincts told her she could trust Dana and Butch, she really didn't know them at all. And the state of mind that Dana was currently in, telling her that *something* landed out here near Paradox that may or may not be radioactive might send her over the edge.

"Maybe they can't get to us," she said. "None of our vehicles work. Maybe they get close and they lose power to their vehicles too."

"Why? What could be causing it? The earthquake?"

"I don't know. Whatever it is, I'm sure it'll work itself out." She leaned closer and nudged her shoulder. "Despite what Mr. Filmore says, I don't think the end of the world is near."

"I hope you're right."

CHAPTER SIXTEEN

As Hal nibbled on the elk jerky that Dusty had brought, he wondered what Jean was having for supper. His stomach rumbled just thinking about the meal she'd have fixed up on his plate. Maybe one of those tender cutlets she'd fry up and then smother in gravy. That would hit the spot about now.

"I got another boiled egg here," Graham said. "Anybody want it?"

"I'll eat it if nobody else wants it," Jim said.

"I don't even have an appetite," Dusty said as he got up from the circle and walked over to the creek.

Hal noted that was the third time he'd done that. Walked over and gazed upstream like he was looking for something. He turned and glanced at Curtis, who shrugged and went back to his own meal.

After a few minutes of silence, Carl got up too and walked over toward Dusty. As far as Hal could tell, they weren't talking, just both of them looking upstream, toward the west. He and Curtis again exchanged glances.

"Maybe he misses his wife," Curtis offered. "I know I do."

"I don't miss her so much as her cooking," Jim said, causing the others to laugh.

"It's been nice not to have her yakkin' in my ear all the time," Graham said, "but yeah, I sure do miss the wife's biscuits and eggs in the morning."

"She make gravy too?" Hal asked.

"Oh, yeah. Nice, creamy sausage gravy," he said. "Hate to say it, but it's better than what my own momma used to make."

Hal nodded. "Jean makes a pretty good gravy herself." He watched as Carl walked off farther upstream. "Wonder what the hell's up with them? Neither one has said more than a handful of words all evening."

"Don't know," Curtis said.

Dusty finally turned around and came back, but he didn't sit down. Hal couldn't stand the suspense.

"What's up with you?" he asked. "Something out there?"

Dusty turned to look at him, and Hal could swear his eyes were glazed over. It was several seconds before Dusty answered him.

"Yeah. I think something's out there." He turned and pointed upstream to where Carl still stood. "Up the creek. Up on Baker's Ridge."

"What? You seen something with your binoculars?" Curtis asked.

"No. I just...*feel* like something's out there."

Hal watched him, noticing the nervous twisting of his hands together. "What is it, Dusty? You think the crew from that helicopter is out there or something?"

"I don't know. Could be."

"Carl? What you think?" Jim called.

Carl turned around and made his way back to them. "What?"

"Dusty thinks something's out there. Maybe the crew of that helicopter."

Carl nodded. "Up on the ridge," he said slowly. "There's something up on the ridge."

Hal turned, his gaze following the creek to where it turned then he looked higher, up to Baker's Ridge in the distance. It was only a silhouette now, what with the sun having already set behind it. And besides, it was too far away to see anything with the naked eye, so he couldn't imagine what they thought they saw there. Dusty hadn't even pulled his binoculars out of his pack one time.

"Don't see anything," he said.

"It's damn near dark," Graham said. "How could you see anything?"

Carl and Dusty lifted their gazes to the ridge, staring intently at it, but neither said a word. Dusty turned and walked back to the creek. After a few seconds, Carl did the same, taking his spot upstream as he continued to stare off to the west.

CHAPTER SEVENTEEN

"That was an excellent stew, Anna Gail," Dana said. "Thank you."

Butch laughed. "Better than my mother's rabbit stew?"

Dana gave him a fake smile. "I'll take chicken over rabbit any day."

"She *loved* my mother's stew," Butch told the others. "Until that one fateful day in high school when she happened to go into the kitchen when Mom was cutting up the rabbit."

"Must you tell this story?" Dana asked.

Butch ignored her. "She screamed so loud, we all thought something horrible had happened. She knocked me right over as she ran out of the house," he said with a laugh.

"I was traumatized," Dana said in her defense. "In fact, I was afraid to eat *anything* at your house after that."

Anna Gail laughed. "Oh, I used to cook rabbit stew when Richard and I first got married. Had his mother's recipe. I pretended to like it, but it was never one of my favorites," she said. "What about you, Corey? Have you had rabbit stew?"

Corey shook her head. "No, can't say that I have. I'm afraid my reaction would be similar to Dana's, though," she said.

For some reason, Dana doubted that. She turned to Anna Gail. "Can we help you clean up the kitchen?"

"Well, actually, if you don't mind helping Holly, that would be nice," Anna Gail said. "I've got to take Richard a bowl for his supper before it gets dark."

"I don't mind at all," Dana said.

"Will he stay there all night?" Corey asked.

"Knowing Richard, he'll stay there until the power comes back on, however many days that'll be," she said. "I don't believe it's necessary to guard the place like that, but there's no arguing with him."

"I didn't have a problem at Tommy's," Butch said. "We've got an account with him anyway, so he put the hay and cubes on our tab like always."

Anna Gail nodded. "Yes, we have quite a few accounts like that too. They come and settle up once a month when they get their paychecks." She stood up and took her bowl to the sink. "Did he mention if he was going to stay open?"

"I think he's kinda like Richard," Butch said. "Seems like he's just hanging out at the store there. Just in case," he said, his voice trailing away.

Dana glanced over at Corey. Despite her claims that the world wasn't coming to an end, the good folks of Paradox apparently thought differently.

It didn't take long for the three of them to clean up the kitchen. While they worked inside, Butch went out to check on the horses and to tie them up for the night. Before long, Anna Gail returned and lit several candles in the house and turned the generator off. Without the constant rattle of the generator's engine, an eerie silence settled around them.

"You almost forget how quiet it is when that thing is shut off," Anna Gail said. "Oh, and Richard told me that Gilbert had come over to visit. Seems they're devising some sort of plan to try to retrieve the fuel from Gilbert's tanks."

"They should try to override the safety valve trigger," Corey said. "There's probably a release switch..."

Dana, Butch, Anna Gail and Holly all stared at her. Corey shrugged. "Well, that's what I would do...but what do I know?"

Again, Dana had a sense that Corey wasn't who she claimed to be. No one could be that calm and unaffected by the past few days' events. Especially someone who was in the company of complete strangers.

She held Corey's gaze with an unspoken question. While Corey seemed to acknowledge the question, she left it unanswered as she turned away.

"I think I'm going to go outside and enjoy the cool evening, watch some stars," Corey said to no one in particular. "That's okay, isn't it?"

"Of course," Anna Gail said. "Don't mind me. Since the power's been out, we've been heading to bed earlier than normal. I guess I'd forgotten how very dark it can be out here without porch lights on." She smiled almost apologetically. "I've lived here in Paradox my whole life and have never had anything to fear. But lately…well, once full dark settles, I'd rather be inside."

"Well, I'm supposed to be camping," Corey said. "And I like the night sky."

"Use the kitchen door," Anna Gail said. "I'll leave a candle on the counter for you so you can find your way to the bedroom."

"I'll be on the sofa," Butch said. "Try not to scare me when you come inside."

"Try not to shoot me," Corey countered as she glanced at the rifle that was leaning against the wall.

Dana followed Anna Gail and Holly to the back of the house where the bedrooms were. She had no idea what time it was. The days were getting longer and she assumed it was after nine.

"Thank you again for giving up your bed," she said to Holly.

"It's okay. I don't mind sharing with Mom."

They left a small candle with her and took the larger one with them. She was surprised that they closed the door behind them. She shrugged, but instead of going into the bedroom, she made her way back out into the living room.

"What's up?" Butch asked quietly.

Dana sat down on the edge of the sofa where he was already sprawled out.

"What do you make of Corey?"

"What do you mean?"

Dana shrugged. "She seems a little…I don't know…odd."

"Odd?" He laughed quietly. "The expression on your face when she was riding behind you on the horse didn't say 'odd,'" he teased.

She gave an embarrassed smile. "Okay…so she's cute. But there's something about her that's not right."

"I don't know," Butch said. "She seems okay to me. Although I don't know why she was camping along the road out there. There's nothing there, really."

"I know. And she said she was from Utah. Why come over here to camp? I mean, I know she said she was heading down to Silverton, but, Butch, come on. It's been a while since I've lived here, but why on earth would you take this route to get to Silverton?"

"You're right about that," he said. "Coming this way through Paradox makes no sense."

She leaned closer. "So who do you think she is?"

"Okay, Dana...I know you and your wild imagination. Escaped convict? Mass murderer? Maybe she's on the FBI's Most Wanted List?"

She slapped playfully at his leg. "I was not thinking any of those things." Then she grinned. "Well, maybe one."

"Let me guess. Escaped convict?"

She nodded. "She seems...shifty. You know my instincts are usually very good. She's not being truthful about something. I can see it in her eyes."

"Maybe that's just how she looks," he reasoned. "It's not like you know the woman."

She tilted her head. "Speaking of that...you owe me twenty bucks," she reminded him.

He shook his head. "Can't believe I lost that bet."

"From a distance, yeah, she looked like a guy. But it was her walk that gave it away," she said. "She's got a rather sexy walk."

"You mean, for an escaped convict?"

Dana leaned back against the sofa and Butch moved his legs out of the way. "So what's with you and Holly? It doesn't look like there's much romance going on here. And my God, she looks like she's still a teenager."

"Yeah, she does. She's being a little distant too. Maybe this whole thing has got her shook up, I don't know."

"And what about her father? He seemed a little crazy."

Butch nodded. "Richard's always on edge. I try to ignore him and stay out of his way."

"Anna Gail is nice, though."

"Yeah, she's always super nice to me."

She stared at him in the shadows, the candle flicking the light back and forth across his face. She wanted to ask more about Holly but decided it wasn't any of her business. She finally sat up.

"I guess I'm going to bed," she said.

"You going to be okay sleeping with an escaped convict?" he asked in an amused voice.

"Very funny," she murmured as she walked away.

* * *

Corey sat on the same bench that she and Dana had used earlier when they'd drank the beer she'd stolen from the fridge. It was a pleasant evening, almost cool. Well, evening wasn't the right word. Darkness had settled and they were all firmly in its grip until morning. There was a sliver of a moon, but it wasn't bright enough to chase the shadows or dim the glow of the stars overhead.

If she had really been camping, this would have been a perfect night to be out by a creek. She could imagine the hypnotic gurgling of the water as it bounced over and around rocks on its way downstream. It was a calm, cool night…spectacular, even in its simplicity. There were no sounds, not even a barking dog to break the silence. There was nothing…nothing except millions and millions of stars. She realized, as she stared out into the night, that she had a smile on her face. This excursion that Harry had her on had at least dispelled the ghosts that she'd been living with. For the first time in more than four months, her team had not been at the forefront of her mind. In fact, had they crossed her mind all day? She took a deep breath, letting the smile slip from her lips. She wasn't really camping, she reminded herself. She was working.

Actually, she wasn't certain what she was doing out here. So some men from Squaw Valley had gone looking for the helicopter? She didn't know where Squaw Valley was and she wasn't certain how to go about asking Butch and Dana for help getting there. Harry had told her to keep things quiet and to go out on her own. She didn't think he anticipated the locals taking up guns and rifles. If she were to ditch Butch and Dana and go off alone, it would cause quite a stir, she was sure. She wasn't from around here. She had no business being here. People were suspicious enough as it was. Suspicious and paranoid—like Richard Filmore.

No, she'd have to talk Butch and Dana into looking for the helicopter. Butch had mentioned that he wanted to head east and follow the creek. Without being obvious and pulling her maps out of her pack, she thought—from what they'd said—that Squaw Valley was to the north or northwest of Paradox, past the road where she'd hooked up with Butch and Dana, who had come from the opposite direction. Without a horse and without Butch and Dana for cover, she'd be hard-pressed to locate the helicopter on her own.

She took one last glance up into the stars, then stood, moving carefully back toward the house. She could see the candle flickering in the window, and she assumed the others were already asleep. She opened and closed the kitchen door quietly, pausing to lock it behind her. She didn't know if that was the common practice around here but considering the circumstances, she assumed Anna Gail would want it locked. Who they were trying to keep out, she wasn't sure.

She picked up the candle, covering it with her hand so that it didn't blow out as she moved through the house. She could hear Butch snoring quietly on the sofa as she passed by it. In the hallway, the door was opened to the room she would share with Dana, but the other two doors were closed. She went inside and held the candle up, finding Dana on the right side of the bed, away from the door. She carefully put the candle on the small table beside the bed and blew it out, plunging the room into complete darkness.

"I'm not asleep," Dana whispered.

"Sorry."

She heard Dana roll over and sigh. "It's too dark to sleep."

Corey laughed quietly. "You've been living in the city too long, huh?"

"I have night lights inside my apartment," Dana said. "Since I was a kid, I've always had some kind of light."

"To keep the monsters away?"

"Well, so that I'd be able to *see* the monsters if they came in," Dana said.

Corey pulled the covers back on her side. "I'll try to keep any monsters away from you," she said lightly. "So...do you mind if I take my jeans off? I mean—"

"I don't mind. I'm in underwear and a T-shirt myself."

"Wow. If only my real dates could be this easy," she said teasingly as she kicked her jeans off.

"I don't imagine you'd have much of a problem," Dana said.

The smile faded quickly from Corey's face. "If you only knew," she murmured.

"What?"

Corey got into bed, making sure to leave plenty of space between them. "Nothing." She turned her head toward Dana. "Have I thanked you for rescuing me today?"

"Was it a rescue? You seemed to be doing okay."

"I suppose I would have eventually made it to Paradox," she said. "Although I doubt Richard would have let me inside his store. He apparently doesn't like *my kind*," she said, using his word. Then she smiled. "But I guess he doesn't know that you're *my kind* too. Right?"

Dana let out a quick, quiet laugh. "I would guess that Anna Gail and Holly don't know either. I moved away right out of high school,"

Dana said. "When I come to visit my parents, we don't ever come here to Paradox."

"If you don't mind my asking, how old are you?"

"Thirty-one," Dana said.

"Wow. I wouldn't have guessed that old," she said truthfully.

"What do you mean...*that* old?"

Corey smiled in the dark. "I thought twenty-six, twenty-seven, maybe. You have a youthful appearance. It'll serve you well when you're, you know, *really* old."

"Thank you. I guess." A slight pause before she returned the question. "And you?"

Corey sighed. "I'll be thirty-six next month. Some days I feel fifty-six."

She expected more questions, but Dana had none. As the silence lengthened, she let her eyelids slip closed. She acknowledged how tired she was but doubted sleep would come easily. It never did. Well, not unless she'd end her day with a couple or three stiff nightcaps. She hated to think that she'd resorted to whiskey to keep her sane at night, but in her mind, it beat the hell out of the pills her doctor had pushed on her. Tasted a lot better too, she thought wryly.

Her sleepless night never materialized, though. Dana's even breathing beside her served to dull her senses just enough as she slipped into a surprisingly peaceful sleep.

CHAPTER EIGHTEEN

"What the hell for?" Curtis asked Dusty. "We all looked with your binoculars. There's nothing up there," he said, pointing to Baker's Ridge.

"I'm telling you, there's something there," Carl said, backing Dusty.

"I can *feel* it," Dusty said, echoing his earlier comments. "There's something…pulling me…telling me to check it out. Hell, maybe it's the crew up there or something."

Hal didn't feel any such pull or gut feeling, but Carl and Dusty seemed adamant. Still, heading toward the ridge was in the opposite direction of home…and Jean. If they made it to the ridge and found nothing, that would set them back hours. That would mean yet another night camping out. He didn't know about the rest of them, but he'd had his fill of sleeping under the stars.

He took his cap off and scratched his thinning gray hair. "I don't know, guys. That ridge is a lot farther off than it looks," he said.

"I think we should head on back toward home," Graham said. "If the crew did manage to survive the crash, why the hell would they go all the way up to the top of the ridge? And on foot, no less."

"Well, if they're trying to flag down a search and rescue craft, then that'd be the place to go," Jim reasoned as he rubbed the stubble on his face thoughtfully.

"Haven't heard a single plane or another helicopter in the air since that day," Curtis said. "And that in itself is strange."

"I don't care. I'm going to go check it out," Carl said as he mounted his horse. "You can all go on back if you want."

"I'm going with you," Dusty said. "Something's up there. Let's go see what it is."

As they rode off, Hal and the others exchanged glances and shrugs. It was Jim who spoke first.

"I guess one more night out won't kill us."

Graham nodded. "Suppose not."

Hal looked at Curtis, hoping he'd offer a dissenting vote but he only shrugged again and nudged his horse, following the others. Hal looked fondly down the creek, wondering if he dared make the trek back home by himself. But he figured he'd never live to hear the end of it if he deserted them now. Besides, they were too far out to make it back home in one day, and the prospect of sleeping out alone wasn't too appealing. So he swung Daisy around and gave her a gentle kick, moving her along to catch the others. He reckoned it would be a waste of time going all the way to the ridge, but it was probably best that they all stay together.

It was a quiet ride with no one speaking and that suited Hal just fine. He brought up the rear, his gaze going to the ridge now and again, hoping he'd see a reflection of glass or metal...anything to suggest that something was up there. But a smattering of scrub oaks amongst the rocks was all he saw.

When they came to a clump of trees at the base of the ridge, they stopped to rest. The little creek that flowed past was shallow and most likely dried up during the hottest part of summer.

"I guess this is Little Squaw Creek," Curtis said. "When I was a boy we used to come out this way."

"It looks too narrow for Squaw Creek," Jim contradicted. "I'm thinking this is one of the forks off Paradox Creek that'll meet up with her again downstream."

"It doesn't fork until it gets farther down the valley," Curtis said. "Got to be Squaw Creek."

Hal didn't have an opinion one way or the other. He only knew they weren't lost. They just had to find Paradox Creek again and follow it through the valley until they came to the canyon. Then they'd climb out of the canyon to the old Jeep road and head northeast for home. This was all federal land out here and he'd explored plenty of it as a boy too. Why, he and Graham used to ride ponies down to the canyon all the time. But that was sixty some-odd years ago.

Without saying a word, Carl prodded his horse and crossed over the creek. Dusty quickly followed. Hal reckoned they were anxious to get up to the top of the ridge and see if there was anything there…the mysterious thing that was a pullin' at them.

"I hope we find something up there," Graham said. "I would hate to think my old bones were a rattlin' around in this saddle for nothing."

"Well, they sure think something's up there," Curtis said as he crossed the creek. "Don't know about you fellas, but I'm ready to head back home."

"Wouldn't mind sleeping in my own bed tonight," Hal said. "But I figure by the time we get off this ridge, we won't even make it to the canyon before dark."

"I'm about tired of elk jerky too," Graham added. "Wouldn't mind a decent meal tonight."

"Ain't that the truth," Hal said.

He wondered if Jean was missing him. She'd most likely be lookin' for him to come home already. Maybe she'd even make something special for him. He wouldn't mind another batch of her smothered pork chops. His stomach growled just thinking about them.

The closer they got to the top of the ridge, he noticed that Carl and Dusty were getting farther ahead of them. They were pushing their horses along, despite the lack of a trail.

"They sure do seem to be in a hurry," Jim said.

"That's cause something's pullin' them," Graham said with a smirk.

"Wonder why they're so sure something's up there?" Curtis asked. "I don't feel nothing pullin' at me. Do you?"

"All I feel are hunger pangs," Hal said, causing the others to laugh.

When they finally got to the top of the ridge, there was no sign of Carl or Dusty. The scrub brush was tall enough in places to block their view, and Curtis stood up tall in his saddle, looking around.

"Tracks go this way," he said, pointing to their right.

As they wove through the brush around to the west, a reflection caught Hal's eyes. He pulled Daisy to a stop, but the others kept going. Maybe they didn't see it, he thought. They continued riding on top of the ridge, and he turned once in his saddle, looking back down from the valley where they'd come. The region was arid and rocky, but the slice of green grass and trees that lined the flowing waters of Paradox Creek belied the high desert image of the area. He knew it would be a lot cooler down by the creek than it was up here on the ridge. He wiped the sweat from his brow, then gave Daisy a little kick.

Carl's horse was standing under the shade of a scrawny old oak, her reins dangling free. Dusty's mare stood out in the sun, her reins looped over the branch of a scrub.

"Where are they?" he asked.

They'd reached a deep ravine on the ridge, and Jim pointed to some dislodged rocks. "Looks like they went down here."

"Carl? Dusty?" Curtis called loudly. "Where the hell are you?"

"Down here," Carl called back excitedly. "We found something."

They heard the crunching of rocks and Carl showed up below them, waving them closer. "Dusty found something. Come look."

Hal, like the others, dismounted. He rubbed his sore back as he stood, trying to work the kinks out.

"What is it?" Graham called. "What'd you find?"

"I don't know," Carl said as he hurried in front them, disappearing into the ravine again.

Hal, Jim, Curtis and Graham all stopped, but Carl kept going toward where Dusty stood. A large metal disc of some sort appeared to have crashed into the ravine. Judging by the size, Hal thought nearly half of it must be lodged in the rocks.

"What the hell is that?" Curtis asked in a quiet voice.

"Looks like something from…well, I don't know. That metal sure is slick, though," Jim said. "Is that a…a wing on the side?"

"Don't get too close," Graham called as Carl took a step toward it. "It might be radioactive or something."

"Looks like one of those spaceships they have in the movies," Hal said.

Nervous laughter followed his statement. "Yeah, a spaceship has landed on Baker's Ridge! Let's hope there aren't any Martians inside."

"I'd take Martians over those other things that were in that *Alien* movie," Jim said. "That movie scared the shit out of me."

"It ain't no spaceship," Curtis said. "Maybe it's something that fell from the sky…like a satellite or something."

"I've seen pictures of satellites before and this ain't one," Jim said.

Dusty slid down the last few feet to the edge of it, and Carl followed close behind. Hal noted that Dusty seemed to be in some sort of a trance. Like he was hypnotized or something, oblivious to the rest of them.

"Don't get too close," Graham said again.

"Looks like there's a door or something," Carl called excitedly.

"Well, hell, don't open it!" Jim nearly yelled.

Hal couldn't see what was going on and he took another step closer, but Curtis stopped him with a tight grip on his arm. Dusty was tugging at the door like a man possessed. Hal watched in amazement as Dusty started banging on the door, as if he were knocking, begging to be let inside. One more tug on the door and it flung open, causing Dusty to fall backward against the rocks. Hal's mouth opened in shock as something—an arm?—reached out and grabbed Dusty, jerking him inside the door as if he were nothing more than a child's doll.

Carl screamed, a loud, piercing scream that a frightened woman might make. He turned and tried to run but something grabbed his ankle, causing him to fall. Hal instinctively tried to go to him, but Curtis held him back. In a matter of seconds, Carl was dragged inside too, his screams cut off with finality as the door slammed shut.

"My God…what…what…what just happened?" Hal stuttered.

"Let's get the hell out of here," Curtis said as he pulled Hal with him. "Come on!"

"We can't leave them!" Jim yelled, heading toward the ravine. "Who knows—"

Curtis grabbed Jim's arms and pulled him to a stop. "What are you going to do? Knock on the door? See if they'll let Carl and Dusty out? Maybe see if they'll let you *in*? We don't even know what the hell that is," Curtis said, pointing back down from where they'd come.

"We can't leave them," Jim said again. "We've got to help them."

"Help them do what?" Graham said as he pushed past Hal and started climbing out of the ravine, back toward the horses. "You saw what happened. *Something* is in there."

"But…"

"We're all over seventy years old, Jim," Hal said. "We're no match for whatever the hell is in there."

He didn't wait for an answer. He followed Graham, not even noticing that his back was killing him. Once out of the ravine, he hurried over and grabbed Daisy's saddle, pulling himself up. He was thankful to see that Curtis had followed with Jim in tow.

"We'll go get help," Curtis said firmly. "That's what we'll do."

"Yeah…we'll go get help," Graham echoed. "Head over to Paradox. Maybe they got the power back on."

"Maybe the sheriff is there," Hal added. "I think we're going to need him."

Curtis handed him the reins of Dusty's mare, and Hal pulled her behind him. Jim took Carl's horse and the four of them retraced their route to the edge of the ridge. Hal looked back once, half expecting to see something chasing after them, but it was quiet and still behind them, not even a raven or magpie calling from the trees.

Hal stared back toward the ravine, in his mind, still hearing the awful screams of Carl as he was being dragged inside the door. He clenched his jaw tightly, trying to reconcile the fact that they'd left... that they'd left Carl and Dusty behind. He shook his head slowly, trying not to think about what could have happened to Dusty...to Carl. Trying not to imagine what could possibly be inside the door.

He was old and feeling every bit of his age at this very moment... but he knew without a doubt that whatever was inside that door...it was not human. Carl's screams told him that.

And he wanted no part of it.

CHAPTER NINETEEN

"I say we follow the creek southeast until it meets up with the Delores," Butch said.

"What about that canyon that Anna Gail mentioned?" Dana asked.

"We'll have to skirt it," Butch said.

Corey sat quietly on the ground, leaning up against a tree. Dana was on the bench and Butch was pacing between them. While Corey appreciated that Butch was trying to be the man, that he was trying to take charge and get them out of there, she had no intention of heading south or east *away* from the helicopter. She would try to reason with him and get him to change his mind. If not, then she'd simply have to tell them who she was and what she was doing there. Harry had said it was classified, but she wasn't really certain why all the secrecy was necessary. She understood him wanting to keep the helicopter crash from the media, but if it was a meteor that landed that wasn't enough to warrant a classified mission.

She stood up slowly and brushed her palms off on her jeans. "I think we should try to find the helicopter," she said as casually as she could.

Butch stopped pacing and stared at her. "Why? We have no idea where the helicopter might have crashed," he said. "If there even was a helicopter. Anna Gail heard from Lou Wright who heard from some guys in Squaw Valley. That doesn't help much."

"Where is Squaw Valley, anyway?" she asked.

"It's a little community northwest of here," Butch said. "Just a handful of farms."

"And it's on this creek you've mentioned? Paradox Creek?"

"Yeah, kinda. It's still part of Paradox Valley, but it's on a fork a little farther north. Some call it Squaw Creek."

"How far is that from where you live?"

"It's north of here. We live about thirty miles or so south, down the road we found you on," he said. "The road to Squaw Valley is off that county road. You would have passed it. But we already know they're without power too. If we can get to the river, then the saline plant is there. We can—"

"If a military helicopter went down, then we're more likely to encounter someone looking for it. They'll send in a search team," she said.

"That's too far, Corey," Butch said. "We can be to the Delores in a day and a half, I'd guess, depending on how long it takes us to skirt the canyon."

Corey scratched her head, wishing she could pull out the topo map that Duncan had given her. She had no clue as to what he was talking about. "So the road to Squaw Valley...it's not the same one you were on?"

He shook his head. "No. There's another county road that crosses the creek and goes north. It's a few miles from where we met you," he said. "But we don't know where they saw the helicopter. It'd be like looking for a needle in a haystack."

Dana had remained quiet, and Corey turned to her now. "What do you think we should do?"

Dana looked between the two of them, then shrugged. "Say we make it to the saline plant only to find out they're without power too. Then what? Do we keep going? Will we have supplies?"

"So you want to go up to Squaw Valley?" Butch asked.

"I think maybe we should stay around our own people," Dana said. "You know everyone around here. Out in Squaw Valley, it's mostly farms, a few ranches. They'll have provisions, just like my parents do, like yours do," she said.

Butch shook his head. "The morning's already gone. It'd take us most of the day just to get north of Paradox Creek. Sure, we'll come upon a farm tomorrow, but who's to say they know anything about the helicopter?" He shook his head again. "No. We go southeast along the creek. It's our best chance."

Dana looked over at her with raised eyebrows. "He has a point, I guess."

"Yeah," she agreed. "Unfortunately, he's wrong."

"You don't know this area, Corey," Butch said. "I do. We'll go south, we'll—"

"We'll go north," she said, interrupting him. "And you can call me Captain."

He frowned. "What?"

"My name. It's Captain Conaway," she said.

He arched an eyebrow. "Excuse me?"

"Captain Conaway, United States Army. And I'd like to commandeer you and your horses to help me locate a Black Hawk helicopter," she said. She then gave an exaggerated smile. "Please."

Dana stood up and walked toward her. "Are you kidding me? You're military?"

Corey gave a genuine smile this time. "What? My haircut didn't give me away?" she asked, rubbing a hand over her hair.

"No. I mean…you must know what's going on then? Right?"

"Oh. Yeah. Well…that's kinda…classified."

Dana drew her brows together as she placed both hands on her hips. "*Classified*? Are you freakin' kidding me?" she asked again.

Butch, too, walked closer. "What do you know?" he demanded. "Are we under attack or something? Is that why the power's out?"

She held her hands up defensively. "No, no, no. We're not under attack," she said. "Nothing like that."

"Then why the secrecy?" Dana asked. "I'm assuming you weren't really camping then."

"Look, like I said…it's—"

"Classified," Dana finished for her. She turned to her cousin. "I vote we go to the saline plant."

"Yeah. Me too," Butch said.

Corey raised her eyebrows, surprised at Dana's defiance. "So you think you get a vote now?"

"What? Are you going to *make* us look for a helicopter?"

Corey sighed. This was getting them nowhere and as Butch had said, the morning was almost gone. They needed to be too. She didn't have time to argue with them. She needed them. Well, at least Butch. As he said, he knew the area. She needed him to get her at least as far as Squaw Valley.

"Okay. You win," she said. "I'll tell you what I know, which isn't much." That, at least, was true. Most everything about this mission was speculation only. "The earthquake you thought you felt was most likely from a meteor," she said.

"A meteor?" Dana asked skeptically.

"That's what they tell me," she said honestly.

"And it took out a power grid or something?"

"Or something."

"You're being very vague," Dana accused.

"That's because we don't really know. The meteor showed up as a blip on the radar. As a precaution, a helicopter was sent out... reconnaissance," she said. "Just in case."

"Just in case what?" Butch asked.

"Just in case the blip on the radar was from a hostile aircraft."

"And the helicopter really crashed?"

"Disappeared off radar, yes. No communication with the crew. And the utility company confirmed the power outage in this area."

"Why hasn't someone come to help?" Dana asked.

"A small unit was sent in. Their vehicle became disabled and they hiked back out."

Dana nodded. "Battery died."

"Yes."

"Do you know why? I mean, phones, everything is dead."

"Again, there's only a theory," she said. "I'm the first person to get this far in that's not a local."

"What's the theory?" Dana asked.

"Electromagnetic pulse of some sort."

"What the hell does that mean?"

"I said it was a theory," she reminded Dana. "I'm trying to find the helicopter first. Then the meteor."

"One person? They send in one person? A woman?"

She looked at Butch. "You got something against women?"

"I mean...why not send in troops? People are—"

"Already paranoid," she said. "Like Richard. What do you think would happen if a couple of platoons of soldiers marched in?"

"Are we even on the news? Does *anybody* know?" Dana asked.

She shook her head. "No. They've got the highway down south blocked off so no one's coming in the area. They're trying to determine how large the zone is."

"Why is the military being so secretive if it's only a meteor?" Dana asked.

"Because someone jumped the gun and sent up a helicopter which then crashed," she said.

Butch nodded. "Because this someone didn't think it was a meteor, did they? They thought it was a—"

"A hostile aircraft."

"And you're sure it's not?" Dana asked.

Corey held her gaze. "We're sure."

Dana shook her head. "Okay, still—and maybe I'm too naive—but none of this makes sense. So it's a meteor? What's the big deal? You've got hundreds of people out here without power, without phones. Why isn't someone trying to help us?"

"The loss of a military aircraft and crew in a situation like this… well, it's complicated," Corey said.

"So the military is more worried about bad press than they are the wellbeing of us?"

"We have a missing helicopter and three crew members. That's my only concern," she said bluntly. "Whatever hardship you've had because you don't have your cell phone is secondary, I assure you."

Dana squared her shoulders. "I don't think I like you very much."

Corey shrugged. "I don't really care." She turned to Butch. "I need you to take me to Squaw Valley. I need to find these men who went after the helicopter. The sooner we find it, the sooner help will come."

"And if I refuse?"

"I need your help. And I need you to trust me." She looked over at Dana. "I'm not the bad guy here."

Butch finally nodded. "Okay, Captain Conaway. Against my better judgment, I'll take you to Squaw Valley."

"Thank you." She again glanced at Dana. "You should probably stay here. You can—"

"The hell I am," Dana said. "You're not leaving me here with that crazy man and his rifle."

Corey opened her mouth to protest, then closed it. She hadn't known Dana long, but long enough to know she sported a defiant, stubborn streak. They didn't have time to argue. They needed to get going.

"Okay. Let's see if we can get some supplies from Anna Gail's store. Butch? Can you do that for us?"

"Yeah."

"Tell her we're following the creek south like you wanted to. Nothing else. And whatever you do, don't tell Richard a goddamn thing."

"Right." He paused. "This is probably a silly question....but are you armed?"

Corey lifted one corner of her mouth in a smile. "Yeah...silly question."

CHAPTER TWENTY

Hal knew there was another good hour or more of daylight left, but his back was hurting him so much, he wasn't sure he could take another minute in the saddle, much less an hour. He pulled Daisy to a stop.

"I'm about done for the day," he said.

Jim looked behind them, like he'd been doing since they'd left Baker's Ridge. Hal wasn't sure if he was expecting someone to be chasing them or if he expected Carl or Dusty to show up.

Graham was the first one off his horse. "When I get back home, I may never get on a horse again."

Curtis, too, looked behind them. "I think we should push on," he said nervously. "Hell, we can still see the ridge from here. We're probably only three hours from the canyon."

"If we push on, then we'll leave the creek," Hal said. "That'll put us up on that Jeep road overnight. No water."

"At least we'll be closer to Paradox," Jim said. "We've got to get some help. Let someone know what happened."

"We don't even know what happened ourselves," Graham said.

Hal held on to Daisy while he got his legs under him. Screaming pain in his back nearly made his eyes water. He finally pushed it aside and straightened up.

"We'll get to Paradox tomorrow," he said. "We'll find the sheriff, hopefully, and let him handle it. We'll tell him what we saw and let him take care of it. I need to get back to Jean. I can't expect her to take care of all the chores much longer."

"We all want to get home, Hal," Curtis said as he dismounted too.

The spring grass was thick along the creek and they let all six horses graze. The young cottonwood trees were thick here, but the few scrub oaks didn't offer much in the way of firewood.

By the time they had camp set up and collected what measly firewood they could find, evening was approaching. Conversation was sparse when they bothered to talk at all. They ate the last of Dusty's elk jerky in near silence. Again, Hal wished he was home with Jean, eating his evening meal with her. A nice cold glass of milk would hit the spot right about now too. He looked up into the sky, seeing the twinkling of stars as darkness was beginning to envelop them. He looked to the east, thankful to see the moon. It wasn't much more than the sliver it had been the night before, but at least it was there. It might cast a little light on them tonight.

"What do you think happened?" Jim asked, his voice low and quiet.

"I'm afraid to think about it," Graham said, his voice equally as quiet.

"What are we going to tell their wives? I mean, we just left them there," Jim said. "What are we going to say?"

"We told them not to go down there in the ravine," Hal said. "We told them not to open that damn door. It was like they were... possessed or something."

Curtis nodded. "Yeah. Possessed. Like they weren't even hearing us." He leaned forward, adding another small branch to their meager fire. "It was most likely something awful, though."

"You think that was some kind of...of a spaceship or something?" Jim asked.

"It wasn't no spaceship," Curtis said sharply. "This ain't some damn movie."

"Then what? There was a door," Graham said. "Something grabbed Dusty. Jerked him in like he weighed nothin' more than a little sack of flour."

"Something grabbed Carl too," Jim said. "I saw this...this arm or something." He covered both ears with his hands. "I can't get his scream out of my head. It was like he was seeing a monster or...or worse."

Hal wondered what would be worse than a monster. He could still hear Carl's scream too, even though he'd tried all afternoon to push it from his mind. They were a bunch of old cowards for leaving them there and that's a regret he'd take to his grave. But after seeing what happened, after hearing Carl's wild scream, there was no way in hell he was going after them.

"Not sure I'm going to be able to sleep tonight," Graham said. "I got this weird feeling."

"What kinda feeling?" Curtis asked.

"Like we're being watched...like we're not alone."

"Come on, Graham," Jim said with a shaky laugh. "You tryin' to scare me more than I already am?"

"I'm serious."

"I thought I heard some rocks tumblin' earlier," Curtis said.

"You got the horses tied up good?" Hal asked. "Maybe they was kickin' rocks around."

"Maybe so."

After a while, Jim spoke again, his voice low and quiet like before. "Seems awful dark tonight, don't it?"

"Clouds are moving in," Curtis said. "Not many stars out anymore."

Hal looked up, searching for the little sliver of moon he'd seen earlier. The sky was black dark.

"Wind's pickin' up too," Graham noted. "Hope we don't get a storm tonight."

Hal was about to suggest they put out the fire and go on to bed, but he doubted he'd get any sleep. Anyway, the fire was their only light. He wasn't in a hurry to have the world plunged into total darkness just yet. So he picked up one of the few remaining twigs and tossed it on top of the flames. No need to be in a hurry to put the fire out. They didn't have enough wood to last another half hour.

They huddled around the fire as close as they could get, watching as the flame flickered, eating at the last of the wood. A high-pitched barking howl downstream made Hal's old heart jump in his chest. Yaps and chortles followed. It was a sound Hal had heard his whole life— coyotes—yet tonight, it made the hair on the back of his neck stand up.

"Sounds like quite a few of them," Curtis said unnecessarily.

"I wish we had more wood," Jim said for the second time. "I ain't relishing this thing going out."

"I don't reckon any of us are," Hal said.

He suddenly agreed with Graham's earlier statement. He, too, felt like they were being watched...like they weren't alone. He jerked his head around as he heard a rustle behind the scrub brush. He listened but heard nothing else.

"Something ain't right," Jim murmured in a near whisper. "If we had any moon at all, I'd have half a mind to saddle up and head out."

"Maybe we should have pushed on," Graham said.

At that moment, now that his back wasn't aching quite as much, Hal was thinking that very thing. It was going to be an endless night, most likely.

Another sound behind the brush, rocks scraping together, and all four of them turned to stare. Out of the shadows, a shape materialized and Hal only barely stifled his scream. They all jumped to their feet... well, as fast as seventy-five-year-old men could.

"Carl?"

"What the hell happened?" Curtis asked as he hurried over to him.

Carl said nothing, he simply stood there looking at them. There wasn't enough light left from the flickering fire to make out his features, but Hal saw—or imagined he saw—blood on Carl's shirt.

"Come by the fire," Curtis said, tugging him closer. "What's left of it, anyway. We're out of wood."

"How did you get here so fast?" Graham asked.

"Ran."

"What about Dusty?"

Carl turned his head slowly toward Jim. "Who?"

Hal frowned. His voice...while it sounded like Carl...it didn't *quite* sound like Carl. And what did he mean, he ran? Most likely Carl hadn't run in thirty years or more. Those pencil-thin legs of his would have snapped like a twig if he'd run. He was about to ask him just that when Carl reached out suddenly and grabbed Graham and Curtis at the same time, slamming their heads together with such force, Hal heard their skulls crack like plates of cheap china and they fell lifeless to the ground. Before anyone could react, Carl reached for Jim. Hal didn't wait, he turned and ran toward the creek, to where the horses were tied. Jim's scream was cut off immediately and Hal ran blindly, not daring to think of what Carl had possibly done to Jim.

When he reached the horses, they danced around him. They weren't saddled but with his adrenaline pumping, Hal grabbed the mane of one and tried to pull himself up. He heard movement behind him but what little courage he still clung to wouldn't allow him to look. His attempt to mount the horse, however, was futile.

He finally turned, seeing Carl approaching him. He held his hands up defensively.

"We didn't want to leave you behind, Carl. But what...what could we do? We didn't know—"

Carl tilted his head, much like Lucky did when Hal talked to him. He heard the words but he didn't understand them.

Hal didn't wait another second longer. He bolted into the creek as fast as his shaky legs would take him. As his foot caught a rock and he felt himself falling, he thought he heard dark laughter coming from behind him. Soaking wet, he scrambled to his feet, expecting to feel hands grab him at any moment. He was surprised when he made it to the other side of the creek unharmed.

"Stop."

He jumped, shocked that Carl was standing beside him. How had he made it across so fast?

He didn't have time for the question—and answer—to register. He didn't even have time to scream.

CHAPTER TWENTY-ONE

Dana pulled her gaze from Corey, who was neatly refolding her tent, and glanced at Butch.

"I'm not quite sure what to make of her," she said quietly.

Butch tossed out the last of his coffee. "I thought she fit your sporty Dream Girl image," he said with a smile.

"Oh, she does. Perfectly, in fact. But maybe I was a bit overzealous when I said I liked strong, independent women." She sighed. "She is cute. But she kinda makes me nervous."

"She makes me nervous too. You know, I go for the more mild-mannered, submissive women."

"Like Holly?"

Butch shrugged. "Holly's just Holly. She doesn't have much ambition. I blame her parents."

"Why?"

"She's the baby. They catered to her, much like my parents did to Tony."

"Well, I can't really see the two of you together," she said. "There didn't appear to be any chemistry between you." She leaned closer, keeping her voice low. "You were having sex, right?" She was surprised by the blush that lit Butch's face.

"Well...the one time."

Dana's eyes widened. "She was a virgin?"

He nodded. "And it didn't go well. Since then, we don't do much more than kiss and make out a little bit."

"Jesus, you're lucky she didn't get pregnant."

He rolled his eyes. "I'm not stupid, you know."

Corey tossed down her pack, then squatted beside the fire and poured coffee into a cup. She shook the pot and Dana heard the sloshing of the liquid inside.

"Not much left," Corey said. "Anyone want more?"

"I'm good," Butch said.

Dana shook her head. She wasn't much for camp coffee. She sighed, missing her morning trips to the Starbucks near her office. What would she have today? She closed her eyes for a moment. Oh…a Caramel Macchiato sounded good. Or maybe a Vanilla Latte. She hadn't had one of those in a while.

"How long do you think it'll take?" Corey asked.

"We should be in the valley in less than two hours," Butch said. "We'll make better time following the road." He motioned to the creek. "I thought it was safer to follow the water yesterday. Makes for better camping too."

Corey took the coffeepot and emptied it, then went to the creek to rinse it out. Butch stood and helped Dana to her feet.

"Guess it's time to head out."

Dana sighed yet again, her pleasant memories of Starbucks coffee fading from her mind. Time to get back on the horse. Another day in the saddle. Another day with that woman riding behind her.

While she found Corey nice enough…Captain Conaway, she mentally corrected…their time on the horse was mostly spent in silence. And even though in her mind her Dream Girl was the strong, silent type, she decided she preferred a little more conversation. She smiled to herself. Not that Corey Conaway was actually her Dream Girl. She was a little too aloof for that. She now knew that the friendliness Corey had shown when they'd first met her had been forced. Since her revelation, well, she was all business now.

"How about I take the saddle today and you ride in the back?"

Dana stared at her blankly. "Huh?"

Corey took a step closer. "I said, I'll take the saddle today. You ride in back."

Dana looked over at their horse. Riding on the back of the saddle didn't look all that safe. Not that Gretchen wasn't gentle, she was just big and tall. Dana was a little intimidated by her and she would miss having the security of the saddle.

"You can hold on to me," Corey said, as if reading her mind.

Dana had no time to protest as Corey had already put her foot in the stirrup and had swung up onto the saddle.

"Guess I'm riding in the back," she murmured.

"Toss me your pack," Butch said.

He had taken to hauling all three of their packs since he didn't have an extra passenger with him. She handed hers over to him, then stood beside Gretchen...and Captain Conaway. Corey kicked her boot out of the stirrup, freeing it for Dana. She wasn't sure what to use to pull herself up. When Corey rode on the back, she used the front of the saddle as leverage. Dana was a little shorter than she was and didn't feel strong enough.

Corey held her hand out. "I'll pull you up," she offered.

Without thinking, Dana grabbed Corey's forearm and Corey did the same. Their eyes met for a second or two, then Dana felt herself being pulled up. She swung her leg over and behind the saddle, grabbing onto Corey's waist to steady herself.

"Okay?"

"Doesn't feel very secure back here," she said.

"Like I said...feel free to hold on to me."

A gentle kick put Gretchen in motion, and Dana nearly fell off the back of her. She wrapped her arms around Corey's waist and pulled herself closer. She could feel Corey's quiet laughter against her hands.

"That was mean," she said.

"Yeah, it was. Sorry."

Dana loosened her grip as she got used to the slow, even gait of the horse. Still, she kept her hands on Corey's waist, right above her hips...just in case, she told herself.

They rode on in silence, following behind Butch as he skirted the creek. They were still technically in the canyon, Dana thought, as the rocky wall jutted up to their right, but the grass was a little thicker here, a little greener. The trees had changed too, she noted, as a few pines had taken hold as the canyon slowly gave way to the valley. Before long, Butch headed up, and Dana assumed it was to hook up with the road.

"So...you're from Seattle," Corey said. "Picked a hell of a time to visit your parents, didn't you?"

"It wasn't exactly planned," Dana admitted. "I was running from a marriage proposal."

Corey turned her head to look at her. "Oh, yeah? Your girlfriend popped the question?"

Dana nodded. "Kendra. Although I don't know that I ever actually called her my girlfriend," she said. "We'd been dating about six months. I guess I didn't realize we were *going steady*."

Corey laughed. "So the proposal took you by surprise."

"I nearly passed out from shock." When Corey asked no further questions, Dana asked one of her own. "Where are you from?"

"Utah, currently."

"Really? I mean, that was your story when you were, you know, camping."

"Still true."

"Are you from Utah because you're stationed at the army base there or are you *really* from Utah?"

"Army brat," Corey said. "No place is home." She shrugged. "Every place is home."

"That didn't answer my question."

"Yes, I'm stationed there. And no, I don't live on base. I rent a little cabin out in the foothills."

"So is there a Mrs. Captain in the picture or some little captains running around?"

Corey laughed again. "No and no."

"Why not?"

"I don't like kids."

Dana's lips twitched in a smile. "Lots of Mrs. Captains then?"

"God, no. I'm career military," Corey said. "All of my time and energy has been devoted to that."

"Surely you have a personal life."

"My team is my…" But she stopped, not finishing her statement.

"Your team is what?"

"Nothing."

The silence lingered again, and Dana could feel the tension in Corey's body. She wondered what had brought that on. Perhaps Corey didn't like to talk about herself. Some people were fiercely private and she could respect that…under normal circumstances. This, of course, was hardly a normal situation.

"So is your team out here somewhere too?" she asked after a while.

"No."

"You said they were sending in—"

"There's a unit on foot, yes. They're not my team," Corey said, her words clipped and measured.

Dana blew out her breath, then tried again. "What about your family? You said you were a military brat. Where are they now?"

Corey turned her head slightly and looked at her. "Why all the questions?"

"You started it," she said defensively.

"So I did." She paused. "My father was killed in Iraq about ten years ago. My mother has remarried and lives in Atlanta."

"So not a military man?"

"Not even close."

Dana could hear the bitterness in her voice and wondered if it was because she didn't like the man or just the fact that her mother had remarried. Some children, after losing a parent, couldn't understand how the other parent could go on with their life and find another partner to share it with. She assumed Corey felt a sense of betrayal.

"You're an only child," she guessed. "Right?"

She felt Corey relax a little. "Right. And I know what you're thinking."

"Is it true?"

"Yes. I've gotten past it, though. We're closer now." When Dana would have asked another question, Corey turned around. "What's with all the questions?" she asked again.

Dana smiled at her. "I'm trying to find something I like about you."

Corey gave a quick laugh. "I thought we were kindred spirits. Don't we have a secret bond or something?"

"It'll take a little more than that, I'm afraid."

"Okay. So tell me something about you."

"Such as?"

"Something other than running from a girlfriend you didn't know you had," Corey said. "Brother? Sister?"

Dana nodded. "One of each, both older. Cathy lives in Denver, she's ten years older. James is in San Francisco, seven years older."

"Close?"

"To James, yes. We're kindred spirits, using your words," she said with a smile, picturing her brother's handsome face. "He doesn't come back home, though. My parents, while they're okay having a lesbian daughter, they have yet to accept that their only son is gay."

"So he's not allowed back?"

"No, no. It's not like that. It's just very awkward, uncomfortable... for all of them," she said. "So their relationship is mainly over the phone. I see him a couple of times a year, though, and we talk often."

Dana glanced up ahead, wondering if Butch could hear their conversation. Butch was the only one in his family who treated James the same even after he came out. The others, well, much like her parents, they couldn't accept it. James was a big guy, a football player in high school, a handsome boy who the girls had flocked to. He kept his secret until he left for college. He spent one year in Boulder, then headed off to California. She'd been too young to really understand what it all meant, but she remembered her mother's tears. That's why, years later, when she discovered the truth about herself, she'd been terrified to tell her parents. She'd been afraid of the tears.

"What about your sister?"

Dana sighed. "We're not close. She's on her second marriage. He's fifteen years older than she is. He's very conservative, very Republican. And he *found* Jesus, so he's apparently one of the chosen ones and the rest of us aren't."

"I imagine he's not too fond of you then."

"I don't speak to him," she said. "Cathy and I talk on the phone once, maybe twice a year. It's superficial only. She tells me about her life and her kids and I listen. We don't talk politics or religion…and we certainly don't talk about my personal life."

"Can't say I blame you, I guess. But I'd always wished for siblings. Especially after my father died. I felt…well, it would have been nice to have a brother or sister to talk to," Corey said.

"You mean when your mother remarried?"

"Yeah. Then."

Before Dana could ask any other questions, however, Corey gave Gretchen a gentle kick, picking up their pace to catch up with Butch… and signaling an end to their conversation.

CHAPTER TWENTY-TWO

Jean had just come in the back door by the kitchen, her basket loaded with the vegetables she'd picked from the garden, when Lucky started barking. She tilted her head, listening. It wasn't his normal bark when company came over. This was a ferocious warning bark that he would normally give to a stranger. Jean placed the basket of vegetables on the counter and hurried through the house to the front door. Her eyes widened as she saw Hal walking up. She frowned slightly as he approached. There wasn't even a hint of a limp from his bad back. Maybe this trip had been good for him.

As he got closer, she saw a dark stain on his shirt. Blood? She pushed open the screen door and hurried out toward him. Lucky intercepted her, still barking his fool head off.

"It's okay, boy. It's only Hal," she said, reaching out to touch Lucky's head. Lucky's barking ceased, replaced with a low growl in his throat. Jean noticed that the hair across his back was standing on end.

"What in the world happened to you?" she asked as Hal walked up to her. "Where's Daisy?"

Hal seemed to be a little disoriented, and Jean wondered if he was badly injured. He shook his head slowly.

"Who?"

"Daisy…our horse," she said. "Where is she?"

"Back there," Hal said with a toss of his head toward the barn.

Jean took a step closer to him. He smelled like he hadn't bathed in days, which she supposed was true. "Are you okay?"

He said nothing, only stared at her.

"You have blood on you, Hal."

He frowned. "Blood?"

"Yes. On your shirt. On your jeans." She reached for his hand to lead him inside. "Come on. Let's get you cleaned up."

She was surprised when he pulled his hand away.

Lucky growled again and circled Jean as if protecting her. "What's gotten into him, I wonder?" Jean turned to Hal. "I'm glad you're back, but you stink. Those are the same clothes you left here in. I put a change of clothes in your pack." She headed into the house. "I'll run you a bath, if you want."

As soon as she got to the screen door, Lucky started barking again. She turned around, shocked to see Hal lift a leg and kick at him. She'd never once seen him raise a hand to the dog before.

"Hal?"

"Make it stop," he said, pointing at Lucky.

As Jean looked into his eyes, she felt her blood run cold. That wasn't her Hal looking back at her.

"Lucky," she called quickly, patting her thigh. "Come here, boy." Lucky came toward her and leaned protectively against her leg. "You must be hungry," she said to Hal, her words measured. "You want your favorite? Got that liver already thawed out. I can make a meal real quick," she offered. "I know how much you love liver."

He nodded. "Okay."

She turned and headed inside, coaxing Lucky to follow. The dog had never set foot inside the house before, and he hesitated, looking at her questioningly.

"It's okay, boy," she said softly, tapping her thigh again. "Come with me."

He finally followed her in and she let the screen door close, leaving Hal on the porch. Her heart was hammering in her chest so fast she feared she would have a heart attack and drop dead right then and there. She took several deep breaths as she tried to slow her racing heart.

Hal hated liver. In fact, the only time she'd fixed it, shortly after they married, he'd gotten physically sick. It had been a joke with them over the years, her threatening to fix liver for his supper whenever he went against her wishes...which was not often.

She heard the screen door open and she turned, watching as Hal came inside and shuffled toward her. Lucky growled low in his throat again and Jean put a steadying hand on his head, trying not to be frightened.

"Clean up?"

Jean pointed to the back door of the kitchen. "Outside," she said. "At the well pump."

Hal followed her direction and went out the back screen door. She watched through the window as he studied the old pump for a long moment before lifting the handle. Lucky had gone to the door and was watching through the screen, his low growl telling Jean all she needed to know.

"I don't know what's going on, Lucky, but that's not my Hal out there," she whispered. "But you already know that, don't you?"

Her hands were trembling as she reached for the handle to the fridge. She'd turned the generator off earlier, trying to conserve their fuel supply. There wasn't much left in the fridge anyway, but the freezer still had plenty of meat. Since Hal had been gone, she hadn't bothered with cooking a meal, eating sparingly instead. She'd anticipated him coming back yesterday and she'd taken out some pork chops to thaw. She pulled them from the fridge now, thinking she could fry them up real quick. She wondered if he would even know that they weren't liver.

They were already sizzling in the pan when Hal came back in. She again stared at the blood on his shirt, then quickly averted her eyes. He pulled out a chair and sat down at the table. It wasn't his chair but the one she normally used. Lucky was pressed against her leg and she plunged a hand into his fur, trying to calm herself down. Maybe something had happened...maybe Hal had lost his memory.

Her hand was trembling as she plucked two chops from the pan and put them on a plate. She had nothing else prepared—no potatoes, no vegetables. She handed him the plate and he took it without saying a word. She felt tears well in her eyes. In all the years they'd been married, he had never forgotten to compliment her meal. She moved to the drawers and pulled out a fork and a knife for him. When she turned around to offer them to him, she saw that he had simply picked up the chop with his hand and begun eating.

She continued to stare, unable to pull her eyes away from this man at her table...this man who looked like her Hal.

"Eat," he said gruffly, pointing at her empty plate.

She nodded and took a chop from the pan. She sat in the chair that Hal normally used and used the knife to cut a piece. She wondered if he noticed her hands trembling as she tried to eat. She jumped as he stood up, frightened, and Lucky growled again. Her nerves calmed a little as he went to the stove and took the last remaining pork chop out of the pan with his fingers and brought it back to the table.

She glanced over to the corner by the kitchen door where the shotgun usually stood. It wasn't there and she panicked. Then she remembered...she'd taken it with her that morning to the barn when she'd let the chickens out for the day. She must have forgotten to bring it back in. She didn't know if she had anything to fear from him, but she was frightened nonetheless.

She got up slowly and took her plate over to the sink, hoping he wouldn't notice her uneaten pork chop. "I need to tend to the chickens," she said. "I forgot to put their feed out."

She didn't look back as she went out the kitchen door. Lucky ran beside her, beating her out. She walked faster now, heading toward the barn. She heard the screen door open behind her and she glanced over her shoulder, seeing Hal following her. She started running then, as fast as she could. Her hands were shaking so badly she could hardly get the barn door opened. It was dark inside and smelled of hay and manure. She went to the corner stall where the chickens roosted at night. Her eyes darted left, then right, as she tried to remember where she'd put the shotgun that morning. A couple of chickens came in from the outside, hoping for another handout of feed.

Lucky barked behind her, and she turned, seeing Hal standing in the doorway of the barn, the sun shadowing his features as he came toward her.

She moved backward, hands held up as if to ward him off. When his eyes pierced hers, her knees nearly buckled from fright. Those weren't Hal's eyes. She wasn't even certain that they were human.

Lucky's barking turned vicious as Hal neared, and without looking, Hal kicked the dog, sending him tumbling across the ground with a wounded yelp.

He came closer, close enough for Jean to notice the sour smell that clung to his clothes.

"Hal...don't," she pleaded, her voice cracking with fear. "Please... don't."

CHAPTER TWENTY-THREE

"And we've heard nothing from her?"

Sutter shook his head. "No, sir. But Duncan's on his way. He briefed Conaway. He's also coordinating the squad that went in after she did." Sutter avoided the stare of Harry Brinkley as he went to his door and opened it. Duncan was just entering the outer room and he motioned him inside.

Duncan immediately came to attention and saluted. "General Brinkley, sir."

"Lieutenant Duncan," Brinkley said. "At ease."

"Yes, sir." Duncan looked nervously at Sutter before turning his attention back to the general. "I wasn't aware you were on base, sir."

"You weren't supposed to be," Brinkley shot back. "Captain Conaway. Any contact from her?"

"No, sir, not since we dropped her off. She was able to send one communication, nothing since."

Brinkley sighed heavily, and again Sutter wondered at their relationship. "Okay, brief me on the squad that was deployed."

"Of course, sir. Yes, twelve men. As you know, we compared satellite images from the last month or so. We think we've located the wreckage. It's in a very remote area...but it's on federal land, not private."

"Yes, that's the first good news we've had," Brinkley said. "Go on, Lieutenant."

"Communication is a challenge. In lieu of batteries, we're using a device—a transmitter—that is powered by a direct-current solar feed. But since we don't know what's taking out the power grid or the batteries, we're not sure how these will function inside the zone."

"How long before they reach it?"

"We hope to hear something today, tomorrow at the latest, sir. They were dropped off at the checkpoint at 0900 Tuesday. We still had communication with them an hour later, nothing since."

"So your solar transmitter didn't hold up? Captain Conaway is using this as well?"

"Yes, sir. They're equipped with tracking devices too, but we've not been able to get a signal. The squad that went in, sir, we're monitoring by satellite. They have flares to send up when they find the Black Hawk."

"Okay. Any luck finding this…meteor?"

"No, sir. We've spent hours going over satellite images. Nothing, sir."

"And what's the latest on the power outage? Any update?"

"No, sir. We do know the extent of the outage zone, though, based on their meter feedback." Duncan glanced again at him and Sutter motioned for him to sit. He looked like he was about to pass out.

"The power company is on standby, sir," Sutter said. "Since they're not having any complaints from their customers, it's been easy to get them to wait. I thought it best to keep them out of the zone. They start bringing trucks in that become disabled…well, it won't take long for that to get out."

Brinkley nodded again, but his stare was intense. "We don't want to cause a panic. Our focus right now is finding the helicopter and her crew. If not for your decision to send her up in the first place, we would be concentrating on what took out the power grid instead of on this search and rescue. You better pray it was only a meteor, Colonel."

"Of course, sir," he said dutifully. "I take full responsibility for this situation."

"Yes. The Secretary is aware of that fact, Colonel Sutter."

Sutter wondered if Brinkley meant that statement as a threat. If he did—and the Black Hawk and crew were indeed lost—Sutter had no doubt his next assignment wouldn't be a cushy Stateside gig. A hot, desolate desert base, no doubt. He had enough left of his sense of humor to find that thought ironic. Their base here in southern Utah wasn't exactly a tropical paradise.

"How long do we wait before notifying the families, sir?" he asked, hoping to play on Brinkley's sympathy.

"As soon as we find the wreckage and know for sure what happened. What have you told them so far?"

"A secret training mission, sir."

Brinkley's face hardened. "It's a shame you'll most likely have to contact them again and tell them your so-called secret training mission ended in tragedy, Colonel." He shook his head. "Because of a goddamn meteor."

Sutter avoided his stare but nodded mutely.

General Brinkley stood then, and Sutter and Duncan both snapped to attention.

"I want to be notified directly as soon as you know something, Colonel. The sooner this mess is over with, the sooner we can work on damage control."

"Yes, sir."

As soon as the door closed, Sutter turned to Duncan, trying to mimic Brinkley's stare.

"I blame you for this, Duncan."

"Sir?"

"A four-second blip on the radar."

"But, sir—"

"Goddamn four seconds," he said loudly. "You inferred that it was a hostile aircraft. You said—"

"But, sir, I said—"

Sutter pointed a finger at his face. "*I'm* speaking now, Lieutenant. *You* are listening."

"Yes, sir."

He narrowed his eyes, piercing Duncan with his best glare. "If this ends badly, I won't be the one taking the fall. You, Lieutenant Duncan, will be held responsible. Not me," he said, tapping his own chest. He was pleased to see Duncan swallow nervously.

"Of course, sir. Yes, sir."

CHAPTER TWENTY-FOUR

Corey guided Gretchen behind Butch, but she knew immediately that there was no one around. It was quiet. Too quiet.

"This is Carl Milstead's place," Butch said.

"Don't hear a generator running," Dana said. "Seems awful quiet."

Corey nodded. "I was thinking the same thing."

Butch got off his horse and walked through the gate of the small fence that surrounded the house. He knocked on the door.

"Carl? Rebecca? It's Butch Ingram," he said loudly.

"We'll check the barn," Corey said, turning Gretchen and giving her a little kick. Dana grasped her waist again as the horse trotted toward the barn.

"Hello?" Corey called. "Anyone home?"

They rode around to the side, finding the stables to the barn opened. Three cows, all with calves, grazed out in the field and two horses were eating from a large bale of hay. Chickens were scurrying about, scratching after insects, and there was a goat following after them.

"Doesn't look like anyone's around," she said.

They went back to the house where Butch was waiting. He looked at her questioningly.

"Is the door locked?" she asked.

"I didn't try it. Not many people lock their houses around here, though."

"Let's take a look inside."

"I don't know if we should do that," Butch said. "Just because they don't lock their doors doesn't mean people can go in uninvited."

"Yeah, well, considering the situation, I don't think we need to follow proper etiquette," she said. She turned, offering her hand to Dana who grabbed on and lowered herself to the ground. Corey followed, leaving the reins dangling around Gretchen's neck.

The door was indeed unlocked and she pushed it open. "Anybody home?" she called. They were met with an eerie silence and she walked inside. The main room was neat and tidy, and she walked through it, finding the kitchen. This was a different story. Dirty dishes were in the sink and two plates of uneaten food were on the table. A lone fly buzzed between the two plates and more flies were on the dishes in the sink. A chair was overturned, as if someone had jumped up, knocking it over.

"Let's check the bedrooms," she said quietly.

Butch pushed open one door. It appeared to be a guest room, and it looked undisturbed and unlived in. The other bedroom's door was opened. The bed was unmade, the cover pulled off to the floor. Corey stuck her head in the bathroom. It was clean and tidy, nothing looked awry.

"What do you make of this?" Dana asked. "It seems like a contradiction."

Corey nodded. "I agree. There was some sort of a...a scuffle or something," she said. "The house as a whole is very neat. Nothing is out of place. Living room, for example...nice and tidy. Clean." She pointed at the bed. "Unmade bed doesn't fit in with the rest of the house."

"Bedspread on the floor certainly doesn't fit," Dana added.

"Bathroom is practically spotless," she continued as they walked back into the kitchen. "Here...it looks like a meal was interrupted. I'd say less than a day ago."

"If Carl was one of the guys who went looking for the helicopter, Rebecca would have been here by herself," Butch said.

"You said no one locked their doors," Corey reminded him. "Nobody out here but neighbors...no one to fear." She shrugged. "Can't imagine Rebecca met with some kind of foul play," she said. "Not unless someone went Richard Filmore psycho on her."

Butch shook his head. "Not out here. Everyone is pretty self-sufficient. I'd think that most out here—like my folks and like Dana's folks—have enough fuel and supplies to last a month or more without power," he said. "After that, *then* you might see someone going Richard Filmore psycho."

"So you're saying the folks who live in Paradox aren't quite as prepared as those living out on farms?"

Butch smiled. "Yeah...city folks."

Corey laughed. "Yeah, Paradox is a thriving metropolis."

The smile left her face about the same time Butch's disappeared. "So now what?" he asked.

"Head on to the next farm, I guess."

"A little farther up this road, that'd be Hal and Jean Bulgur's place. Nice folks. Or we can keep going west...Dusty Truchard's place. I can't recall his wife's name."

Corey turned a circle, looking out around them in all directions, trying to picture the map she and Butch had gone over that morning. She faced west where the sun was already starting to fall, signaling that the end to the day was fast approaching.

"Let's try the Bulgur place first," she said. "When I left, they were still trying to determine which grid the helicopter could have gone down in. We need to head west after that, I think."

* * *

It was getting late, and Dana had had about enough of riding behind Corey on the saddle. She took off the cap that Butch had scrounged up for her at the feed store in Paradox and ran a hand through her hair. The cap was a god-awful bright red, advertising Tommy's store, but at least it kept the sun at bay. She sighed, wondering what time it was. For that matter, she wondered what day it was. It seemed like it had been forever since she'd left her parents' place. Would this be their fourth night out already?

"You're sure quiet back there," Corey said.

"Tired." She sighed. "And my ass hurts."

Corey laughed. "I guess tomorrow you're going to want the saddle back, huh?"

"If Captain Conaway will permit it, yes. You know, it *was* my horse."

"You didn't even know her name," Corey countered.

"Makes little difference." She pointed to a gadget that Corey had tied to the saddle. "What's that?"

"Oh…it's a transmitter. Sort of."

Dana perked up. "Like you can talk to someone?"

"I haven't been able to get it to work. It's solar powered, no battery," Corey said. "I was able to communicate when they dropped me off, but the farther I got into the zone, the less effective it was. Apparently, it's affected like everything else." Corey glanced back at her. "It's got a tracking device on it. Even if I can't get a transmission out, I'm hoping they can still track me. But if it's blocked…"

"And it probably is," Dana said.

"Yeah. I'll keep trying."

They could see the farmhouse from the road, and they guided the horses down the narrow lane. A black dog started barking and Dana saw someone standing on the porch. As they got closer, she could see that it was a woman wearing a floral housedress.

"Best let me go up first," Butch said. "Looks like Miss Jean has a shotgun with her."

"Jesus…not another crazy, I hope," Corey murmured. "Do you know them?"

"No," Dana said.

Corey pulled Gretchen to a stop, and let Butch get ahead of them. Dana glanced down where Corey had strapped a gun to the saddle. She had been a little uncomfortable with it there, but now that they were staring down the barrel of a shotgun, she didn't mind it so much.

"Miss Jean? I'm Butch Ingram, down from over the south side of Paradox Valley," he said.

The woman pointed the shotgun directly at Butch. "Don't come any closer."

Dana leaned closer to Corey. "What do you think is up with her?" she asked in a whisper.

"I have no idea."

The black dog stood next to the woman—Jean—but his barking had ceased. She still didn't lower the shotgun.

"Get off your horse slowly," Jean said to Butch. "I surely do know how to use this thing," she said as she waved the shotgun at him.

"Yes, ma'am."

He slid off the saddle and onto the ground, holding his hands up. Dana wondered if he was as nervous as she was. Corey apparently was too, because she untied the bottom strap that was holding her gun.

"Stop right there," Jean said, and Butch did, still holding his hands up.

"We don't mean you no harm, Miss Jean. We're just like you…got no power."

The dog walked closer to Butch, tail still wagging.

"Who are they?" Jean asked, looking over at her and Corey.

"This here is my cousin Dana...she's Louis and Barbara Ingram's daughter," he said and Dana smiled and nodded at her. "And this is... this is Corey. She had the misfortune of going camping around here. We picked her up the other day." He smiled. "Well, I guess it was three days now when we found her on the road. Got my days all mixed up, I guess."

Jean nodded, then pointed at the dog. "Pet Lucky."

Butch frowned. "Okay. He's not going to bite, is he?"

"You better hope not."

Butch stuck his hand out slowly and waited while Lucky sniffed it. The dog's tail was wagging wildly, and Butch then scratched his head as Lucky danced excitedly around him.

Dana sighed with relief as Jean lowered the shotgun finally. "Sorry. I couldn't take a chance," she said. "Not after what happened this morning."

Corey kicked her boot out of the stirrup, and Dana took her arm as she slid to the ground. Corey followed.

Dana walked closer to the woman, offering a smile. "I'm Dana," she said. She pointed behind her. "This is Corey."

"Miss Jean...we heard that some men from the valley here went looking for that helicopter," Butch said. "You know anything about that?"

She nodded. "Yes. My Hal was one of them."

"Okay," Butch said. "I don't guess you know which direction they went, do you?"

"Why do you want to know?"

Corey stepped forward. "We're trying to find it too," she said. "We figure if it's a military helicopter then somebody is bound to come looking for it."

Jean nodded. "They headed off four, five days ago now, I guess. Sunday afternoon. Hal said they were going across the canyon to the other side of the creek. Up by the high ridge."

Dana noticed that her voice was cracking, and she looked like she was about to cry. She walked closer to her and touched her arm. "You know my folks?"

Jean looked at her, tears welling in her eyes. "Yes, I know them."

"Is everything okay?" she asked gently.

Jean let the shotgun slip down until it was touching the ground. "No. I don't think anything will ever be the same again."

Her tears turned to sobs, and Dana instinctively opened her arms, letting Jean Bulgur cry on her shoulder. For all her bravado with the shotgun, Jean was a small, frail woman whose slight body shook with each sob.

CHAPTER TWENTY-FIVE

Anna Gail wished she knew what time it was. She'd always been a stickler for having supper at a decent hour, even during the summer months when the days were long. They had several more weeks before she'd call it summer, but the daytime temperatures sure had been warm lately and it seemed like forever before the sun lowered enough to call it evening time. Of course, longer days meant they didn't have to use the generator for lights. She kept her refrigerator going, though, running it several hours at a time. If this power outage kept up, she'd probably move what was left at the house over here to the store. No sense in them running two generators like they'd been.

She knocked on the back door to let Richard know she was there. She didn't want him accidentally shooting her. That rifle of his never seemed to be out of his grasp lately.

"It's me," she called as she went inside. "I brought supper."

He was sitting in a chair facing the front door, keeping watch. His rifle was resting on his lap. She shook her head.

"You sitting there like that, you'll scare off any customers that we may have."

"We don't need any customers," he said. "This might be all we have to our name soon."

She put the basket on the counter near the cash register. "Oh, Richard, what good would it do us to have all this and our neighbors have nothing?"

"I'm just saying…we need to be careful. We don't have the money to feed this whole town."

"You know they'll make good once the power comes back on," she said. She lifted up the towel that covered the basket. "Made fried chicken today. Had that last hen in the freezer." She went about taking plates out for the two of them and setting up their meal. It was a warm day and she thought potato salad would go good with the chicken.

"Where's Holly?" he asked.

"She went over to Gail's house. Gonna share supper with them. I told her to get home before dark."

He nodded. "We broke into Gilbert's gas tanks today," he said. "Got through that damn safety valve finally."

"Well, good. Maybe now you can relax knowing we won't all run out of fuel."

"Had a hell of a time rigging a pump up, though," he said as he stole a drumstick from the platter and bit into it. "We tied together a bunch of hoses and dropped them into the tanks. We're using a hand pump to siphon the gas out."

"I don't imagine Gilbert is having a problem selling fuel then."

"Had people lined up," Richard said. "He's keeping a ledger of who's getting fuel in the hopes that people will pay up when this is all over with. Good luck with that."

"That's what I'm doing here. What if Gilbert was like you and wanted to keep the fuel all to himself? We've got to share with our neighbors," she said. "I imagine Tommy is doing the same thing up at the feed store."

"Makes me nervous is all," he said. "What are we going to do when it runs out? Then what?"

"Oh, Richard, you act like the power is *never* going to come back on." She scooped potato salad onto a plate and added another piece of chicken and handed it to him. She paused before fixing her own plate. "Of course, I sure thought that we would have heard something by now."

"It's a government conspiracy, that's what it is," he said around a mouthful of potatoes. "God only knows what's happening out there. We may have been invaded by Russia or even the Chinese."

She didn't contradict him. That was the second time he'd said that. She, for one, thought no such thing.

"I wonder if Butch and those girls made it to the saline plant yet? Surely they'll find out something there. Someone will come to help then."

"Saline plant? I heard that Butch and those gals were spotted heading up north, toward Squaw Valley," he said.

Anna Gail shook her head. "No. He said they were going to follow the creek all the way to the Delores if they had to."

"Well, apparently they changed their minds. Makes you wonder about him traveling with those two gals."

"One is his cousin, Richard."

"Yeah, and the other one ain't hardly no woman, I'll tell you that."

"Oh, she was a little different, I suppose. But she seemed nice enough."

"Different?" he scoffed. "Lot more than *different*. We don't need her kind around here."

"Guess we don't need to worry about that now," she said. "We probably won't ever see her again anyway."

CHAPTER TWENTY-SIX

Corey stared at the barn door, wondering what they were about to find in there. Jean's story of a crazed man—her husband—chasing after her was certainly riveting and a bit scary.

"I can't believe Jean shot Hal," Butch said as he stood beside her. "You think he was really...you know, possessed, like she said?"

"She seemed to think so." Of course, she too was having a hard time wrapping her mind around the fact that this elderly woman had confessed to shooting her husband...her husband of fifty-some-odd years.

She glanced behind them, but all was quiet. Well, except for the humming of the generator. Jean was kind enough to offer them a meal, and Dana had stayed with her to help. Corey wasn't sure if it was the prospect of cooking that was so appealing to Dana, or if she was simply avoiding whatever they might find in the barn. Regardless, she had eagerly offered to stay behind with Jean. Corey couldn't say she blamed her.

"We should probably hurry," Butch said. "Clouds are rolling in. Gonna get dark early tonight."

She followed his gaze to the west. "Looks like a storm."

He nodded. "Be nice to get some rain on the fields. We'll be looking to bale hay later this summer."

"I was actually thinking more of us getting wet if we're trying to bury him."

Butch shrugged his shoulder with a heavy sigh. "I can't believe she shot him," he said again. "Are you sure we should bury him? I mean, shouldn't we wait for the authorities?"

"Wait how long?" she asked as she opened up the barn door.

The last of the sunlight streamed inside, the shadows almost dancing in every corner. She could see particles of dust floating in the light and she walked inside, finding Hal's body where Jean had said it would be. There was already a musty smell of decomp, which surprised her. It hadn't been that many hours ago that Jean had shot him.

He was lying on his back, eyes opened...dull and lifeless. His arms were out to his sides, palms up. One leg was buckled, the other out straight. As she stared at him, a frown formed.

"There's no blood," she murmured, almost to herself.

"What?"

She pointed to his chest where the obvious shotgun blast had hit. "No blood. Powder burns on his shirt, nothing more."

"What the hell does that mean?"

"I'm almost afraid to take a guess," she said. "Come on. Help me move him."

She bent over, intending to grab him by his ankles, but Butch never moved. She looked up at him, and he was staring at the body, a rather pensive expression on his face.

"Butch?"

Butch slowly slid his gaze toward her, and she noticed that he had a faraway look in his eyes. "I don't think we should move him."

"We can't just leave him in here," she said. "Grab his wrists. Let's pull him out."

Butch looked back at the body but didn't move.

"What's wrong with you?" she asked.

"I don't think we should move him," he said again, his speech slow and even.

She looked around the barn, seeing the shadows creeping closer. There was only a trickle of sunlight coming inside now. She didn't have time to argue with him. She'd seen her share of dead bodies before—plenty—but this one made her uneasy. The last thing she wanted was to be caught inside the barn after dark. She tugged his legs and tried to drag him toward the door.

"I said no!"

Butch shoved her away, hard enough for her to land on her ass. "What the *hell* is wrong with you?" she asked as she got to her feet.

"Leave him alone," Butch said loudly, holding his hands out as if shielding the body.

"We cannot leave a dead man in here and let that poor woman deal with him," she said, pointing toward the house. "If you're not going to help me, then get the hell out of my way."

Butch took a protective stance over the body with a fierce shake of his head. "No!"

"Jesus Christ, man, what's gotten into you?"

"I...I can't. He needs to stay here. Right here."

The shadows were heavy now and Corey could feel them pressing against her. She had an urge to run out the door and into the light. The sun was fading fast, but if they hurried, they could still have him buried before full dark. She was about to try one more time to get Butch to help when he jumped and glanced down at his feet.

She followed his gaze, her eyes widening. Hal's hand had opened and was clinched tight around Butch's ankle. Corey grabbed Butch and pulled him away, but Butch turned on her, swinging his arm as if to hit her. She easily deflected him and spun him around, forcibly shoving him out the door.

He turned and charged her, wrapping his arms around her and taking them both to the ground. She rolled, taking the brunt of the force on her shoulder as she kicked him off her. She scrambled to her feet, only to have him charge her again. At the last second, she jumped to the side, then grabbed him, jerking him around. A fierce kick to the groin dropped him to his knees, and he curled into the fetal position, cupping himself as he writhed in pain.

"Sorry," she murmured. She ran a little ways toward the house, then stopped. "Dana!" she yelled. "Dana! I need some help!"

She went back to Butch, who was trying to get to his feet. She pushed him down again. "Stay down or I'll tie your ass up," she threatened.

She heard the screen door slam and turned, seeing Dana and Lucky hurrying toward her. Dana's eyes widened and she looked at her accusingly.

"What did you do to him?" Dana squatted down beside him. "Butch...are you okay?"

Corey's eyes were drawn to Lucky, who had stopped several feet away. The dog let out a low growl, the hair on his back standing on end. She quickly grabbed Dana and pulled her up.

"Stay away from him."

Dana jerked her arm away. "What the hell is wrong with you?"

"Something's wrong with *him*, not me," Corey said. "Look at the dog."

Lucky was staring at Butch, showing his teeth now, his growl turning into a sharp bark.

Butch struggled to his feet, then took a lunge at Dana. Corey intercepted him and twisted his arms behind his back, disabling him. Butch kicked at her legs, and she twisted his arms tighter until he cried out in pain.

"Oh, my God," Dana said as she backed up. "What's going on?"

"Let's get him to the house," she said, dragging Butch along with her.

Lucky darted around them, his barking subsiding the closer they got to the house. By the time they got to the back door, Lucky's tail was wagging and he was licking Butch's hand. Corey loosened her hold on Butch and let him stand. He looked at her with wide eyes, then shook his head as if trying to clear it.

He turned his gaze to Dana, blinking several times. "What's going on?"

Dana put her hands on her hips. "You tell us."

He looked at his hands, turning them over. "Did we get Hal buried already?"

Jean held the door open, and Corey led Butch inside. Jean looked between them and Corey could see the fear in her eyes.

"Something happen with Hal?" she asked in a shaky voice.

Corey nodded, then settled Butch down in a chair. "Butch, you think we should bury Hal?"

He looked up at her, confusion on his face. "Well, we can't leave him in there," he said.

Corey ran her hands across her hair several times, trying to figure out what was going on. The fact that a dead man had his fingers wrapped around Butch's ankle was still foremost in her mind.

"You going to tell me what's going on?" Dana asked quietly.

Corey nodded, then looked back at Butch. "Do you remember anything that happened?"

"We were…" He looked away from her, a frown marring his features. "We were going to bury Hal. You wanted…you wanted me to help you." He glanced at her again, his eyes widening. "He grabbed me. He grabbed my ankle."

Jean gasped. "Hal? But—"

"He's dead," Butch said. "How could he—"

"You freaked out in there," Corey said bluntly. "It was like you were…possessed," she said, using Jean's word of how she described Hal. "You wouldn't let me move him. You kept saying to leave him. Then you took a swing at me."

"When I came out," Dana said, "it was like you weren't there. You looked at me, but you didn't really see me. You tried to attack me."

Butch shook his head. "I would never hit you. What are you talking about?"

Corey rubbed her forehead, trying to decide what to do. It would be dark soon. There was no way they could bury him now. But she didn't think burying him was the answer.

"I think we should burn the body," she said.

Jean held a hand to her chest, her eyes wide. "Burn Hal?" She shook her head. "No. No, you can't. Not my Hal."

"You said yourself that it wasn't Hal," she reminded her. "He tried to kill you."

"Doesn't mean we need to burn him like he was nothing," she said. "That's my husband."

"I don't like the idea of burning a body, Corey," Dana said. "That's going too far."

"Something's not right with him. I'm not sure it's just a body anymore."

"What are you talking about?"

"You saw what happened to Butch. Like he was being manipulated—controlled—by something." She turned back to Jean. "When you shot Hal…there wasn't any blood, was there?"

"No," Jean whispered. "It was like…like he was already dead."

Dana grabbed Corey's arm, turning her around to face her. "What is it that you're suggesting?"

"I don't really know," she said honestly. She pointed at Butch. "You stay here. Help Miss Jean."

"But—"

"Dana's going to help me."

"I am?"

"We need to hurry. It'll be dark soon." She glanced at Jean. "Make sure he stays."

"Are you going to…to burn my Hal?"

Corey stared at her. "That man out there is not your Hal. Whatever it is, it's dangerous."

She nodded slowly. "Okay." She touched Butch's shoulder gently. "I'll get him to peel potatoes."

Corey motioned Dana out the door, then on impulse, called for Lucky. The dog followed obediently.

They walked in silence to the barn. It was dark inside, and she half-expected the body to be gone. But it was where she'd left it. As she got nearer, rustling in the stall made her jump, and Dana gave a startled gasp too.

Corey smiled with a relieved sigh. "Chickens," she said.

Dana covered her nose and mouth, but Corey hardly noticed the smell.

"He...he really grabbed Butch?"

"Look, I'm as scared as you are."

"I doubt that. My teeth are chattering," Dana said.

"Let's drag him out," Corey said. "Take his leg."

"I can't believe I'm doing this," Dana murmured as she grabbed his foot.

He was lighter than Corey expected and they moved him easily. Lucky was waiting outside the barn, and again, he emitted a low growl as he circled the body.

"Let's go around back," Corey said. "No need for Jean to see this."

"We're going to get into all kinds of trouble for doing this, aren't we? I mean—"

"I don't like doing this any more than you do," she said as they drug him around to the back of the barn. "You heard Jean. When she shot him, there was no blood. Whatever the hell is going on, this isn't her husband. That's why we need to burn him." She stopped and straightened up. "You should have seen Butch," she said. "He refused to let me move him. He pushed me down when I tried to. Like I said, he was possessed." She pointed to the body. "It was like Butch was protecting it."

Dana took a few steps away as the wind picked up. She looked to the sky as if only now noticing how dark it was. Lucky was standing several feet away, whimpering.

"We should hurry," Dana said. "I got a really bad feeling."

"You and me both, honey," she murmured as she turned and headed back toward the barn. Dana ran after her.

"Where are you going? What are you doing?"

"Looking for some diesel or something. You stay with the body."

"The hell I will," Dana said. "You're not leaving me alone out there."

"Okay. Look for some fuel. Diesel, kerosene, anything."

"What about what she's using for the generator?"

"I don't want to use that unless we have to. When we leave here, she's going to still need her generator," she said.

Luck was on their side, though. Just inside the door of the barn she found several containers of fuel. She took one outside into the waning light and opened it up, smelling it.

"Diesel," she said. "Run to the house. See if Jean's got some matches or a lighter. I'll meet you around back."

"Okay."

"Take Lucky with you," Corey said. "Lucky seems to have a sense for…well, if something isn't right."

"Maybe you should take him with you."

"I'll be with the body." She looked at Dana. "In case something happens to me," she said pointedly.

"Oh, Jesus…you don't mean—"

"Bring her shotgun back with you. Or Butch's rifle."

"No. Jesus…you're talking crazy. Wait for me here," Dana said as she ran toward the house.

Lucky stayed with her, and Corey reached out and stroked the dog's head. "Crazy, yeah. This whole damn thing is crazy," she murmured. What she was thinking was crazy too. Could Duncan have been right? Could the alleged meteor have really been something else?

She didn't have long to ponder the question as Dana ran back to her. She held up her hand.

"Got matches."

"Let's go."

Again, Corey wouldn't have been surprised if the body was missing, but it wasn't. She didn't think about what she was doing as she doused it with the diesel. She knew, without wood for fuel, the fire would do little more than char the body. Char it beyond recognition. Tomorrow, they would bury what remained.

She struck a match and tossed it on the body. The flame ignited the diesel immediately and she jumped back, watching in fascination as the fire consumed the body like it was nothing more than a straw man. She walked over to where Dana was standing near the corner of the barn.

A loud clap of thunder sounded, and Dana moved closer to her, their shoulders touching. Across the valley to the west, they could see lightning.

"Storm'll be here soon," she said quietly.

Another loud clap of thunder sent them back toward the house. Just before they reached the back door, the dark sky seemed to explode with lightning and as Lucky leaned against her leg, Corey could feel the dog trembling.

"Don't like storms, boy?"

She'd no sooner said that when Jean opened the back door and beckoned the dog inside. Dana followed, then looked back at her questioningly.

"Be there in a second," she said.

She walked around to the side of the house, watching the lightning. It seemed to be shooting from all directions. She went a little farther away from the house, scanning the horizon. Each lightning strike, no matter where it originated in the sky, seemed to strike the same place. She watched in awe as a streak cut the dark sky, illuminating a far distant ridge. Thunder rumbled around her as more strikes followed, all drawn to the same ridge. She wondered if it was possible for something to attract lightning or if lightning strikes were random.

When the first drops of rain fell, she turned and made her way back to the house, pausing once to look back to where the lightning was concentrated, trying to memorize the location in her mind. But another loud clap of thunder followed by the beginning of a downpour sent her scurrying inside.

CHAPTER TWENTY-SEVEN

After the big meal they'd had last night, Dana was surprised she had any appetite for breakfast, but Corey had gone out at daybreak with Jean to gather eggs. She wondered if perhaps Jean had wanted to see Hal—to see what was left—for some sort of closure.

When she'd served breakfast, Jean had apologized for having no bacon, but the sausage patties she'd taken from the freezer were excellent, not to mention the fried potatoes.

"How do you stay so thin?" Corey asked as Dana took another helping of potatoes.

"She's gained seven pounds in the last year," Butch offered.

Dana glared at him. "Will you shut up? That wasn't to be shared with anyone."

"I love a woman who can eat like a man," Jean said.

Dana groaned as both Butch and Corey laughed. "I'm not sure that's a compliment, Miss Jean."

After a while, Corey stood and went to the back door, looking out. Because of the rain last night, it was cool and crisp this morning. Dana had taken her first cup of coffee out to the porch to enjoy it. Of course, her eyes were drawn to the barn, and she couldn't help but remember how they'd ended the day.

When they'd finally sat down to supper, conversation had been nonexistent. She wondered if any of them would even be able to eat. But Jean had served them smothered pork chops and gravy, telling them it had been one of Hal's favorite meals. It wasn't until she'd taken the first bite that she realized they hadn't eaten since that morning. They finished off the pork chops and mashed potatoes and Jean had seemed pleased that they had.

There wasn't much discussion about them staying the night with Jean. As before at Anna Gail's…she and Corey shared a bed and Butch took the sofa, the other spare room having been converted into Jean's sewing room. No one commented when Butch propped his rifle next to him or when Jean went off to her room with Lucky by her side and the shotgun cradled in her arms. It wasn't until Corey opened her pack and pulled out a handgun that the reality of it all hit her. She was normally terrified of guns. For some reason, the fact that Corey had one and was taking it to bed with them offered her some comfort.

Because they were possibly in danger. Only they didn't know from who or what.

That thought made her move a little closer to Corey during the night, fearing she would get no sleep. She was surprised, then, when she awoke hours later with dawn creeping in their window…and Corey already up and dressed.

This morning, everyone seemed to be a little more talkative and relaxed, even Jean, although her puffy eyes were evidence that she'd had a tearful night.

"I need to tell you all something," Corey said as she finally turned away from the door.

Dana arched an eyebrow. She could tell by the tone of Corey's voice that she was in Captain Conaway mode now.

"Miss Jean, sit down," Corey said gently. "We'll all help clean up from breakfast in a bit."

Jean nodded and took her coffee cup back to the table with her, sitting down beside Butch. Lucky was lying on the floor on the other side of Butch, and he handed the dog the last of his fried potatoes, causing Jean to shake her head disapprovingly.

"Yesterday morning was the first time Lucky's been in the house," she said. "Look at him now. Didn't take him long to learn how to beg."

Corey pulled out her chair and sat down next to Dana. She rested her elbows on the table and tapped her fingers together nervously.

"First of all…Jean…I'm not a stranded camper that they randomly rescued. I'm Captain Conaway, US Army. I was sent here to try to locate the helicopter and crew." She glanced at Dana. "And also to find the location of a possible meteor that may have hit out here."

"A captain in the military?"

Corey nodded.

"Well, I'll be," Jean murmured. "And a meteor?"

Corey nodded again. "It was assumed the meteor had hit something, perhaps, that had taken out the power grid."

"So what we thought was an earthquake was really a meteor?"

"That's the assumption."

"If you're here, then someone knows we're having trouble out here, right?" Jean asked.

"Yes. Only no one knows what kind of trouble or what's causing it." Corey again looked at her, then over at Butch. "Something I didn't share with you earlier was the possibility that it perhaps wasn't a meteor."

"You already said that at first they thought it might be a hostile aircraft."

"At first, yes, but that was dismissed almost immediately." Corey paused. "There is a possibility that what landed was a...well, a UFO." She met Dana's gaze head on. "A spaceship."

Dana would have thought she was joking if not for the seriousness of her expression. She didn't know whether to laugh or cry at that moment.

"A spaceship?" Jean asked with a gasp. "Like in the movies?"

"It was a possible theory that was largely dismissed by the upper brass," Corey said. "The lieutenant who briefed me was the one who suggested we not totally disregard the possibility."

"What is it you're trying to say?" Dana asked. "After what we've been through, don't try to spare us now." She pointed out the door. "We burned a body last night, for God's sake."

"I don't want to frighten anyone."

"Too late for that," she shot back.

Butch held his hand up. "First of all...are you *serious*? A UFO? *Really*?"

"When it was first brought up, I dismissed it as well," Corey said. "Frankly, I thought he was crazy. But his message to me was that we should not dismiss the possibility just because it seemed implausible. His words."

"And what makes it plausible for you now?" she asked.

"I'm not sure, really, but I wanted to be upfront with you all. The fact that something is killing the power grid, jacking with cell phones and batteries...and after seeing Hal," Corey said, glancing at Jean.

"I'm sorry, but you shoot somebody at point-blank range in the chest with a shotgun…well, there should be a hell of a lot of blood. There was nothing on him but powder burns."

Jean nodded. "It wasn't Hal. Lucky knew it before I did. I thought at first, maybe he'd hit his head or something. Maybe that was why he seemed so confused, so disoriented. But his eyes…they were cold, lifeless. My Hal had twinkling blue eyes," Jean said, her own welling up again with tears. "It was my Hal's body…but that wasn't my Hal."

Dana stared around the table, not really believing what she was hearing. Was Corey—Captain Conaway—*really* suggesting that a spaceship from some distant planet landed here and the occupants were…what? Killing people and taking over their bodies?

"What do you think happened my Hal?" Jean asked quietly, her tear-filled gaze on Corey. But she lowered her eyes quickly. "I probably don't want to know, do I?"

"Just because this happened to Hal doesn't mean there's a UFO out there," Dana said. "There could be another explanation."

"You said last night that Carl Milstead was the one that came over to get Hal," Butch said. "Do you know who else went with them?"

"Because the Milstead place was empty," Corey added.

"I couldn't guess where Rebecca would go off to, not without a car," Jean said. "We were their closest neighbors." She shoved her coffee cup aside and clasped her hands together, her fingers moving nervously. "Let's see. There was Jim and Graham with him when he came up." She looked over at Butch. "Do you know them? Graham Ellis and Jim Holman?"

"Yes, ma'am, I know them."

"Hal said that they were meeting over at Dusty Truchard's place. I believe Curtis was along too."

"Curtis Benson?" Butch asked.

Jean nodded. "Hal left here on Daisy, our horse." A quick smile lit her face. "Poor Daisy. She hadn't been ridden in more years than I can count." Her smile faded just as quickly. "When Hal came up yesterday, he was walking. When I asked about Daisy, at first he didn't know what I was talking about. Then he said he left her over at the barn."

"We didn't see a horse there, Miss Jean. I put ours out in your corral there. Was empty," Butch said.

"Whatever happened to Hal, I don't suppose Daisy fared much better."

Dana looked at Corey. "What are we going to do now? We're going to head back to Paradox, right? We're going to go get help, right?"

Corey shook her head. "My mission is to locate the helicopter. If the squad on foot finds it first, I'm to concentrate on where the...the meteor went down."

Dana bit her lip. She didn't want to go on. She didn't want to find the helicopter and whatever else might be out there. She wanted to get the hell out of here. Even going back to Seattle and facing Kendra was more appealing than this. Of course, until they had power back, that was out of the question.

"Might be better to have three horses," Butch said. "Riding double like you are, we're limited on the supplies we can carry."

"What do you have in mind?" Corey asked.

"There were two horses at the Milstead's place. I say we go back there and commandeer one," he said. "With the captain's order, of course."

Dana stared at him. "You really want to keep going?"

"Do we have a choice?"

"Yes! We can head back home and check on our parents. We can—"

"And do what?" he asked. "Wait? We don't even know what the hell we're waiting on."

"You don't have to go if you don't want to," Corey said to her. "I'm sure you can find your way back to Paradox. I tried to get you to stay there when—"

"Stop it," Dana said, holding up her hand. "I know you told me to stay. You don't have to go over it again."

"I want to go with you all," Jean said, her voice quiet.

Corey shook her head. "Miss Jean, no offense, but Butch tells me it's rough terrain out there. We'll most likely have to camp out a couple of nights, maybe more. It might be too much for you."

"I can't stay here," Jean said. "I may be seventy-five years old, but I can still ride a horse. I won't slow you down."

Dana wondered if Jean didn't want to be here because she would be alone, without Hal, or if she was simply afraid to be alone because of what Corey had just said. She wondered at her own reason for wanting to leave. Yes, she was concerned about her parents, but was that why she was ready to bolt back home? Or was it because she was afraid of the unknown? Afraid of what might really be out there? Regardless, she realized she felt safer with Corey than without. Despite her outburst that she wanted to leave, that she didn't want to continue on, she knew they were better off with Corey. Miss Jean must have felt it too.

"We can't leave her here," Dana said.

Tears welled up in Jean's eyes again. "I'm scared to stay here alone. Let me go with you, Captain. Please."

Dana saw Corey's expression soften and she nodded. "Okay, you come with us. I imagine it's a good idea to have Lucky with us anyway. He seems to have a sixth sense."

The relief on Jean's face was visible and Dana felt it too. Yes, she was scared. They all were, even Corey. Yet Corey had maintained her resolve to find the helicopter as she was ordered to do. Dana had no doubt that if Butch decided he didn't want to continue, if he wanted to abort this mission and head back home, that Corey would go on without them. There was something, something deep inside—deep in her soul, perhaps?—that wouldn't allow that to happen. They would stick together. All of them.

CHAPTER TWENTY-EIGHT

Jean let Dana tend to the breakfast dishes as she escaped to her bedroom. She knew she'd lied to the captain. She hadn't been on a horse in more than thirty years. What business did she have getting on one now?

But she couldn't stay here. Not after…well, after what had happened with Hal. She opened her closet door and leaned against the jamb, her eyes closed as she pictured Hal's handsome face, his twinkling eyes. He was a gentle, kind man…and she'd killed him. Whatever in the world would she tell their boys? How could she tell them that the awful sour smell of his breath reminded her of the dead raccoon that had gotten trapped under their porch that one summer? How could she explain that she'd grabbed the shotgun at the last second, fearing for her life as Hal's hands had wrapped around her neck? How could she tell them that she'd pulled the gun between them, not caring if she shot Hal or herself at that moment? How could she tell them that she had been so afraid of him that she lost control of her bladder?

She wiped the tears from her eyes. Would they even care? Hal Jr., would be the only one, she guessed. Peter and Johnny…why, she wasn't even sure how to get ahold of them. She had an address for Peter. Who knew where Johnny was? Hal Jr., kept in touch with them some, she knew that.

Well, when this was all over with, she'd deal with it then. She needed to stop feeling sorry for herself. There would be plenty of time for that later. For all she knew, she might end up in jail. Would anyone believe that she'd shot Hal in self-defense? Surely they would. If these three did, two of them total strangers to her, surely her neighbors would.

Of course, who knew where her neighbors were? Carl Milstead had been with Hal. Now they say Rebecca wasn't at home either. The captain and Butch were on their way over to borrow their horses. Steal was more like it, she thought, but what choice did they have?

With a heavy heart she went into her closet, trying to find something suitable to wear. She was never one to wear jeans or even pants, for that matter. She preferred her loose-fitting cotton dresses. In the winter, when doing chores outside, she'd put on insulated coveralls over her old pair of wool pants. She turned her gaze to Hal's side of the closet, seeing his neatly hung jeans and work pants. They would be too big for her, of course. And too long. But she'd have to make do with them.

She decided that jeans would be more suitable so she pulled one pair off the hanger. Hal's jeans. And he would never wear them again. Profound sadness overtook her, and she thought her heart might break right then and there.

She'd met Hal when she was fourteen, married only two weeks after her seventeenth birthday. Neither of them finished high school. Hal's daddy had just died...kicked in the head by a mule. Hal was the youngest of four and the only one still at home. They'd married and moved here to the farm, taking over right where his daddy had left off. Hal's momma, Doreen, was never the same after that. She wasted away to nothing, dying in her sleep one night at the young age of forty-eight, leaving her and Hal with the farm. Hal Jr., was already born then and Jean had been pregnant with Peter. They'd made a good enough living out here, and they'd turned the old farmhouse into their own home, upgrading and remodeling it whenever there was enough money left over. It hardly looked like the same old house they'd first moved into.

She wondered what would happen to it now. Even if she could bear to stay here by herself, she'd never be able to keep it up. She could manage her vegetable garden and tend to the chickens. But when it came time to harvest those chickens...well, that was Hal's job. Same with the few pigs they kept some years. She could slop them up and fatten them, but Hal took care of supplying the pork chops and roasts.

She wiped her cheeks as her tears fell again, and she sat down heavily on the bed, still clutching Hal's jeans to her chest. How long she sat there, she didn't know. She heard movement behind her, and she turned, finding Dana standing in the doorway and watching her with sympathetic eyes.

"I guess it hasn't set in yet, huh?" Dana asked gently.

Jean shook her head. "No. I have to remind myself that he won't be coming back."

"Do you want to talk?"

"Oh, I was just reminiscing," she said. "And wondering how I'm going to make it here on the farm without him." She tried to smile. "Feeling sorry for myself is more like it."

Dana came fully into the room and sat down beside her, putting a comforting arm around her shoulders.

"You seem like a strong, capable woman to me, Miss Jean. I imagine you'll be just fine."

Jean nodded. "I suppose. I don't want to end up like Hal's momma. When his daddy died, I think his momma didn't want to go on without him. She stopped eating. Stopped living. She willed herself to die, I think. I don't want that to be me."

"I saw pictures in the living room by the TV. You have children? Grandkids?"

"Three boys. Two of them left here and never came back. Hal Jr., lives up in Grand Junction. His kids are grown now, but they don't come around. We don't see him much either...a few times a year."

"I'm sorry."

She shrugged. "They never took to the farming life. It's not for everyone."

"I know. I was the same way. It makes me realize that I should visit my parents more often," Dana said.

"Where did you move off to again?"

"I left for college—Boulder—then moved to Seattle," Dana said. "I've made a life there, friends, a good job. I don't get back here often enough."

"I guess you're wishing you hadn't picked this particular time to visit," she said, offering Dana a small smile.

"It's certainly been an adventure." Dana stood up. "And it looks like it's only beginning."

With a sigh, Jean got to her feet too. "Do you believe what the captain says?"

"You mean about the possibility of a UFO out here somewhere?" Dana shook her head. "I think I'm afraid to believe it. Because it's… crazy."

Jean nodded. "I don't want to believe it either. But my Hal…there's *something* out here that shouldn't be. Maybe the captain is right."

Dana looked at her quizzically. "Why do you call her 'Captain' and not Corey?"

"Anybody who serves our country like she does deserves respect," she said. "I'm sure she's earned her title. If you look at her, *really* look at her, deep in her eyes…she has a tortured soul."

"You think so?"

"Like she's seen too many horrors of war, be my guess. But she seems competent. I suppose we must trust her."

Dana nodded. "Yes. I think I'm actually glad she's here. She has taken charge, that's for sure." Dana took a deep breath. "So…you need help with anything?"

"I'm trying to find some clothes to wear." She smiled at Dana quickly. "Don't tell the captain, but I haven't been on a horse in many, many years. I'm having to resort to wearing Hal's jeans. Do you think she'll notice?"

Dana smiled back at her. "I'd guess she probably already knows you haven't been on a horse in years. I doubt that matters to her, anyway."

"Well, let me get these together, then I'll bake that bread I've got rising. We'll need to start on lunch. I reckon the captain will want to head out as soon as possible."

CHAPTER TWENTY-NINE

Sutter stood with his back to the door, staring out his window. His blinds were nearly closed, keeping the midday sun from streaming inside, but he'd opened them a fraction, enough to let him know that there was life out there. He hadn't been home in forty-eight hours. Hadn't seen his wife. Hadn't had a decent meal. All because some goddamn meteor had blipped on their radar screen for four lousy seconds.

Sure, maybe he'd jumped the gun by sending out a Black Hawk. But what if it had been a hostile aircraft? Then Brinkley would be praising him for taking action so quickly. Instead, he was getting his ass chewed at nearly every meeting with him.

He turned as his door burst open, finding Duncan rushing inside.

"What the hell, Lieutenant?"

"I'm sorry, sir, but we've had contact from the squad," he said excitedly. "Just a few minutes ago."

"Fill me in," he said, motioning for Duncan to sit as he resumed his seat behind his desk.

"It wasn't much and the transmission was broken, but we were able to clean some of the static out."

"I don't care about that, Duncan. What the hell did they say?"

"Sergeant Wilcox communicated that they found the Black Hawk, sir."

"And the crew."

"No crew, sir."

"So they survived? They left on foot?" he asked hopefully.

"It was badly damaged, sir. Charred from the fire. They were going to search the perimeter, hoping to find tracks."

Sutter ran his hand over his hair, back and forth. "But we have an exact location now?"

"Yes, sir."

"That's good news, Lieutenant." He leaned back in his chair. "Good news. So the squad makes it but still no word from Conaway?"

"No, sir. Nothing."

He shook his head. "I still don't know why Brinkley wanted to send her in. Waste of time, if you ask me."

"Yes, sir."

He leaned forward again, wondering if Duncan could see the relief on his face. "Let me notify General Brinkley. At least there's hope that the crew made it out alive."

Duncan hesitated. "There's one other thing, sir."

"What is it?"

"One of the supervisors at that saline plant out there lives in Paradox. Because the road was closed due to the rock slide, he stayed at the plant. But he's been unable to contact his wife or his neighbors there in Paradox and apparently he got worried, sir."

"And?"

"Well, he drove all the way around to the north and tried to come down one of the forest service roads there, sir."

"And his vehicle became disabled," he finished for him. "Now what?"

"He hiked back out. It's pretty desolate out there. I think he was several hours on foot before he found someone to help him. Sheriff's department is involved now."

"Is the Department of Transportation still cooperating?"

"I believe they want to reopen the road, sir."

"Which means people will try to drive into Paradox, only to have their cars stall."

"Yes, sir." He paused. "I'm hearing there will be something on the news tonight...a Grand Junction station, sir."

"Great," he said dryly. "Okay. I'll inform Brinkley. Thank you, Lieutenant."

Well, they'd managed to keep the local authorities out of it far longer than he'd thought possible. And now it had made the news. Well, they had known that it was only a matter of time before it leaked out. But, he reminded himself, that was General Brinkley's problem, not his. His only problem was the three missing crew members and it looked promising that they'd walked away from the crash. He'd let Brinkley worry about the media.

CHAPTER THIRTY

Corey and Dana were making sandwiches from the bread that Jean had baked. The bread was still warm, and Corey couldn't resist slathering a piece with butter and eating it right then and there. She didn't think she'd ever had real homemade bread before. She looked up from her chore as Jean came in and she had to hide her smile. Dana had already warned her that Jean would be wearing Hal's clothes. The jeans were several inches too long and had been rolled up, revealing pristine white socks and an ancient pair of athletic shoes. A belt was cinched tight around her waist, holding the pants up, and she had a flannel shirt tucked inside.

"No need to say anything, Captain. I'm aware of how awful I look," Jean said as she nudged her out of the way. "Dana and I can finish this."

"You don't look awful, Miss Jean. Quite charming, in fact." She was surprised that the compliment brought a blush to Jean's face.

"My bag is by the door," Jean said. "It's only a light blanket and a pillow. I daresay this is the first time I've traveled and did not bring a change of clothes."

"Hopefully we won't be gone more than two nights," she said. "I'll go see if Butch needs help." She paused. "We need to get going soon. The day's almost wasted."

"You'll thank us for these sandwiches later," Dana said with a smile. "Or you can have one of your little freeze-dried things instead." Dana turned to Jean. "She inhaled a piece of bread earlier with enough butter on it to clog an artery."

"Like I didn't see you sneaking a piece too," she countered. "We leave in ten minutes."

Dana laughed. "If only we had a clock to determine those ten minutes."

Butch was leading all four horses up to the house when she went outside with Jean's bedroll.

"No problem with the saddle?" she asked. They'd only found one saddle at the Milstead's place. Jean had pointed them to an old one in their barn, but she warned it hadn't been used in forty years or more.

"It's in pretty good shape," he said. "I oiled the leather real good. It should hold up." He motioned to the house. "We about ready to head out?"

"Yeah. They're finishing up with the sandwiches. Jean had a leftover pork roast in the freezer that she took out this morning. We'll eat good tonight, at least."

"I thought I smelled bread baking," he said. "My grandmother used to bake bread all the time."

"She still alive?"

He nodded. "Nursing home up in Grand Junction. Dana's grandmother too," he supplied. "Dementia," he added. "She doesn't talk much anymore."

"I can relate," she said. "My grandfather died of Alzheimer's. He was only seventy-six."

The screen door opened on the front porch, and Dana stood there with two bags in her hands. She looked between the two of them and frowned.

"Why so glum? Did something happen?"

"Plenty's happened," Butch said. "But nothing new. We were just talking."

Dana came down the steps and handed Corey one of the bags. "Try not to eat them all," she said with a wink. "They're for breakfast."

Corey peeked inside, expecting sandwiches. "What is it?"

"Pigs in a blanket," Dana said. "Or sausage rolls, if you prefer. And if we stay with Miss Jean much longer, I'll be as big as a house."

"I guess you're starting on another seven pounds then," she said. She gave Dana's body a teasing perusal. "I don't think seven pounds would harm you, though."

"Clothes tend to hide imperfections, don't they?"

It was too easy and Corey couldn't resist. "I don't know. If you want to show me later, you know, without clothes, I'll be happy to give you an assessment."

Butch laughed, and Dana's eyes widened as her face turned red. "Oh, my God…are you *flirting* with me?"

Corey wiped the smile from her face. "Of course not. This situation is far too dire for flirting." Then she grinned. "I was simply offering my services." She wiggled her eyebrows. "I can assist you with…a lot of things. I'm very…talented."

Dana's face remained red, but she met her gaze. "I'm sure you are, *Captain*."

"She's your Dream Girl, all right," Butch said.

Dana turned on him with a glare. "Not…a…*word* out of you," she said as she pointed threateningly at him, causing him to laugh louder.

"Dream girl? Do I want to know what that's about?" she asked.

"No, you do not," Dana said curtly.

Jean came out carrying a wicker basket with a handle. She looked questioningly at them. "What's so funny?"

"Nothing," Dana said quickly. "They're tormenting me, is all. And enjoying it far too much."

"It's nice to hear laughter." Jean looked over at her. "I guess I'm ready. I don't see the point of locking up the house, do you?"

Corey went to her and took the basket from her hand. "Whatever you feel comfortable with, Miss Jean."

"I packed a little dog food for Lucky," Jean said.

"We can share ours with him too," Butch said. "He'll be fine."

Corey stood back as Butch helped Jean up and onto the saddle. The horse they'd chosen for her was the young mare from the Milsteads. They'd thought maybe they'd put her on Gretchen since she was so gentle, but she was also huge compared to the mare.

"I guess now's a good time to confess that it's been a few years since I've actually been on a horse," Jean said as she took the reins from Butch. "I'll be lucky if I don't break a hip or something."

"We'll travel slow enough," Corey said. "You'll be fine."

She and Dana both went over to Gretchen. Dana grabbed the reins before she could and she pushed her aside.

"I'm fairly certain that this is *my* horse," Dana said.

"Again…you didn't even know her name," Corey said as she went over to the white stallion. He was spirited and probably more than she could handle. It wasn't like she was experienced around horses. She had hoped that Butch would volunteer to ride him, but he'd stuck with his mount, not even suggesting a change. Her only saving grace was that he was smaller than Gretchen and thus not quite as intimidating.

She rubbed his head a few times, then grabbed the saddle horn and pulled herself up. He danced sideways as she swung her leg over the saddle and she pulled up on the reins, trying to quiet him.

"Please don't throw me off," she murmured as she leaned down and patted his neck.

"How long's it been since you've been on a horse?" Jean asked.

Corey grinned. "I rode a pony on my twelfth birthday," she said. "Of course, now Gretchen the last few days. She's a sweetheart."

"Which is why I have her," Dana said with a flirty smile.

"I think the captain should be on the stallion anyway. It's fitting," Jean said. "However, I do recall a story once where he tossed Carl into the creek. You might want to be careful when we get there."

Butch led the way, and for the most part, they rode single file. It didn't take long to come upon the creek, and Butch turned west, heading upstream. The afternoon was slipping away from them, and Corey wondered how many hours they could travel before dark. Out of habit, she glanced at her wristwatch. It was an old-fashioned watch with a face and hands. Not the kind that needed daily winding, unfortunately, but one that was battery operated. Or had been. It was stalled at 5:14, the time they'd dropped her off at the checkpoint. How many days ago was that now? she wondered.

"Miss Jean, you might know this better than I do," Butch said. "The horses can't follow the creek up the canyon. On the map, it looked like there's an old road of some sort up here. Do you know for sure?"

"Yes. Hal said they would most likely follow the Jeep road along the south rim of the canyon. Back in the day, before they built the new road to Paradox, this was the only route."

Butch pulled his horse to a stop. "I'm not familiar with this area," he said to Corey. "I don't know how far to follow the creek before we can't anymore. Might be best to head up to the south rim now and follow the Jeep road. Maybe we can pass the canyon and get back to the creek before dark."

Corey pulled out her binoculars and scanned the ridge above them, then up ahead where the creek flowed. They'd gone over the topo map several times, but neither of them could determine how far along the creek they could go before the canyon swallowed it up. It still looked relatively flat, and she thought they'd still be able to climb to the ridge later. Of course, they'd probably make better time following a road instead of picking their way across the many boulders and rocks that lined the creek here as they got closer to the canyon. Better safe than sorry, she supposed.

"The Jeep road follows the creek, right?" she asked.

"Yeah, it winds around the top of the canyon ridge," he said.

"Okay…let's head up then. It'll get dark early down here in the canyon."

It was a fairly easy climb to the top, and the horses made it without any problems. The Jeep road was in pretty good shape, and they picked up the pace a little as she kicked her stallion into a trot. They were on the south side of the creek now, and the view down into the canyon told her that they'd made the right choice. It had narrowed considerably, and she knew they'd be scrambling to find a way out had they stayed down below.

The sun was getting low in the sky by the time they passed the steepest part of the canyon, and the creek again leveled out into a green valley below them. She saw movement along the creek and whipped out her binoculars, surprised to find three horses but no riders.

"What is it?" Butch asked. "Cattle?"

"Horses," she said. "Take a look." She handed over the binoculars to him.

"Looks like they're tethered."

"I don't see any people," she said. "Do you?"

"No. No movement."

Corey turned in her saddle, looking at Jean. "How many riders went out with Hal?"

"I think it was going to be the six of them," Jean said. "Carl, Dusty, Jim, Graham, Curtis and my Hal."

"Could be their horses," Butch said quietly.

"Let's head down then," Corey said. "It'll be a good place to stop for the night, if nothing else."

It was steeper than it looked, and it was slow going to get down to the creek. At one point, Jean's mount slipped, and she let out a little scream but held on until the horse righted herself.

"You okay back there?" Corey called over her shoulder.

"I'm still in the saddle," Jean said. "Won't mind putting my feet on the ground again, though."

Corey looked back at Dana. "You?"

Dana gave her a slight smile. "Me and Gretchen are doing fine."

When they got closer to the creek, Corey could make out the remnants of a camp. There appeared to be four bedrolls laid out, a couple of backpacks, a coffeepot sitting on rocks beside a fire ring.

"Oh my goodness," Jean said excitedly. "That's…that's our Daisy."

Corey held her hand up, signaling them to stop. "Stay here," she said as she rode closer. She pulled her horse up and slipped from the saddle, still holding onto the reins.

She saw the discoloration on the rocks and assumed it was blood. She looped the reins on a limb of a small bush and then followed drag marks. More blood, she noted. A lot of it.

"What is it?" Butch called.

She looked at him, then slid her glance to Jean. "Got blood," she said.

She whistled for Lucky, who was already in the creek splashing around. He bounded over to her and sniffed the ground. He gave a low growl and the hair stood up on his back as he seemed to be following a scent trail. She went after him into a clump of bushes. She saw no tracks and found no more blood, but Lucky seemed to sense something. He barked a couple of times, then retraced his steps back to the bedrolls. Finally, he seemed to shake himself, then with a wag of his tail, he headed back to the creek and jumped in.

She looked back at the others and shrugged. "I guess it's okay."

Butch helped Jean from the saddle, and Jean held on to him as she found her balance. She murmured her thanks, then went directly toward the bedrolls. She stopped at one, staring down at it. As Jean's shoulders slumped, Corey knew it had been Hal's. She looked over at Dana, who nodded before going to stand next to Jean.

"Was that Hal's?" Dana asked gently.

Jean wiped at a tear on her face. "That old quilt. Wasn't hardly nothing left of it. His momma made it for us right before we married. That...that was his pack. It never occurred to me that he didn't have it with him when he came home."

Butch walked over to where the three horses were. They appeared to be skittish and Corey watched as he spoke to them in a quiet, calm voice. Only two were still tethered and he soon had the other secured as well.

"They're okay," he said.

"What should we do with them? Turn them loose?"

Butch shrugged. "They might make their way back home. Might not." He led all three to the creek and let them drink. "I suppose we could take them with us."

"Well, we can't leave them here," Dana said.

"We're not leaving my Daisy here, Captain," Jean added.

Corey sighed. It would slow them down, no doubt, but she knew it would be pointless to argue. "Then let's head out and find a place to camp."

CHAPTER THIRTY-ONE

Dana nibbled on the pork sandwich, trying not to jump at every little noise. The fire was still burning brightly but beyond the circle they sat, it was black dark.

"I don't think I'll be able to sleep," she finally said.

Corey added another limb to their fire. "We'll take shifts," she said. "Two at a time."

Dana had hoped that would be the case. Whatever fate those men had met—and it was most likely something very terrible—she wanted no part of. Had they been killed in their sleep? No, their bedrolls had looked undisturbed. Had something lured them out?

"I'll take the first watch," Butch said.

"I'll partner with you," Jean added. "My body is tired, but my mind isn't."

Corey's tent was up, and she'd already offered it to Jean. Dana wondered if they could take turns sleeping in it. The tent would offer no protection from…well, from an attack of…of some sort, but at least it would provide a sense of security. Albeit a false sense.

"Do you know how to use a gun, Dana?" Corey asked.

Dana nodded. "I've shot before, yes. It's been a lot of years, though."

"We should be okay tonight," Corey said. "Lucky will be on guard too. He'll alert us if anything comes up."

The dog was lying between Butch and Corey, hoping for a handout. Dana had noticed that Corey had given at least half of her sandwich to him. She probably wasn't hungry. Dana had seen her sneaking sausage rolls a couple of times during their ride today. Still, Corey seemed awful quiet this evening.

"Got a little moon tonight too," Butch added. "Once it gets higher in the sky, it'll give us some light."

Dana hugged her knees to her as she stared into the fire. "Seems so strange to be out here like this, doesn't it? Like we're the only people left on earth. No sounds. No cars or trucks. No planes."

"We haven't heard any planes because they've designated this area as a no-fly zone," Corey said. "An unplanned military training exercise is the excuse. Whatever is jamming signals and killing power and batteries…well, they have no idea the reach of it."

"You think we've made the news by now?" Dana asked.

Corey shrugged. "Probably."

"That won't really mean anything for us, though, will it?" she asked.

"Hard to say. Depends on how much press it's getting and how truthful the answers have been. One reason the power company didn't try to rush in was because they were told a radioactive satellite fell to earth," Corey said. "That's one way to keep people out."

"Unbelievable," she murmured.

"I know." Corey met her gaze across the fire. "You should get some sleep. Why don't you take the tent?"

Dana looked over at the tent which was a good distance away from the fire. She looked back to Corey. "I'm…I'm scared." She looked away for a second, embarrassed for being so frightened. Even Jean seemed to be holding up better than she was. But…what the hell? She swallowed down her pride and looked back at Corey. "Can we both fit in there?"

Corey smiled slightly and nodded. "I guess we can squeeze in."

"Good. Because I'm not going in there alone." She started to get up, then stopped. "And you'll bring your gun, right?"

Butch laughed. "I thought you hated guns."

"Yes. But I hate scary monsters worse," she said as she got up. She really wanted to brush her teeth but didn't dare go to the creek alone. Her teeth would have to wait until morning.

Corey got up too and brushed her jeans off with her hands. "I know we don't have clocks but watch the moon," she said to the others. "Give us about three or four hours' sleep and then we'll relieve you."

They all looked overhead at once, finding the moon. It was about a quarter of the way up. Dana had no idea how Butch would be able to tell when four hours had passed. Corey went over to Butch and sat down beside him.

"Here…follow my arm. Break the sky up into eight sections. When the moon gets to four, wake us up. It's not exact by any means," Corey said, "but it's the best we can do."

"Okay."

"Miss Jean? You sure you'll be okay on the first shift?" Corey asked.

"Like I said before, I know how to use this shotgun, Captain."

Corey nodded. "You know, you don't have to address me as 'Captain,'" she said.

"I address you as 'Captain' for the same reason you address me as 'Miss Jean.'"

Corey smiled at her. "I understand."

"I hope that's okay," Jean continued.

"Yes, ma'am. That's perfectly fine. And I'll try my best to get us all out of here in one piece."

"We would all appreciate that, Captain."

Dana thought it was a sweet exchange between the captain and Miss Jean, and she couldn't help but smile. Of course, she too hoped Corey got them all out of here safely. She went to where she'd laid her bedroll and picked it up, waiting for Corey.

Corey motioned to the tent and Dana followed. Corey didn't seem to be having any trouble seeing.

"I hope your night vision is better than mine," Dana said. "Because I can't see a damn thing."

"I imagine if something comes up tonight, Lucky will be the first to hear and see it," Corey said.

"Something?"

Corey squatted down and reached for the bedroll. "Something…a person, a wild animal." She glanced up at her. "Little green men from another planet."

Her voice was teasing, but Dana could find no humor in the statement.

"If you're trying to put me at ease, that's not helping."

"No?" Corey stood up again. "You want the side against the wall or the door?"

"Not the door," she said as she got down on her knees to crawl inside. "If something comes in, I want them to have to go through you before they get to me."

"Okay. Be right back."

Dana's eyes widened. "Where are you going?" she asked quickly.

"To get my pack. And my gun."

"Hurry," she said tensely. She sat down on her bedroll, her eyes glued to the door. It wasn't so bad, though. She could see the fire and make out Butch and Jean. Lucky was lying between them.

When she heard Corey come back, she scooted over, giving her room. The tent was obviously intended for one person or a couple who didn't mind getting cozy with each other. Corey got in next to her and lay down but did not zip up the tent.

"Or would you rather I close it?" Corey asked. "I thought you might feel better if you could see the fire."

"Is there enough wood to keep it going?"

"He'll add to it enough to keep a flame, not much more," Corey said.

"Okay." She stretched out on her back. "I hate sleeping in clothes."

"Feel free to take them off," Corey said. "I won't mind."

Dana again recognized the teasing in her voice. "Is that how you handle stress? By being playful? Teasing?" She heard Corey's quiet sigh before she answered.

"I haven't been playful or teasing with anyone in…in nearly five months now."

Dana rolled her head to the side, seeing Corey's profile in the shadows of the tent. She appeared to be staring at the ceiling. It wasn't any of her business, she knew, but curiosity got the better of her. As Jean had said the other day, if you look deep into Corey's eyes, you see a tortured soul, although Corey did well to hide it. Had she lost someone? A lover?

"Want to talk about it?" she asked quietly.

Corey turned her head to the side to look at her. "I've done a lot of that already. Faked my way through it, got cleared."

"What happened?"

Corey sighed again. "You should get some sleep. We'll have a long day tomorrow."

In other words, Corey didn't want to talk about it. But Dana's curiosity was high. She bit her lip and closed her eyes, trying to keep her questions inside, trying not to pry. It didn't help. She tried another approach.

"You've been a little distant today."

"Have I?"

Dana nodded in the shadows. "It's like your mind is elsewhere. What's going on?"

Corey laughed quietly. "I don't even know what's going on *here*, much less what's in my mind."

They were quiet for a moment, then Dana remembered a conversation they'd had earlier. "Tell me about your team," she coaxed.

Corey turned her head quickly toward her. "What about them?" she asked abruptly.

"You mentioned them once, but not again."

"So?"

Dana shrugged slightly. "Intuition, I guess…they're not here with you. Are they on your mind?"

Corey turned her head away from her, staring up at the ceiling. Her long, heavy sigh made Dana regret her question.

"No, they're not here with me. They won't ever be with me again."

So it wasn't a lover she'd lost. It was her team.

"Tell me about them," she whispered.

"God…they were my…my family. They were all I had, really. We were so close, all of us. They were my team, yet they didn't treat me like their commander. We worked as one, no one greater or lesser than the others."

Dana didn't say anything. She lay there quietly, listening to the shift in Corey's breathing. She could hear her own as well as she tried to guess what had happened to them.

"We were on assignment, in Pakistan," Corey continued. "Bad intel all around. We were ambushed. It was a bloodbath."

"Were you injured?" Dana asked quietly.

"Yeah. Yeah, I was. I probably should have died right there with the rest of them." She paused. "Sometimes I wish I had."

Dana reached over and touched her arm. "Please don't say that, Corey."

"It's the truth. I'll be honest, I was a basket case. Took a couple of months to recover—physically—but then, I couldn't deal with my loss," Corey said. "I certainly couldn't function as a soldier. The shrink they sent me to wasn't helping at all, and I got sick of talking about it."

"So you faked your way through it?"

"Yeah. Got cleared when I shouldn't have. But Harry—that's General Brinkley—is a family friend, and he put me on special assignment," she said. "For the last four months I've been living in solitude at my little cabin, doing pretty much nothing. Existing, not living." She turned her head toward Dana. "He's the one who brought me in on this mission. I think he—and everyone else—expected it to be fairly routine."

Dana gave a nervous laugh. "Routine?"

"I know. I'm still holding out hope that it was just a meteor."

Dana realized her hand was still touching Corey's arm. She didn't pull away, however. "I'm sorry about your team," she whispered in the darkness.

Corey didn't say anything but again, Dana heard a quiet sigh.

"Goodnight, Dana."

The words were spoken quietly, and Dana returned them, letting her eyes slip closed. They were on their backs, their shoulders touching. She relaxed, trusting Corey to keep her safe for the few hours of sleep they were allowed.

CHAPTER THIRTY-TWO

Corey heard movement and—as she was trained to do—was wide awake within seconds. It was only Butch stirring, adding more wood to the fire. Jean was no longer sitting up and Corey spotted her prone figure on Butch's bedroll. For a moment, she panicked. But then she remembered Lucky and found the dog sitting beside Butch, undisturbed. She relaxed again, only then noticing that Dana was curled up next to her, her hands wrapped around Corey's arm securely.

It felt nice and brought some solace to her as well. She doubted Dana even knew that she did that. The nights they'd shared a bed, first at Anna Gail's house then at Jean's, Dana had moved close to her during sleep. Last night at Jean's, Corey had been tempted to pull Dana into her arms, seeking the same comfort that Dana apparently had been looking for. In the end, she had remained still. They were strangers, thrown together in an uncertain and stressful situation. There was no need to complicate things.

But the contact felt good, she acknowledged. It had been so long since she'd shared her bed with anyone…she couldn't remember the last time she'd even had a lover. And when she'd lost her team…well, she'd lost her only close friends. Since then, her interaction with others was strained, to say the least. Her life lately had been empty and void of any human contact. Harry had been right to kick her ass into gear. If he hadn't sent her out on this mission, she'd still be holed up in the cabin, watching the days waste away...much like her life had been doing.

However, it appeared that this particular mission wasn't one that she was trained for. She'd never been up against a nameless, faceless enemy before. Maybe if she had her team...maybe they could figure it out. Here, she was relying on three civilians, one of whom was seventy-five years old. Butch could most likely handle his rifle, but after the incident in the barn with Hal, she wasn't certain how far she could trust him. And Dana? Dana hated guns. But first thing tomorrow, she was going to get a quick lesson. She'd give Dana her Beretta. It was easier to use than the new Glock she had. She could already hear the argument Dana would have, but it wouldn't be up for discussion. They all needed to be armed. They all needed to be prepared.

Prepared for what, however, was still the question.

* * *

"Hey...wake up," Corey said as she nudged Dana with her elbow.

After they'd relieved Butch and Jean, Dana had stayed awake for maybe an hour, then had rested her head against Corey's shoulder, falling asleep again. Corey didn't mind. It felt good just having someone there with her, even if they were asleep. Lucky, too, had dozed off, but he'd jerked awake a couple of times, staring off into the darkness. She'd followed his gaze, her hand tightening around the Glock she held, but after a few seconds, Lucky would settle down again. Other than that, the night was quiet and still...and dark. Now, dawn was approaching, turning the sky nearly purple as the darkness was pushed to the west. She needed to get the fire going again. She had an uneasy feeling, and she wanted to head out early. There were too many unanswered questions running around in her mind. Mainly, if six men started out, why were there only four bedrolls and three horses? What happened to the other two men? And of the four remaining, Hal made it back home, but without a horse. How did he get there? And where were the other three men? Judging by the blood she'd found and the drag marks, they were badly injured. Were they able to get on a horse and make it to Paradox for help? She shook her head. Too many questions and no damn answers. Well, hopefully they'd find the helicopter soon. They might even stumble upon the squad that Sutter sent in. That was what she really hoped for, but it would be blind luck if they did.

She glanced over at Dana and nudged her once again. "Dana... wake up," she said, louder this time.

Dana's eyes fluttered open, then she lifted her head, finding Corey's gaze.

"I fell asleep," she said unnecessarily. "Sorry."

"It's okay. It's been quiet."

Dana ran her hand through her hair a couple of times, then rubbed her eyes. "The sun will be up soon," Dana said. "I'm not sure I've ever looked forward to a sunrise as much as this one."

Corey holstered her gun, then moved to the fire, using a stick to stir the embers. A few small twigs caught easily, sending sparks and smoke swirling up.

"Wake the others," she said, a little more abruptly than she intended. "I want to get out of here as soon as possible."

Dana stared at her as if sensing something was wrong. "Do you think we're in danger here?"

"Just a gut feeling," she said honestly. "I feel like we should move on, that's all."

Dana got up quickly. "I'll trust your gut then."

It wasn't long before the four of them were sipping coffee and nibbling on the sausage rolls that Jean had made for them. No one was attempting to carry on a conversation, and she assumed they were all dog-tired. Corey was used to existing on a few hours' sleep a night. They were not.

It wasn't a particularly cold morning, but the fire chased away some of the chill in the air, as did the hot coffee. She finished the last of hers then stood, silently signaling an end to their breakfast. The sun was still low in the sky by the time they saddled up and headed out with three extra horses in tow.

They continued following the creek and conversation was nearly nonexistent. Whether it was from fatigue or fear, Corey didn't know. She looked back at Dana a couple of times with raised eyebrows, and Dana had given her a brief smile each time. She was being a trooper, she'd give her that. And Jean...well, Jean was holding her own, riding confidently in the saddle—this time on the horse she called Daisy. Lucky was leading the way, pausing several times to splash in the creek before running back out again.

"He sure does love the water," Butch commented, breaking the silence. "I may join him for a bath soon."

"That sounds nice," Dana said. "Will we camp along the creek again tonight?"

Corey knew the question was directed at her, and she turned in her saddle. "I hope we come upon the helicopter soon. Hard to say where we'll camp."

"What are the chances it's somewhere along the creek?" Butch asked.

"When they originally flew in, they were using the creek as a landmark," she said, repeating what Duncan had told her.

"When you said you'd been camping...that was just for show?" Dana asked. "You hadn't really been out?"

Corey nodded. "That was my cover story. But technically, I did spend one night out," she said. "They dropped me off at the checkpoint, and I hiked the road until dark. Then back at it the next day."

"I don't understand why it was such a secret."

Corey sighed. "Does it really matter now?"

Dana shrugged but didn't reply.

Silence again as they continued on, the horses' hooves rolling the rocks from time to time. Lucky barked once and took off through the creek to the other side, chasing a rabbit that they'd scared up from its daytime hiding place. Butch called him back, and the dog stopped, returning to them but not before splashing around in the water first. Corey thought a bath sounded good, but she did wonder how the four of them could accomplish that feat. There was only a smattering of trees and brush near the creek but not enough to provide any kind of privacy should they get in the water. She let a small smile play on her lips...maybe she and Dana could share a bath.

She sighed and brought her attention back to the task at hand. There was no time for any nonsense like frolicking in the water naked. Even if it did sound like fun. Because there was no time for fun either.

She estimated they'd ridden three or four hours when they came to a fork in the creek. She got her binoculars out and stood up tall in the saddle, scanning the area in front of them and across the creek too, just as she'd been doing every several hundred yards or so. She was actually shocked when she spotted something. So shocked, in fact, that she passed right over it. She swung the binoculars back around, her heart beating excitedly. It was the wreckage. *Finally.* Before she could tell the others, Butch spoke.

"Looks like there was a camp over there," he said. "Recent fire ring."

Corey lowered the binoculars, nodding where he pointed. They were close to the helicopter, and all she wanted to do was push on, but she knew they were tired and most likely hungry.

"Let's rest," she said.

"Thank God," Dana said. "My ass is numb." Then she looked quickly at Jean. "Sorry, Miss Jean. My *butt.*"

"I know what an ass is," Jean replied. "Mine's pretty numb too."

"I'll help you out of the saddle, Miss Jean," Butch said.

Corey landed on the ground easily, then walked over to hold Daisy as Butch took Jean's arm and helped her down. Dana was moving around and holding her lower back as she stretched her legs.

"I'm pretty certain that once this is over with, I won't want to see a horse or a saddle again for a long, long time," Dana said.

"It's an adventure," Corey teased.

"Yes. I keep telling myself that," Dana said. "Can we take time to eat something?"

Corey shook her head. "No. I think I spotted the wreckage," she said. "We need to go."

"You did?" Dana asked excitedly. "That's good, right? Why didn't you say something?"

"Where?" Butch asked.

Corey turned and pointed across the creek, down past the fork. "About a thousand yards or so, I'd guess." She walked to the creek and splashed water on her face, only to have Lucky join her, his tail wagging wildly as if he wanted her to throw something for him. She picked up a rock and absently tossed it into the creek. To her surprise, he dove after it, sticking his head under the water and coming up with a rock. It wasn't *her* rock, but still…

"I'll be damned," she murmured when he brought the rock to her and looked at her expectantly. She picked it up and tossed it in again, a smile on her face. She'd always liked dogs, but they'd never had one. Her mother said they moved around too much to keep one. Corey's protest that other families had them fell on deaf ears. When she was older, she realized that had simply been her mother's excuse.

"Out at the farm," Jean said, "we never had a ball for him. So he'd bring us sticks or pinecones or, yes, even rocks. Hal and I were too old to keep him entertained, though." Her voice faltered a bit with the mention of Hal's name, but there was still a little smile on her face as she watched Lucky in the water.

One more toss of a rock, then Corey turned away from the creek and took up the reins on the white stallion she rode. She remembered Jean's earlier warning that he'd tossed Carl Milstead into the creek once. They'd have to cross the creek now and she wondered if she'd end up soaking wet before it was over.

"Let's head out," she said.

Butch again helped Jean while Dana held the horse, then they too climbed back in their saddles. Butch crossed the creek first, pulling two of the extra horses behind him. She followed, hoping no one saw the tight grip she had on the saddle as her horse ducked his head several times, his nose touching the water. But she made it across without incident, and she allowed herself to release a relieved sigh.

She glanced up at the sun, noting that they were heading northwest now. She shielded her eyes, then slipped her sunglasses back on. She kicked her horse, urging him into a faster trot. Now that they were close to the helicopter, she was anxious to get there. Lucky ran beside her, his tongue hanging out, and she swore there was a smile on his face. She imagined this was the most activity the young dog had had in his life and he appeared to be enjoying the trip.

She glanced behind her, seeing that the others had also picked up the pace, even Jean, who was bouncing in the saddle, both hands gripping the saddle horn tightly. Dana appeared to be having no problems on Gretchen as she pulled the other mare behind her. She nodded and gave Corey a quick smile.

It took them a good while to reach the helicopter, and she assumed it had been farther away than it appeared. She stopped several yards away from it and the others did as well. When Lucky would have gone to investigate, she called him back.

"Stay here," she murmured, touching the dog's head. "Let me take a look first," she said to Butch.

She walked closer, her boots crunching over rocks, her eyes darting around, looking for signs of the crew. They wouldn't have been able to survive the crash, she knew. There was evidence of a fire, but it hadn't consumed the craft, which was odd. Still, there should be bodies.

She stepped over a twisted piece of metal, peering into the remains of the cockpit. Hard to tell if that was blood she was seeing, but she assumed that it was. But where was the crew?

"Well?" Dana called.

She turned around and held up her hand, signaling them to stay put. "No crew. I want to check the perimeter for tracks."

"Been a few days…and we had rain the other night," Butch warned.

She nodded as she walked away from the wreckage, her eyes glued to the ground around it. As Butch had said, any tracks would most likely have been washed away in the rainstorm. But if the crew wasn't here, Sutter's squad must have made it to the wreckage. They would have taken the bodies with them.

But where the hell was the squad?

She blew out a frustrated breath, then walked back to the others with a shake of her head.

"Nothing."

"No bodies?" Butch asked. "You think they could have survived that?"

She shook her head. "No. Most likely the other squad found the wreckage before me."

"If they were on foot and we're on horseback, what are the chances they would have beaten you here?" Dana asked.

She shrugged. "I don't know. They left a day after me," she said. "But maybe from satellite images they were able to spot the wreckage so they knew exactly where to go. I feel like we've been riding all over the damn place. Wouldn't have been hard to beat us here."

"True."

"So now what?" Butch asked.

Corey sighed. Yeah…now what? Look for the so-called meteor? How in the hell was she supposed to find that out here? It was blind luck that they found the helicopter in the first place. What were the chances she'd stumble upon the…well, whatever the hell it was that landed out here? She looked over at Dana. Not to mention she had the safety of these three civilians to worry about. No, the best thing would probably be to head back to Jean's place. They would have shelter there, they would have food. And it would be safer than being out here.

"I guess I need to get you back. At least to Jean's," she said. "My assignment is to find the meteor."

"I thought you were convinced it wasn't a meteor," Butch said.

"Wait a minute," Dana said as she walked closer to her. "You mean, leave us at Jean's and then you're heading out again?"

Corey nodded. "You'll be safer there. Maybe you could go on to Paradox. I'm sure Anna Gail—"

"No." Dana stared at her. "We all stay together. You're not dumping us off and then heading back out here alone. That's crazy."

"What's crazy is having the three of you out here with me when we don't know what the hell we're looking for. Besides, we don't have much food left. My supplies were for one person, not four," she said. "My mission is to—"

"Well, fuck your *mission*," Dana said loudly. "Miss Jean shot a man who looked like her husband and he didn't bleed. We burned his body, for God's sake, because you were afraid it wasn't just a body, remember?" She turned and pointed at Butch. "And he *freaked* out and attacked you—and me—when he was near the body. Whatever the hell is going on out here, I won't feel safe at Miss Jean's house," she said, her voice nearly quivering now, "not if you're not there."

God. She took her cap and sunglasses off and rubbed her hair vigorously, trying to decide what to do. Dana was right. She couldn't leave them there alone.

She slipped her cap back on and met Dana's frightened gaze. She finally nodded. "Well, I guess we'll be eating rabbit for dinner then." She was surprised by the quick, tight hug Dana gave her.

"I'm on a diet," Dana murmured. When she pulled away, Corey could see the relief in her eyes. "Thank you," Dana whispered.

Corey nodded, then turned to the others. "I guess we head back to the creek."

Butch looked at her sheepishly. "I'm sorry that I, you know, freaked out and attacked you."

Corey slapped his shoulder as she walked past him to her horse. "Not your fault." She paused to glance at Jean before getting on her horse. "How you holding up?"

Jean nodded. "I think Dana's right. We should stay together." Then the corners of her eyes crinkled up as she smiled. "I like rabbit. Tastes like chicken."

Corey felt some of the tension leave her as she laughed. Taking the three of them with her probably wasn't the wisest decision, but it was the right one.

CHAPTER THIRTY-THREE

It was a bit early to be stopping for the day, but since they'd found the helicopter, Corey's sense of urgency faded a little. Her uneasiness seemed to grow, however. Back at the creek, they investigated the previous campsite they'd found. Most likely, Hal and his group had camped there several days ago. They'd also most likely collected any available firewood as none was to be found.

"So they camped here, then were heading back home," Butch said, looking down the creek. "The camp where we found the horses, though, there were only four bedrolls."

"Four bedrolls and three horses," she said. She glanced over at Jean. "Hal was on foot?"

Jean nodded. "He said he'd left Daisy by the barn." Jean patted the neck of her horse. "Obviously that was a lie. He came walking up in the front, like he'd come from the road."

If Hal was in his mid-seventies, like Jean, there was no way he could have made it all the way back home on foot. Not that fast. Of course, it wasn't really Hal, was it?

"What are you thinking?" Dana asked.

Corey shook her head. "Nothing. Everything." She got back on her horse. "Let's keep going. There's no firewood here anyway." Dana still stared at her and Corey winked at her, trying to set her mind at ease. "We've still got to catch a rabbit, you know."

Dana rolled her eyes. "Again with the rabbit," she murmured.

* * *

Dana sat down next to Jean, who was sitting on a large rock. Even though it wasn't dark yet, the fire was burning brightly. Fortunately, there'd been no luck finding a rabbit, and they'd shared the last sandwich and two containers of the meals that Corey had. If they were out much longer, then yes, Dana would be forced to eat a rabbit. Sad really, since she knew that Paradox Creek was teeming with trout. She'd take fresh trout over a bunny any day. Shame that they hadn't thought to bring fishing gear along.

She watched as Butch strolled along the creek, his gaze shifting up toward the ridge several times. She glanced over at Corey, who was also watching him.

"He's acting a little weird," she said finally.

Corey turned to her. "Yeah, he is. I hate to say it, but he's got that look in his eyes again. Like when we were in the barn."

"Great," she said dryly.

"When we keep watch tonight, do you mind taking a turn with him?"

She nodded. "Okay." Then, "Are you worried about him?"

"A little, yeah. He keeps looking up at that ridge," Corey said. "Is it significant?"

Dana shrugged then glanced at Jean. "Miss Jean? Is that ridge something out of the ordinary?"

"That's Baker's Ridge," she said. "Highest point in this area." Her gaze slid to the ridge in question. "Back in the day, Ernest Baker and his brother—can't remember his name—held off an Indian attack for three days up there at the top. By the time help came, the brother was dead and Ernest was found with no less than six arrows in him," she said matter-of-factly. "He lived into his eighties."

Dana looked at Corey and exchanged a smile with her.

"Miss Jean, can you see this ridge from your house?" Corey asked.

Jean nodded. "There's a view of it out the kitchen door. Why?"

"During the storm the other night, it looked like the lightning was concentrated up on the ridge here. I remember thinking that no matter where the lightning strike originated, it seemed to be drawn to this particular ridge."

"Would something attract it?" Dana asked. "Like iron or something?"

Corey shrugged. "I don't know enough about it to say. Lightning being attracted to something could be a myth. But the lightning from that storm was definitely hitting the ridge."

The light had almost faded from the sky, and Corey added a few more sticks to the fire. They were camping in an area with lots of small trees and scrub brush. There'd been ample firewood, and they'd all helped gather it, even Jean. Corey again had her tent set up and Dana assumed they would take turns sleeping. Since she would take the shift with Butch, she wondered if Corey would offer to share the tent with Miss Jean.

She looked over as Butch made his way back to the fire. She raised her eyebrows at him.

"What's going on?"

"What do you mean?"

"You've been a little standoffish," she said.

He squatted down beside the fire. "I think there's something up on the ridge," he said quietly.

"Like what?" Corey asked.

"Don't know. Just…something," he said vaguely.

Dana met Corey's eyes across the fire, wondering what she was thinking. She didn't have to wonder long.

"Maybe we should ride up there tomorrow…take a look," Corey suggested.

Butch jerked his head up. "Yeah. We should take a look." He stood. "We can head out right now. We can—"

"How about we wait until morning?" Corey said. "Let's get some rest, then we'll check it out in the morning."

That seemed to pacify him, and he nodded. "Okay. Yeah. We'll check it out in the morning."

"Why don't you get some sleep," Corey suggested. "I'll take the first shift."

"I'll stay up with you," Jean said.

Dana saw Butch hesitate, so she stood up too. "Come on," she said to him. "Let's sleep in the tent. It makes me feel a little safer."

* * *

After Dana and Butch went inside the tent, Corey turned to Jean. "If you're tired, I'll be okay by myself."

Jean shook her head. "My sleep is filled with dreams I'd just as soon not have." She motioned to Lucky, who was lying beside Corey. "He seems to have taken a liking to you."

Corey reached out and ran her hand across his fur several times. "I never had a dog. I think I would have wanted one just like him."

"Your folks wouldn't let you?"

Corey placed another stick on the fire. "No. I didn't understand it at the time. My mother always made some excuse as to why I couldn't have one. When I got older, I realized the excuses were only excuses. My mother didn't want a dog, but she didn't want to be the bad guy, so she made up other reasons."

"When my boys were young, we had a couple of dogs running around. Barn cats too. The youngest, Johnny, he loved that old ugly mutt named Bruno. Never knew a boy could cry as much as he did when that old dog died." Jean sighed. "When it was just Hal and me... well, we didn't give a thought to having a dog around. We had enough to handle with the farm animals that we kept."

"Where did Lucky come from?"

"The Bensons had a momma dog," Jean said. "They brought two of the puppies over one day and next thing I knew, this fat black thing was in my lap nibbling on my fingers," she said with a laugh. "You should have seen the look on Hal's face when he realized that we were keeping him."

"Benson? Is that one of the guys who went out with Hal?" she asked.

Jean nodded. "Yes. Curtis. Their place is farther out east of us." Jean stared at her, her gaze thoughtful. "You think any of them made it back home?"

Corey hesitated only a second. "No. I don't think so. Where we found the horses...there was a lot of blood. I think they met with... with foul play," she said cautiously, not wanting to upset Jean.

"I wonder if any of them made it back, though...like my Hal did," Jean said, her voice little more than a whisper.

"I hope not, Miss Jean."

Jean's face was solemn as she nodded. "I surely do hope not too."

CHAPTER THIRTY-FOUR

For the first time in her life, Dana was afraid…afraid of Butch. Or maybe afraid *for* him. As soon as Corey had gotten them up to take watch, Butch had grabbed his rifle and made his way to the creek. Each night the moon was a little brighter, and she could make out his features. His back was to her, his gaze fixed on what she assumed was the ridge. It was too dark to see it but it was out there…and it was almost as if it were calling to Butch.

She'd huddled as close to the fire as she could, Corey's gun gripped tightly in her hand. When coyotes started howling close by, she'd nearly jumped out of her skin. The coyotes seemed to break whatever spell Butch had been under, and he made his way back to the fire. When he sat down, he didn't say a word. She admitted she was afraid and she came very close—several times—to getting up and waking Corey. But she knew that Corey's shift had lasted much longer than theirs would. So she stifled her fear, telling herself there was nothing to fear in the first place. This was *Butch*, for God's sake.

And now, as daylight was slowly creeping over the valley, the new day couldn't come fast enough. In fact, she wanted it to come so badly that she got up, startling Butch in the process. She made her way over to the tent, smiling slightly as she found Lucky lying beside it, as if keeping guard.

She bent down and petted his head, then reached inside, touching Corey's shoulder. Corey jumped, her eyes wide.

"It's just me," Dana whispered.

"What's wrong?"

"It's almost daylight," she said. "And…I'm scared," she admitted.

Corey looked past her to where Butch sat. As they watched him, he got to his feet, walking aimlessly back toward the creek, his gaze lifted up to the west…and the ridge.

"He hasn't said a single word the whole time we've been up," she said.

Corey sat up and rubbed her face with both hands.

"You're exhausted, aren't you?" Dana asked unnecessarily.

Corey gave her a half smile. "Don't have time for that, I'm afraid." She looked over at Jean, who was watching them. "Did we wake you?"

"I'm always up with the chickens," Jean said. "Now's no different."

Dana stood and got out of the way as Corey crawled out of the tent. She straightened up, raising both arms over her head in a big stretch. Her eyes were closed and Dana watched her, noting the smooth skin on her face, the lips that were turned up slightly in a smile. She wondered if they'd met under different circumstances, would she still find Corey attractive?

"What?"

Dana blinked, finding Corey staring at her. She shook her head. "Nothing."

She went back and got the fire going, thankful that there was still enough coffee. The supplies they'd gotten from Anna Gail's store were dwindling, but the bag of ground coffee was still half-full. She smirked. Or half-empty, she thought.

Miss Jean came over, holding her hands out to the flames. "Sitting out here with the captain last night, I was a little chilled. The tent was nice," she said.

"Did you sleep okay?"

"Yes. Until those coyotes came by. Of course, they woke the captain too."

The sun wasn't up yet, but dawn had replaced darkness and she could see around them. "Where is the captain?" she asked.

"She said she was going to the creek to clean up," Jean said.

Corey came walking up then, her hair wet. She, too, held her hands out to the fire.

"Surely you didn't bathe," Dana said. "The water is freezing."

"Yeah, I dunked my head, trying to wake up," Corey said. "That cold water will do it." She ran her fingers through her damp hair several times.

"I had a scare with cancer a while back," Jean said, seemingly out of the blue.

"Oh? Are you okay?" Dana asked.

Jean waved her question away. "Twenty-five years ago or so. Anyway, I lost all my hair during treatment. Had me this god-awful wig to wear. Hal hated it," she said. "When it was just the two of us, I'd take the thing off...bald as a cue ball." She looked over at Corey. "I remember when my hair got to be about like yours. I was so happy for it to be growing back." She shook her head. "Why in the world would a woman cut her hair that short?"

Corey laughed and again rubbed her hair. "Been in the military my whole life, Miss Jean. I wanted to be just like my father. My mother screamed when she found me in the bathroom with my dad's clippers."

"I take it she was too late?" Dana asked.

Corey nodded. "I had half of it done. After she stopped screaming, she started crying as she finished the job for me."

"Well, I suppose it looks okay on you," Jean said. "Can't say I'd want it for myself, though." Dana laughed and Jean looked at her. "It's a look that fits the captain. I don't think you need to be experimenting with it either."

Dana smiled at her. "Don't worry. I kinda like my hair the way it is."

Corey turned, glancing over at Butch. "I'm going to go talk to him. See what's going on."

"Okay. Coffee will be ready soon."

CHAPTER THIRTY-FIVE

There was a small creek at the base of the ridge, and Corey stopped, thinking it was a good place to take a break. Butch was anxious, and she wouldn't have been surprised if he ignored her and kept on going.

"Take a break," she said, her eyes holding his firmly.

He looked past her, up to the ridge, spying the trail they would take. He turned back to her. "Got to get to the ridge. There's something up there."

It was a mantra he'd been repeating all morning. She nodded. "So you say. But let's take a short break before we head up. Looks like it'll be quite a challenging climb."

She got off her horse, then grabbed the reins of his mount, holding it tightly. She wondered if he was contemplating jerking away from her. She finally saw his shoulders relax, and he nodded.

Corey looked over at Jean, who was struggling to get out of her saddle. She hurried over to give her a hand.

"This would be Little Squaw Creek, I think," Jean said as she walked closer to it.

"Is this what flows down by your place?" Corey asked.

Jean shook her head. "This little one hooks up with Paradox Creek farther down. Then it forks off again and we call that Squaw Creek that runs through our valley. It eventually flows back into Paradox

Creek again before it reaches town," she explained. She lowered her voice. "He seems a little out of sorts today, doesn't he?"

"I'll say," she murmured.

Dana and Butch were kneeling at the creek, splashing water on their faces. Yeah, he was certainly out of sorts, she thought. If he'd mentioned the ridge once, he'd mentioned it a hundred times. It was like he was obsessed with getting to the top. He had that faraway look in his eyes, like he wasn't really with them. It was a look she remembered from Jean's barn, when they'd found Hal's body.

And she admitted—at least to herself—that it frightened her a little. She figured she could handle Butch, though. It was what they might find at the top of the ridge that scared her.

As they'd ridden closer to the ridge that morning, she'd pulled her binoculars out several times, hoping to spot something up there. All she could see were rocks and scrub brush, nothing out of the ordinary. She'd even tried her solar transmitter again. Thus far, it had been useless. But she'd tried to get a signal that morning and was shocked to actually hear static. The other times she'd tried it, there was nothing but silence. She had broadcast a quick message in case the transmission was really getting through. She'd try it again up on the ridge. Maybe it was only being down in the valley that was impeding the signal. Up high on the ridge, it might be a different story.

She met Dana's worried eyes as she came over to her. Corey gave her what she hoped was a reassuring smile.

"What's wrong?" Corey asked quietly.

Dana wasn't afraid to hold her gaze. "You look worried, therefore I'm worried."

Corey dropped the pretense and nodded. "Yeah, I'm a little worried about Butch."

"I know. He's...well, he's not his normally cheerful self, that's for sure. But it's something else entirely. I've never seen him this... this *weird* before," she said as she glanced back toward him. He was standing off by himself, his head cocked back as he stared up at the ridge. "Do you actually think it's a good idea for us to go up there?" Dana let out her breath. "Because I've got a really bad feeling."

"If there's something...well, something *bad* up there, Lucky will warn us," she said. "Of that I'm certain." She took her cap off. "Let me take advantage of the water. Then we should head out. It's a steep climb. It'll probably take us a good while to get up there."

They'd decided to leave the three extra horses at the creek instead of taking them up with them. Corey and Dana decided, anyway. Butch had been noncommittal, continuing to stare blankly up at the ridge as if not even hearing their conversation. Or not caring. She thought it would be best for Dana and Jean to stay behind too, but she knew better than to suggest it to Dana. But she thought she'd try with Jean.

"Miss Jean, maybe you should stay down here, make sure the horses are okay," she said lamely. Jean saw through her feeble attempt at an excuse.

"Captain, if something's up there, I can face it as surely as you all can. Besides, I'd just as soon not be down here alone."

She looked over at Dana, who shook her head.

"Don't even suggest it," Dana warned. "I'm going with you. We should stay together."

Corey nodded. "Okay. Then let's head up."

The words were barely out of her mouth before Butch give his horse a kick and they nearly bolted across the small creek. Lucky ran across too, then looked back, as if waiting for the others to follow.

The trail appeared steeper than it actually was and the horses didn't labor at all. It seemed to be nothing more than a game trail, but it climbed at an easy angle. Butch was getting farther and farther ahead of them, though, and her calling him back was to no avail. When they got close to the rim, he again kicked his horse and then disappeared out of sight as they topped the ridge.

"Goddamn it," Corey muttered as she, too, gave her horse a kick.

Butch was nowhere to be seen when they all crested the top. The scrub brush was thicker so she stood up in her saddle looking for him. Maybe the dog would come to her if Butch would not.

"Lucky," she called and then whistled.

The black dog darted back toward them, stopping with his tongue hanging out. Then he disappeared back into the brush and Corey followed, assuming Dana and Jean were right behind her.

She hadn't gone more than thirty or forty yards farther before the unmistakable smell of rotting flesh hit her. She tried to ignore it, but it was strong and she covered her nose and mouth.

"Oh, my *God*," Dana said behind her. "That's awful. Is that what I think it is?"

"I'm afraid so." She glanced behind her, seeing both Jean and Dana pulling their shirts up around their face to try to stifle the smell.

Corey spotted his horse, but Butch wasn't anywhere around. Lucky was whining as he stood beside the horse, his intelligent eyes going to Corey, then away, looking into what appeared to be a ravine of some sort. She finally spotted Butch as he was scrambling down it.

She jumped off her horse, taking the time to grab the extra rope Butch kept on his saddle before running after him. Lucky was right on her heels, urging her down.

"Corey?" Dana called.

"Stay there," she yelled back without looking.

She caught up to Butch about halfway down the ravine and she spun him around. His eyes were nearly feral, and she was certain that he wasn't really aware of her presence. He swung wildly, trying to swat away her hand as he headed down again.

"Butch, look at me," she said. "I need you here with us. I need your help."

She knew her words were pointless as he never broke stride.

"Stop," she said sharply. "You're not going down there."

She grabbed his arm and tried to twist it behind his back, but he turned on her, his angry eyes flashing. She was ready for his swing and she blocked it easily. With her elbow, she popped him hard in the chin, causing him to stumble backward.

"Sorry about that," she mumbled as she pushed him to the rocks and quickly folded his hands behind him, her knee pressed hard against his lower back. He cried out in pain, but she ignored him, using her other hand to wind the rope around his wrists.

"Let me go!" he yelled.

"Nope," she said as she pulled him to his feet. He tried to run, but she kicked him on the side of his knee, causing his leg to buckle. She wrapped the rest of the rope around his torso, then hauled him to his feet again.

Dana was coming down the ravine to meet them and the look in her eyes alternated between worry and concern…and fear.

"What the hell is wrong with him? It's like he's—"

"Possessed," Corey finished for her. "Let's get him out of here."

But Dana's eyes were looking past her, down into the ravine. "Oh…my *God*," she murmured, pointing. "It's…it's…it's…"

Corey turned following her gaze. *Oh, fuck.* Duncan's words "run like hell" rattled around in her brain and she wanted to do just that.

"Let's get the hell out of here," she said quickly as she jerked Butch up ahead of her. He tried to kick her, and she responded with her own kick to his hamstring, causing him to fall to his knees again, his face planted against the rocks. By the time they got him out of the ravine, his face was bloody and swollen, the fight all but gone from him.

"Good Lord," Jean said as she rushed over to them. "What happened?"

"We need to get him out of here," Corey said, not explaining. "Help me get him on his horse."

"We're going back down to the valley, right?" Dana asked urgently as all three of them had to hoist Butch into the saddle. "Right? We're going back down?" she asked again when Corey didn't answer.

Corey took her by the shoulders, facing her. "You and Miss Jean take Butch down to the little creek. I'll be—"

"No! You're not staying up here by yourself." Dana pointed toward the ravine. "Whatever's in that…that *thing* is making Butch crazy. I'm not leaving without you."

"Goddamn it, Dana. There's no time to argue. You smell the decomp too. I've got to check it out," she said.

Dana's eyes were practically pleading. "Please come with us," she whispered. "You don't know what's up here."

Corey surprised herself by pulling Dana into a quick, tight hug. When she released her, she met her eyes, trying to reassure her that everything would be all right. "I'll be fine. I'll have Lucky with me. I've got to check it out, Dana. That's all I'm going to do. Then I'll be right behind you."

"You promise? You promise you won't do anything stupid?"

At that, Corey smiled. "I promise."

They loosened the rope around Butch and used it to tie him to the saddle. She took the reins from around his horse's neck and handed them to Dana once she'd gotten back on Gretchen.

"Don't stop at the little creek down there," Corey said. "Head back the way we came, toward Paradox Creek." When Dana would have protested, Corey walked closer, resting a hand on her thigh. "I'll be right behind you. But you need to get Butch as far away from here as possible."

Dana finally nodded. "Okay." She turned to go, then stopped Gretchen. "Please be careful."

"You too."

CHAPTER THIRTY-SIX

Dana took the lead, pulling Butch's horse behind her as they headed down the trail, back toward the valley. Jean was behind them, holding tight to Daisy's saddle. She expected Butch to protest, but he was mostly quiet, his head hanging low, his chin resting on his chest. She didn't understand him…not at all. Obviously *something* was affecting him. Maybe the same thing that had taken over Hal. But no…Hal hadn't really been Hal. Butch was still Butch. At least she hoped.

There were no words spoken between the three of them as the horses maneuvered their way down from the ridge. It seemed steeper on the way down, for some reason, and she was relieved when she saw the little creek come into view…Little Squaw Creek, according to Jean.

But as she'd learned, distances were hard to judge up here, and it seemed to take forever before they reached the creek. The three horses they'd left behind were still there, reminding her that they would need to lead them along too. She went to cross, but Gretchen lowered her head into the water, drinking thirstily.

"I guess we can stop for a minute," she said, glancing back at Jean. "You think that's safe?"

"I imagine so," Jean said, turning and looking behind them. "I hope the captain isn't long, though."

"You and me both," Dana murmured.

She got off Gretchen and walked over to Butch. She touched his leg, and he lifted his head. She could tell his eyes were still glazed and she wondered if he even knew where he was. But then he uttered the words she'd heard all day. Words she didn't want to ever hear again.

"We need to get up to the ridge," he said. "Something's up there."

"Yeah...we've already been. There's nothing up there. We're leaving," she said.

He sat up straighter. "No! There's something up there. I know it."

She looked at Jean, noting her worried look. "We'll go back tomorrow, Butch," she said, hoping to appease him. "Maybe we'll find it then. But it's getting late."

"There's still time. We should go up. There's something up on the ridge."

She stared at him, wishing the Butch she knew and loved would come back...but the eyes that she looked into weren't familiar to her in the least. She looked past him, to the trail that they'd just come down from, hoping to see Corey. After a few seconds, she let out a weary sigh, again glancing at Jean.

"I guess we should do as the captain said. Head back toward Paradox Creek."

Jean nodded. "Yes. She'll catch up with us. I have faith in her."

Dana went back to Gretchen and pulled herself back into the saddle. "I hope we don't get lost."

"No, we'll head to the other ridge of the canyon there," Jean said, pointing. "The creek flows along it. We won't get lost."

When they crossed the little creek, Dana again got off Gretchen and gathered the reins of the three horses. She was already pulling Butch and his horse behind her. Could Jean lead all three of them?

"Tie one to Butch's saddle," Jean suggested. "I'll take the other two."

Dana nodded. "Good idea."

Once they were on their way, she wondered if that was even necessary. The horses seemed to be as uneasy as she was, seemingly wanting to put distance between them and the ridge. She imagined the three horses would have followed along regardless if they were tied or not.

"You think the captain will be okay?" Jean asked after a while. "I thought she'd be down by now."

Dana glanced behind her, looking back toward the little creek. "Yeah, I thought we'd see her by now too."

She tried not to worry. She didn't want to upset Jean. But damn, she couldn't help it. Whatever that...that thing was down in the ravine, it wasn't something from *here*. And that scared the hell out of her.

* * *

Corey stood at the top of the ravine, looking down on...what? A fucking spaceship? She couldn't really wrap her mind around that thought and she tried to push it aside. She brought her binoculars to her eyes, scanning the area. It was obviously *something*, that was for sure. She adjusted the focus, thinking she was seeing things. Was that a door?

"God...what the hell?" she murmured nervously. She felt Lucky at her side, leaning against her leg. He was most likely as afraid as she was.

She continued to scan the area, stopping when she saw a discoloration on the rocks. Blood. Lots of it. But clouds were building to the west, obscuring the sun, making early shadows in the ravine. She lowered the binoculars, then walked back to her horse, Lucky right at her heels.

She swung up in the saddle, coaxing the horse around to the side. She needed to get to the other side of the ravine. She hoped there would be a place to cross, but if need be, they'd go down to the bottom and up the other side. As they walked the edge of the ravine, the smell of decomp nearly overwhelmed her. She did like Dana and Jean had done earlier, holding her shirt up over her mouth and nose, but it did little to suppress the smell.

The ravine ended abruptly and she wondered if the impact of the... the *craft* had created the ravine in the first place. She maneuvered her horse around to the back side, her mouth and nose still covered. She glanced down, seeing Lucky sticking close to her, the hair standing up on his back.

"That can't be good," she murmured to herself.

Her horse stopped, rearing his head up and down, refusing to go any farther. She finally saw what she'd been smelling. Bodies, not far from the craft. She slid out of the saddle, pausing to wrap the reins around a limb, not wanting her horse to take off without her.

She took a couple of steps closer, then turned. "Lucky, come on, boy," she said quietly, tapping her leg. For some reason, she felt better with him near.

She didn't need her binoculars to see, but she used them anyway. The bodies were laid out, in a neat line, next to each other. She gasped when she realized what their state was. They'd been eaten. Some partially. Some more than others. She counted twelve bodies, most still partly clothed. Five were wearing army fatigues. Three were covered in the remnants of flight suits. The other four appeared to be civilians.

"Jesus Christ," she whispered as she lowered the binoculars. That had to be the squad that was sent in. But there would have been ten, maybe twelve soldiers. Not just five. *Oh, God.* Where were the others? And how the hell did the helicopter crew get up here?

Her hands were shaking as she stared at the bodies. Were the others like Hal? Were they...were they out, looking for...for *what*?

She heard rocks falling—rustling—in the ravine and she jerked her head around, expecting to see...*something* coming for her. Lucky whimpered beside her, then growled as he took a step away, heading to her left. She stopped him with a hand on his head.

"I know, boy. I'm scared too. Let's get the hell out of here."

She hurried back to her horse, nearly embarrassed as she swung up onto the saddle. She was a soldier, for God's sake. A team leader. A captain. But none of her training had prepared her for *this*. She turned the horse around, kicking him hard, urging him into a gallop. Lucky darted ahead of her, leading the way. She swore she heard the craft shift, heard metal on metal, heard the creaking of hinges, and she imagined the door opening...imagined *things* coming out...looking for her, running after her. Had they heard her? Did they know she was there? She crouched low in the saddle, nearly hugging her horse's neck as they bolted off the ridge and down the side as if running from the devil himself.

When she heard thunder off in the distance, she slowed, only then daring to look behind her. The trail was simply a trail, looking as benign and nonthreatening as a trail could look. She slowed the horse to a walk, continuing to look behind her. A gust of wind whistled down the ridge, causing the brush to rustle around her. It was enough to send her on her way, and she gave her horse a kick, sending him hurrying down the trail once again.

When they got to the bottom and reached the creek, she expected to find Dana and Jean waiting for her. Even though she'd instructed Dana to keep going, she doubted that she would. She didn't know if she was glad she'd followed her order or sorry that she hadn't waited on her.

It had been a tough ride up and then down the ridge and she let her horse drink, even though she was anxious to catch up with the others.

Even Lucky seemed to be eager to get going. He'd only splashed into the creek long enough to lap up water, then had moved to the other side, waiting on her.

As soon as her horse lifted his head, Corey urged him across the creek. She broke out into a trot, glancing over her shoulder several times, making sure no one was following her. Lucky kept up with their pace, but she knew the dog must be exhausted. In the distance, she could see horses and she pulled her binoculars out, relieved to see Dana, Jean and Butch ahead of her. She slowed her pace, allowing Lucky to catch his breath. Dana was going slow, she noted, and she knew she'd catch them before they made Paradox Creek.

It was only then that she allowed her mind to contemplate what she'd seen. Yes, it appeared to be a spaceship, and God, she couldn't really believe she was thinking that. And, yes, obviously something was inside it. Were they using some kind of telepathy or something? Was that why Butch was so affected? But why only him? Why not all of them?

She didn't have a clue to the answer but judging by the indention in the ravine, the spacecraft had crash-landed, burrowing into the rocks. Even then, it appeared to be intact. It was like a thick disc, not quite like in the movies she remembered. There were wings on each side, but they were small in proportion to the craft, nothing like the wings you'd find on jets and planes.

She shook her head, trying to lose the image of the bodies all lined up in a row. But where were the others? Did they get away? Did they escape? Or were they like Hal? Were they…infected or something? Had their bodies been taken over? Was something killing them and then using their bodies?

"Jesus…you're thinking crazy stuff," she murmured. Yeah, she was. She also felt like she was in a goddamn movie. Unfortunately, she knew she *wasn't* in a movie.

This was really happening.

And she was honest enough with herself to admit that she was scared.

Scared to death.

CHAPTER THIRTY-SEVEN

Sutter stared at Duncan, his eyes glaring. "Where is your goddamn squad?" he asked tersely.

"I...I don't know, sir. We've had no—"

Sutter slammed his fist on his desk, causing a sheet of paper to flutter to the floor. "*Why* haven't you had communication, Duncan? That's what I want to know."

"They haven't checked in, sir," Duncan said for the third time. "I assume the solar transmitter is not working."

"Two days since we heard from them. They should have made it to the checkpoint by now."

"Yes, sir, they should have."

"And Conaway? Anything else from her?"

"No, sir."

Sutter paced beside his desk. He knew General Brinkley would be there within the hour, and he had nothing to give him. Not only did they have a missing helicopter and crew, now they had a missing squad as well. Conaway had given them some hope, at least. Her message on Saturday had been too garbled for them to make out much of it, but they knew she'd found the helicopter. There was no mention of her meeting up with the others, none that they could make out, anyway.

The only other words they got were something about following a creek and going up to a ridge. Duncan assumed the creek was Paradox Creek. But the ridge? It could be anywhere out there.

"Sir?"

Sutter turned slowly, almost forgetting that Duncan was still in his office.

"Do you think it's time to send in troops? I mean, maybe not a whole company, sir, but at least a platoon or two?"

"I imagine General Brinkley and I will discuss that," he said. "It's in the news now. We can't keep a lid on it any longer. Once they opened up the highway again, they got stalled cars going into Paradox, dead cell phones. Yeah, it's time to send troops in and see what the hell is going on." He sighed. "And we'll need to come up with a plan for damage control."

"I guess it'll be the true definition of foot soldiers then," Duncan said.

Sutter looked at him sharply. "Are you trying to be funny, Duncan? Are you making a joke about this?"

"No, sir. Of course not. I was just—"

"All of the damn technology we have at our disposal, none of it works inside this zone. We're not trained to operate that way, Duncan. There's got to be communication." He stared at him. "Why the hell can't we figure out something to use?"

"We tried the solar—"

"I know we tried the goddamn solar transmitter," he said loudly. "Find me something that *works*," he demanded.

"Yes, sir. They've been working on it, sir. So far—"

Sutter held up his hand, silencing Duncan. "Save it. I'm tired of excuses. General Brinkley is tired of excuses. The only saving grace we have with him is that we've had some communication from Conaway."

"Yes, sir," Duncan said obediently.

Sutter sighed. "Get out of here, Duncan. I'll let you know when Brinkley arrives. I'll let *you* brief him."

"Of course, sir."

Sutter sat down in his chair with another weary sigh. How could an obscure four-second blip on radar cause this much chaos?

CHAPTER THIRTY-EIGHT

At the sight of Corey riding toward them, Dana's relief was so profound, she hadn't realized how tense her body had been. She relaxed her shoulders and let out a thankful sigh. She didn't want to admit it, but she had been afraid Corey wouldn't make it back, had been afraid *something* would get her. Hurt her. Kill her.

God, stop it.

"Do you see the captain?" Jean called from behind her.

"I do," Dana said, trying not to let Jean see how worried she'd been. But she slowed her pace nonetheless, wanting Corey to catch up to them. It seemed like it had been hours since they'd left the ridge but with the clouds in the west, she had no way of knowing how low the sun really was. She stared at the dark clouds now, wondering if they'd get rain later…and hoping they wouldn't.

She glanced behind her, looking at Butch. He met her gaze, then blinked several times. He seemed to be coming back around. For that, she was very relieved. Even so, he hadn't spoken much, just a few repeated references about the ridge…and the mysterious *something* that was up there. Yeah, there was something up there, all right. And she wanted to get as far away from it as possible.

As Corey got closer to them, Dana finally stopped altogether, deciding to wait for her. She looked back at Jean, as if for confirmation.

Jean nodded. "Yes, let her catch up to us."

"I don't like being separated. I think we should stay together," she offered as an excuse.

Jean pushed at the gray hair around her ears, moving it away from her face. Her skin was red from their days in the sun, and Dana wondered why she hadn't brought a hat to wear.

"Are you going to tell me what you saw down in that ravine?" Jean asked.

Dana gave a shaky laugh. "I'm afraid to say it out loud," she admitted.

"The captain looked pretty shook up about it too. I imagine her fears were confirmed then."

Dana nodded. "It looked like...well, like something from a space movie," she said. She let her eyes drift to Butch. "And he was trying to get to it. Corey had to fight him."

Her words didn't seem to register with Butch, who made no comment. Or maybe they did register and he simply had no explanation.

"What do you think the captain will want to do now?" Jean asked.

"I hope we're getting the hell out of here," Dana said truthfully. "I don't mind saying, I'm plenty scared, Miss Jean."

Jean nodded slowly. "Yes, I think I'd like to get far away from here too." She looked at her thoughtfully. "But how far is far enough?"

Dana had no answer for her. Instead, she kept her gaze locked on Corey as she came closer, close enough now to make out her features. Close enough to see the concern etched on her face. And close enough to see that she had Lucky in the saddle with her.

Corey slowed her horse as she got nearer, her eyes finding Dana's. Dana held them, trying to read them. They were filled with worry, which in turn only heightened Dana's own anxiety. She said the first thing that came to mind.

"Are you okay?"

Corey nodded but didn't stop. "We should keep going."

"What...what did you see?"

Corey shook her head. "We'll talk later. Let's get to the creek and we'll rest there."

As they headed out again, Jean's voice broke the silence. "Is Lucky okay?"

"Yeah...he ran out of gas," Corey said. "I had a hell of a time getting him up here, though. He weighs close to a hundred pounds, I'd guess."

Lucky was practically lying in Corey's lap, his tongue hanging out as he panted. She imagined the dog was exhausted. They'd had quite a trek already today, not to mention him having to run up and then down the ridge.

There was no more conversation as they made their way slowly toward the creek. Corey turned around several times, looking behind them, and Dana wondered who or *what* she thought might be following them. At last, the dry, rocky and barren terrain turned green as they reached the valley grass that surrounded the creek. It was cooler near the water, and she was thankful to get out of the saddle for a bit.

"Untie Butch," Corey instructed. "I need him to help me get Lucky down."

Dana wasn't sure if it was safe to untie him, but she did as Corey asked. It was only then that Butch seemed to realize that he was even tied to the saddle in the first place.

"What's this?" he asked.

Dana met his gaze. "So you wouldn't get yourself killed," she said frankly.

He blinked at her several times. "Did I...did I freak out again?"

"Yeah, you did. And it's a good thing we don't have a mirror." She stepped back, letting him get out of the saddle.

While he walked over to Corey to take Lucky from her, Dana went over to Jean and helped her down.

"Thank you," Jean murmured. "I'd be hard-pressed to do that on my own."

Dana noticed that Jean seemed to have aged years since they'd first met her. Her shoulders were curved, and she leaned forward as she walked, her steps shuffling.

"Are you okay?" Dana asked quietly. "Sore?"

Jean nodded. "I guess I was a little ambitious when thinking I could still ride a horse. My back doesn't seem to want to straighten up."

But she was smiling, and Dana followed her gaze, landing on Lucky. He was lying down in the water, lapping at it as it flowed by. Dana was thirsty too, and she took one of the bottles from the pack on her saddle, drinking a few swallows before putting it back.

Corey was kneeling by the creek, splashing her face and head with water. Then she stood, wiping her hands over her wet hair, front to back. Dana walked over to her.

"Are we in trouble?" she asked quietly.

Corey nodded. "Yeah, I think so."

Dana met her eyes. "What did you find?" Dana thought she might not answer her as Corey's gaze looked past her, back toward the ridge. But she turned to her again.

"Bodies. Twelve of them. The three crew from the helicopter, four civilians and five...five from the other squad that was sent in," Corey said, her voice cracking with emotion. "They'd been...well, they'd been partially eaten."

Dana gasped. "*Eaten?*"

"That's what it looked like to me," Corey said.

"Dear God," Dana whispered. "What are we going to do?"

"The squad would have had ten or twelve soldiers," Corey said. "So...the others either escaped or..."

Dana reached out and grasped her arm. "Or? Or they're like Hal? They could come for us?"

Corey nodded. "Yeah. So we need to get away from here. And fast."

"Good. You won't have any argument from me," she said as she took a step away. "In fact, let's go right now."

Corey stopped her when she turned. "How's Butch?"

"Quiet. I doubt he has any recollection of what happened," she said.

"The farther away we get from the ridge, the less hold it'll have on him," Corey said. "At least I hope so. It's like...some kind of thought transference, like telepathy or something."

Dana nodded. "Like something takes over his mind, his body. Why only him? Why not all of us?"

Corey shrugged. "I don't have a clue." She gave Dana a nervous laugh. "And I don't want to find out."

Dana's eyes bored into hers, and she again reached out and touched her arm. "You're scared," she said. It was a statement, not a question. "I'm terrified myself, Corey. Please...you can't be scared too. We need you to get us out of here."

Corey took a deep breath and nodded. "I'll do my best."

CHAPTER THIRTY-NINE

If Corey had to do it all over again, she'd have insisted that the others stay at Jean's house. Or even better, head back to Paradox and find shelter there. She imagined that Anna Gail would have put them up, even if there were protests from her husband. But she hadn't insisted, and there was no point in using hindsight now. Of course, if she were being completely honest, she was glad that they were with her. After what she'd seen on the ridge, her imagination was running wild as it was. Maybe it was the old safety in numbers theory, but she felt a little more in control—of herself and the situation—having Dana, Jean and Butch with her. And Lucky, she added, as she glanced at the dog that was alternating between walking beside her horse and jumping in the creek.

The clouds that had rolled in earlier were moving off, taking the threat of rain with them. The sun peeked out from time to time, brightening the day. While it wouldn't be long before sunset, it wasn't quite as late as she'd thought. They needed to get much farther away from the ridge before they stopped for the night. Of course the prospect of spending a night out, with them again taking turns at keeping watch, was not very appealing. Especially not when she wasn't sure if she could trust Butch. And certainly not after…well, not after what she'd seen up there. She turned and glanced behind her,

her eyes drawn to the ridge. It still seemed so close. *Too* close. Because whatever was up there, if it was indeed a...a spaceship of some kind, then the occupants were definitely not friendly. She wondered how long it'd be before General Brinkley sent in troops. Hell, she didn't even know what day it was. How much longer would Harry wait on communication from her? She hoped he'd already given up on her and had given the go-ahead to send in help. Although help would be on foot and it could take days before they showed up out here. They probably didn't have days.

No, she thought their best bet was to get back to Paradox and wait for help. They were out of food, except for three measly meals that she still had. Maybe Lucky would scare up a rabbit. She figured Dana would be hungry enough to eat it.

She pushed her thoughts away as she looked behind them once again. It was only then that she noticed that the sun had disappeared behind the ridge. They'd still have a good hour of daylight before the shadows crept in. That should get them far enough away. The problem would be finding a place to camp where there was enough firewood to last through the night. There were pockets of trees along the creek, but most of them were young cottonwoods and they weren't dropping limbs.

She turned around one more time to look behind them, then did a double take. She frowned and narrowed her eyes, trying to make out what the movement was.

"What is it?" Dana asked.

Corey reached for her binoculars. "Thought I saw something," she said as she pulled her horse to a stop and turned around, facing the ridge. Her eyes widened as she saw three people running, coming toward them. She looked past them, wondering if something was chasing them, but there was no movement anywhere behind them. She was about to tell the others when she looked again. Yeah, they were running. But they were as fast as a horse.

"Is that somebody running?" Dana asked.

"Jesus...*Christ*," Corey muttered as she continued to stare through the binoculars.

"They're running pretty fast, aren't they?" Butch asked as he, too, held binoculars to his eyes.

"Corey?"

She finally lowered her binoculars and turned to the others. "Three people, two wearing army fatigues. The other a civilian, an older woman." She glanced at Jean. "A woman about your age. Gray hair, looks like it's pulled back in a knot or something."

"Looks like Rebecca Milstead," Butch said.

Jean looked back at her with frightened eyes. "Yes, that sounds like Rebecca, Carl's wife. She has long gray hair that she always twists up into a bun," she said. "But she can't run. She had hip surgery not more than two months ago. She was still using a cane to get around."

"Oh, God," Dana said. "That means—"

"That we need to get the hell out of here," Corey said. "And fast."

They kicked their horses into a gallop, but as she looked over her shoulder, she could tell that they were gaining on them. If anything, they appeared to be running faster now. But how could that be?

"Keep going," she yelled as she pulled her horse to a stop again.

"No! We stay together," Dana yelled back at her as she, too, pulled Gretchen to a stop.

"Goddamn it, Dana…get the hell out of here!"

She took one more look with her binoculars, thinking that the people chasing them looked like ragdolls running, their legs flopping about as they practically flew across the ground.

"Corey…come on," Butch said urgently. "Let's go."

"They're going to catch us," she said quickly. She pulled out her gun. "Keep going," she said. "I'll take care of them."

"Corey, no," Dana said.

"Go!" she said more forcefully, pointing ahead of them.

"Dana, let's do as the captain says," Jean said, her voice shaking with fear.

Butch pulled his rifle out. "I'll stay too."

Corey glared at him. "You ever shot anybody, Butch? This isn't a goddamn movie. Now get the hell out of here. You take care of Dana and Miss Jean. Let me do my job."

He nodded curtly, then turned his horse, tugging two of the extras behind him. Dana held the reins of the third horse, but she stopped and looked back at her.

"I'll be so pissed if something happens to you."

Corey gave her a quick smile. "Not half as pissed as I'll be." She motioned to the others, who had already headed out. "Go on. Take Lucky with you. I'll catch up."

She didn't wait for a reply. She turned and headed back the way they'd come, shocked to see how close the three were to her already. She rode fast, straight at them, only then noticing that two of them had weapons dangling at their sides. When she felt she was close enough, she took aim with her Glock, praying the shot wouldn't spook her horse.

She fired six rounds in rapid succession, knocking all three to the ground. Her horse reared up, kicking his front feet out, and she held on tightly, trying to steady him. He danced excitedly, his hooves pounding the ground, causing dust to stir around them. She urged him closer, seeing one of the soldiers moving and trying to sit up. There was no blood on any of them so she had no qualms about shooting them again. She managed a shot to the head for each of them before her horse twirled around, trying to toss her off.

"Easy, boy," she said. "It's okay. All over with."

But he wouldn't settle down so she turned him and gave him a swift kick. He took off like a lightning bolt, nearly losing her in the process. She let him run as she bent low in the saddle, her face nearly touching his mane as they galloped through the valley, trying to catch up with the others.

* * *

"Here she comes," Dana said as she pulled Gretchen to a stop. "Thank God."

She looked over at Jean, whose knuckles were white as she gripped the saddle horn. She didn't even have a hold of Daisy's reins but thankfully Daisy had stopped.

"You okay, Miss Jean?"

Jean shook her head. "No. I'm scared."

Dana nodded. "Me too."

"I counted nine shots," Butch said. "You think she killed them?"

"I don't know. I hope so," she said, not caring how callous that sounded.

Corey slowed her horse as she got closer, finally bringing him down to a trot, then a fast walk. The white stallion was breathing hard and foam flew from his mouth as he shook his head several times. Dana met Corey's gaze, wanting to ask a hundred questions.

"I think they've been disabled," Corey said. She looked over at Jean. "They were like Hal. There was no blood when I shot them."

"Oh, dear Lord," Jean murmured. "And Rebecca was one of them. That means that...that Carl must have gone to her like my Hal came to me."

Corey nodded. "I have no idea what's happening here or what we're up against. My guess is they sent a squad of ten, possibly twelve soldiers in to look for the helicopter. Five were dead, up on the ridge. This is two more. So if we assume ten, then three are unaccounted for."

"Carl is unaccounted for too," Butch said. "Right? If he...if he visited Rebecca like we think."

"He could have visited all of our neighbors by now," Jean said, her voice cracking. "God only knows how many of them there are. They could be out here...watching us, waiting for us."

Dana heard the fear in her voice but didn't know what to say to ease it. Hell, she was eaten up with fear too. Not just fear for themselves—fear for her parents, fear for Butch's parents as well.

"We keep going," Corey said. "We ride all night."

"Where to?" Dana asked.

"We're going back to Jean's place."

"Do you think it's safe?"

Corey nodded. "It's safer than being out here, that's for sure. We need a place to rest and we need some food. We can get both of those at Jean's."

"Then what?"

"We'll decide that once we get there," Corey said.

"We should go back to Paradox," Butch said.

"That's probably safest," Corey said. "Or we can try to reach the checkpoint."

"Where they dropped you off?" Dana asked.

"Yes. I'm guessing it was at least thirty miles or more down that road, though," Corey said. "Maybe more. Unless we really push the horses, that means we'd have to camp at least one night."

"I'm not crazy about that idea," Dana said honestly. "I say we push the horses."

"Yeah. And I'm not crazy about riding into Paradox only to find out that Carl Milstead beat us there."

Without another word, Corey gave her horse a nudge, riding past her. Dana sighed. What the hell had they gotten themselves into? She should have taken her mother's advice and stayed with them. She'd be completely oblivious to what was happening out here then. That is, until someone—some*thing*—came up to the house.

Of course, that thought made her worry more for her parents. What if Carl Milstead hadn't gone into Paradox? What if he'd gone past the road to Paradox and continued on to her parents' farm?

She squeezed her eyes shut for a moment, pushing those thoughts away. Her parents were safe. Surely, they were safe.

CHAPTER FORTY

Anna Gail made her way to the back door of the store with supper, as had been her custom for the last several evenings. She knew Richard was inside, facing the front door, a rifle in his lap, scaring away any potential customers. Of course, she relieved him in the mornings and she always propped the front doors open invitingly. Their neighbors would come by then, picking up a few items which they promised to pay for later. She had no problem with writing IOUs. But really, most who came by didn't really come to shop. Most came to gossip and complain that the power wasn't back on yet. She assumed that most missed having TV or, like Holly, missed their fancy cell phones.

She knocked twice on the back door before opening it.

"Richard, it's me," she called.

She brought her picnic basket to the counter, not even noticing that Richard hadn't so much as looked her way yet. Tonight's supper was simple and everything out of cans. Richard always thought she fussed over this casserole whenever she made it, but elbow macaroni and a can of chili was the base to which she added beans, tomatoes and corn and lots of cheese. Richard loved it, so whenever she wasn't in the mood to cook or lacked the time to put out a proper meal, this was her fallback.

She finally realized that Richard hadn't spoken, and she glanced over at him, seeing him staring out the windows.

"What is it?" she asked.

"Carl Milstead from over in Squaw Valley," Richard said, motioning outside. "Walking down the street like he's in a hurry."

Anna Gail followed his gaze. It wasn't dark yet, but evening was fast approaching. "I wonder where he's going at this hour?"

"Looks like he's heading over to the feed store."

"You think Tommy is still open?"

"He sleeps there," Richard said. "They'd have stole him blind if not."

"Oh, Richard," Anna Gail said with a shake of her head. "Carl looks filthy, doesn't he? You think they're without water up there too?"

"Hell, he's got the creek right there by the house," he said. "You'd think he would have at least cleaned up before he came to town."

Anna Gail went back to her picnic basket, pulling out the still-warm casserole. "You don't think he walked all this way, do you?"

"He's got horses. Why would he walk?"

Anna Gail shrugged and scooped out a large portion of the casserole onto a plate and handed it to him.

"Where's Holly? She over at the neighbor's again?"

"No. She's at the house, cleaning up the kitchen. I told her I'd come back and have dinner with her. I want to get back before dark."

He nodded as he took a bite, his moan telling her that he liked it. Richard was never much for compliments, but his quiet moan was enough for her.

Anna Gail looked back out the window, but Carl was out of sight. "We should have called Carl over and asked if he ran into Butch and those gals," she said.

Richard shook his head. "No need for him to come over. He'll probably want to come in and take food."

"Well, if they need food, we'll write up a receipt like we've done for the others," she said.

"We're never going to see a dime of that and you know it."

It was a statement he said frequently, and now, as usual, she ignored it. It did no good to contradict him. He wasn't going to change his tune.

"If you're ready for lights, I'll get the generator going," she said, already heading out to the back to start it. They ran it periodically now. They didn't have much left in the coolers and what they could, they froze. The freezers were holding up, even running it as sparingly as they did.

The generator cranked on the first pull, and she noticed that Richard had chained it and the three gas containers to the post in the back, as if thinking someone would come by to steal it. She didn't know of a single person in town who didn't already have a generator and now that Gilbert had his pumps working, no one would run out of fuel. What Richard was so paranoid about, she couldn't fathom.

Darkness was settling around her, and she knew she needed to hurry if she was to make it back home before full dark. She went back inside to get the casserole dish before taking her leave.

"I'll take another helping of that," Richard said, holding his plate out to her.

"Sure. There's plenty," she said as she scooped out another large serving.

She'd just handed the plate back to him when the bell jingled over the front door. Carl Milstead stood there, staring at them.

"Oh, my goodness," she said before she could stop herself. He smelled something awful, and she very nearly covered her nose and mouth from the stench. His clothes were absolutely filthy, and the smell reminded her of when that old white dog of theirs had rolled in that deer carcass one year. They couldn't stand to be around him for nearly a week.

"Damn, Carl, you smell like you haven't bathed in a month or more," Richard said bluntly. "Get the hell out of my store."

Anna Gail frowned as Carl stood there, staring at Richard as if he didn't hear him. Then…quick as a cat, Carl lunged at Richard, his hands going around Richard's neck, choking him as Richard's arms flailed around, hitting Carl hopelessly on his shoulders. Anna Gail dropped the casserole dish and screamed as she ran toward Carl. She grasped his arm, but Carl flung her hard against the wall as if she was nothing more than a fly he'd swatted away. She felt herself falling, sliding down the wall as if in slow motion. She tried to hold on to consciousness even as the light started to fade around her. She watched in disbelief as Carl Milstead tossed Richard's limp body over his shoulder and hauled him out into the night. As her eyes started to close, she knew what she'd seen was impossible. Richard was thirty years younger and at least fifty pounds heavier than Carl Milstead.

But she could hold on no longer, and she surrendered to the blackness, falling into an unconscious heap on the floor.

CHAPTER FORTY-ONE

Corey was dog-tired and knew the others were as well. She'd tried to keep the conversation going, hoping to keep them from falling asleep in their saddles. However, what little conversation she tried was met with fewer and fewer replies. They'd stopped several times to rest and walk around a little. The moon was a little brighter, nearly half-full, and it cast enough light for them to see. Following the creek had been easy, but they had the deep canyon to navigate. Butch suggested they head up to the Jeep road on the ridge and that had taken them awhile to reach the top. Once on the road, conversation again ceased and she finally gave up. Once past the canyon, they could have gone back down and followed the creek again—it would have been shorter. They decided to stay on the road, thinking it was safer than trying to get down the steep embankment in the dark.

She looked up into the sky now, guessing it was two or three in the morning. Their pace was slow and methodical. Even Lucky was laboring as he followed along beside her. She'd thought about stopping and taking him into the saddle with her, but they were getting close and she didn't want to take the time.

After what seemed an eternity, Jean—who Corey suspected was nearly asleep—pointed weakly ahead of them.

"There's the road. We're almost there."

The Jeep road dumped into the county road they'd taken that first day when she, Butch and Dana had left Paradox heading to Squaw Valley. If her memory was right, they'd pass the Milsteads' place first.

"It's so dark...and quiet," Jean said. "I don't guess I've ever been out here this late at night."

"Or maybe this early in the morning," Corey corrected.

"Wonder what time it is? I feel like I could sleep for a couple of days," Dana said. "After I eat, of course. Don't know about the rest of you, but I'm starving."

"Yeah. Let's hope Jean still has something left in her freezer."

"The chest freezer in the utility room has plenty of food," Jean said. "It may be starting to thaw by now, but it should still be okay, I'd think."

Corey's stomach rumbled at the thought of food. She couldn't decide what she wanted more...sleep or a meal.

When they passed the lane that would lead to the Milsteads' place, all four of them looked down it. Corey wondered what they might be expecting but all was quiet. They kept going and before too long, they came upon Jean's lane. The trees that lined the road cast shadows and blocked out the moon's light, but Lucky led the way and the horses followed behind. She could almost feel the tension leave them when Jean's house came into view.

"Didn't know I'd miss the old place so much," Jean said as they neared. "Wonder how my chickens made out? Hadn't seen a fox in a while but that doesn't mean they're not around."

"I hope there are plenty of eggs to choose from," Dana said. "I wouldn't mind three or four for breakfast."

"No wonder you gained seven pounds," Butch said with a laugh.

"I'm fairly certain I've lost every bit of that and more on this trip," Dana replied.

"And you didn't even have to succumb to eating a rabbit," Corey added.

Dana laughed. "I'm so hungry, I'd eat one right now."

They stopped in the front and unloaded their packs, dropping them on the ground beside the horses.

"Miss Jean, if you and Dana could get the generator going, I'll help Butch with the horses," Corey said.

"I think sleep is going to win out over food," Dana said around a yawn. "Shocking, I know, but I think I'm too tired to eat anything."

"Yeah. Go get some rest," Corey said. "We'll have to take turns keeping watch. Just in case," she added.

"We're all exhausted," Dana said.

"I'll take first watch," she said. "We can't take a chance, Dana. We don't know what's out there."

Dana nodded. "Okay. You're right. We'll take turns."

Corey and Butch led all seven horses to the barn, with Lucky walking beside them. The moon was getting lower and she thought it wouldn't be long before it dropped out of sight...taking what little light there was with it.

They didn't take much care with the saddles, simply hanging them across the board fence that lined the enclosed pen.

"There was hay left in the stalls," Butch said. "I imagine they'll find it if they're hungry."

"It'll be daybreak in a few hours," she said. "We can check on them then."

They heard the rumbling of the generator and saw lights come on inside Jean's house. It was a welcome sight, for sure.

"Come on. I'm ready to get inside," she said, turning to go.

"Hey...I need to apologize," he said.

She stopped. "Why?"

"For getting all crazy on you again."

She tilted her head, trying to read his expression in the darkness. "Do you remember anything?"

He shrugged. "Not really. My face hurts, though. Did you punch me?"

She smiled quickly. "You took an elbow to the chin. I'm afraid the rest of the damage was done by you falling on rocks." Her smile faded quickly. "I'm not sure why it affects you and not me. Or Dana and Jean either," she said. "The closer we got to the ridge, the more obsessed you became with it. When we got close, we could all tell that you weren't really *with* us, if you know what I mean."

"I remember camping at the creek. I remember feeling this...this pull, this overwhelming feeling that I had to get to the ridge. Like something was pushing me, guiding me up there. I don't really remember anything else until you rode up with Lucky in your lap and I was tied to my saddle."

"By that time, we'd already been to the ridge and back."

"What was up there?"

"What we feared," she said evenly. "I found twelve bodies."

"Twelve?"

"Most military, four civilians. Probably the men who were with Hal," she said. "They're...they're using them for food, it seems."

Butch gasped. "What the hell? But I thought they…I don't know…took over their bodies or something. Hal was—"

"They obviously use some of them…hell, Butch, I don't know," she said as she ran her fingers through her hair. "I'm just shooting in the dark here, but it's like they use their bodies as some sort of vessel or something."

"They kill them, then…then what? Get inside them? But they're *dead*. How can they—"

"I don't know. This is so far out of my realm, I can't even take an educated guess," she said honestly.

Butch stared at her. "We keep saying 'they' but what the hell *are* they?"

Corey reached down and stroked Lucky's head as he leaned heavily against her leg. "I don't know what they are and I sure as hell don't want to find out."

When they got back in the house, the kitchen was empty. Corey had a moment of panic, her eyes darting around. Then she heard movement down a hallway and followed the sound. Jean was staring into her chest freezer. She glanced up at them and gave a weary smile.

"For the first time that I can ever remember, I don't know what to cook."

Corey went closer and closed the freezer. "You're exhausted, Miss Jean. Go get some sleep. I'll take kitchen duty."

"I'm too tired to argue with you, Captain."

Corey smiled gently at her. "I assume Dana's already in bed. You go too. I'll try not to mess up your kitchen." As Jean shuffled off, she turned to Butch. "You should get some rest too. I'll need to be relieved soon."

"You sure? I can stay up with you," he offered.

"Sleep on the couch. At least you'll be close by if I need you."

He didn't protest. "If you find yourself falling asleep, you come wake me."

"I will."

She and Lucky went back into the kitchen, and she sat down heavily in a chair. Lucky laid down on the floor beside her. She imagined he was as hungry as the rest of them, probably more so.

"Wonder where she keeps your dog food?" she asked. "Bet you'd probably rather eat people food anyway," she murmured as her hand again found his fur. It was comforting, somehow, to run her fingers through his thick coat.

She rubbed her eyes with her other hand, trying to convince herself she wasn't as tired as she felt. It wasn't so much the hours she'd been awake. She'd pulled forty-eight hours before. No, it wasn't the hours. It was the situation, the stress—fear of the unknown—and the responsibility she felt for these three people who had banded with her. How many days now? Had it been a week? More? She was too tired to try to count back, too tired to care. It didn't really matter anyway. They had become her team and she felt responsible for them. They had formed a bond in a very short time, and she felt the need to protect them all. She only wished she knew what enemy they were up against. Because of that, she wasn't so sure going back to Paradox was the best option. They didn't know what they'd find there. No, she needed to get to the checkpoint. She needed to let Brinkley—Sutter—know what they were up against. Then whoever he sent in wouldn't be coming in blind. That is, if he hadn't already sent in another squad into the zone.

She blew out her breath, then stood. She needed something to occupy herself or she'd fall asleep sitting in the damn chair.

"So let's cook something."

She went back to the freezer and opened it, finding it well stocked. She thought some sort of a casserole would be safe to make. She took out a package of ground beef, then found a smaller package and took that as well. It was on top and starting to thaw already. Back in the kitchen, she unwrapped the packages and put the meat in a cast-iron skillet, then put that in the oven, hoping to speed up the thawing process.

She was thankful when the gas oven turned on. She'd feared that Jean had blown out the pilot light when they'd left the other day. She then turned her attention to the pantry. She found a bag of rice and a box of macaroni pasta. Either would serve the purpose, she supposed. She looked through the cans, picking up a cream of mushroom soup. Two shelves of the pantry held homemade canned goods, and she turned them around, finding what she thought were stewed tomatoes.

She rolled her eyes. The concoction she was contemplating didn't even sound good, despite how hungry she was.

"There are onions in the bin," Jean said from behind her.

Corey turned and smiled at her. "Can't stand someone in your kitchen, huh?"

Jean gave her a tired smile. "What are you planning on whipping up there?"

"Some sort of casserole, I guess," she said. "I thought it'd be easier to feed the four of us that way." She pointed to the oven. "Got ground beef in there thawing."

Jean nodded. "Let me help you."

"You should be resting."

"I think I'm too tired to sleep," Jean said as she picked up the coffeepot from the top of the stove and went about filling it with water. "My old bones have been rattled around more these last few days then they have in the last twenty years."

"I was just thinking that I feel so exhausted, not because of the number of hours that I've been up, but rather the stress of the situation we find ourselves in," she said. "But for you, I guess that stress is doubly so. None of us have lost a loved one."

"To be honest with you, Captain, it hasn't really set in yet that my Hal is gone. I'm seventy-five years old. I met him when I was but fourteen. It's hard for me to even remember a time when Hal wasn't in my life," Jean said. She shuffled to the table and sat down. "I reckon I'll grieve properly once this is over with. Then I'll have to face my boys. How can I possibly tell them that I shot their daddy?"

Corey said down opposite her at the table. "I mean no disrespect here, Miss Jean, but the thing you shot might have looked like Hal, but it wasn't him. It wasn't human. Not any longer."

Jean met her gaze. "Do you know what's happening here, Captain?"

"Not really, no."

"What did you find up there on the ridge? I know you must have told Dana. She doesn't hide her emotions very well."

"She's scared like the rest of us, I guess."

"I've seen enough dead animals in my life to recognize the smell that was up on the ridge," Jean said. "But I'm guessing whatever you found wasn't an animal. You said something about seeing five of that squad you said they sent in."

Corey hadn't had any intention of telling Jean what she'd seen up there, but perhaps she should. It might do her good to know that at least Hal hadn't been dinner for whatever the hell was in that spaceship.

"What was it?"

Corey got up, retrieving the coffeepot that had been percolating on the stove. She took down two cups and filled them both.

"There were twelve bodies up there. Three were from the helicopter crew. And the five from the team, yes." She set the cup down in front of her. "The other four were civilians. Males, best I could tell."

Jean sipped from her coffee. "The men that went with Hal." It was more of a statement than a question.

"Most likely," she said. She held the coffee cup between her hands, enjoying the warmth. "They met with a worse ending than Hal, I think."

"What do you mean?"

"They were eaten," she said. "At least, that's what it looked like to me."

Jean's hand was shaking, and she spilled coffee on her table. She didn't seem to notice. "Maybe wild animals…maybe coyotes or something found them."

Corey shook her head. "They were very near the…the aircraft that we found. They were neatly laid out in a row."

Jean took a steadying breath. "Aircraft?"

Corey shrugged. "I thought that sounded a little saner than saying spaceship."

"So it was? A real life UFO? Like in the movies?"

Corey nodded slowly. "Yeah. Like in the movies."

Jean closed her eyes for a moment. "Lordy, what have we gotten ourselves into?"

Corey reached across the small table and took her hand, feeling how frail it felt in her own. "I'm going to do my very best to get us out of this mess, Miss Jean. It's mostly my fault we're in it in the first place."

Jean squeezed her hand tightly. "It's not your fault, Captain. Don't blame yourself."

Corey pulled her hand away. "I shouldn't have ever insisted that Butch and Dana bring me here. They wanted to head in the opposite direction, toward some saline plant out there," she said with a wave of her hand. "They'd be safe then. They wouldn't be mixed up in this. *You* wouldn't be mixed up in this."

"You were only doing your job, weren't you? Following orders? And I'd have been left here all alone if you hadn't shown up. Who knows if I'd even still be here? Maybe Rebecca or Carl would have come…" Jean's voice faded and she shook her head. "You had no way of knowing all this would happen," she said reasonably. When she picked up her cup, her hand was no longer shaking. "You said you'd been in the military your whole life, that you wanted to be like your father. Yet I sense it's more than that." She put her cup down again. "You want to be *better* than your father?"

Corey was shocked at Jean's astuteness. It was something she'd barely even admitted to herself, let alone another person. Jean's eyes held hers, the wisdom of her years showing in that simple glance.

"My father was a highly decorated soldier," she said. "And yes, I wanted to be like him." She pushed her coffee cup away from her, staring past Jean as she recalled all the times he'd missed her birthday, missed Christmas or missed a soccer game. She brought her eyes back to Jean. "I worshipped him, yet I was…invisible to him." It was something she'd thought often enough but saying it out loud brought tears to her eyes. "He wanted a son to follow in his footsteps. I tried my best to be that son for him." Jean's glance moved to her hair, and Corey self-consciously ran a hand over it. "Yeah…my hair too."

"It's grown on me," Jean said with a smile.

Corey wiped at tear that had escaped her eye. "I never knew if he was proud of me or not," she said. "I hoped he was but he never said. But he was killed…over in Iraq. My career was just starting, really. After he died…well, yeah, I wanted to be better than him. A better soldier, a better *person*."

"Are you married? Do you have a family?"

Corey smiled quickly and stood up, going for more coffee. "No, no. Not married. My mother remarried. Actually, she married pretty quickly after he died. It was a bit of a challenging time for us," she admitted. She refilled Jean's cup. "I realize now that as bad of a father as he was, he was probably much worse as a husband."

"Our perception of things when we're young does tend to change with age," Jean said. She stared at her intently, her eyes not showing the weariness of earlier. "So you're not married and don't have a family of your own. You've made the military your life then?"

"It's what a lot of us do. To be a good soldier—the *best* soldier—it's what you must do. My father knew that too. Only he could never cut the ties with my mother and me."

"That sounds like a sad, lonely life to me," Jean said.

Corey shrugged. "I'm used to it."

"We all need love, Captain. We all need…*someone*."

"I don't know. Do we? I've made it this far without it."

Jean stared at her for a long, uncomfortable moment, and Corey wondered what she was thinking. Jean finally pushed herself up, leaning heavily on the table for support.

"I guess that meat is thawed out enough," she said. "I best see what I can whip up."

Corey nodded but said nothing. Then Jean turned, meeting her gaze again.

"I think Dana was asleep even before her head hit the pillow," Jean said. "Maybe at daybreak, you could go out to the barn and fetch us some eggs." She took the skillet from the oven. "After we eat, you need to get your own rest, Captain."

"As do you." She watched as Jean put the soup can and tomatoes back into the pantry. "What are you going to make?"

"I thought I'd make a breakfast casserole," Jean said. "I'll doctor up this beef and use it instead of sausage. I'll make a biscuit batter and mix that with eggs and this meat. That ought to bake up just fine. I think I'll make up a little gravy to go with it too. Hal always loved my gravy."

Before long, Jean was chopping up an onion and browning the meat on the stove. The smell made Corey's stomach growl. Even Lucky was brought out of a deep sleep by the aroma wafting through the kitchen.

"Best feed Lucky something or he'll be begging us later," Jean warned. "I keep his food in the closet there by the back door," she said, motioning with her head. "His bowl is still out back, I guess."

Corey got up and went out the kitchen door to retrieve his bowl. While still dark, the sky was beginning to lighten toward the east. To the west, the sky was dark and clear and filled with stars, the moon having set not long after they'd gotten there. She stood outside, looking up into the sky, listening to the quiet...listening to nothing. Then off in the distance, down by the creek, an owl hooted in the trees. A moment later, another answered, his call fainter than the first and farther away. Back and forth they went and she closed her eyes, feeling a little peace settle around her, if only for a few minutes.

CHAPTER FORTY-TWO

Dana moaned quietly, hanging in that tiny space that separates sleep and wakefulness. It was a dream she'd had before, many times. But it felt different this time. Warm, soft. Comfortable and natural. Her hips moved, instinctively trying to find purchase against the body that was pressed close to her. Yes, a delicious dream. Only this time, her dream lover wasn't faceless…wasn't nameless. She knew exactly who she was.

The throbbing between her thighs chased the dream away, bringing her closer to wakefulness. She tried to hold on to it a little longer but her eyes fluttered open.

Jesus Christ.

Not a dream. She was clutching a real live person to her. A person who was watching her with tired, but amused eyes.

"I'm so sorry," she murmured quickly as she moved away from Corey.

"Dreaming about your wedding night?" Corey asked quietly. "What was her name again?"

Dana blushed as she moved even farther away from her. "Kendra. And no, I wasn't dreaming about *her*." Their eyes held and Dana felt herself blush even more. "Well, this is embarrassing," she said as she moved to the edge of the bed. Then she stopped. "Wait a minute. Where are my clothes?"

Corey's eyes closed. "I found you on top of the bed. I thought you'd be more comfortable without your jeans...and under the covers," she said sleepily.

"That was sweet of you," Dana said as she stood up, standing there in nothing but a dirty T-shirt and her underwear. Then she frowned. "Wait a minute," she said again. "You're *clean*."

Corey's eyes blinked open for a second and she smiled slightly. "Shower," she mumbled.

"Oh, that is so not fair."

Corey smiled, but her eyes remained closed. "Be quiet."

Dana smiled too, taking a few seconds to stare at her. Corey's face looked relaxed for once, and Dana noted again how attractive she was. With a quick sigh, she turned, but Corey's hand reached out and grabbed her wrist.

"With luck, maybe I'll dream about you too," she whispered, her eyes still closed.

Oh, God. Dana bit her lip, watching as Corey's hand slipped away. She could tell that Corey had already fallen asleep. Her eyes roamed over her again, then she made herself turn away.

"No, no...this is *so* not the time for this," she whispered to herself as she picked up her dirty jeans and quietly left the room, closing the door behind her.

In the hallway, she pulled on her jeans, then walked barefoot into the kitchen. Butch was sitting at the table drinking coffee. His rifle was across his lap, and he turned when she came in.

"Good morning," he said.

"You've showered too," she said accusingly.

He smiled. "Yeah. And it was great. I'll turn the generator back on if you want to go grab one."

She looked at the dish on the stove, and her stomach growled. "As soon as I eat something," she said, pausing to take a nibble off one corner. "What is it? It looks good."

"Jean called it a breakfast casserole. It's pretty good."

Dana took a plate out and put a generous helping on it, then scooped a ladle full of gravy and put that on top. She filled a coffee cup and joined Butch at the table. She studied him for a moment.

"Your face doesn't look as bad as I thought it would. A few bruises," she said.

"Not too sore," he said. "Corey got me pretty good on my chin, though."

Dana took a bite of the casserole and moaned loudly. "Oh, God… this is delicious. I'm glad she made a big pan. I'll probably eat half of it. This is the best gravy." Then she stopped chewing and sniffed the air. "But what's that I smell?"

Butch laughed. "She's got a big roast in the oven. Now *that* looked good."

"There goes my seven pounds," she said around another bite. She looked out the window at the bright sunshine. "What time do you think it is?"

"I don't know. Nine…ten, maybe."

"Corey stayed up a long time then. Did Jean stay up with her?"

"Jean was already in bed when Corey woke me." He pushed his coffee cup aside and stood up. "I should go check on the horses," he said. "Make sure they have water."

She nodded. "How long do you think we'll stay here?"

He shrugged. "Don't know. But she needs more than a few hours' sleep. The horses need some rest too."

She stopped to sip her coffee. "You think we'll stay another night?"

"I guess we'll have to wait and see. If it's late afternoon, I don't see the point of heading out, only to have to stop a few hours later. Unless she plans to ride all night again."

"I'm not really crazy about that," she said. "That was a little spooky last night."

"If we left early, we could make it to Paradox easy in one day," he said.

"Corey didn't really sound like she wanted to go to Paradox, though," she reminded him. "And I tend to agree with her."

"You do?"

She nodded. "Paradox might not be safe. How many days have we been gone? Plenty of time for one of those…those *things* to have gotten there." She put her fork down. Talking about it made her appetite disappear. She sighed. "I'm *so* ready for this to be over with."

"Yeah. I'm ready to get back to the farm, check on things."

"I know. I'm worried about Mom and Dad."

He paused at the back door. "I guess when we first started out, we should have followed the creek south instead of going into Paradox to begin with."

She shook her head. "We had no way of knowing all this would happen. Going to Paradox was the logical choice."

"I guess."

When he opened the back door, she called after him. "Take Lucky with you."

CHAPTER FORTY-THREE

Corey felt someone watching her, but even in her deep sleep, she knew it wasn't hostile. She forced herself awake, opening her eyes only a fraction, finding Dana standing at the edge of the bed.

She tried to smile. "You've showered," she murmured sleepily.

Dana nodded. "Yeah. It was great, actually." She paused. "I've come to take your clothes."

Corey managed a laugh. "Wow. That's the best offer I've had in a while." She shoved the covers off her. "Am I still dreaming?" A blush lit Dana's face and Corey was almost sorry she'd teased her. Almost.

"Butch hooked up the generator to Jean's washer," Dana said. "We thought we'd throw all our clothes in there at once. Butch and I didn't exactly bring a whole wardrobe with us."

"I see. So if you weren't able to wake me, were you going to strip me naked?"

"Well, that could have been fun."

Corey grinned. "Okay. Then let's pretend I'm still asleep."

"No, no, no. Too late now, honey. Hand them over."

Corey didn't know how to reply to that, and she was nearly embarrassed by the rapid beating of her heart. Instead of saying anything, she stood up, stretching her arms over her head, loosening up her shoulders. "I didn't plan to sleep this long. I guess the day is wasted."

"Depends what you mean by wasted," Dana said. "Jean's been cooking. I've already gained my seven pounds back and then some, just from what I ate today."

Corey turned her gaze to Dana, letting her eyes travel down the length of her, thinking she'd be far too thin if she actually lost the seven pounds she claimed she'd gained. She raised her eyes back up, meeting Dana's.

"Your clothes," Dana said, holding out her hand.

Corey pulled her shirt over her head without thinking, holding it out to Dana. She'd never been self-conscious, and it didn't faze her now, but Dana's eyes weren't locked on her breasts. Instead, they were wide in shock as they traveled over her body...landing on her now-healed wounds.

"My God," Dana whispered.

Corey touched the scar on her side, the scar that Dana's eyes were glued to. Shrapnel had barely missed her vest, and she rubbed the wound now, not really feeling the scar beneath her fingers.

"I kinda forgot about them," she said. She let her hand drop. "I kinda forgot about a lot of things these last few days."

Dana raised her head, meeting her eyes head on. "Is that a good thing?"

Corey nodded. "Yeah. It's a good thing. My team...everything that happened...it's been consuming me for so long. Eating at me." She shrugged. "Yeah...it's a good thing."

Dana smiled slightly, her gaze now—finally—landing on her breasts. Under her perusal, Corey had to resist the urge to cover herself with the shirt she'd just pulled off.

Dana moved her gaze from her breasts back to her eyes. Corey searched them, surprised to find a hint of desire there...a hint of arousal. Then Dana held out her hand, clearing her throat slightly before speaking.

"Your shirt?"

Corey nodded and handed it over.

"And...and your underwear?"

Corey licked her lips, finally chewing on her lower one nervously. She nodded, bending over to remove them as well.

Dana took them and turned, heading to the door. But she stopped, swinging her head around again.

"If...if the circumstances were different," she said, her voice quiet in the room. "Well...if things were different..."

Corey nodded slightly as their eyes held. "Yeah…if things were different. Because I feel this…this attraction between us too."

Dana held her gaze for a moment longer, looking like she wanted to say something, but she didn't. She simply left the room, leaving Corey standing there naked.

"Okay…well, this is awkward," she murmured. Her pack, which contained another pair of dirty jeans and a couple of shirts, was where she'd left it…in Jean's living room. She walked to the edge of the door and stuck her head out into the hallway. "Hey…a little help here," she called.

* * *

"That's probably the best meal I've ever eaten," Corey said as she leaned back from the table and rubbed her full belly.

Jean nearly beamed at the compliment. "My momma taught me how to bake a tender roast when I was barely ten," she recalled. "Although the secret to the gravy came from my granny. She always said a meal wasn't a true meal unless there was gravy to go with it."

"And there's enough left over for sandwiches," Dana said. "That is, if we can keep Corey from going back for thirds."

"I could eat a third helping myself," Butch said. "That was delicious, Miss Jean."

"Oh, I do love to cook," she said. "And my Hal used to…" She looked away. "Well, it doesn't matter."

Corey looked across the table at Dana, who then reached over and took one of Jean's hands gently in her own.

"We'll get through this, Miss Jean," Dana said.

Jean looked up again. "Yes. I'm counting on the captain to get us out of here. I suppose there's not enough time left today to get started."

Corey shook her head. "I think we'll be safer here tonight. I'd like to leave at first light, though. If we could be up and packed and get out of here early, then I'm hoping we can make the checkpoint in one day's ride."

"Still against going into Paradox?" Butch asked. "If we take the road to the checkpoint you've mentioned, then there's no water along that route."

"Can the horses make it?" Dana asked.

"They'll have to," Corey said. "We don't know if Paradox is still safe. Let's get to the checkpoint. We know there'll be help there."

"I'm worried about my parents, Butch's parents," Dana said. "And my other aunt and uncle, they're at Butch's house."

"I know. That's why we need to get some help in here. I need to let Colonial Sutter, General Brinkley know what's going on."

"How do you even explain this?"

"Yeah. They'll think I've lost my mind," she agreed.

"Okay," Butch said. "I guess you're right." He pushed his chair back from the table. "I'll go tend to the horses."

"Might see if those hens laid any eggs," Jean said before he opened the screen door.

"Yes, ma'am, I'll do that." He paused, then tapped his leg for Lucky to follow him.

"How much fuel do you have left for the generator?" Corey asked, noting the silence now with it off.

"Butch says only a little more than a gallon is left in the can," Jean said. "That'll get us through tonight and tomorrow morning. Unless you think we should run it all night for lights."

"Might not be a bad idea," she said.

"I've got some kerosene lamps," Jean said. "They belonged to Hal's parents. Back in the day, there was no generator. That's what we used when the power was out."

"I guess we could start with that," she said.

"Well, I'll help you clean up the kitchen," Dana offered.

"I can do it," Jean said. "Why don't you take the captain out to the clothesline and see if those clothes are dry? With this wind we've had today, I imagine they're ready to come in."

Dana smiled teasingly as she looked at her. "So? Does the captain want to fold clothes?"

"Sure. I'm quite handy at doing laundry," she said.

As Jean had predicted, the clothes were dry. It brought back a childhood memory, one of her mother hanging their clothes out in the tiny backyard they had when her father was stationed at Fort Hood. It was summer and blistering hot, and she remembered her mother commenting that it had taken less than an hour for the clothes to dry that day.

"What?"

She blinked, chasing the memory away. "Huh?"

"You were staring at the jeans and smiling. Old memory?"

She nodded. "We moved around a lot. It wasn't often that we had any kind of a yard. One time when we did, I recall my mother taking advantage of the clothesline."

Dana nodded. "Growing up, the only time we used the dryer was during the winter, and even then, not always. I remember helping my mom hang out clothes twice a week. I hated it." Then she smiled. "I loved the way they smelled, though." She took a shirt and brought it to her nose now. "No dryer sheet can beat this."

"I believe that's my shirt. Don't get all slobbery with it."

Dana laughed. "I'll try to control myself."

Lucky's sharp barks interrupted their playfulness, and Corey dropped the clothes she held into the basket and took off running toward the barn. She touched her hip when she got closer, realizing she'd left her weapon back at the house. Lucky continued to bark, and she turned, finding Dana right behind her.

"Get back to the house," she said quickly. "I don't have my gun."

Dana stared at her.

"Don't argue. Go get it."

Dana nodded, then turned and ran back toward the house. Corey walked cautiously around the side of the barn, then jumped into the enclosure where their horses were. They seemed agitated as they shied away from her but maybe it was only from Lucky's barking.

She slipped quietly into the barn, finding Butch against the wall, his hands held up defensively. A soldier was watching him, an M16 rifle held casually in his hand. Lucky was between them, his bark ferocious, but the soldier didn't seem to notice, his gaze was fixed on Butch.

"Hey," she said as she walked up.

He turned slowly, staring at her.

"Get out of here, Corey," Butch said. "He's...he's not real. And he's got a gun."

"Private...I'm Captain Conaway," she said, ignoring Butch. When the soldier failed to acknowledge her and did nothing more than stare, she murmured, "And you have no idea what that means, do you?"

The man slowly turned his head back to Butch, then looked down at Lucky. "Stop."

"Lucky...come here, boy," Corey said. Lucky's barking turned to growls, and he took a few steps in her direction, then turned back and started barking again, his lips curled back, his teeth glistening.

The soldier pointed his rifle at Lucky, but Butch stepped forward. "No!"

The man's finger wasn't even on the trigger, and Corey doubted he was cognizant enough to know how to fire it, but she couldn't be sure. As she contemplated what to do, the soldier—quick as a lightning bolt—lunged at Butch, slamming him against the barn wall with such force that the boards rattled around them. She flung herself at him, tearing him away from Butch. They tumbled to the ground and she rolled over, hopping to her feet. Just as the man took aim at her, a shot sounded behind her, sending him careening backward.

She jerked around, finding Dana standing in the doorway, holding her Glock in her hands. She was shaking wildly, and Corey wondered how she'd even managed to get a shot off.

"That was damn close to hitting me," Corey said as she pulled the rifle away from the crumpled soldier.

"But it missed you," Dana said as she handed the Glock to Corey and hurried over to Butch. "God, he's not moving. Please say he's not dead."

Corey bent over him, holding a finger to his neck. She detected a faint pulse. She put her hand behind his head, trying to lift it, when she felt the wet stickiness of blood.

"He's alive," she said. Then she pulled her hand out, showing it to Dana. "But injured."

"What should we do?"

"Is there a doctor in Paradox?"

Dana shook her head. "I don't think so. At least, there never was. The closest is in Moab, I think. Maybe Jean might know."

"I'm afraid to move him," Corey said.

"We've got to do something."

Lucky came over to them, sniffing Butch, his tail wagging. Corey reached out and ruffled his fur, then caressed his head.

"Good dog," she said softly.

But Lucky pulled away, a low growl in his throat. They turned, finding the soldier trying to sit up. Corey aimed her gun at him, shooting him twice in the chest. He fell back down again.

"No blood," Dana whispered.

"No. I need to burn the body," she said. "It's the only way to be sure."

"What about Butch?"

"Go get Jean. Let's see if we can't rig up something to carry him with. I'll pull this guy out and take care of him." She touched Dana's thigh as they knelt beside Butch. "Then we need to get inside the house and lock up. It'll be dark soon."

Dana looked at her. "I'm really scared."

Corey nodded. "Me too."

CHAPTER FORTY-FOUR

Dana swirled the amber liquid in her glass before taking a sip. It burned her throat but she didn't care. As Jean had said, they could all use a stiff drink. Jean had surprised them when she pulled a stepstool out of the closet and stood on it to reach the top cabinet beside the fridge. There were two bottles in there. One was a clear liquid, vodka or gin, she supposed. The other, a bottle of scotch whiskey that Jean had said Hal saved for special occasions. It was three-quarters full, if not more. She was surprised by the sadness that struck her at seeing the nearly full bottle. Apparently there had been very few "special occasions" in their life. Or else they didn't deem them special enough at the time to warrant the drink. Now, of course, it was too late.

Corey tossed back her shot, apparently savoring the taste as she licked her lips. Then she got up, going to look out the kitchen door, something she'd done several times already.

After they got Butch inside, Jean had cleaned his wound and wrapped his head. The bleeding had stopped, and once they'd cleaned it, it wasn't as bad as she'd first imagined, although she still thought he needed stitches. Butch came around, complaining of a headache. He didn't seem to recall what had happened in the barn, though. He fell back into semi-consciousness, scaring her even more.

They settled him on the sofa and Jean had patted her hand, telling her that he'd be okay in the morning. He just needed time to rest his scrambled brain, she said. Corey seemed to be in agreement so Dana tried to push her worries aside.

She knew Corey had burned the soldier's body. Corey didn't have to tell her; she'd smelled it while she was outside getting their clothes in. Later, she and Jean had watched out of the kitchen window as Corey filled the generator with the last of the fuel before starting it up. When Corey had come back inside, she'd closed and locked the doors. Then she'd gone around the house and closed all the windows, shutting out the pleasant breeze that had been blowing all day.

They'd taken turns with showers, then had settled around the kitchen table. Conversation was minimal, if at all. She was glad they'd taken the day to rest. She doubted any of them would get any sleep tonight. Corey had said the plan was still to head out at first light if Butch was well enough to travel. She didn't have to add, that was, if they made it through the night.

"You want another splash?" Jean asked.

Dana looked at her glass, surprised that it was empty. She didn't remember drinking it all. She nodded. "Just a little."

"It takes the edge off, doesn't it?"

Dana smiled at her. "I'm not sure even drinking the whole bottle would take the edge off. I don't think I've ever been more frightened in my life, Miss Jean."

Corey turned from the window. "This one made eight. There should only be two still out there," she said. "Of the ten soldiers, anyway. If it was a twelve-man squad, then four more."

"And Carl Milstead," Jean added. "And maybe more by now."

"Keep our weapons with us at all times," Corey said. "We'll be okay."

Dana glanced down at the gun in her lap. She didn't have to look to know that Jean had her shotgun resting across her thighs. And Corey's gun was in the holster at her hip. Even Butch's rifle was beside the sofa next to him.

"And we have Lucky to warn us," Corey added. "I don't know what we'd have done without him."

Dana nodded, remembering the scene in the barn. She'd gotten there just in time to see the man send Lucky sprawling. Then he seemed to fly across the ground. He was on Butch so quickly, Dana had hardly noticed the blur of his actions. Then Corey had lunged at him, and as they tumbled to the ground, Dana knew she had to do something. The man would have been able to kill both Corey and

Butch in a matter of seconds. She fired without thinking, praying she didn't hit Corey in the process. She'd learned to shoot at an early age, but it was never something she enjoyed, and as she got older, guns frightened her more than anything.

She glanced again at the gun in her lap, a Beretta 9mm. Corey had given her a quick lesson that one morning when they'd been camping along the creek, telling her it would be easier for her than the Glock. She hadn't told Corey that her father owned a Glock or that it was the first handgun she'd ever fired…at the tender age of ten. She'd simply taken the Beretta from Corey, thinking she would have no use for it anyway. She had no intention of firing a weapon. Of course, that had all changed in a matter of seconds.

Corey was again staring out the window, and Dana followed her gaze, seeing the last light fade from the sky, replaced by darkness that seemed to be swallowing them up much too rapidly. Even though the generator's rumble had faded to the background, she was glad for the noise. Without it, it would be deathly quiet in the house.

When Corey turned, Dana met her eyes. Corey gave her a gentle smile.

"If you want to try to get some sleep, now's your chance," Corey said.

Dana shook her head. "I don't want to be back there alone. Besides, I'm too scared to sleep."

"That old bed back there is just a double," Jean said. "It wouldn't take much for you to drag the mattress out to the living room. Someone needs to keep an eye on Butch during the night anyway."

"You wouldn't mind if we did that?" Dana asked.

"Maybe we'll take turns using it," Jean said. "I'm not looking to go back to my room alone either."

Dana looked at Corey for confirmation and she nodded. "Keep Lucky with you," Corey instructed to Jean when the dog started following them. Jean called him back and he obediently went to her.

"I think Lucky's become attached to you," Dana said.

"Yeah, I think so," Corey said. She stopped beside Butch and touched his face, then felt his neck. She nodded. "Pulse is strong, steady."

"What if he can't ride? Then what do we do?"

"We'll worry about that in the morning," Corey said. "Come on."

Dana was thankful they'd lowered all the blinds. She didn't want to see outside. Not that they could see anything. It was too dark. Not unless someone was right at the window, pressing his face against the glass. She turned away from the window quickly.

"What's wrong?"

Dana shook her head. "I was...I was imagining someone outside the window, looking in at us."

Corey walked over to her and touched her face, caressing it lightly before letting her hand drop away. "I won't let anything happen to you. I promise."

Dana felt herself shaking. "They're so...so *fast*," she said. "Like when they were running after us. We were on horses, yet it was like they were flying. And the one in the barn...he was on Butch so fast, I didn't have time to even blink."

Corey put her arms around her and pulled her close, and Dana sank against her. She was trembling now, almost uncontrollably, and Corey rubbed her back, soothing her.

"It's going to be okay," she whispered.

"Is it? We might make it out, but what about my parents? Butch's parents?"

"Dana...we've got to get help first," Corey said. "I know you're worried about them. And you *should* be. They won't be prepared like we are. They won't know what's going on. Someone they know could come to them and...and..."

"You're not helping," Dana mumbled against her chest.

"I'm trying to be honest with you, that's all."

Dana pulled away from her slightly, not enough to separate completely, though. "You've been so strong through all of this," she said. "We've seen so much...so much *shit* these last few days, this last week, however long it's been. Yet you're still in control. It's like nothing bothers you."

Corey met her eyes and Dana noticed the sadness there. "It's because I've seen a lot of shit over the years." Then her eyes crinkled up in a forced smile. "It'll take more than this to freak me out." Her smile faded quickly, though. "That's not to say that I'm not scared. Because I am."

Dana held her gaze. "I think that's what makes you so unique. You're strong. You've been a rock for all of us. But you don't pretend that you're not as scared as the rest of us."

She reached out and ran her fingers across Corey's cheek, surprised by the softness of her skin. Her hand seemed to move of its own volition and she didn't stop it as it wound around Corey's neck. Her gaze dropped to Corey's mouth, then found her eyes again. She was aware of her heart beating just a little faster than it should, aware of the anticipation she felt as their eyes held. But her eyes slipped closed as Corey leaned forward, brushing her lips with her own, lingering long enough for Dana to want more.

"Now's probably not a good time to start this," Corey murmured as she pulled away. "Even though I'd really, really like to."

"I'm afraid if we wait we won't get another chance," Dana said as she moved closer again. "Just for a few moments, let's pretend that everything is normal."

Her plea was apparently enough to convince Corey as arms wrapped around her again. Dana moaned at the contact, her body pressed tightly against Corey's. When soft lips found hers once more, she deepened the kiss, relishing the intimate contact, savoring the few seconds they allowed for themselves. She felt the change in Corey, and she opened to her, her tongue touching Corey's in a dance as old as time. At that moment, she knew without a doubt that Corey was the one who'd been haunting her dreams all these years. She felt it in her heart, in her soul. She clutched Corey even harder, trying to get as close as possible to her.

Inevitably, their kiss came to an end, but Corey didn't untangle from her. They stood there for countless seconds, just holding each other as their breathing returned to normal. When Dana felt in control again, she moved away from Corey enough to look at her, to look into her eyes. Did Corey recognize the connecting of their souls like she just had?

Corey seemed to read her mind and she nodded. "I haven't had a lover in more years than I can count," she said quietly. "I never really missed it. You…you make me want to have that in my life again. I hope we get a chance."

"I hope we do too." Dana finally separated fully from her, knowing this wasn't the place or time for all this. The situation didn't allow them that. Not yet.

"Your…your life's been the military? That's all?"

Corey nodded again. "It was one or the other," she said. "I didn't feel like I could be my best at either one if I couldn't devote one hundred percent of myself."

Dana stared at her, noting the sadness in her eyes again. "Maybe you were wrong. Maybe you can have both."

Corey's gaze dropped slowly to her lips, then back up. "I hope so. I truly hope so." She glanced over at the bed. "We should get this moved. Jean's probably worried about us."

Dana reached for her side of the mattress, noting that she wasn't trembling from fright any longer. No, she was trembling from desire now. Damn the circumstances, she thought. For years and years, this woman had been haunting her dreams. Her nameless, faceless Dream Girl...always just out of reach. She looked over at Corey, who had folded up the end of the bedspread and tossed it on top. This woman, real flesh and blood, was also out of reach...for now. But at least her Dream Girl was no longer faceless. Corey's strong face, her gentle dark eyes were now etched in her mind forever.

* * *

Jean was getting anxious when the girls didn't return, and she made her way into the hallway, catching bits and pieces of their conversation. She stared in shock as they embraced, her eyes wide as they kissed. She turned around quickly and went back into the living room, finding Lucky squatting on his haunches beside Butch.

"Oh, my goodness," she murmured.

Never in all her seventy-five years had she seen two women kiss. Not even on TV, though she'd heard about it on the news and such. They could even get married now, she knew that much. It wasn't right. She and Hal had thought it was a crazy concept. How could two women or two men have the same loving relationship as she and Hal? It wasn't possible. But the captain? And Dana?

"Oh, my goodness," she said again.

She went back into the kitchen and stared at the glass she hadn't finished, the whiskey still there. She picked it up quickly and drank it all in one swallow, then coughed as it burned her throat.

"Are you okay?" Dana asked, patting her back gently. "Go down wrong?"

Jean turned to her, afraid to meet her eyes. "I'm fine," she said.

"Let me get you some water."

Jean watched as Dana filled a glass and handed it to her.

"I'm not used to that, I guess," Jean said.

"I know. Me either. Anytime I have any kind of a drink, I always mix it with something. Coke or juice or something," Dana said. Then she tilted her head, staring at her. "What's wrong, Miss Jean?"

Jean hesitated for only a moment. "I...I saw you."

Dana frowned. "You saw what?"

"You and the captain." She was surprised by the blush on Dana's face.

"I see. You saw us...kiss?"

Jean nodded. "Are you...I mean, you and the captain, are you—"

"Are we gay?" Dana nodded. "Yes." She smiled and held her hands up. "But don't worry, Miss Jean. Now's not exactly the right time for… for romance." Then Dana's smile disappeared, and her expression turned thoughtful and a bit wistful as she stared past her. "Perhaps if we make it out of here in one piece, maybe then," she said. Dana looked back at her. "We have this…this connection between us—me and Corey."

Jean didn't know what to say and Dana laughed quietly.

"You don't understand, do you?"

"No."

Dana shrugged her shoulders. "No, I guess you don't. It doesn't matter anyway, Miss Jean. The circumstances are what they are. We're just trying to get out of here alive. Right now, that's all that matters."

They both turned when the captain came into the kitchen. She looked between them, her gaze landing on Dana's with a question in her eyes. Dana smiled at her and the captain then looked at Jean.

"Everything okay?"

"Yes," Dana said quickly. "Just chatting. Got the bed set up?"

"Yeah, it's ready. You feel like a nap?"

Dana shook her head. "Not quite yet. But I suppose I could go sit with Butch."

As soon as Dana left, the captain winked at her. "She'll be asleep before too long."

Jean went to the stove. "Should I put some coffee on? Gonna be a long night, I suppose."

"That'd be nice, Miss Jean, thank you."

Jean scooped coffee grounds into the top, then secured the lid before turning on the gas stove. She went back to the table and sat down in her chair, noting that the captain was sitting in Hal's spot. She couldn't stop thinking about the embrace she'd seen the captain and Dana share…the kiss that was much too intimate for an old woman her age to be witness to. Still, Dana's words echoed in her mind. They had a *connection*.

"You know, Dana is a nice girl, isn't she?"

Corey nodded. "Yeah, she is. You know her folks?"

Jean nodded. "Know of them, of course. Seen them around town a time or two. They're much younger than us so we never socialized with them." Then she laughed. "Not that Hal and I did much socializing. We were content being here at the farm together." She shook her head sadly, knowing the farm—this house—would never be the same again. "My boys never did take a liking to the farm. It was like they couldn't wait to leave here. Hal and I never understood that."

"I guess it's like Butch and Dana. Butch stayed here with his parents, Dana moved off."

Jean nodded. "Young people have more opportunities now. When Hal and I were young, there wasn't much choice. Jobs weren't plentiful, not around here. Still aren't."

"Do you regret not having a chance to leave the valley?"

Jean shook her head. "No, no. I don't recall there ever being a time that I wished I was somewhere else. This was home. We were happy. I can't imagine being anywhere else." She eyed the captain, waiting until she met her gaze. "You have regrets, Captain?"

"Sometimes, yes."

"Sometimes wishing you hadn't followed in your daddy's footsteps?"

The captain smiled, a half smile that didn't really reach her eyes. "Sometimes I can't imagine having any other life than what I have. And sometimes I long for a completely different life."

Jean reached across the small table, lightly touching her hand. "Like now?"

The captain sighed. "I tell myself that if I wasn't here right now, who would be? Who would be here with you and Dana? Would they be taking care of you?"

"So it's fate after all that's brought you here. Is that what you think?"

The captain stared at her. "Do you believe in fate, Miss Jean? Do you believe in God?"

Jean thought about the old Bible that was in the nightstand next to her bed. She couldn't remember the last time she'd held it in her hands, the last time she'd even opened it up. It had been her grandmother's, given to her when she and Hal had wed. It was well-worn, but she had to admit that most of the wear was from her grandmother's hands and not hers.

"After Hal and I married and moved in here with his mother... well, she wasn't in a good place," Jean said. "My family was church-goers. Hal's too. Back then, everyone was. But after his daddy died, well, his mother turned her back on God. She refused to go to church, she blamed God for taking her husband from her. She'd never missed a service her whole life before that. Devout, in fact." She got up and went to turn down the coffee, then pulled two cups from the cabinet. "Hal and I still went, even without her. For a while. I don't remember when we stopped going. Once the boys were born, we should have taken them, but I guess it was too easy to stay here. We had already fallen into a pattern."

"You didn't answer my question."

Jean turned to her. "If you'd asked me last week, I'd have said yes. About God, that is. Now…I'm not so sure."

"And fate?"

Jean brought their coffee to the table and set a cup in front of the captain. "Life is funny sometimes," she said. "When good, unexpected things happen, we often say it's fate…or destiny. Bad things happen, we say we're unlucky. But fate isn't always good, is it? Was it fate that my Hal rode off to look for a helicopter? Or was it just bad luck on his part?" She met the curious eyes across from her. "Or did God not care enough about Hal to spare his life? Not care enough about me to bring my husband home?" She took a sip from her coffee and closed her eyes. So much had happened, she really hadn't had time to think about it before. But now…now she realized she was angry with God, much like her mother-in-law had been.

"I don't believe…that there's a God," the captain said.

She looked over at her. "No?"

"No. Bad things, as you say. I've seen a lot of them. There's been too many people killed in the name of God. No *loving* God would allow all of that."

"Some things can't be explained, I guess."

"Yeah. And God works in mysterious ways," the captain said with a bitter laugh. "That's bullshit."

"So you think it's only fate that's brought you here?" She looked at the captain questioningly. "Are fate and God not one and the same?"

"Maybe luck brought me here."

"Good or bad?"

The captain laughed. "I guess it depends how you look at it."

Jean smiled at her. "Well, I certainly feel like it's good luck on my part. I'm sure Dana feels the same."

"Yeah, I guess there's no place that I'd rather be right now than here, hanging out with you guys."

Jean laughed loudly. "Oh, Captain, surely you don't mean that. Have you grown that fond of us?"

"Well, yeah I have. I've grown quite fond of you." Her smiled faded a little. "There's not anybody else I'd trust here with you, that's for sure."

"Trust to keep us safe, you mean?"

The captain nodded.

Jean leaned back in her chair, relaxing for the first time in hours, it seemed. "Thank you. For being here to keep us safe. And for the chat. It felt good to laugh."

The captain smiled at her as she set her coffee cup down. "Thank you for that," she said. "I suppose I should go check on Butch...and Dana."

Jean nodded. "I'll be fine right here."

As soon as she left, Jean's mind returned to the kiss she'd witnessed. Could it be that Dana and the captain really did have a connection like she and Hal had? She supposed it was possible. They surely did seem to be fond of each other, that was for sure.

CHAPTER FORTY-FIVE

Corey looked skeptically at Butch as he tried to pretend he was okay and fit enough to ride. If she thought they had any other choice, she'd insist they wait it out another day. But something was going on. She could feel it. They all could. And it had nothing to do with the gunfire they'd heard during the night. Nothing to do with the gunfire they'd heard as they were saddling up the horses at daybreak.

"That last shot sounded like it came from the other side of the creek," Jean said quietly. "Down across the bridge, there are only a few families that live out that way." She shook her head slowly. "I sure hope they're okay."

"I hope you're not suggesting we go check on them," Dana said as she pulled herself on top of Gretchen.

"We can't take a chance," Corey said to Jean. "Not with Butch injured. We need to get out of here."

"Yeah, we do," Dana agreed. "Because I've got a really bad feeling."

It was something Dana had said several times before on this trip, and Corey had to agree with her. She met her gaze and nodded. "Me too," she said as she swung up in the saddle, pulling up on the reins as the white stallion danced around.

"I hope the other horses will be okay," Jean said.

"They'll find their way to the creek," she said. "There's plenty of grass."

After much debate, they'd decided it best to only take the four horses they would ride. The other three, they'd left in the corral where they had access to the stalls where there was hay, but they'd left the gate open. Butch thought they'd be fine until someone could come back and round them up.

"And my chickens," Jean added with a sigh.

Well, Corey would miss fresh eggs, that was for sure. What they hadn't eaten for breakfast, Jean had boiled up the rest and they'd packed them, along with the sandwiches they made with the leftover roast from yesterday.

They'd slept very little last night, catnaps, not much more. But it gave Jean time to cook, and she'd baked two loaves of bread. The smell alone was enough to keep Corey from sleeping, and Jean had allowed her to eat a warm slice with butter while Dana was sleeping. They'd practically devoured one loaf for breakfast with the scrambled eggs and sausage Jean had whipped up. The other loaf was made into sandwiches.

Now, with the sun's light starting to poke through the trees that lined Jean's lane, they headed out in single file, Lucky leading the way and Dana bringing up the rear.

Despite her apprehension, it proved to be an uneventful morning. That is, if she ignored the gunfire that occasionally broke the silence. She hadn't shared with the others, but several of the blasts were from automatic weapons, most likely M16s. That told her that Brinkley had indeed sent in more troops...or her assumption of the number in the original squad was off. Or else somehow those weapons ended up in the hands of civilians...or worse.

She kept those thoughts to herself. When they'd reached the main road, they'd paused. Left would take them toward the cutoff to Paradox, where Dana and Butch had picked her up all those days ago. Right would take them to the checkpoint. Butch had voiced his opinion—Paradox would be a lot closer. Corey knew that it would, but they had to get out of the zone. She needed to report back to Sutter and Brinkley. They needed to know what was really going on out here. Besides, her gut told her the checkpoint would be safer than Paradox anyway. Dana echoed that sentiment.

"All this shooting we've heard," Dana had said. "Who knows what the hell is going on in Paradox? I vote for the checkpoint."

"I trust the captain," Jean had said, leaving Butch no choice but to agree.

So they turned right, leaving the trees and valley behind as the road left the creek and headed west, through the arid high desert of rocks and the occasional clusters of scrub brush. They rode mostly in silence, a comment here or there breaking in from time to time. It was another sunny, warm day, and with the sun hot overhead, she thought a break for lunch was in order. A clump of trees—if three scraggly oaks could be called a clump—would provide a little shade. She pulled her horse to a stop and glanced behind her.

"How about a break?"

"I wouldn't mind getting out of this saddle for a little bit," Jean said. "To use Dana's words…my ass hurts."

They all laughed, easing some of the tension. Corey swung down, then held Daisy while Jean got off.

"I'm hungry," Dana said.

"Surprise, surprise," Butch replied.

Dana went over to him and helped him down. "How are you feeling?"

He gave a false smile. "Not too bad if I ignore the bass drum in my head."

Corey turned him around, noting that the knot on the back of his head was still pronounced, although it wasn't quite as bad as last night. He needed a doctor to check him out, and she hoped they weren't doing a disservice to him by traveling. However, there had been little choice, she knew.

He seemed to read her thoughts, and he squeezed her forearm quickly. "I'm going to be fine, Captain. Probably just a hell of a concussion, that's all."

"Your vision was blurred this morning," she reminded him. "How is it now?"

"It's fine," he said quickly. Too quickly.

She knew he was lying, but she didn't press. It would do no good. The situation was what it was. And that meant another four or five hours until they reached the checkpoint, if her guess was right.

They stood in the shade of the trees and ate sandwiches, sharing with Lucky from time to time. The dog, however, didn't seem all that interested in food. He seemed to be more alert than normal, his ears held at attention as if listening for predators…or something worse. When he walked out into the middle of the road, looking across it into the vast expanse of nothingness, she followed him.

"What is it, boy?" she whispered. "You hear something?"

"You think we're being followed?" Dana asked beside her, her gaze on Lucky. "He's acting like something's out there."

"I know. But with this terrain, there's not a lot of places to hide, not enough trees or brush to conceal someone. I imagine we'd see them coming, if we were being followed," Corey said.

"I saw you with that solar transmitter thing that you have. Any luck?"

She shook her head. "Mostly static. I've sent a few messages in the last couple of days, but I don't know if they're getting through or not."

Dana nodded. "So, at the checkpoint, they'll have power? Phone? You'll be able to contact someone?"

"Yes. They'll be outside of the zone. I'll call my commanding officer immediately," she said, wondering if she should bypass Sutter and simply call General Brinkley instead. Dana's eyes were searching hers and Corey lifted an eyebrow questioningly.

"My parents," Dana said quietly. "I'm really worried about them."

"I know you are."

Dana chewed on her lip nervously. "Once we get Butch and Miss Jean to safety…do you think…well, could we—"

"You want to come back here?"

"I feel like I'm deserting them. Like I'm just leaving them behind to fend for themselves," Dana said. "Which, of course, is the truth."

Corey didn't know if she was surprised or not by Dana's suggestion. She knew Dana was scared. Hell, she was too. Once they got out of here, would Dana *really* want to come back?

"All the shooting we've heard," Dana continued. "That can't be good. I grew up in a family of hunters. I've been around rifles," she said. "Some of those didn't sound like rifle shots."

"No. Automatic weapons," she said quietly, glancing over to where Jean and Butch were still leaning against the tree. Were they listening to their conversation? If so, they were hiding it well.

"So maybe they've…they've learned how to shoot now."

"Or maybe it's another team that was sent in," she said.

"Then who are they shooting at?"

"Don't think the worst, Dana."

"I'd rather be prepared for the worst to happen than to think everything's going to be okay. Because we both know it's not."

Lucky barked once and took another step toward the edge of the road. Corey followed his gaze, but she saw nothing out of the ordinary. Nevertheless, she felt the urge to push on. Dana apparently did too because she gripped her arm and pulled her back toward the others.

"Let's go," Dana said urgently.

They helped Butch and Jean back on their horses, then took off at a little faster pace than normal. However, Lucky didn't seem agitated any longer, so Corey slowed her horse to a walk and finally exhaled.

"I'm nervous as hell," Dana said. "I feel like we're being stalked."

"How much farther to the checkpoint?" Jean asked.

"I don't know. Nothing looks familiar," she said. "They dropped me off on Monday, about five. I hiked until dark, then started out again the next morning at first light." She looked over at Dana. "I guess it was late afternoon when I met you and Butch."

"So...on foot, what, ten, twelve hours or so?"

"I'd guess."

"Should take half that with horses," Butch said. He shielded his eyes as he looked toward the sun. "We should get there well before dark."

"From where the checkpoint was, they calculated it to be about forty miles from the Paradox turnoff," she said.

"Quite a hike," Dana said.

Corey smiled. "Why do you think I was so thrilled when you offered me a ride on Gretchen?"

Dana smiled back at her. "I thought it was because you were getting to ride behind me."

Butch laughed. "I don't think now's a good time for flirting, Dana."

"If not now...when?" Jean chimed in.

Corey laughed at the blush that lit up Dana's face. Indeed. If not now, when? Of course, that thought sobered her. As soon as they were safe, would Dana head back to Seattle? Would she forget about Corey? And who knew where Corey's next assignment would be? Would they give her another team to train? Could she handle that again? Hell, did she even want to? As she'd told Jean, most times she couldn't imagine having any other life than what she had. Except for those times when she longed for any life *other* than this. Since losing her team, those times came far more often now. She'd attributed it to her grief, nothing more, feeling that it would pass. Yet here she was, whether she wanted to be or not, taking on the responsibility of trying to get them all out of here safely, this new team of hers, a team of civilians. She pushed the stress of it all aside...it was what she was trained to do. Still, the stress weighed on her, she could feel that. If there wasn't an outlet for it soon, she feared she would crash and burn. And if she was feeling that way, how must they feel? Did Jean, at seventy-five-years-old, feel helpless? Did Butch feel helpless right now with his banged up head and blurred vision? And Dana? Did she feel helpless?

No. Jean had been the first to experience the craziness of what was going on. She'd had the courage to shoot her own husband with a shotgun. Butch had experienced—twice now—the telepathic pull of this unknown entity and had managed to survive it, albeit with a little help. He'd survived a vicious attack too, and even though the last thing he should be doing now was riding a horse, he hadn't once suggested that they delay their escape because of him.

And Dana? God, Dana had been a trouper through it all. She wasn't shy about voicing her opinion, wasn't shy about admitting that she was scared. Yet when Corey needed her, she'd been there, firing a weapon she had no business firing, firing it without flinching. Corey smiled to herself, thankful Dana had managed to not hit *her* in the process.

No...no one was feeling helpless. But feeling the stress? Yes, she imagined it weighed heavy on all of them.

CHAPTER FORTY-SIX

Dana smiled as she glanced at Lucky, who was perched in Corey's lap, riding in the saddle with her.

Even though their pace had slowed, Lucky had been laboring and at one point had simply laid down on the road, refusing to go another step. They'd stopped to rest for a few minutes, then she and Jean had helped lift Lucky up on the horse with Corey.

They were getting close, or so Corey had said. The sun was sinking lower in the sky, but she guessed they still had a couple of hours of daylight left. It had been a hot, almost blistering day and without the benefit of traveling next to the creek, the horses were starting to labor as well.

She glanced behind her, wondering how Butch was holding up. Even though he repeatedly said he was fine, she could tell he was not. He had a tight grip on the saddle, and she suspected that he might be feeling a bit dizzy or maybe it was just the effects of his blurred vision.

"Look up ahead," Corey said.

Dana saw sunlight reflecting off a windshield, and she felt relief flood her as she dared to hope it was the checkpoint. Corey had stopped her horse and she pulled out her binoculars.

"It's the checkpoint. We made it," Corey said with a laugh. "We actually made it."

"Thank you, Captain," Jean said. "I never doubted you for a minute."

Dana pulled her horse up beside Corey's, a big smile on her face. "It's kinda anticlimactic, isn't it?"

"What? You'd rather have us running for our lives as we're being chased?"

"No. Been there, done that," Dana said. Her smile faltered just a bit. "You're *sure* this is the checkpoint, right?"

"The soldiers appear to be real soldiers, if that's what you mean."

"I'm worried about Butch," she said, her voice low. "I think he needs a doctor."

Corey nodded. "Yeah. There's probably a medic here, at least. Judging by the number of tents, I'm guessing there's at least a platoon here."

As they got closer, she saw two of the soldiers step out onto the road, watching them. She held back, letting Corey go first. They appeared to be a little wary, and she noticed that both of them were holding their weapons in front of them.

She looked back at Jean, seeing the concern in her eyes.

"I think we're okay," she said quietly, then turned her attention back to Corey.

"Corporal Perez," Corey said with a curt nod.

Dana's eyes widened as both soldiers snapped to attention, saluting her quickly even though she wasn't in uniform.

"I'm sorry, ma'am. I didn't recognize you. Glad you made it back safely, Captain," he said.

"You still have power here?"

"Yes, ma'am. We're out of the zone."

"Great. Who's in charge?"

"Lieutenant Jones, ma'am."

"Can you get him? We'll need to get Colonel Sutter on the horn."

"Of course, Captain." He paused. "Need help with the dog?"

Corey nodded. "Yeah. He could use some water too, if you have it."

"What about a doctor?" Dana called.

Corey pointed back at Butch. "Got an injured man. You got a medic?"

"Yes, ma'am."

They took Lucky from the saddle, and Corey slid to the ground, stretching her back and legs as she looked back over at Dana.

"I'll be right over there," Corey said, pointing to an area where vehicles were lined along the road.

Dana nodded. "Okay."

Dana got off Gretchen, then went over to help Jean down. She couldn't help but smile up at her. They were safe. The day had been, as she'd said, anticlimactic. Other than the sporadic gunfire they'd heard that morning, which eventually had faded away, making the afternoon quiet and as nonthreatening as a walk down a country road could be. But after all they'd been through, she had a nagging feeling that it was only the calm before the storm. She hoped that wasn't the case.

"We should have asked them what day it is," Dana said to Jean. "I don't have a clue."

Two soldiers came up, holding Butch's horse steady as he got off. Dana hurried over to him to help.

"What kind of an injury, sir?"

"Head," Dana answered for him. "He has a gash on the back, some swelling. He had blurred vision this morning." She looked at Butch. "Still?"

"A little," he admitted.

"Okay. Come with me. I'll have the doc take a look."

Dana held his and Corey's horse, then looked at the other soldier. "I don't guess you have any water for them, huh?"

"I can probably round up something, ma'am."

"Thanks." When he turned to leave, she stopped him. "Oh...what day is it?"

He frowned. "Day?"

"Yeah, you know...Saturday, Sunday?"

"Oh. It's Tuesday, ma'am."

Dana sighed as she looked at Jean. "The power went out Saturday, more than a week ago already."

"I lost track of the days too," Jean said. Then she motioned to where Corey was standing, a phone held to her ear. "The captain looks like she's yelling."

Dana nodded. "Yeah, she doesn't look too happy."

"That's because whoever she's talking to probably doesn't believe her," Jean said.

Dana watched as Corey made a fist and pounded the side of the vehicle, her voice almost loud enough for her to hear. "I'm going to go see what's wrong," she said, handing the reins to Jean. As she approached, Corey pounded the vehicle again.

"Goddamn it, I *know* it's farfetched. You think I'm making this shit up?" she yelled.

Dana touched her arm and squeezed tightly, feeling how tense Corey was. Corey met her eyes, holding them.

"Colonel Sutter, if you would just get Lieutenant Duncan for me. He'll—" Corey paused. "I know you're in charge, but you're not hearing me." Another pause. "I'll go directly to General Brinkley if I have to." Corey's jaw clenched. "Thank you," she said tersely. "Now, if you'll get Duncan."

"They don't believe you?" Dana whispered.

"He's a goddamn jerk," Corey said.

"Who's Duncan?"

"He's the one who suggested that it might not be a meteor," Corey said.

"Okay, good. He'll believe you then," she said.

"I hope so."

Dana motioned to one of the large tents that were set up off the road. "I'm going to go check on Butch. Miss Jean has the horses and Lucky."

"Okay." When she turned, Corey grabbed her arm and pulled her back. "I haven't forgotten."

Dana frowned.

"About your parents," Corey clarified.

Dana nodded briefly. "Thanks."

* * *

After what seemed an eternity, Lieutenant Duncan finally got on the phone.

"Captain? Colonel Sutter says—"

"Just listen to me, Duncan." She blew out a breath. "You were right all along. It wasn't a meteor. It's some kind of a spaceship."

There was only a slight pause. "*Jesus*," he nearly hissed. "Are you serious?"

"Frankly, I wish I wasn't," she said. "We've got to quarantine this area. We need to send in more troops. We need—"

"Captain, we've deployed two platoons, thirty men in each," Duncan said.

"When?"

"Two days ago, ma'am."

She ran her hand over her hair. "Do you still have communication with them?"

"Not any longer, no."

"And you've not heard from the original squad, have you?"

"No, ma'am. Not since we got a message that they'd found the helicopter. It was a garbled message, but we were able to make out that much, at least."

"They're gone," she said bluntly.

"Gone? What do you mean?"

"Dead. Killed. Or worse," she said.

"But—"

"Just listen to me," she said, cutting him off. "They...they use the bodies somehow. Like a puppet or something. They take over the body. It's a dead body, but it's still a functioning body," she said, her words coming quickly. "They take it over, use it, manipulate it. Like a puppet," she said again. "They...they speak, but it's not normal." She remembered Jean's description of Hal. "Like they're disoriented."

"Excuse me, ma'am...but *they?*"

"Yeah, *they.* Whoever—*whatever*—is in the goddamn spaceship," she said loudly. "It's up on Baker's Ridge, that's what the locals call it. We need to deploy a missile, hit it head on. We need to take it out. We need—"

"Whoa, Captain...that's *way* over my paygrade."

"Listen to me, Duncan," she said. "It looks like it crash landed. It burrowed into the ridgetop, making this ravine, this crevice, maybe two hundred feet long," she said. "The craft itself appears to be intact, but I'd say nearly half of it is buried in the rocks. Whatever it's made out of, it's some kind of very hard metal. There didn't appear to be any damage at all from the crash. There was no explosion, no fire. Hell, I don't even know if a missile will take it out." She took a breath, trying to slow down as she realized how fast she was talking. "I know this all sounds crazy, Lieutenant, but I assure you, it's very real. You've got to convince Sutter. The troops you sent in are in danger. We need to quarantine this whole area," she said again.

"I'll...I'll tell him everything you said, Captain. But...well, he's not going to believe me. I've heard that you and General Brinkley are close...well, I mean—"

"Are you suggesting I need to go over Colonel Sutter's head, Duncan?"

"I'm suggesting it wouldn't hurt, ma'am. Of course, please don't tell Colonel Sutter I suggested it."

She again ran her hand over her hair. "We heard gunfire this morning. Some last night as well. Where were the troops headed?"

"One platoon was going to the crash site. The helicopter," he clarified. "We got a hit on the tracking devices. Five of them, anyway.

They were up on one of the ridges. The second platoon was going there."

"Oh, shit," she murmured. "That's Baker's Ridge. I saw the bodies. There were twelve bodies up there. The three crew members, five from your squad and four civilians," she said. "It looked like they were using them for food."

"Oh, God," Duncan said. "So we sent them up to Baker's Ridge? That's where you said the…the spaceship was?"

"Yes. It's at the top of Baker's Ridge, in the crevice. And we're in a world of hurt, Duncan. If that squad made it up there, made it even close to the ridge, then we've got to assume they've been compromised." She closed her eyes for a moment. "Fill Sutter in. I'm going to call General Brinkley."

She disconnected before he could say more. Yeah, the squad had most likely made it to the ship. That's why there was so much gunfire. They were using the weapons now. Whoever the hell *they* were.

She stared up into the darkening sky, trying to remember Harry's direct number. When she called, he answered on the second ring.

"It's me," she said. "And you were right. It's a clusterfuck any way you look at it."

CHAPTER FORTY-SEVEN

As the last of the light faded from the sky, Dana stood beside Jean and watched as Daisy was loaded into the trailer along with Gretchen. She wasn't certain how Corey had managed to get the trailer here so quickly. Since Corey had gotten off the phone, she'd been rather quiet and hadn't offered much information. Of course, they hadn't had any time alone to talk, but she assumed that was going to change.

"I really wish you wouldn't go back there, Dana," Jean said once again. "Let the soldiers go in."

"They're my parents," she said. "If we go south, like Butch suggested, then I think we'll be okay." Dana hugged her tightly. "And you'll be okay too. Try not to worry about us." She started to pull away, then hugged her again. "And please take care of Butch for me."

"Are you sure the captain doesn't mind that we stay at her place?"

Dana shook her head. "She's the one who suggested it. With luck, it'll only be a couple of days," she said, echoing Corey's words of earlier in the day. Corey had already given Butch the keys to her SUV, which was parked at the base, along with her house keys. "And speaking of the captain, let's go find her."

They spotted Corey and Butch leaning over the hood of a Jeep, looking at a map, both of them holding flashlights over it. It was odd to see flashlights that worked, but according to Corey, they were three hundred yards from the outage "zone," as she called it.

Corey looked up as they approached. "Hey. Got the horses loaded?"

"Yes. Looks like they're about ready to leave," she said, pausing to ruffle the fur on Lucky's head. She motioned to the map with her other hand. "We have a plan?"

"Yeah, I think. If you head directly south from here, you'll hit Cat Creek," Butch said, pointing across the road. "Just follow the creek all the way to the bridge, then get out at the road."

Dana nodded. "At the same bridge we got out on. Only from the other direction."

"Right. Get out at the bridge. There's that drop-off downstream. You know the horses can't make that," he reminded her. "You'll need to go around it."

"Okay. Follow the creek how far?" she asked, looking at the map.

"Follow it back to the county road, where you and I first hooked up with it," he said, tapping his finger on the map. "Right here." He stood up. "And you'll check on my folks too, right?"

"Promise," she said.

He sighed. "I should be going with you. I could—"

"Your job is to take care of Miss Jean," Corey said. "You'll be safe at my place. Besides, you need to get some rest. You had no business being out on horseback today as it was."

"Why can't some of the soldiers go with you?" Jean asked.

"They've got their hands full," Corey said. "And...well, we're kinda going in unauthorized." Corey looked over at her. "And against orders," she added.

"Will you get into trouble?" Dana asked.

"Doesn't matter," Corey said dismissively.

Dana knew she had been on the phone four different times, but she didn't know who all Corey had spoken to. She hoped Corey would fill her in later.

"Captain Conaway? We're all set, ma'am."

"Thanks." Corey said to the soldier who had walked over, then turned to Butch. "Time for you two to get out of here, I guess. You remember the directions to my place?"

Butch nodded. "I'll find it." He then hugged Corey quickly, then did the same to her. "You take care of my horse," he said. "I'll see you in a few days."

"I will. I'm sure Gretchen will be happy for a reprieve," Dana said. While Gretchen had held up pretty well, she was ten years older than Butch's mare. He had suggested they switch and Corey had agreed.

Jean walked closer to Corey, then brought her into a hug. Dana felt a tear in her eye as she watched them.

"I'm surely glad it was you that came to our rescue, Captain," Jean said. "I'll look forward to seeing you in a few days. Maybe I'll cook up something special."

Corey laughed. "I warned you there wasn't a whole lot of food at my place."

"I'll find something, don't you worry." Jean then turned to her and, once again, she and Dana exchanged a hug. "You take care of the captain," Jean whispered into her ear.

"I'll try."

Jean patted her cheek affectionately. "Yes…and she'll take care of you."

She and Corey stood next to each other, their shoulders brushing, watching as the truck and trailer pulled away, the taillights glowing in the darkness.

"Seems strange to see—hear—a truck," she said.

"Yeah, it does." Corey turned to her. "I've got the tent all set up. Our bedrolls are in there." She motioned with her head. "Down off the road a little ways." She handed Dana a flashlight. "Take Lucky. I'll be there in a minute."

Dana stared at her. "I can wait," she offered, not really wanting to go off by herself.

Corey smiled quickly. "You're safe here, Dana. I'm just going to find us some water bottles and get my gear packed for the morning. I want to get an early start. Before daybreak," she said. "Which means no time for coffee."

Dana wrinkled up her nose. "No coffee?"

"Will I be able to live with you?" Corey teased.

"Well, you'll be taking a chance, that's for sure." When Corey would have walked off, Dana called her back. "Are you okay, Corey? You've been…well, really, really quiet. A little…distant."

Corey walked back over to her, reaching out a hand to stroke Lucky's head affectionately. "They all think I'm crazy. Even Harry."

Dana tilted her head slightly. "That's General Brinkley? The family friend?"

"Yes. Although he wasn't quite as vocal about it as Colonel Sutter. Sutter said I was out of my fucking mind."

"I see. Guess we're all out of our fucking minds then," she said, eliciting a small smile from Corey.

"I recommended a missile strike," Corey continued. "I don't think Harry was convinced."

"A missile strike? Oh, my God! Where?"

"Baker's Ridge. It's federal land. My thought is to hit the ship and hopefully kill whatever's in it."

Dana couldn't stop her hand from reaching out to Corey, and she felt her fingers slip around her arm. "But what about those that *aren't* in the ship anymore?"

"I know," Corey said quietly. "I conveyed all of that to Harry. All my concerns, my fears," she said.

"If he's not convinced of a missile strike, then what's the alternative? More troops? That hasn't exactly worked out for them," she said.

Corey paused. "What I'm really afraid of is that they *will* believe me and someone will make the decision to try to capture these…these things, whatever they are, and want to study them. Research." Corey ran a hand over her hair. "Hell, try to communicate with them."

Dana shook her head. "They haven't been out here, they don't know what these things are capable of. I mean, we don't have a clue as to how they kill, how they take over these bodies." She stopped. "And I can't believe we're having this conversation as if it's perfectly normal to be discussing aliens and body snatchers. Maybe we *have* lost our fucking minds."

Corey lifted a corner of her mouth in a smile. "That would be a far simpler explanation, wouldn't it?" Then her smile faded. "But we know that's not the case." She shrugged. "When they realize that what we're saying is true, then there'll be this big, massive cover-up and they'll try to explain it with something even more absurd than a UFO."

Dana watched her walk away, then she turned and pointed the flashlight down the hill, finding the tent. She flashed it around her, finding nothing but rocks and a few scrub bushes, neither large enough for someone to hide behind.

She glanced down at Lucky, who was looking up at her. "Are you scared too?" All she got was a wag of his tail in response. She sighed as she touched his head. If she lingered here long enough, Corey would come back, then she wouldn't have to go to the tent alone. But she didn't want to be that needy, clingy person who was afraid of her own shadow. As Corey had said, they were safe here. They were outside of the so-called "zone." Of course, the "zone" was only an imaginary line, easily crossed by…well, by whatever was out there.

She flashed her light around one more time, again seeing nothing out of the ordinary. But she jumped, her heart lodging in her throat as a chorus of coyote howls bounced over the barren landscape.

"They sound close. *Really* close," she whispered to Lucky, who had emitted a low growl. She looked behind her, seeing the lights from the large tents set up at the checkpoint, seeing movement as a few soldiers walked about. The sight chased some of her fears away. Some, but not all.

Another sigh, then she made herself move, heading to Corey's tiny tent. Their horses were staked nearby, and the white stallion swung his tail absently, back and forth, as if swatting at a fly on his back. The horses didn't seem concerned with the coyotes—or anything else. She swung her pack off her back and placed it beside the tent. Lucky immediately laid down beside it.

She bent over and opened the flap on the tent, then crawled inside, never once even considering turning the flashlight off. Of course, she didn't know why she was bothering getting in the tent in the first place. There was no way she would even contemplate closing her eyes until Corey returned.

After she took her boots off, she lay back, curling one arm behind her head, her eyes wide as she stared at the door, listening for movement outside. Lucky would alert her, she knew. Nonetheless, she wanted to be prepared for…well, she just wanted to be prepared. She reached to her side, finding the gun she'd placed beside her. She was shocked by the comfort that brought her.

Comfort, yes, but she still didn't dare relax.

After what seemed like hours, she heard Lucky stir, and she cocked her head, listening. Then she heard footsteps on the rocks, heard Corey's soft murmur as she greeted the dog. Dana finally let out a relieved breath, feeling some of the tension leave her body.

"Hard to sleep with that light on, isn't it?"

"Um, no," Dana said. "It's hard to sleep when you're paralyzed by fear."

Corey kicked her boots off, then got in beside her. "Lucky will be on guard," Corey said. "Besides, they'll have three on watch duty at all times." Corey turned to her. "I briefed them. They looked at me like I'd grown a second head or something."

"Why doesn't anyone believe us?"

Corey reached over and took the flashlight from her, plunging the tent into darkness. "Would *you* believe us if you hadn't experienced it?"

She paused only slightly. "No. I'd say you'd lost your fucking mind."

Corey's laughter rang out, and Dana joined her. It felt good to laugh. But their merriment ceased almost as quickly as it had come.

"I want to get up very early," Corey said. "About three. We should still have a little moonlight."

"It's weird having *time* now, you know?"

"I know. And we won't have it for long, I suppose." Corey turned her head toward her. "Try to get some sleep. It'll be a long day tomorrow."

"You don't sound tired," she said, "but I know you're exhausted. What's your secret?"

"Years of practice," Corey murmured.

Dana rolled to her side. "Do you mind if I use you for a pillow?"

Corey shifted. "Would you like me to hold you?"

"That would be really nice."

She could feel rather than see the smile on Corey's face as she pulled her nearer. Dana sighed contentedly as she snuggled against her. She felt as safe as she'd ever felt, nestled here in Corey's arms. Oh, how she wished they'd met under different circumstances. Yes, they had a connection between them. A part of her wondered, though, if that was only because of the situation they found themselves in. If they weren't under this constant duress, would they still be pulled together like this? Would this attraction be as strong?

As Corey's hand rubbed lightly against her back, she thought that surely it would be. It felt too right being with her. Was it fate that brought them together? Was it their destiny that they meet like this? In her heart...in her soul...she knew the answer and she pressed herself even closer to Corey.

"Close your eyes," Corey whispered. "You're safe."

"I know." She didn't close them, however. She lifted her head slightly. It was too dark to see, of course, but she was still able to find Corey's mouth. It was a soft, gentle kiss, nothing more. This wasn't the time or place for more, but their kiss was enough to ignite a flame inside her, making her wish she'd not kissed her in the first place. It only served to whet her appetite for more.

And they couldn't have more. Not yet.

She groaned in frustration as she pulled away, again resting her head against Corey's shoulder as she pulled her closer again.

"I know," Corey said quietly. "God...I know."

Dana smiled in the darkness. Yes, they were connected. Corey apparently could read her mind. She finally closed her eyes then, a smile still lingering on her lips as sleep claimed her.

CHAPTER FORTY-EIGHT

Sutter stood at the window, staring through the half-opened blinds, seeing nothing really, just watching as lights flickered in the darkness. He took a deep breath, then finally turned, finding Duncan standing at his desk.

"At ease," he murmured, motioning to the chair.

For once, Duncan seemed to be at a loss for words. He sat quietly, his hands fidgeting with a file he was holding.

"Do you believe her?" Sutter asked. Duncan opened his mouth to speak, then closed it again. Sutter was aware of his nervousness and he waved an impatient hand at him. "Well?"

"Do you really want my opinion, sir, or do you want—"

He leaned forward, staring directly at Duncan. "We don't have time for games, Lieutenant. I'm well aware of what has transpired in the last ten days. I'm well aware of what your stance on this has been since the beginning. What I want to know is…do you believe her?"

Duncan nodded. "Yes, sir. I do."

"You actually believe that a spaceship landed? That it made it all the way through space without being detected by satellite? That it invaded our airspace without being detected by radar?" He leaned back. "And I'm not talking about the goddamn four-second blip either.

Her story is…it's too farfetched to be true. You're an intelligent man, Duncan. Surely you can see that."

"It's too farfetched to be fabricated, sir."

Sutter slammed his fist on his desk. "I told her she was a fucking lunatic. And you know what she did? She called Brinkley directly," he said loudly. "Did you know that?"

Duncan hesitated only a second. "No, sir."

"He's flying in tonight," he said with a shake of his head. "I've got two platoons unaccounted for, not to mention the squad that we sent in at the beginning. I'm ready to send a whole goddamn battalion in to find them." He paused. "But you know what he's got his mind set on? A goddamn long-range missile strike, all because *Captain* Conaway thinks it's the best form of action." He slammed his fist on his desk again. "I'm a goddamn colonel! He took Major Godfrey away from me and now has *you* handling his duties. *You!* A goddamn lieutenant!" Sutter felt his face turn red, felt his heart as it beat loudly in his chest. "And now…a goddamn *captain* is apparently giving orders around here!"

Duncan stared at him obediently. "Yes, sir."

Sutter took a deep breath, trying to get his anger under control before he had a stroke. His hand was shaking as he reached for his water bottle.

"Jesus Christ, Duncan…never in my life would I have believed it would come to this. There've been UFO sightings since the dawn of time. There's always an explanation, Duncan. Always."

"Over the years, Air Force pilots have reported seeing—"

"Air Force," he said disgustedly. "What the hell do they know?" He stood up and walked to the window, staring out for a second, then closed the blinds on the night. "Regardless. Whether she's right or wrong, this whole incident will get buried so deep, so fast, it'll make your head spin."

"But why, sir? We've been searching for life on other planets forever," Duncan said.

Sutter turned to him. "Yeah. *Searching*, Duncan. Never finding. If it gets out to the general public that a spaceship landed here—without our knowledge—and that the…the *extraterrestrials* or whatever the hell you want to call them, are killing and eating people," he said and laughed humorlessly. "And taking over their bodies like a *puppet*, she said. God, I can't believe Conaway really believes that. Anyway, can't you see the mass hysteria? It would be total madness, Duncan."

"So to protect the masses, we keep them in the dark," Duncan said quietly. "For their own good, of course."

Sutter could hear the disdain in his voice. "That's exactly right, son. For their own good." He returned to his desk and sat down again. "Everything about this operation will be classified, Duncan, whether they find little green men or not. Homeland will take over. Or maybe the clowns from the FBI." He snorted. "Hell, goddamn NSA might want to take over." He narrowed his eyes at Duncan. "What I'm trying to say is, if there's even a hint of a leak, it will be dealt with swiftly."

"Yes, sir."

He leaned back in his chair and looked around his office. "And I imagine I'll be relieved of my duties. In hindsight, sending out a Black Hawk wasn't the best decision I ever made."

"If I may, sir...had you not, we wouldn't have known what was going on. The power outage, the cell phone towers...that would have all been left to the local authorities."

"Yeah. And I wouldn't have two platoons missing either, Lieutenant."

"Of course, sir."

Sutter gave him a fake smile. "Well, Duncan, maybe after they clean house here, you'll get a cushy assignment like Major Godfrey did," he said sarcastically. "Out in a desert hellhole."

"Yes, sir."

CHAPTER FORTY-NINE

Corey fumbled with her watch, illuminating the face. It was three twenty. Dana was still curled at her side, and even though she knew she should get up, should wake Dana...she allowed herself a few moments to savor the closeness, the contact of another person. It had been so long since she'd felt this...this connection with someone. Even though she knew they needed to go, needed to hit the trail, she couldn't deny herself these few moments.

She'd only known Dana a little more than a week, yet it felt like a lifetime. How could that be? How could she feel like she'd known her forever? How could she feel like Dana was a part of her...that'd she'd always been a part of her?

"I'm awake," Dana whispered as she tightened her hold. "By the way, you make a wonderful pillow."

Corey smiled in the darkness. "No one's ever said that to me before."

"Maybe you haven't slept with the right person before," Dana murmured.

Her smile faltered only slightly. Dana was right, of course. She'd been so focused on her career, she rarely gave her personal life any thought. She'd had lovers, sure. Most, however, were forgotten the minute she'd left their beds. She never missed having someone in her life, someone permanent. She had her team. That had been enough. Now that they were gone, the void seemed large, much too large to try to fill.

"What are you thinking about?" Dana whispered.

Corey sighed. "Just…just thinking."

"I see. None of my business, huh?" Dana pulled away from her and rolled to her back. "I didn't think I'd sleep, but I guess I did." She turned her head slightly. "Did you?"

"Uh-huh," she said. She sat up, bending her head back and stretching her neck. "I don't think I woke up once."

"What time is it?"

Corey again touched her watch, the hands glowing in the dark. "Almost three thirty."

Dana sat up too and rubbed her face with both hands. "You know, the only things that should be out and about at this hour are vampires."

Corey laughed. "Vampires?"

"You know what I mean."

Corey found the flashlight and turned it on, watching as Dana shielded her eyes from the light. "Sorry."

"No, no. Light is good. Now if you could produce some coffee, it'd be perfect."

Corey got out of the tent and took the light with her. Lucky was right outside the door, his tail wagging when he saw her.

"Good boy," she said quietly as she patted his head. She turned back to Dana. "Fifteen minutes. I'm going to get the horses ready."

"Okay. I'll take the tent down."

* * *

Dana yawned as she followed behind Corey, still longing for a cup of coffee. Corey had said her eyes would adjust to the darkness and they had. Still, riding horses at three thirty in the morning was just not normal. Of course, it was her parents they were going after. She should be thankful that Corey was taking her, regardless of the ungodly hour and regardless that they hadn't taken time for coffee. Corey had mentioned last night that they were going back in without authorization and against orders. She knew nothing of military protocol, but she assumed Corey would get into some sort of trouble. Corey didn't seem to be concerned about it, though.

"You okay back there? Still awake?"

"I'm still awake," she said. Then, "You're not going to get, you know, court-martialed or something, are you?"

Corey laughed. "Colonial Sutter would probably try to charge me with treason if he could. But no, considering the circumstances and everything that's happened, I don't think my reprimand will be severe," she said.

"But you're going to get into trouble?"

"Disobeying an order does have consequences," Corey said. "It won't be my first time. Probably not my last."

"I see," Dana said, although she wasn't sure if she really understood. No one in her family had ever been in the military. In fact, she didn't know a single person who had been. "Well, thank you for doing it, despite knowing you'll get into trouble. Because if you'd said no, I would have attempted to go back alone."

"I know. And I couldn't let you do that."

She nodded in the darkness, knowing Corey would not have let her go out on her own. She only hoped the outcome was a favorable one. She wouldn't be able to forgive herself if something...well, if something bad happened.

"I hope we don't regret this," she said quietly, voicing her concerns.

"I think Butch was right...this route we're taking should be safe. With luck, we should make it there by noon or a little after," Corey said.

"It seems like we're going slow."

"Yeah. Once it's daylight, we'll pick up the pace."

Dana looked to the sky, thinking it would be another hour before dawn approached. Of course, the days were getting longer. Sunrise seemed to come earlier and earlier. And last night, there was still a little light in the sky even as the clock ticked close to nine. She remembered the long summer days of her childhood when she and Butch could still be outside playing well after supper. Late June, early July, the days had seemed to last forever.

She just wished this one would hurry up and get here...because she was ready for it to be over with.

CHAPTER FIFTY

Corey shifted in the saddle, her back sore. She guessed it was nine, maybe ten already. Her watch had stopped working shortly after they'd entered the zone. Once the sun had come up, they'd made much better time and had only stopped once to take a break and stretch their legs. Lucky, on the other hand, had plopped down to rest, his tongue hanging out as he panted. He hadn't even bothered to get in the creek.

They were following Cat Creek and it was much smaller than the creek they'd followed back and forth the previous week. Cat Creek was little more than a trickle in places, then widening in spots as it flowed across a bed of rocks. Cat Creek followed a small canyon which was rocky and arid, nothing like the lush valley that Paradox Creek flowed through.

"You ever been out this way?" she asked, tossing a glance over at Dana, who was riding beside her.

Dana shook her head. "When we were kids, we explored the creek downstream, past our farms. We never went beyond the county road."

"That's where we'll get out?"

"We'll get out at the bridge," Dana said. "We could follow the creek a little farther, but there's a steep part—a drop-off—nothing but rocks."

"That's where Butch was saying the horses couldn't go," she said.

"Yeah. But if we stay above the creek, we can still see it. It crosses under the county road then. That's the road we'll take to my parents' place."

"We started out so damn early, I thought we might be there by now," she said. "Once we get to the bridge, how far do you think?"

"Maybe an hour," Dana said. "Probably a little longer. It's not an easy ride. Lots of rocks. There's not really a trail." Dana stared at her. "You're ready for this to be over with too, huh?"

Corey nodded. "It's been quiet. Brinkley acted like they were going to send in a whole damn battalion. Maybe he changed his mind."

"You expected to hear gunfire?"

"Yeah."

What she really hoped to hear was a missile strike up on Baker's Ridge. But if that was going to be the plan, they would have done it at daybreak. Unless it was still being discussed, that is.

"How far are we from Baker's Ridge?" she asked Dana.

"Oh, a long way," Dana said. "It's northwest of Jean's house. Once we get out at the bridge, we'll be about fifteen, twenty miles south of Paradox. That's Highway 90. Our farm is still several miles east of there."

"Highway 90 is where they had the so-called rock slide," she said, wondering if the road was still closed. "So you can't see the ridge from here?"

"No."

"Yet when this thing crash-landed up there, you heard it?"

"Didn't hear a crash, no. It felt like an earthquake," Dana said. "It didn't last long, ten seconds at most." She pointed up ahead. "There's the bridge."

It was still a couple of hundred yards away, but the sight of it made Corey feel like they were getting close. She didn't realize how tense she'd been, and she rolled her shoulders a couple of times, trying to relax.

But as they neared the bridge, just when she thought that the quiet morning would signal an uneventful day, they heard gunfire. They stopped their horses, looking around them.

"How close?" Dana asked quietly.

"Hard to tell. The sound echoes here in the canyon," she said, her voice quiet too. "Two shots."

"I'm not an expert on guns, but that sounded like a normal rifle."

Corey nodded. "Yeah. Hunting rifle, probably."

"I don't want to think the worst, but maybe…maybe one of them made it down this far. Maybe—"

"It could be anything. Let's just keep our eyes open," she said as she gave her horse a gentle kick.

They found an easy path out of the canyon and up to the road. Corey hurried to the other side, not taking the time to look around. They were out in the open, and she wanted to get off the road. Not that there was much cover anyway. A few small trees here and there but mostly scrub brush scattered among the rocks. The creek was down to their right—they followed along from above. It didn't take long for them to reach the drop-off, and she paused to watch as the water tumbled over boulders and down to the bottom some fifty feet below.

They skirted the rocks and climbed a little higher, finding more level ground. Up ahead, she could see where the creek flattened again, its rapid pace over the rocks changing to a slow, even crawl, making barely a ripple in the surface.

"This is where Butch and I came up," Dana said.

Corey saw what appeared to be game trail, and Lucky took the lead, his nose to the ground, tail wagging. They followed him back down to the creek, where he apparently lost interest in the scent he was following. He plunged into the water, his face tunneling under it, then he shook himself and began to drink. The water barely reached his belly.

"Is the creek this shallow all the way?"

"No. Down past our place, it's decent size. Enough to trout fish," Dana said. "And swim in."

"Oh, yeah?"

"Water was cold as hell no matter what time of year," Dana said with a laugh. "But when you're kids, you don't seem to notice, I guess. Butch and I spent a lot of time there."

Corey nodded. "I regret not having that."

Dana frowned. "Having what?"

"Childhood memories like that," she explained. "We moved around so much, it's really all a blur."

"Your childhood and adult life both," Dana said. "I don't suppose you've ever had the chance to put down roots."

She shrugged. "My choice. I guess I never thought I would regret it," she said truthfully. Actually, ever since she and Jean had talked, she realized just how much she did regret some of her choices in life. Like never taking the time to find love. She sighed, still fearing it was too late for her now. She looked over at Dana, about to tell her that very thing when she heard a sound off in the distance that she knew well.

She glanced quickly to the sky, scanning it, hearing the swoosh of air as the missile shot through it.

"What is it?"

Before she could comment, the explosion shook the ground and her horse danced sideways upon the rocks. She pulled up on the reins, trying to steady him.

"What the hell was that?" Dana asked urgently.

"Missile strike," she said. "But the explosion, the ground shaking… not just from the missile. It must have made a direct hit." She turned her horse around. "Stay here," she said as she retraced their steps, guiding the stallion back the way they'd come. Once at the top, she stood up tall in the saddle, shielding her eyes against the sun. She finally found what she was looking for. Smoke.

She glanced down at Dana. "I'm guessing it's Baker's Ridge," she called. "At least I hope so. Got smoke in the air. Looks a hell of a long way off."

She turned her horse again, going back down the trail to the creek. Dana's eyes searched hers.

"So you think they hit the…the spaceship, right?"

"Yeah."

"And we're hoping it's not like…radioactive and stuff…right?"

Corey grinned. "Oh, yeah…hoping like hell." She gave the horse a kick. "Let's push on."

CHAPTER FIFTY-ONE

Dana felt a sense of relief when they finally reached the small county road. As Cat Creek left the canyon and entered the valley—Lion Valley—scrub brush disappeared, replaced by trees and grass. Even though she didn't make it home much anymore, this, at least, was familiar to her. They left the creek and followed the road, heading toward the tiny dirt lane that would take them to her parents' farm.

"We're close, right?"

"Yes," she said. "A few more miles." She motioned to the dog in Corey's lap. "How's he doing?"

"He appears to be comfortable," Corey said. "One of us might as well be."

Dana smiled, knowing Corey was teasing. She had been the one to insist that Lucky ride. It had been a long day, and Lucky's pace had slowed considerably. Getting him onto her lap was no easy task, but he seemed happy with the change.

"Have I mentioned lately how hungry I am?"

Corey laughed. "This makes eight times, I believe. Maybe your mother will have something. I'm a little hungry myself."

Dana's smile faded. "I hope she's okay. It seems like I've been gone for a month."

"I know."

Dana turned to her. "When this is over with, am I going to see you again?"

Corey shrugged. "Seattle is a long way from here. Besides, you know, you have a marriage proposal to deal with."

Dana rolled her eyes. "Don't remind me. Of course, I'm sure she thinks I'm not answering my phone on purpose. Maybe she's gotten the message."

Corey watched her, and Dana finally turned from her stare, wondering what thoughts were going through her mind.

"If you aren't in love with her and have no intention of marrying her, why didn't you just tell her that when she asked? Why run?"

Dana bit her lower lip. Yeah…why *had* she run? She glanced over at Corey and gave an almost apologetic shrug.

"I panicked," she said. "I think—in the back of my mind—I was afraid I'd say yes."

Corey raised an eyebrow questioningly.

Dana wondered if now was the right time to be having this conversation. No, of course it wasn't. She continued on, nonetheless.

"Ever since I was a young girl, I've had this…this vision of who my mate would be. I didn't know I was gay when I was that age, obviously, but I was aware that my image of this person was genderless." She glanced at Corey again, smiling. "When I got older, this vision that I had in my head…in my heart…was no longer genderless. She became my Dream Girl." She laughed. "Silly, I know."

Corey smiled too but said nothing.

"Every year that passed…every year I got older, I began to fear that I'd never find her."

"So you were ready to give up?"

"No. At least I don't think so. But how long is long enough?" she asked. "How long should I search for this person before I accept that I might never find her?"

"So you were afraid you'd settle for Kendra?" Corey guessed.

Dana remembered the very brief conversation she'd had with Kendra. "I was so shocked when she asked me; I was actually speechless for several seconds. And when I did speak, I blurted out exactly what I was thinking, 'Are you out of your *mind*?'" she recalled with a laugh. But her smile vanished. "I think she was so sure I'd say yes that it was her turn to be speechless." She waved her hand dismissively. "Anyway, it was an awful ending to the date and that night, as I lay in bed—alone—I was having a hard time picturing my Dream Girl and I feared I was losing her." Dana looked over at Corey, who was watching her. "And I was afraid I'd say yes. So I ran."

Corey's stare never wavered. "And now?" she asked quietly.

Dana held her gaze. "And now I don't want to settle. I want...I want my Dream Girl."

Corey nodded. "Then I hope you find her."

"I hope she *lets* me find her," Dana countered, her eyes never leaving Corey's.

* * *

"Here's the lane to the house," Dana said. "Hard to believe that it was only what? Nine? Ten days ago that I left here."

"Yeah. A hell of a lot has happened," Corey said. She looked over at Dana. "And we need to be careful."

"What do you mean?"

"No offense to your parents, because I don't know them, but after this much time, they might be Richard Filmore crazy," she said.

Dana laughed. "My father is *nothing* like Richard Filmore. He won't be guarding the house with a rifle."

Dana sounded confident, but Corey wasn't so sure. It had been nearly two weeks without power, without communication. That kind of stress sometimes made people do crazy things. Of course, being out here alone, without the influence of a paranoid storekeeper like Richard Filmore, might mean they were still operating like there's nothing out of the ordinary going on. If you ignored the explosion of the missile strike, that is.

"What? Are you worried he's going to shoot us?" Dana asked.

"It's crossed my mind," she said truthfully.

"Corey, I promise, they're normal people. But if you're worried, let me ride up first," Dana said.

"I think Lucky's going to beat you to it," she said, motioning to the dog that was trotting up to the house ahead of them. Since his ride on the horse earlier, he seemed to have replenished his energy level. Unfortunately, there was no creek for him to play in here.

Dana pulled her horse to a stop where the lane ended and the yard began. The house was a smaller ranch-style with a long porch on the front that wrapped around to the back. A porch swing hung on one side and, while inviting, she wondered how often it got used.

"Mom?" Dana called as she slipped off her horse. "Dad?"

Corey got down too, and she held the reins loosely in her hand as she looked around.

"Mom?" Dana called again as she hurried up to the porch.

The front door was open, leaving only the screen door as a barrier. Dana opened it, then paused to look back at her. Corey noticed the worried look in her eyes.

"Maybe they're out back," she suggested.

Instead of going inside, Dana let the screen door close again and she walked back over to her.

"I'm scared. What if—"

"Let's go around back," she said.

They led the horses behind them and went around the side of the house to the back. As at many of the farms they'd been to, the barn wasn't far from the house. The back porch was larger than the front and looked like it had been added on to over the years, making a deck out in the yard. She saw an old cast-iron smoker and a gas grill next to it. They both looked well-used.

"Mom?" Dana called.

Corey saw movement to the side of the barn and tensed as chickens ran around the corner. Lucky's ears perked up, and Corey put a hand out, touching his head. He barked once when a woman came into view. She looked startled, then a smile lit her face.

"Mom!" Dana ran toward her and Corey relaxed again.

"Dana! Oh, my. I'm so glad to see you," she said as they embraced.

"Are you okay?"

"Of course. I told you we'd be fine. Took longer for the power to come back on than we'd thought, but we made out just fine."

Corey's eyebrows shot up. "The power's back on?" She looked at her watch, shocked to see it working again. Had the missile strike done that?

"Yes. Came back on about an hour ago, maybe two." She and Dana walked closer and Corey noticed the suspicious look in her eyes. "Who are you? And where's Butch?"

"Mom…this is Corey. Butch is…he's fine." Dana looked around. "Where's Dad?"

"He just got back. He's inside," she said, motioning to the house.

Dana and Corey exchanged a quick glance. "Back from where?" Dana asked.

"He went over to Joe and Fredda's yesterday." Dana's mother clasped her hands together, wringing them. "And I'm worried sick," she said.

"Who is Joe and Fredda?" Corey asked.

"Butch's parents," Dana explained. "My dad and Joe are brothers. Mom and Fredda are sisters." Dana stilled her mother's hands. "What's wrong, Mom?"

"I know something's happened. I can feel it. And your father won't say. He came back and has hardly said a word to me. I don't know if Fredda and Joe are okay. He didn't say a word about George and Tina. You know they were still staying with them."

"How…how long has he been back?" Dana asked.

"Just a little while before you got here. I came out to see if I could find some eggs. I thought I'd bake up something special since the power's back on."

Dana ran her fingers through her hair nervously. "I…I went to the door. I called out," she said. "No one answered. Is he…is he all right? Does he seem like himself?"

Dana's mother shook her head. "He won't talk to me. And I know he got into something. He's got bloodstains on his shirt and he acts like he doesn't even know where it came from. That's why I know something's wrong. Something must have happened to Joe and Fredda. And Irene and Paul…we haven't seen them in two days. I've been a nervous wreck. Something—"

"I'll go take a look," Corey offered.

Dana grabbed her arm. "Take Lucky."

She met Dana's worried eyes. "You and your mother stay here."

Dana stared at her. "I should…I should go with you."

"Stay here," she said firmly, then glanced at her mother. "Stay with your mom."

"Wait," Dana's mother said. "Why do you have a gun?" She had a puzzled look on her face as she looked between them. "What's going on, Dana?"

"I can't explain now. We need to check on Dad first."

Corey hesitated, looking back at Dana, meeting her gaze once again. Sadness filled her eyes, and she knew Dana was fighting back tears. But Dana squared her shoulders and nodded.

"Be careful," Dana whispered.

"What's going on?" her mother demanded.

"Let's go back to the barn, Mom."

"No! I want to know what's going on."

"Mrs. Ingram…please, stay here," she said.

Her mother stared at Dana. "Dana? What's going on? Who is she?"

"Mom…*please*," Dana begged. "Just trust me."

Corey took a deep breath, then headed to the back porch, Lucky right at her heels. God, she didn't want to do this. But it was all too familiar. Just like Hal. Just like the soldier in Jean's barn.

She went up on the porch. There were two doors and she chose the one closest to her, pulling open the screen door. It was quiet and dark inside. She paused, then walked in, beckoning for Lucky to follow. The dog seemed to understand, and he padded in front of her, his ears alert as he looked around the kitchen. She reached out, flipping on the light switch and the overhead bulb came on, chasing the shadows away. The kitchen was neat and tidy, although pots were out on the stove, ready to be used for dinner. A sound out in the hallway pulled her gaze from the stove.

She tilted her head, listening. She slowly moved her hand to her holster and unclipped the leather strap, taking out her weapon. Lucky growled low in his throat, and she felt her adrenaline kick in, felt her senses come alive as she crept quietly to the door.

She swallowed nervously as she took another step, then paused as Lucky brushed by her, his growl louder now. He went out into the hallway, his growl turning into a sharp bark.

"Mr. Ingram?" she called. "You there?"

Lucky's barking turned vicious, a sound Corey recognized, and she tightened her grip on her gun. She went out into the hallway, finding Lucky, the hair on his back standing at attention. It was a short hallway and it opened up into the living room. The shadows were heavy inside, despite the glow from a lamp on an end table.

"Mr. Ingram?" she called again.

Lucky's incessant barking took on a frantic sound, and as Corey rounded the corner into the living room...she gasped, her heart nearly stopping dead in its tracks.

"Jesus Christ," she murmured.

* * *

Something was wrong. She could feel it.

"Dana, why in the world would that woman let that *dog* into my house? You know how I feel about that."

Dana held her hand up. "Mom...stop."

She stared at the house, trying to decide what to do. Lucky's bark—it was different. It sounded panicked.

"I will not stop. You're acting very strange." Her mother started walking toward the house. "If you won't tell me what's going on, I'll find out for myself. What is she? Law enforcement or something?"

Dana grabbed her mother's arm and pulled her to a stop. "Yes. Something like that," she said. She went to her horse and opened her bag, taking out the gun Corey had given her.

"What in the world?" her mother asked, her voice high-pitched with shock. "You *hate* guns."

Dana ignored her as she ran toward the house. "Stay here!"

"The hell I will!"

Dana knew Corey had gone into the kitchen, but Lucky's barks were farther back in the house. She went to the living room door instead, pausing to catch her breath before opening it...pausing to try to calm her nerves somewhat. She felt her mother come up behind her, and she turned to her, meeting her gaze.

"Something is wrong," she whispered.

"Your father—"

"No. I don't think Dad's here."

"Of course he is. I told you—"

"Please trust me. I'm begging you...please, just trust me."

Her mother stared at her for the longest time, then finally nodded. Dana blindly reached for her mother's hand and squeezed her fingers briefly before opening the door.

The barking was louder now, and she walked inside, her gun held out in front of her. The stench hit her immediately and she only barely resisted covering her nose and mouth.

"What on God's green earth is that smell?" her mother whispered.

Dana felt her heart pounding in her chest, and she was aware of the gun trembling in her hand. There were four of them, all standing along the back wall, watching Corey and Lucky.

Her father. A soldier. An older man she'd never seen before. And Richard Filmore.

They turned when she walked fully into the room, all now staring right at her as if they'd forgotten Corey and Lucky were even there.

"Get the hell out of here!" Corey yelled.

Everyone seemed to move at once and she fired her weapon at the same time Corey did. Unfortunately, they'd both taken aim at Richard Filmore, their shots sending him tumbling back against the wall.

Her mother screamed loudly behind her, and Dana turned, shooting the soldier as he reached for her mother. She swung back around, but Corey's shot had taken out the other man, sending him sprawling to the floor. She stared in shock as her father grabbed both Corey and Lucky at the same time, flinging them into the hallway wall so violently that the pictures hanging there fell from their hooks.

Everything slowed to a crawl, and she was amazed at the clarity. A picture of her and Butch was the last to fall, and she watched as it hit the floor, the glass shattering upon impact. Corey and Lucky lay in a heap and seconds passed as slowly as minutes. Her mother's screams faded to the background as her father turned to her, his angry eyes boring into hers.

She held her gun up, pointing it at him, her hands shaking so badly she couldn't take a shot. He took a step toward her, his mouth quivering, as if trying to smile. It came out as a snarl instead.

As he took another step toward her, she fired, missing badly. Her mother's screams started again, and she felt her mother try to pull her back and she shook her off. Taking a deep breath, she grasped the gun with both hands, pulling the trigger three times in quick succession, all three hitting her father in the chest. He fell to his knees, then back... finally stilling.

"Oh, my God! Oh, my God!" her mother shrieked as she flew to her father, cradling his head as her tears fell. She looked at Dana accusingly. "What have you *done*?"

Dana bolted into action, running past her mother to Corey. She rolled her over, seeing blood seeping from her mouth.

"Corey," she whispered.

She was relieved to hear Corey moan, and she wiped at the blood, seeing a cut on her lip. She touched her face gently, then turned to glance at her mother. Her wails filled the house and Dana went to her, trying to pull her up.

"Get away from him," she said.

Her mother slapped at her hands, her eyes wild. "You *shot* him!" she screamed.

"Get away from him!" Dana said forcefully, pulling her mother with her.

"You *killed* him!"

Dana grabbed her mother's shoulders and shook her. "That's not him!" she yelled.

Her mother slammed her hands into Dana's chest, hitting her hard as she screamed, tears running down her face. Dana tried to still her hands but failed as her mother's palm caught her across the cheek.

"Goddamn it!" she yelled, pushing her mother back forcefully against the wall. "It's not him!" She pointed at the man lying on the floor, the man who looked like her father. "It's not him," she said again, softer now. "Look," she pointed. "There's no blood."

As they both looked at him, his arm began to twitch. Dana stared in amazement as he sat up, lifting his head to look at them. His eyes were black and lifeless and this time when her mother screamed, it wasn't with grief and sorrow. No, this time it was with fear.

Dana lifted her arm, about to shoot him again when another shot rang out, the bullet ripping through his head. She turned away from the body, gathering her mother in her arms, trying to calm her as she shielded her from the sight of her husband lying on their living room floor.

"Come on," she said, pulling her mother into the hallway.

Corey was slumped against the wall, her eyes half-opened. One hand was clutching Lucky to her, the other still holding her gun.

"I'm so sorry," Corey murmured.

Dana knelt down beside her. "No. Thank you," she whispered. Then, "Are you okay?"

"Yeah. Blacked out for a minute there. I'll be okay."

Dana brushed her cheek gently, then reached out and touched Lucky's head, hearing him whimper.

"Yeah...I think he'll be okay too," Corey said. As if to prove her right, Lucky's tail wagged weakly.

Dana squeezed her hand. "Let me get my mother settled. I'll be right back."

She took her mother into the kitchen and pulled out a chair, pushing her down into it. Her mother's eyes were wide, darting around the room nervously. Dana took a glass and filled it with water, then set it in front of her mother.

"We'll need to leave soon," she said. Her mother met her gaze, but Dana wasn't sure she'd heard her. "That...that man. Who was he?"

Her mother frowned.

"Richard Filmore was one," Dana said. "And a soldier. But who was the other one?"

Her mother opened her mouth to speak, then closed it, her eyes blinking several times.

"Mom?"

Her mother looked down. "It was...it was Carl Milstead," she said, her voice little more than a whisper. "He lives...way up in Squaw Valley, I think."

Dana leaned down and hugged her. "I know you don't understand what's going on," she said. "I'm not sure I can even explain it. But that wasn't Dad. And that wasn't Mr. Filmore and that wasn't Carl Milstead." She stared at her. "And that wasn't a real soldier. Do you understand?"

Her mother looked up at her, her eyes searching. She finally shook her head. "No. I don't think I do."

Dana sighed. "No. Of course not." She sighed again. "You've got to trust me, Mom. *Please*?"

CHAPTER FIFTY-TWO

Corey hated leaving the horses behind. In fact, she was shocked by how much she was going to miss the white stallion. But the pasture had plenty of grass this time of year and the water pump was working again at the trough. They should be fine for a while. She knew Dana was watching her and she turned to her.

"How do you feel?" Dana asked.

Corey tilted her head thoughtfully. "I think the question should be, how do *you* feel?"

She saw Dana take a deep breath, saw her put on a brave face. "I haven't really processed it yet." She waved back toward the car where her mother was. "And Mom is in shock. She won't...she won't talk. She's totally unresponsive now."

Corey went to her and pulled her into a hug, holding her tightly. "I'm so sorry," she whispered. She felt Dana's hands clutch at her shirt, folding it into her fists.

"I shot...my father," Dana said simply.

Corey felt the wetness of her tears, even though Dana made no sound. She held her while she cried, rubbing her back soothingly. Dana said she hadn't processed it yet, but her tears said otherwise. She'd lost her father. Butch's parents were apparently gone too. And her mother was nearly catatonic. Yes, she'd processed it, whether she believed it or not.

Dana pulled away, wiping her nose with the back of her hand. "Sorry."

Corey had no comforting words for her, and she didn't bother with some trivial apology or empty words of remorse. She knew from experience that neither would do any good. So she merely took Dana's hand, holding it gently as they headed over to the car. Dana's mother and Lucky were in the backseat. They'd already stored their packs in the trunk and she'd found a container of fuel to top off the tank.

"You want me to drive?" she asked.

Dana nodded. "Yes. I'll show you the way."

It felt strange to be in a car again after all these days on horseback. As she pulled away, she glanced back to the barn, seeing the white stallion watching them. Dana followed her gaze.

"They'll be okay," Dana said. "Hopefully, we'll be able to come back soon. I mean, if—"

"I know. Hopefully it'll all be over very quickly."

When they got to the end of the lane, she turned right on the county road. She looked in the rearview mirror, seeing Mrs. Ingram staring blankly ahead, never blinking.

"Where does Butch live?" she asked Dana.

"There's a cutoff road up here, to the right. Why?"

"Let's swing by there. Just in case," she murmured.

Dana nodded. "Thank you. I promised Butch—"

"We both promised him," Corey reminded her.

She looked once again in the mirror, seeing no reaction from Dana's mother. As Dana had said, she was in shock. She'd just witnessed something that was extremely traumatic. Corey knew very few people would have come out of it unscathed. She was only thankful Dana was holding up as well as she was. She had a feeling she was going to need her.

But her fears weren't warranted, it turned out. Her aunt and uncle's house was indeed empty. However, it was obvious there had been a struggle. Chairs were tipped over in the kitchen and a lamp was smashed next to the sofa.

Dana was staring at a spot on the living room rug. She turned to Corey. "Is that blood?" she asked quietly.

Corey nodded. "Looks like it."

"Aunt Fredda kept an exceptionally tidy house," Dana said. "Except for the kitchen. She, like my mom, was always cooking or baking something." Dana impatiently wiped a tear away. "I can't believe this is happening."

"I know, honey," Corey said gently. "But right now, we need to get your mom out of here."

Dana nodded. "Yes. Okay."

Back out at the car, Lucky was sitting up in the backseat, watching for them. Corey paused at the window, reaching inside to ruffle his face.

"You feeling better, boy?" she asked softly.

He had been limping badly and she feared his front leg or shoulder was broken. But he seemed to be putting a little weight on that leg now. She slid her gaze past Lucky to Dana's mom. Like before, she simply stared straight ahead, as if unaware of what was going on around her.

"I'm really worried about her," Dana whispered beside her. "I wish Miss Jean was here. Maybe she could talk to her."

Corey nodded. "Hopefully tonight."

They looked to the sky as thunder rumbled off to the north. She'd just now noticed the thick clouds overhead.

"Wonder what time it is?"

"Have you checked your cell since the power came back?"

"Yeah. Battery is apparently really dead. I've got a charger for the car. I didn't even think to grab it," Dana said.

"Well, I'm sure it's late afternoon. Hard to tell with the clouds. Four? Five?"

She got inside and slammed the door shut, waiting for Dana to do the same. Before she started the engine, she glanced at her.

"I think we should go into Paradox."

Dana's eyes widened. "Why? If they made it this far south, then surely they're in Paradox."

"Most likely, yes. But I need to be able to give an accurate report when we get out." She met Dana's gaze. "And I think we owe it to Anna Gail to check on her and Holly."

Dana bit her lower lip, but nodded. "You're right. I don't want to go there, but…you're right."

They drove on in silence, and Corey wondered if Dana was doing as she was—checking their surroundings for people on foot. Well, not exactly *people*. Dana had said that the fourth man had been Carl Milstead. According to Jean, he had been with Hal when they'd first set out to look for the helicopter. His body should have been badly decomposing by now and she assumed that it was, judging from the smell. On the outside, he still appeared to be human. But obviously, *something* was inside him, controlling him. If she'd had her wits about her, she would have examined the bodies better. But the truth was, she was afraid to be alone with them. Dana had been consoling her mother, and even though Corey knew they should have burned them, she didn't want to take the time. Besides, she wasn't sure that Dana—or her mother—could have handled that. As it was, she only hoped that the bodies were disabled enough to be useless to them.

Which brought another thought. Whatever was inside of them… did it simply die if it couldn't find another host?

She jumped when a hand touched her thigh, and she smiled quickly at Dana. "Sorry."

"The turnoff to Paradox is coming up," Dana said. "To the left."

Corey nodded, then reached down and covered Dana's hand with her own, holding it against her thigh. She didn't say anything and neither did Dana. She glanced in the mirror once, but Mrs. Ingram's expression hadn't changed. She was still staring straight ahead, her eyes wide and unblinking.

She slowed when she approached Paradox. It looked even more deserted than before, if that was possible.

"Looks like a ghost town," Dana said quietly, echoing her own thoughts.

Corey pulled to a stop in front of the grocery store. She wasn't surprised to find the doors closed.

"Since Richard was…well, I mean—"

"I know," Corey said. "The chances of finding Anna Gail are slim." She left the car running, then got out. Before she closed the door, she looked back at Dana. "Get behind the wheel," she said.

"Why?"

"In case…in case something happens," Corey said. "You can—"

Dana shook her head. "No. I'm not leaving you."

Corey lifted up a corner of her mouth in a quick smile. "Well, I was kinda thinking in case we needed to make a quick exit, you'd have the car ready to go and I'd just have to dive in."

"Oh," Dana said sheepishly. "Okay."

"So yeah, try not to leave me behind."

Dana smiled briefly, then glanced to Corey's hip where her holster was, eyeing the gun briefly before looking back at her. "I should probably come with you. Or at least Lucky should."

Corey shook her head. "Stay with your mom." She glanced in the backseat at Lucky, who was sitting up, watching her. "And I think Lucky has done his duty for the day." She turned back to Dana. "I'll be okay. Come get behind the wheel," she said again.

Corey waited until Dana hurried around the car, then she closed the door. She turned, eyeing the store before walking across the sidewalk. The afternoon was growing late and thick clouds had settled overhead. A low rumble of thunder sounded, and she looked up just in time to catch a lightning bolt shooting across the sky followed by another clap of thunder. She could smell rain and she hoped they made it out before the storm hit.

She walked close to the window and cupped her face, peering inside, hoping like hell there was no one with a gun pointed at her. Of course, she knew Richard Filmore was gone. But that didn't mean his rifle was.

"Anna Gail?" she called. She pulled her face from the window and knocked on the glass, then moved to the door. "Anna Gail? You in there?" She tried the handle but it was locked. She looked again through the glass on the door, but the inside was dark with shadows.

"Anna Gail? It's Corey. And Dana," she added. "We were the ones with Butch the other day." She waited, still hearing nothing from inside. She jiggled the handle again, then shrugged. But just as she was about to turn away, she heard a thump from inside, as if something had banged against the wall or the counter. She put her face to the glass once again. "Anna Gail? Holly?"

"Should we try their house?" Dana called from the car.

"Let me try the back first. I thought I heard something," she said as she went to the side of the building and rounded the corner.

She pulled her gun from her holster...just in case, she told herself. She was aware of each beat of her heart, the sound echoing in her ears as she crept along the wall. A sound behind her made her jump and she twirled around, finding Lucky limping toward her. She smiled, her relief so great she nearly laughed at her nervousness.

"Thought I needed help, huh?" she whispered as she touched the dog's head. Most likely Dana had thought she needed help. Well, she was glad he was here. His presence calmed her a little.

However, at the back door, she refrained from sticking her face against the glass. Again...just in case. Yeah, just in case there was a rifle pointed at her. Instead, she reached for the doorknob, shocked when it turned easily. She pushed the door open—waiting, listening. All she heard was her heart pounding in her ears.

"Anna Gail?" she called. "Holly? Anybody here?"

She pushed the door all the way open and Lucky went in ahead of her. Corey watched him, looking for the signs she'd come to recognize, but there was no growl from Lucky, no bark. He disappeared around the counter and she heard a startled scream from inside.

"Holly?"

She followed Lucky around the corner, finding the young woman huddled against the wall, her father's rifle wrapped in her arms. It was obvious she had no clue how to use it. She put her own gun back in its holster, holding her hands up.

"You remember me? Corey?" she asked quietly. "You okay?"

Lucky's tail wagged as his wet nose nudged Holly's face. Corey could see tears in her eyes and she squatted down beside her.

"Where's your mother?" she asked gently.

At that, Holly's body shook with tears and Corey untangled her fingers from around the rifle and pulled it away from her.

"Come here," she said as she pulled Holly up. "What happened?"

"Where's…where's Butch?" Holly asked.

"He's…he's not with us now, but he's fine. Where's your mother?" she asked again.

Holly pointed to the small office, and Corey glanced past the door, seeing a body on the floor. She hurried toward it, finding Anna Gail half-covered with a sheet, her head resting on a pillow. There was dried blood on the pillow, and Corey bent down, her hand trembling as she reached out, touching Anna Gail's neck. Her skin was cold to her touch and there was no pulse.

She turned, finding Holly standing in the doorway, her eyes locked on her mother's face. Corey slowly pulled the sheet up, hiding Anna Gail's face from Holly.

"What happened?"

"I don't know," Holly said. She blew her nose into a wad of tissue she was holding. "I found her in the store, on the floor."

"When?"

"I think…three days ago," Holly said. "She didn't come home. She…she brought supper to my dad and she didn't come back." Tears started again. "It was dark, but I was worried. And scared. So I walked down to the store," she said.

"Was your father still here?"

Holly shook her head. "No. And I haven't seen him. Mom was… she was alive, but I didn't know what to do." She blew her nose again. "I've been staying here with her."

"What about people in town?"

Holly shook her head, her eyes scared. "No. Something's going on. I didn't dare go back outside. I locked the doors."

Corey frowned. "The back door was unlocked."

Holly nodded. "When I saw it was you, I unlocked it. But I was too scared to go outside." Her eyes darted to the window. "Something's going on. I've heard screams. I've heard gunshots."

"Yes. Something's going on," she agreed. She looked back down at Anna Gail's body. "When did she die?"

Holly's tears started again and she wiped at them. "This morning. I was sitting with her, holding her hand. And she just stopped breathing." She looked at Corey helplessly. "She never woke up. She never opened her eyes. She never talked to me. And she...she just died," she sobbed.

Corey took the younger woman into her arms, holding her tightly as she cried, trying to offer her some comfort, however meager it was.

Lucky whimpered beside her, and she knew it was time to go. She loosened her arms, letting Holly pull away.

"Come on. We need to go."

"Go where? I can't leave her. I can't—"

"Holly, you said yourself, there's something going on. You're not safe here. Come with us. Dana and her mother are outside in the car."

Holly's eyes widened. "The car?"

Corey had been so used to there being no electricity, it didn't occur to her how dark the store was. She reached for the light switch and turned it on. Holly gasped.

"The power's back? I didn't know. All the coolers and the freezer, they're all hooked up to the generator now. I should...I should plug them in. Mom would want—"

Corey grabbed her shoulders. "Holly, let it go. We need to get out of here. It's getting dark."

Holly pulled away from her. "No! This is my mom's store. I'm not going to let everything spoil. She would never forgive me if I did."

A loud rumble of thunder sounded, loud enough to shake the glass. Lucky pressed close against her leg.

"Okay," she said, thinking it would be quicker to do it instead of arguing with her. "Let's hurry."

There were three coolers and one freezer. The cords were a tangled mess as Richard had hooked up extension cords between them all. Corey flipped on lights so they could see better, even though she thought it was a terrible idea. If any one of...of *them* were in town, they were just calling attention to themselves. Of course, with Dana sitting outside in a running car, it wasn't exactly inconspicuous.

Another clap of thunder made them both jump, and Lucky tucked his tail and whimpered. Corey couldn't take the time to reassure him that he was safe. Instead, she fumbled with the cords, finally finding the one for the freezer and plugging it in. It hummed to life and she went to help Holly.

A horn honked outside twice, then a third time.

"We need to go," she said. She found the last cord and shoved it into the outlet, then pulled Holly with her to the front door.

She jumped back as a lightning bolt sizzled across the sky, the roar of thunder vibrating around them in almost the same instant... its boom still echoing long after it hit. As if on cue, the dark clouds opened up, sending a downpour of rain over Paradox. Dana honked the horn again and Corey saw what the urgency was. Four people, two in army fatigues and two civilians, were hurrying down the street toward them. One of the civilians, a woman, had an M16 slung over her shoulder.

She ran with Holly toward the car and jerked open the back door. Lucky beat Holly inside as he nearly jumped into Mrs. Ingram's lap. Corey simply shoved Holly in and slammed the door.

"Hurry!" Dana said urgently.

Corey opened the front door, then paused, squinting through the rain. The woman had taken aim with the rifle.

"*Christ*...let's go!" She dove inside, barely getting the door closed before Dana sped away. A spray of bullets sounded, but the woman had missed badly.

Corey sat up, wiping the rain from her hair. Dana had a death grip on the steering wheel, her knuckles nearly white as the car skidded around the corner.

Corey touched her arm, seeing Dana jump. "It's okay. You can slow down now."

Dana glanced at her. "Anna Gail?" she asked in a whisper.

Corey shook her head. "No. She was injured. She died this morning."

She turned in her seat, finding Lucky still in Mrs. Ingram's lap. Lucky was trembling and Dana's mother had a grip on him, holding him tight against her. She looked up, surprised to find Mrs. Ingram looking back at her.

"He's scared," she said quietly.

Corey nodded. "Yes. He's scared of storms." She glanced at Holly. "This is Dana's mom...Butch's aunt."

Holly nodded. "Yes, I know."

Yes, of course she did. It wasn't like Paradox Valley was inhabited by thousands of people. This area was probably more than a hundred square miles—and she felt like they'd traveled over nearly all of them—but most here not only knew everyone else, they also knew where everyone lived. She turned back to the front, the windshield wipers barely keeping up with rain.

"Can you see to drive? Should we pull over until it lets up?"

"Are you out of your mind? There's no way I'm stopping," Dana said. "We'll turn right up here. That's the road to the checkpoint."

"So another thirty miles or so, close to forty," she murmured. It was already dark, but she knew that was because of the storm. Dana had the lights on, but they did little to cut through the rain. When another rumble of thunder hit, Lucky again whimpered. She heard Mrs. Ingram whispering to Lucky, but she didn't turn around to watch.

A few tense miles later, the rain began to let up and a short time after that, it stopped altogether. She finally allowed herself to relax as the sky lightened. Off to the west she could see the break in the clouds and streaks of the waning sunlight. They should make the checkpoint before dark.

And after that, they'd keep driving, into Utah. Another hour and a half, two tops, they'd be at her house. Maybe then, they could put this nightmare behind them.

It would be easier for her than the others, though. They'd all lost someone. Dana still had her mother, but Butch and Holly had lost both parents. Jean, too, would be all alone. From the little she'd learned from Jean, her sons weren't involved in her life. Maybe that would change now.

Or maybe not. And that thought saddened her.

CHAPTER FIFTY-THREE

"Shouldn't we be there already?" Dana asked.

"Coming up real soon, I think," Corey said.

Dana felt Corey's eyes on her, and she glanced quickly at her. "What?"

"You okay?" Corey asked quietly.

Dana glanced in the mirror, seeing her mother still holding Lucky. "I think so," she whispered. "Mom at least seems responsive."

"It's been a hell of a day...hell of a week," Corey said. "A lot for everyone to process. You and I, we've had more time."

"I know."

Yes, they'd had more time. They knew what was going on. She'd lost her father, and she didn't even want to think about what might have happened to him. The man she'd shot wasn't her father. She'd told herself that over and over again, but that didn't make it any easier to take. Her mother didn't have a clue as to what was happening. All she knew was that her daughter had fired a gun at point-blank range and killed her husband. Even if they could explain, even if her mother came to realize what had really happened, Dana wondered if her mother would ever get that image out of her mind.

And poor Holly. She probably had no idea what had happened to her father. And now her mother was gone too. Dana hoped that she and Butch would lean on each other.

Oh, Butch. He was going to be heartbroken. And Dana would have no answers for him. There was little evidence as to what had happened to his parents. He would have a hard time finding closure.

"There. Up ahead," Corey said.

Dana saw the vehicles but frowned. "It's getting late. Almost dusk. Shouldn't there be lights on already?"

"Yes." Corey shook her head slowly. "Shit," she murmured.

Dana glanced at her sharply. "Oh, no. You don't think—"

"Let's just be on guard," Corey said.

Dana slowed as they approached the checkpoint. As before, barricades were across the road and a Jeep was parked on the side. Beyond that, tents were still erected and several vehicles lined the road. It looked very much the same as it had when they'd left that morning. Yet, something was different.

"It looks too quiet," she said.

"I know. No activity. I've only counted four soldiers."

"There were at least twenty or more yesterday," she said.

"That's Corporal Perez. Stop up here and let's talk to him."

She gripped the wheel tightly as she saw Corey pull her weapon onto her lap.

"Dana…you do exactly as I say," Corey whispered, never taking her eyes off Perez. "If I say floor it, you smash right through the barricades."

Dana swallowed nervously. "Okay." She glanced in the mirror, seeing her mother's eyes wide with fright. She met them and nodded. "Be ready, Mom."

The car crawled to a stop, and Corey stuck her head out of the window, glancing up at Perez. He showed no sign of recognizing her. From the backseat, Lucky's low growl turned into a bark.

"You're Private Jones, right?" Corey asked. "I'm…I'm Major Conaway."

Perez stared at her, then moved his rifle in their direction. Corey shot him twice as both her mother and Holly screamed. Dana didn't have to wait for Corey's instruction—she slammed her foot on the accelerator, smashing through the barricades as her mother's shrill scream still echoed in her ears.

There seemed to be gunfire all around, and she dodged a soldier standing in the road, nearly sending the car careening into a parked truck. Corey hung out the window, firing behind them and Dana glanced in the mirror, seeing three men running toward them— running faster than the vehicle.

"Drive!" Corey yelled. "Keep your head down."

"I can't do both!" she yelled back.

A spray of gunfire blasted out the back window, and Dana ducked down, causing the car to swerve again. It spun to the side, nearly spilling Corey out of the window. Dana grabbed her jeans by her waist, pulling her back inside as she jerked the steering wheel to the right, sending the car spinning in the opposite direction. The car's front bumper hit a Hummer and bounced off, driving over the side of a tent in the process. She was shaking so badly, she could hardly keep her hands on the steering wheel.

"Jesus Christ, Dana!"

"I'm trying," she shot back.

She finally got the car back on the road and floored it, sending them all flying back against the seats. Another glance into the mirror showed the men far behind. There were only two now.

"Stop the car," Corey said, putting a hand on her arm.

"What?"

"Stop the car, Dana," Corey said again.

Dana slowed, finally stopping. She was breathing as fast as if she'd been running herself and she made herself loosen her grip on the wheel. But her eyes widened as Corey opened the door and got out.

"What the hell? Get back in the goddamn car!"

"You go on," Corey said. "I'll catch up."

"Goddamn it, Corey! Get in the car. I'm not leaving you."

Corey slammed the door closed and stuck her head in the window. "I've got to take care of this, Dana. And we need something to communicate with. I've got to report this."

"No! You cannot go back there alone."

"I'll be right behind you. Trust me."

Their eyes met and Dana held them. "Oh, God...Corey, I need you here with me. Please don't do anything stupid."

"Not a chance." Then Corey winked at her. "Take care of my dog."

"*Your* dog?"

Corey tapped the side of the car, signaling for her to drive off. Dana again gripped the steering wheel, then after taking a quick breath, she drove on, leaving Corey standing at the side of the road. Lucky was barking sharply, looking through the back. With the window missing, she was afraid he would try to jump out and follow Corey.

"Mom…hold him."

"I've got him."

"Those were soldiers," Holly said, her voice cracking with nervousness. "Why were they shooting at us?"

"They weren't really soldiers," Dana said.

"Then why would she leave? Is she *crazy*?"

"No. She's my Dream Girl," she murmured to herself.

CHAPTER FIFTY-FOUR

"This wasn't one of your better ideas, Conaway," she muttered as she jogged back toward the checkpoint.

Yeah, because obviously they were using the weapons now. Not that they were great shots. Thankfully. Of course, these things, whatever they were, were smart enough to engineer a spaceship, smart enough to land on an inhabited planet...surely they were smart enough to figure out how to use a weapon. Unless these weapons were so rudimentary to them, they were like a child's toy.

What do you want? For them to shoot lasers at you or something, she thought. Her attempt to amuse herself vanished when a man jumped out from behind a truck. He was on her so fast, she hardly had time to react. She pulled the trigger twice as they tumbled to the ground. She rolled away, then shot him once more, sending him flying backward, landing against the fender of Jeep. He slid slowly to the ground, lying motionless. Without thinking, she walked closer and shot him in the head.

She grabbed his rifle then headed toward a tent. There was a soldier on the ground, blood covering his face, his chest, his legs. She nearly gasped. For all the shooting they'd done, all the...the *disabling*, as she liked to call it, there was never blood. This man had been killed and left. He hadn't been taken and his body used as a host. She knelt beside him and felt for a pulse but found none. His flesh was cold to her touch. She stared at him, wondering if his throat had been cut. But then she saw it, a wound to the neck. She stood up. His legs had been shot as well. Was that why he'd been left? The others—Hal, the soldier in the barn, even Dana's father—all had blood on their midsections. Were they killed that way? Or, Christ, was that simply the entryway for these...these *things* to get inside? With those thoughts running through her head, she bent down and took his weapon as well, slinging it over her shoulder with the other. Then she patted his pockets, finally finding what she was looking for—a cell phone. She turned it on, silently cursing as the familiar "Enter Passcode" screen popped up. She slipped it into her pocket anyway. If she couldn't find a phone, then she'd have to use this one to make an emergency call. Hopefully the 911 operator wouldn't think it was a prank call.

She snuck around the outside of the tent quietly, listening for movement. The light was fading fast from the sky and the shadows were creeping in closer. She had no idea how many of *them* there were. She'd counted four when they'd first arrived, not including Perez. By the sound of the gunfire, there had to be more. Many more. The two guys who were chasing after the car seemed to have disappeared.

"Yeah...but to where?" she whispered.

Hell, maybe there were only four. Maybe the others had already dispersed, heading to...well, the mothership was hopefully destroyed, so not up on Baker's Ridge. Then where? There weren't any houses out here. Squaw Valley? Judging by the gunfire they'd heard when they'd left Jean's place, Squaw Valley was already compromised. Paradox was compromised. Paradox Valley was compromised. Hell, where would they go next? South to the highway? East to Bedrock and the saline plant? North all the way to Grand Junction? Or continue west into Utah?

"*Jesus.*" How were they ever going to contain this?

Well, she needed to contain *this* area and she needed to find a cell phone. Then she needed to get the hell out of here. She pulled the clip from her Glock—only two shots left. Her extra clips were in her pack, in the trunk of Dana's car.

Real smart, Conaway.

She took one of the rifles off her shoulder instead. The magazine appeared to still be full—thirty rounds—but before she could slam it back into place, a voice sounded beside the tent.

"You."

She spun around, seeing the hulk of a man standing not ten feet behind her. They stared at each other and her eyes widened. His hands…his fingers were curled, his nails long and claw-like. An image flashed through her mind of those claws ripping her belly open. She pushed that image aside as she fumbled with the magazine, her hands shaking slightly as he took a step toward her.

"Hey, there," she said, her voice trembling with nervousness. "I'm…I'm Colonel…oh, what the hell, I'm *General* Conaway," she said. "You're like, a private, right? Hell, maybe you want to be a colonel today, huh?" The magazine finally slipped into the rifle and she slammed it home.

"Stop."

"No, no…you stop," she said, swinging the rifle up. But he was too fast, jerking the rifle out of her hands as easily as if she'd been holding a slippery greased pipe. She dove to the ground and rolled, pulling her gun out of her holster at the same time. She fired the two remaining rounds, hitting him low in the stomach.

To her surprise, he emitted a loud, pitiful scream and clutched himself, as if trying to keep his insides from spilling out. There was no blood, only a milky white liquid.

"So that's where you are, you son of a bitch," she muttered.

She picked up the rifle he'd flung down and aimed it at him, sending eight or ten rounds into his midsection. Like a puppet whose strings had been cut—he tumbled to the ground, his legs folding under him and he lay still.

She scrambled to her feet, moving quickly away from him…away from *it*. Only then did she realize how dark it had gotten. She looked to the west, seeing the fading light clinging to the horizon.

She had no business being out here. Everywhere she turned, the shadows seemed to be moving, closing in on her. She wanted to run blindly down the road and before she could do just that, she ducked into one of the tents, peering through the darkness, hoping to find… what? A flashlight? A phone?

She bumped into a cot with her knee, wincing at the pain. But then she stepped on something soft, something that rolled and moved under her foot. She jumped back with a stifled scream, listening, hearing nothing but her own breathing…and the booming of her heart.

* * *

"Why are we stopping?" Holly asked.

Dana turned in her seat, looking behind them, hoping to see headlights approaching. Surely that's what Corey had intended, right?

Grab a Jeep or a Hummer or something, once she took care of *things*. She glanced at Holly, then her mother.

"I'm waiting on Corey," she said.

"She told you to go on," Holly said. "She said to—"

"I know what she said. I'm still going to wait. And if she doesn't come soon, then I'm going back for her."

"No! They were shooting at us," Holly said. "We can't go back."

The shadows were pronounced now, and she wasn't able to see Holly's expression but she knew the girl was frightened. She was too.

"It's not the guns we have to worry about," she said quietly.

"I don't understand what's going on," her mother said, "but we shouldn't put ourselves in danger because of her."

Dana didn't want to be angry with her mother, but she was. It was because of Corey that they were all alive to begin with. Her mother didn't know it, but she'd probably been only minutes away from an unthinkable death had they not shown up when they had. But as she'd said, her mother didn't understand what was going on.

"Her name is Captain Conaway," Dana said. "She's…military. She was sent in after the…after the power outage." She bit her lower lip, wondering how on earth she was going to explain this. "Something landed up on Baker's Ridge, northwest of Squaw Valley."

"Was my daddy right?" Holly asked. "Are we under attack?"

"No. At least, not in the conventional way," she said. "Whatever landed up on Baker's Ridge…well, it was a UFO."

Silence filled the car for several seconds. It was her mother who broke it.

"That's nonsense. There was an earthquake. We all heard it, felt it."

"There was no earthquake, Mom. And there was no meteor, which is what the military thought at first," she said.

"That's crazy talk. There's no such thing as UFOs," Holly said defiantly.

"I so wish that was true," she said.

She looked past the sound of their voices to the dark, empty road beyond them. Lucky seemed to follow her gaze, and he whimpered quietly, still lying across her mother's lap.

* * *

Corey pressed against the inside of the tent, trying not to imagine what she'd stepped on. An arm? A leg? A *snake*?

Oh, Jesus…please not a snake.

As if she didn't have enough to worry about, thinking that a seven-foot long rattlesnake might be sharing the tent with her literally made her tremble. She didn't have many fears or phobias…but *snakes?* In her mind, she could imagine the snake being eight, even ten feet long, its tongue flicking out as it slithered along the floor, searching for her.

She was about to bolt out of the tent when she heard running outside. She held the rifle at the ready, planning to shoot anything that moved, man or snake. Two people, running fast, sped past the tent entrance. Running very fast. Running much *too* fast. She stepped out, firing several rounds in their direction. She heard, rather than saw them fall. She hurried over, seeing their dark shapes on the road. One was getting back up and she shot again. As before, she aimed for their midsections, getting off ten or twelve rounds before she made herself stop.

She didn't take the time to assess the damage. She went to a Hummer and leaned against it, trying to calm her breathing so she could hear. She could feel the perspiration on her face and she impatiently wiped it away, her eyes scanning the terrain around her. There was no movement, no sound.

She crept around the Hummer to the driver's side and opened the door. The interior light came on and she glanced beside the steering wheel, shocked that there were actually keys dangling from the ignition switch. Her eyes widened ever further when she saw a phone plugged into a charger.

She got inside and quietly closed the door, then turned the key. It started immediately and she put it into gear, pulling out onto the road, running into the side of a Jeep in the process. She turned on the lights, then gasped as the shape of a man appeared in her line of sight, heading toward her. He was running fast, only ten or twenty yards away. She stomped on the gas pedal, holding tight to the wheel as she plowed into the man, sending him flying out in front of her. She held her breath as she ran over him, hearing—feeling—the back wheels as they crushed him.

She looked in the mirror, seeing nothing but emptiness behind her. She finally took a breath, then sped on. She wanted to catch Dana before she crossed over into Utah. But knowing Dana…she would be waiting for her.

CHAPTER FIFTY-FIVE

Dana's heart jumped to life when she saw headlights down the road. She pointed.

"There. That's got to be her," she said.

"What if it's not?" her mother asked.

"It is." She wasn't sure how she knew, but she did. It was almost as if she could *feel* Corey. She started the car again and pulled to the side, leaving the lights on. But, just in case, she pulled her gun onto her lap as she waited. Just in case, she told herself.

The dark Hummer slowed, then pulled to a stop beside her car. She waited for what seemed to be an eternity as the window on the passenger's side lowered.

"Got car trouble, ma'am?"

She smiled with relief. "Well, I seem to be missing a passenger," she said.

When Corey got out of the Hummer, Dana opened her door and got out too. In the glow of the headlights, they stood watching each other. Dana wasn't sure who moved first but she found herself in Corey's arms, and she held on to her tightly.

"You're okay?" she whispered.

"No worse for wear," Corey said.

They pulled apart, but Dana kept a hand on Corey's arm. "Is it... is it over?"

"I called General Brinkley. He already knew the checkpoint had been compromised. To quote him, they're bringing in troops from all goddamn directions."

"What does that mean for us? For you?"

Corey sighed wearily. "We're going to my house. I'm running on fumes right now. I've got to report to Colonel Sutter first thing in the morning for a debriefing. Harry will be there too."

"But you won't have to come back out *here*, right?"

"No. I won't have to come back."

Dana finally let her relief show, and she nearly cried from it. It was over. For them, this nightmare was over. She found herself in Corey's arms again and she clung to her, the relief she felt so profound, so *overwhelming*, that it nearly brought tears to her eyes.

"Come on. Let's get out of here," Corey said. "We'll take the Hummer. Leave your car. It's shot to hell anyway."

Dana smiled when Corey and Lucky greeted each other. Lucky got a two-handed rub on his ears and Corey got a wet, sloppy kiss. But Lucky's limp seemed more pronounced and she noticed the worried frown on Corey's face as they took their packs from the trunk.

"How's your mother?" Corey asked.

"She seems to be coming around. She no longer looks shell-shocked. She doesn't understand what happened, though. I tried to explain. They both looked at me like I was crazy," she said.

"When they talk to Miss Jean and Butch, they'll know it's the truth," Corey said. "They'll need time to process it, just like we did."

Dana paused. "Did we? I don't remember processing it. It just... well, it just happened and we went with it," she said.

"We didn't have time to do anything else," Corey reminded her. She reached down and rubbed Lucky's head as the dog leaned against her. "He needs a vet."

"I can take him tomorrow," Dana offered. "I imagine your debriefing will take several hours."

"If not most of the day," Corey said.

The drive into Utah was made mostly in silence, and Dana leaned back in the seat, feeling her eyelids getting heavy. It felt like it had been days since she'd slept. She didn't know how Corey was still functioning. She sat up straighter, blinking several times, trying to stay awake. She turned in the seat, glancing into the back. Both her mother and Holly were looking out of their respective windows, saying nothing…and most likely seeing nothing. Lucky lay on the seat between them, his head resting in her mother's lap. That made her smile. Her mother wasn't fond of dogs, never had been. The last dog they'd had, James had brought home as a puppy when Dana was still young. But as soon as James had graduated high school and moved off, the dog had mysteriously disappeared.

She looked over at Corey, who was staring straight ahead. As if sensing her watching, Corey turned, meeting her gaze in the soft glow of the dash lights.

"Do you want me to drive?" she offered.

Corey smiled. "You're about to fall asleep."

Dana smiled too. "How can you tell?"

"Your bobbing head gave you away."

"Yeah, well three something this morning was a *long* time ago," she said around a yawn. "And speaking of sleeping, will there be room for everyone?"

"There are two beds and a sofa," Corey said. "We can draw straws for the floor."

"I vote Butch," she said quickly. But that thought only reminded her that Butch would have to be told about his parents. She wasn't looking forward to that. Her shoulders sagged and she sighed.

As if reading her mind, Corey reached over and squeezed her hand, then let her fingers entwine with Dana's. Dana's own squeezed around them, and she covered their joined hands with her other one, holding Corey against her.

What was going to happen now? How could she possibly go back to Seattle and leave her mother here alone to pick up the pieces? Would her mother even want to go back to the farm? If not, then what in the world would they do with it? And what about Butch? Would he go back to his parents' house and work the farm on his own? She closed her eyes and sighed. And poor Holly…what would she do? Did she have siblings? And Miss Jean? She seemed so strong, but would she be able to come back? Or would her sons force her out, force her to live with one of them?

A light squeeze on her fingers brought her eyes open again. She rolled her head, finding Corey watching her. She smiled slightly, nodding at Corey's unasked question.

Yes, she was okay. She had to be.

CHAPTER FIFTY-SIX

Unable to even think about sleeping, Jean sat in the rocking chair and pushed it into motion. She'd been pleasantly surprised to find one on the porch. Young people didn't seem to appreciate rockers anymore. For her, there was nothing more relaxing. Why, after supper, she and Hal took to their rockers almost daily during the summer months. And they'd talk and tell stories, stories they'd each heard dozens and dozens of times already. But they still laughed at the tales as if it was the first time they'd heard them.

The sadness that had been hovering over her for days now seemed to be settling down as if it planned to stay a while. She had wondered when it would hit. Every time it reared its head, she would push it down. There hadn't been time to wallow in sorrow, which was exactly what she'd wanted to do. She'd been too busy for that. She had the girls to take care of. And Butch.

Now? Butch was lying down again, as he'd been doing for most of the day. But she'd kept herself occupied. As the captain had warned, the cupboards were practically bare. In the freezer, she'd found nothing but a steak and a lone chicken breast. She'd browned the chicken and served it over rice for breakfast, which Butch hadn't seemed to mind. So while he rested, she'd taken the captain's vehicle—and a credit card she'd found on her dresser—to the nearest grocery store. She'd bought enough food for a week, at least, but she didn't think the captain would mind, even though she'd been shocked at the cost. Living on the farm, she was used to growing her own vegetables, used to the chickens providing them eggs, used to Hal providing them meat. It pained her to pay for a carton of eggs when she knew, back home on the farm, her chickens' eggs were going to waste.

But she wanted to have a meal prepared in case the girls made it back today. Butch had told her that it would be tomorrow, at the earliest. He told her it would take them most of today just to reach the farm. Regardless, Jean had made a beef stew that she'd simmered all afternoon. Come suppertime though, it was only she and Butch who enjoyed the meal.

She clutched her hands together, her fingers worrying as they rubbed back and forth. Oh, she hoped Dana's parents were okay. How awful would it be if the girls got there, only to find the house empty? Or worse. Lord, she hoped that wasn't the case. Dana had been through enough already.

With her toe, she pushed the rocker a little faster. The light had long left the sky, but it was a pleasant evening. And it was getting late, she assumed. Best she be thinking about bed instead of sitting out here worrying.

Worrying never did anyone no good. That's what her granny always said. What will be, will be, whether you liked it or not. She'd learned that plenty of times over the years.

"Child, there's no sense worrying over something you can't control."

She smiled, amazed that she could still hear her granny's voice in her mind after all this time. Her smile faded though. Those words of wisdom were never truer than they were now.

So as she rocked the minutes away, she tried to push her worry aside, much as she tried to push her sorrow aside. It would do no good for Butch to come out and find her with tears in her eyes. No good at all.

Instead of tears, she closed her eyes, picturing Hal's face as she'd seen it hundreds of times, his blue eyes twinkling, his laugh lines pronounced as he smiled. She could almost hear his gentle compliment as she served him supper.

"Looks real good, Jean."

Her rocker slowed as a tear escaped her eye, followed by another and then another. She couldn't stop the flow, and she gave in to them, her heart breaking as silent sobs shook her. She wrapped her thin arms around herself, seeking comfort. It was a pitiful reminder that she was now all alone. There was no one to console her. Not ever again.

* * *

Corey slowed as she turned onto the road that would take her to the cabin she rented. It wasn't anything fancy, but it was quiet and it had been her solace in those dark days when she was recovering from her injuries...and the death of her team. That seemed like a lifetime ago.

The front porch light was on, which startled her. She rarely used it. She assumed Jean and Butch, not being familiar with the area, would feel safer with it on.

She nudged Dana, who was still holding her hand. She jerked her head up quickly.

"We're here," she said quietly.

Dana yawned. "Sorry. I fell asleep."

Corey glanced in the mirror, finding Holly asleep as well. Mrs. Ingram was awake, however, and she met her gaze in the mirror.

Corey drove to the side of the cabin and stopped the Hummer. She opened the back door, holding her hand out to assist Dana's mother, then she lifted Lucky off the seat. His tail wagged when she put him on the ground, and he limped off to the side, sniffing around a tree before lifting his leg.

She slung her pack over her shoulder and handed Dana hers, then headed up to the steps. She was surprised to find Jean sitting in the old rocker.

"Captain? Dana? Is that you?"

"Miss Jean? What are you doing out here this late?" Dana asked as she walked over to Jean. The rocker creaked when Jean tried to get out of it, and Dana held her hand out, helping Jean up.

"I couldn't begin to think about sleep, worrying about you like I was," Jean said. "Butch said not to expect you until tomorrow." She looked behind them to where Mrs. Ingram and Holly stood, then she looked back at Dana.

Without another word, Jean folded Dana in her arms and held her. Corey was shocked to see Dana's shoulders shake as she cried. She looked away from them, glancing to Dana's mother, who had tears in her own eyes.

"I'll...I'll get Butch," she said, not knowing what else to do.

She found Butch on the sofa, asleep. She nudged his shoulder gently, seeing his eyes flutter open. He grinned when he recognized her.

"You made it back," he said sleepily, sitting up.

"How's the head?"

"Lingering headache, that's about it," he said as he rubbed the back of his head. "Dana?"

"Outside. They're on the back porch."

He met her eyes. "My mom and dad?"

She swallowed, then shook her head. "No. I'm sorry."

"Oh, Jesus," he whispered, burying his face in his hands.

"Dana's dad…well, he didn't make it," she said quietly. "We went to your place, but it was empty."

He looked up. "Then maybe—"

"There was blood. Signs of a struggle," she said. "I'm so sorry." She stepped back. "Dana's mom and Holly are with us."

"Anna Gail?"

"No. She was injured. She died. Richard was…well, he's dead too."

"Oh, my God."

He stood up, then walked past her to the back door. She watched through the window as Holly flew into his arms. She then slid her glance to Dana, who was now holding her mother. Jean stood off to the side, one hand still resting on Dana's shoulder.

Corey sighed heavily, then closed her eyes for a second, wishing she had some words that would take away their pain.

"Captain?"

She opened her eyes, finding Jean standing in the doorway.

"You…you want a bite to eat?"

Corey smiled wearily at her. "You actually found something to cook here?"

"Not exactly, no. But it wasn't too hard to find a grocery store."

"Well, I'm past the point of hunger, I think. Besides, I'd probably fall asleep at the table."

Jean nodded as she came closer. It was only then that Corey noticed the puffiness of her eyes. She searched them, her expression gentling.

"Are you okay, Miss Jean?" she asked quietly.

"Oh, feeling sorry for myself is all," she said dismissively. "I was missing my Hal." She took Corey's hand and squeezed it. "I'm glad you're back safe and sound. I don't imagine it was without incident. Lucky seems to be favoring his front leg."

Corey nodded, then looked outside to where Lucky was standing by the door. She patted her thigh, beckoning him inside. His tail wagged, and he limped over to her, sitting down beside her and leaning against her leg.

"I'm not sure that we would have made it through all of this without him," she said as she rubbed his head.

"Dana's daddy…I guess—"

"He was like Hal," Corey said. "We got there just in time. He was inside their house along with a soldier, Richard Filmore and Carl Milstead."

"Oh, my Lord. Carl Milstead? He made it all the way down to that part of Paradox Valley?"

"We couldn't find Butch's parents or the aunt and uncle who were staying with them," she said. "Their house was empty, signs of a struggle."

"Oh, poor Butch. I think the not knowing will be the hardest," Jean said.

Corey looked out through the window again to where the others were still standing outside. There were tears from all four, she could see that.

"It'll take them some time to get over this, I guess." She turned to Jean. "You too, I imagine."

"Time heals, Captain. There'll be good days and bad, I reckon. But it don't matter much which one you're having…the sun will still rise the next day. For us, life goes on." She paused. "For now, at least."

Corey nodded, knowing all too well what she was trying to say. No matter what happens, whether you lose your family or you lose your team in a brutal attack, the world keeps on spinning, day after day after day.

"Now, why don't you go get cleaned up, Captain? Get yourself off to bed. I'll tend to the others."

"Going to be kinda cramped sleeping," she warned.

"We'll manage. Get some sleep. I'll plan a big breakfast for in the morning."

Corey nodded. She took one last look out the window, then shuffled off toward her room. She wasn't really surprised to hear Lucky hobbling after her.

* * *

Dana pushed open Corey's bedroom door quietly, pausing before going inside. Lucky was on the rug beside the bed and he lifted his head to look at her, then relaxed again. She ran her fingers through her damp hair, then used the towel she carried to dry it a little more.

Her clothes were filthy and she had no clean ones, but she simply couldn't sleep without a shower. She'd been surprised to find a pair of cotton shorts, a T-shirt and undies folded neatly on the counter in the bathroom. Although it was only a thoughtful act on Corey's part to leave the clothes, she still felt a little naughty as she slipped on Corey's underwear.

She lifted the covers back on the bed, pausing again as Corey shifted to her back. Corey must have felt her presence. She leaned up on an elbow for a second, then lay down again with a tired sigh.

"Hey."

"Sorry. I didn't mean to wake you," she whispered.

Corey patted the bed beside her and Dana got in, moving closer to her.

"Did everyone find a place to sleep?"

"Uh-huh," she said. "And please don't ask me how I am," she said.

"Okay."

"Because I really don't know. So much has happened and I still can't wrap my mind around it all," she said. "My mom is heartbroken and she doesn't grasp everything that happened. I don't know that I've grasped it. But hell, I'll be okay." She paused. "But don't ask me how I am."

"Okay," Corey whispered. "I won't ask."

She sighed. "Would you hold me?"

Corey rolled to her side and gathered Dana in her arms, pulling her close. Dana's eyes closed and she tugged Corey's arm even tighter around her.

"You're safe," Corey murmured. "I won't let anything happen to you."

"I know." She snuggled even closer to her. "You're not going to disappear on me, are you?"

"Not a chance."

"Good."

They were quiet, and she thought Corey had fallen asleep. She sighed, no longer able to keep her eyes open, but Corey's soft voice made them flutter open once again.

"Am I your Dream Girl?"

Dana brought their clasped hands up and kissed the back of Corey's gently. "You are," she said simply.

Corey pulled her tighter. "Good."

CHAPTER FIFTY-SEVEN

Four months later

Jean felt like a lazy bum as she set her rocking chair in motion. It was getting on to be suppertime, but she thought it could wait a few more minutes. She was enjoying the sight of the girls out in the garden too much.

Never in her life had she seen a grown woman get so excited about digging potatoes. But the captain was like a kid at Christmas, excitedly showing off her prize time and again when she unearthed a big one. Dana was helping her, although not with the same exuberance as the captain.

She smiled, surprised at how content she felt. And she supposed she needed to stop referring to Corey as "the captain." Her retirement became official when the calendar flipped over to September. She seemed much too young, and Dana had explained that even though Corey had fifteen years' service, she still didn't qualify for early retirement. Some general had pulled some strings, she'd said. Well, Jean thought that was only right, after what all the captain had been through.

After she'd rescued Dana's mother and Butch's gal Holly, they'd still given the captain no rest. It was two weeks before they'd even let them come back to the valley and even then, they weren't allowed to stay. Thankfully, the town of Paradox fared better than they'd thought. It wasn't quite the ghost town that Dana had suspected. Most of the residents were locked up tight in their own homes, afraid to step foot outside. Still, it was another two weeks before the area was deemed safe to return to. Safe from what, most on the outside never knew. She was amazed at the different ways the government could spin something. There was never a single mention of a spaceship landing up on Baker's Ridge. Well, regardless of what they were saying, she had been still too afraid to stay at the farm alone. Hal Jr., had suggested she move in with him. She knew she should be pleased that he cared enough to even make the offer, but the thought of moving into the city, living in his tiny house, didn't appeal to her in the least.

The captain, however, had the perfect solution. Jean had jumped at the proposition of the captain and Dana moving in with her at the farm. She'd assumed that Dana would move back to Paradox Valley and stay with her mother for a while, but her mother had flat-out refused to go back to their farm. Barbara ended up moving in with Butch, and Dana had put the home and farm up for sale. Dana had flown back to Seattle, only to return a week later with a rented van loaded down with her things.

Jean had moved into the spare bedroom, letting Corey and Dana take over her and Hal's old bedroom. It was too large for one person, she reasoned. But the truth was, without Hal there, she couldn't find much peace in the room anyway. Besides, the spare room was right next door to Johnny's old bedroom, the room she'd converted into her sewing room. She had a mind to set up her quilting rack again, something she hadn't had the itch to do in years.

Laughter pulled her out of her musings, and she watched as Corey picked Dana up and spun her around. Lucky danced around them, barking excitedly at their antics. When the captain set her back down, Dana slipped her arms around Corey's shoulders and pulled her close for a kiss. Jean felt her face blush as she watched them, even after all these months of living with them. Those two were so affectionate; it warmed her heart to watch them. It was obvious they were very much in love. It reminded her of when she and Hal were young. He used to chase her around the garden too.

She took a deep breath, once again savoring the contentment she felt. As she'd warned the captain, there'd been good days and bad, but for the most part, they'd put the nightmare behind them. There were no funerals and she felt guilty for not giving Hal that, but the town of Paradox held a memorial service for those who were lost. The tiny Baptist church had been overflowing, and the captain had sat on one side of her and Hal Jr., on the other and she'd cried her eyes out once and for all. Dana's brother and sister had come too and all of Butch's family. There were so many tears, Jean wondered if they'd ever stop. Of course, they did. As she'd told the captain once, the sun was still gonna rise the next day. Life would go on.

And it had. They'd formed their own little family group here, and she was content to know that she'd be able to live out her remaining years here at the farm. She had the girls to take care of...and they would take care of her. She suspected that Hal Jr., was relieved at that prospect. She nodded to herself and she noted the smile on her face. She glanced around her surroundings, seeing four horses now in the pasture instead of only her Daisy. The white stallion was the most prominent of the bunch, even though Gretchen stood several hands taller than he did. Her gaze slid back to the garden where Dana and Corey were again working on the potatoes. Lucky lay at the edge, watching them. Oh, that dog sure had taken a liking to the captain. He hardly let her out of his sight. She knew that they had bonded during the ordeal, but she suspected that he also enjoyed the once-a-day trek they made to the creek where the captain would throw rocks in the water for him. She and Dana accompanied them some days, but mostly, it was a private time for the captain and Lucky.

Well, she had supper to start. Best get to it, she thought, even though it would be a simple meal tonight. Tomorrow—as they did nearly every Saturday—Barbara, Butch and Holly were all coming over to spend the day with them. She would cook up a big roast with her special gravy that Dana liked so much. And of course, some of the potatoes and carrots from the garden.

She looked once more at the girls, then got out of the rocker and moved back inside to the kitchen. As she was chopping an onion, she heard a phone ringing. She looked around, scanning the cabinet. She finally found the captain's phone and walked over and picked it up.

"Hello," she said.

"Yes, hello. I need to speak to Captain Conaway, please."

Jean looked out through the window, seeing Corey and Dana still in the garden. "I'm sorry, but she's not inside right now. She's out in the garden, got dirt clean up to her elbows," she said. "Digging potatoes."

"Oh, I see. Well, would you please be so kind as to get her for me?"

Jean frowned. "Who is this?"

"General Brinkley, ma'am. Please. It's rather urgent."

Jean didn't like the sound of his voice, and she had half a mind to hang up on him. But she would do as he said. She put the knife down and went outside, taking the phone with her.

* * *

"Hey, Miss Jean. Look at this one," Corey said, holding up a large potato. "I think we should have this bad boy for supper. What do you think?"

Jean nodded. "How about I fry us up some potatoes to go with that chicken?"

"Sounds great." Oh, yeah, she loved Miss Jean's fried chicken.

"Oh, Captain, here, I almost forgot," Jean said, handing her phone to her. "You have a call."

"Okay, thanks," she said, wondering who would be calling her. She used her phone so rarely, she almost forgot she had one. "Hello, this is Corey."

"Captain Conaway, I understand you're in the garden. From the sounds of it, you're digging potatoes. I imagine that's a stress-free job."

She smiled. "Hey, Harry. Yeah, we're digging potatoes for the second day now. I had no idea how much fun it would be." She could tell by the sound of his voice that this wasn't a social call. She took a few steps away from Dana and Jean. "So…what's up?"

"Got a bit of a situation," he said. "I wanted to keep you informed. Just in case," he added.

She frowned. "Just in case what?"

"There's a small community south of you. Brush Canyon. Along the Delores River," he said. "Nothing more than a dot on the map out in the middle of goddamn nowhere."

"Never heard of it," she said.

"No, I don't suppose you have. Got four people missing. Reports of strange behavior. Found a body…partially eaten."

"Jesus," she whispered. She walked closer to the barn, keeping her back to Dana and Jean. "Are you saying what I think you're saying?"

"Nothing's confirmed yet. The body, it could be wild animals got to it, that's all. But after what happened in Paradox Valley…well, we don't want to take a chance. Don't want to waste time with bullshit protocols."

"Harry…you're not asking me to assist, I hope. Because—"

"No, Corey. Your retirement is official. No worries there. I only wanted to make you aware of the situation." He paused. "In case it gets out of hand again."

"Okay. I appreciate that, Harry." She glanced behind her, seeing Dana and Jean watching. "Please keep me in the loop, if you can."

"Will do. You take care of yourself, Corey. I hear farming is pretty hard work."

She smiled quickly. "Best decision I ever made. I've finally got a home, Harry. A home that I don't ever have to leave."

"I was hoping that was the case. You deserve it." He cleared his throat. "Well, you take care, kiddo."

Her smile faded after she slipped her phone into her pocket. Christ, were those...those *things* still out there? Somewhere? No. They'd gotten them all. Surely to God they had.

"Everything okay?" Dana asked.

Corey turned, forcing a smile onto her face. "Yeah, yeah. Fine. That was Harry," she said. "Everything's fine."

Dana eyed her suspiciously. "You sure?"

"Yeah. He was just checking on me." She walked over to her and slipped an arm around her shoulders. "He wanted to know how I liked the farming life."

"Really? And what did you say?"

This time, Corey's smile was genuine. "I told him it was the best decision I'd ever made."

Dana smiled sweetly at her and moved into her embrace, kissing her lightly on the lips. "Well, I happen to agree with you." She turned to Jean. "Isn't that right, Miss Jean?"

Jean nodded. "I think she makes a very good farmer. You both do."

Corey laughed. "Well, it's a start. I *still* refuse to kill any of our chickens, though."

"All in good time, Captain," Jean said as she turned away. "I reckon I best get to supper and fry up this prized potato of yours. We'll eat in an hour, girls."

"Yes, ma'am," Corey said.

As soon as she walked away, Dana linked arms with her. "You sure everything's okay?"

"Promise."

Dana searched her eyes, finally nodding. "Okay. Then let's go put up all these potatoes you insisted on digging. I hear a shower calling my name." She smiled up at her. "In fact, I think you should join me. Sharing a shower with you has become one of my favorite things to do."

Corey laughed. "Yes, I know. Remember what happened the last time, though? You were so loud, Jean thought you were under attack or something."

Dana laughed too as she tugged Corey with her. "I *was* under attack. Only it was friendly fire."

Corey pulled her to a stop, turning her to meet her eyes, her expression serious now. "I love you, you know. Very much."

Dana's expression was gentle, and she reached out a hand, lightly caressing her cheek.

"I love you too." Then she grinned. "My little farm girl, with dirt on her face."

Corey laughed. "I thought I was your Dream Girl."

"Oh, sweetheart, you are definitely *that*. I'm just sorry it took me so long to find you."

Corey leaned closer, kissing her softly on the lips. "Not as sorry as I am."

They embraced tightly, then pulled apart when Lucky—tail wagging wildly—squeezed in between them.

"I swear, he's so jealous," Dana muttered as she ruffled the fur on his back.

Corey squatted down beside him and took his head between her hands. She smiled and closed her eyes as a cold, wet tongue swiped across her face.

Dana laughed, then pulled her back up. "Come on, Farmer Brown. Shower time. We don't want to be late for supper."

Corey sighed contentedly as they headed to the house with their baskets of potatoes. She paused, looking behind her to the south, where the low clouds were starting to reflect the reds and yellows of sunset. She wondered how far Brush Canyon was from them.

"Corey?"

She turned back around. "Hmm?"

Dana tilted her head, watching her. "You sure everything's okay?"

She met the steady gaze that held her own. Was she really protecting Dana by keeping this from her? After all they'd been through, was that fair? But it was because of all they'd been through—Dana, her mother, Butch, Holly and Jean—that she kept silent. Their pain was still just below the surface. Over the summer months, they'd bonded, they'd formed a new family and laughter had gradually replaced tears... happiness had replaced sadness. They were healing.

"Honey?"

Corey nodded. "Yes. Everything is perfect."

Bella Books, Inc.

Women. Books. Even Better Together.

P.O. Box 10543
Tallahassee, FL 32302

Phone: 800-729-4992
www.bellabooks.com